# Skylark

*Also by Jo Beverley*
*in Large Print:*

Winter Fire
St. Raven
Dark Champion
Tempting Fortune
Hazard
The Devil's Heiress
The Dragon's Bride
Devilish
Forbidden Magic
An Unwilling Bride

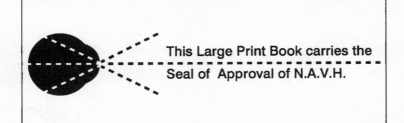

This Large Print Book carries the
Seal of Approval of N.A.V.H.

# Skylark

## Jo Beverley

Thorndike Press • Waterville, Maine

Published in 2004 by arrangement with NAL Signet, a division of Penguin Group (USA) Inc.

Thorndike Press® Large Print Core.

The tree indicium is a trademark of Thorndike Press.

The text of this Large Print edition is unabridged. Other aspects of the book may vary from the original edition.

Set in 16 pt. Plantin by Elena Picard.

Printed in the United States on permanent paper.

**Library of Congress Cataloging-in-Publication Data**

Beverley, Jo.
  Skylark / Jo Beverley.
    p. cm.
  ISBN 0-7862-6622-8 (lg. print : hc : alk. paper)
  1. Inheritance and succession — Fiction. 2. Mothers and sons — Fiction. 3. England — Fiction. 4. Widows — Fiction. 5. Large type books. I. Title.
PR9199.3.B424S44 2004
  813'.54—dc22                    2004049841

*To my sisters, Stella, Marian, and Eileen,*
*because sisters play a part in this book,*
*and sisters are special*

As the Founder/CEO of NAVH, the only national health agency solely devoted to those who, although not totally blind, have an eye disease which could lead to serious visual impairment, I am pleased to recognize Thorndike Press* as one of the leading publishers in the large print field.

Founded in 1954 in San Francisco to prepare large print textbooks for partially seeing children, NAVH became the pioneer and standard setting agency in the preparation of large type.

Today, those publishers who meet our standards carry the prestigious "Seal of Approval" indicating high quality large print. We are delighted that Thorndike Press is one of the publishers whose titles meet these standards. We are also pleased to recognize the significant contribution Thorndike Press is making in this important and growing field.

Lorraine H. Marchi, L.H.D.
Founder/CEO
NAVH

* Thorndike Press encompasses the following imprints: Thorndike, Wheeler, Walker and Large Print Press

# Chapter 1

*The Berkshire Informer,* October 7, 1816:

*We hail the return of Johnny Tring, despaired of by his family when lost at sea six years ago. As a result of the might of His Majesty's navy and the bravery of Britain's sailors, he, along with nearly two thousand other unhappy Christian souls, has been liberated from durance vile in the cruel hands of the Mahometan corsairs of Algiers. Most of these unfortunates were from hot Mediterranean lands. How much deeper must Tring's gratitude be to Him on high when now restored to Berkshire's cool and green Elysium.*

*More likely a nasty shock to the system,* Laura Gardeyne thought, tucking her woolen shawl more closely around herself. The chancy sun had slid behind clouds again, and a cool breeze rustled the newspaper and the dying leaves in the oak above her seat.

But still, to be released from slavery and imprisonment must gladden any heart.

Her son ran up to her. "Mama, may I have my ball?"

As a child must gladden any heart. She smiled at three-year-old Harry and gave him the ball and a canvas bag. "Why not ask Nan to build a tower with your blocks? Then you can try to knock it down."

He ran back to his nursemaid, a sturdy bundle of energy in nankeen trousers and a short blue jacket. Free, as happy children are always free. As adults rarely are.

She gazed around this small piece of Elysium. The park of Caldfort House was lovely, even on a dull day, designed as it was in the natural style. The grass that ran from the house to the River Cald was kept neatly short by sheep and dotted with majestic old trees.

Caldfort House itself stood on a rise, square, pale, and dignified — the very picture of a modern country home.

What had Lovelace written?

> Stone walls do not a prison make,
> Nor iron bars a cage.
> Minds innocent and quiet take
> That for an hermitage.

8

It worked in reverse, too. An idyllic setting could be durance vile. In fact, she remembered where the phrase *durance vile* came from: Robert Burns, the Scottish poet.

*In durance vile here must I wake and weep.* . . .

Her son's laughter broke her mood and she shook herself out of poetic melancholy. It was not at all in her nature, and compared to most, she was a fortunate woman. She was a widow, to be sure, but that sadness was nearly a year old, and she had a handsome jointure that meant she need never fear poverty.

And she had Harry, the joy of her life.

She watched him roll his red leather ball again and demolish at least half the blocks. He was developing a good eye for a three-year-old, but then his father had excelled at every type of sport. Harry got his dark curls from her. The rest of him was pure Gardeyne — square chin, brown eyes and hair, and the promise of height and strong build.

His next attempt sent the whole tower flying. Laura put aside the paper and applauded. "Well done, Harry! Well done!"

He hurtled to her for a hug, then back to roll his ball at the rebuilt target. It hit only the corner, but it made a sound like an explosion. He raced back to her again. "Mama! Mama!"

Laura caught him up, thinking, *Thunder?*

But crows had risen cawing into the gray sky.

It had been a shot!

Laura realized immediately what had happened, but she still held her son close. "Don't be frightened, Minnow. It's just your Uncle Jack enjoying some sport."

The maid came over. "Shall I take Master Harry in, ma'am?"

"No, of course not. Reverend Gardeyne would never aim his gun near us, and Harry's enjoying himself, aren't you, darling?"

After an uncertain moment, Harry nodded and scrambled off her lap to run back to his game.

With hard-won skill, Laura kept a slight smile in place as she watched, then as she let her eyes move to the coppice wood that spread between the house and the village of Cald St. Edwin's. The shot had come from there, but the wood offered no extra information. The crows had settled, and there was nothing to see.

Surely she'd spoken the truth. Her brother-in-law would not be careless about where he aimed his gun. Jack Gardeyne was vicar for the local parishes of St. Edwin's and St. Mark's, and a good one. As with all Gardeynes, however, hunting, shooting, and fishing were the true joys of his life.

In six years of marriage, Laura had grown accustomed to living among dogs, horses, and firearms. Guns hadn't bothered her until recently. Until she'd begun to suspect that the Reverend Jack Gardeyne would like Harry dead.

Now sweat trickled down her spine. She tried, as she did all the time, to convince herself that no man, especially a vicar, would wish harm to his innocent nephew. Even if the child did stand between him and a title, a fortune, and all the hunting, shooting, and fishing he could want.

She wasn't convinced, and she couldn't stop herself from hovering over Harry's play as if watching could hold off disaster. No one could watch a child all the time, however, and as he grew older it would become impossible. A boy must be allowed to explore and have adventures, but as things stood now, Laura didn't know how she could bear to let him out of her sight.

She noticed that he was throwing the ball more wildly and becoming frustrated.

Time for his nap . . .

Then she leapt to her feet and ran.

Harry had hurled the ball right past Nan. It was rolling down toward the river and he was chasing it, but that wasn't what alarmed her. A black dog had streaked out of the woods with the same intent.

The dog got there first and snatched the ball in its sharp teeth. Harry had already reversed. He'd spun around and was fleeing toward safety — toward her. She swung him into her arms and held him close, murmuring reassurances that she could hardly hear over her own thundering heart.

"Don't be cowardy custard, Harry! Bouncer won't hurt you."

Laura glared over her child's head at the source of the hearty voice. Jack Gardeyne was strolling toward them, jolly smile in place.

How could anyone see him as a monster? He was a fleshy man, portly around the middle, but strapping, like all the Gardeynes, and full of vigor and bonhomie. He carried a gun under his arm, but safely pointed down.

In his casual country clothes he looked as harmless as could be, but his free hand gripped the legs of a dead pheasant, its limp head brushing the grass. Laura was not mawkish about dead animals, but at this moment the corpse made her shiver.

"Your uncle's right, darling," she said, hiding her tension. "His dog won't hurt you."

She made it a statement for Jack rather than for her son. When Nan hurried up, Laura passed Harry to her, then went to his retriever and grabbed the ball. "Release, Bouncer!"

Bouncer snarled deep in his throat.

Though fear leapt inside, Laura didn't let go. She wanted Jack to know that he faced not only a small child but her. She stared a demand at him.

His smile set a little. "Bouncer, release! Heel!"

The dog let her have the ball and turned to settle at his master's side. It was surely her imagination that saw a sneer in its panting expression.

Jack shook his head. "Laura, my dear, dare I suggest that perhaps you are a little overprotective of Harry?"

He'd started this line recently, trying in subtle ways to separate her from her son. She feared that he was slowly turning his father, Lord Caldfort, to his side.

"He's only three, Jack," she said, drying

the ball on her handkerchief. "There'll be time to toughen him up later." She attacked back. "I'm surprised to see you out. We received word that Emma's confinement had started."

"Nothing for a man to do there," he said. "In the way, in fact. I've been through this three times before, remember."

"But I hope all is going well."

"Midwife said so. Hoping for a boy, of course, this time. Father would be pleased. Always good to have a spare as well as an heir."

Laura's throat tightened, but she looked straight at his cheerful face. "I'm sure it is, though it's unlikely that anything will happen to Harry, isn't it? Children don't die as frequently as they used to."

"God be praised! But still, His divine will takes some innocents. Wise men pray for the best, but prepare for misfortune." He nodded. "Good day to you, Sister. I'll drop by to see how Father is, then get back home."

She watched him stroll toward the house, corpse dragging on the grass, trying to persuade herself that the threat was entirely in her imagination.

Jack Gardeyne was a man of God, and a good enough vicar in his way. He ran the services responsibly, preached excellent sermons, and organized the care of the less fortunate of the parishes. He was a good father and a kind husband. In fact, he seemed to care for his Emma more than Hal had cared for her once the first bloom was off their marriage.

She looked at Harry and saw he was limp in Nan's arms, his head on the maid's shoulder.

"Time to go in, Minnow," she said as if nothing unusual had happened, and bent to gather up the blocks and ball, wishing Jack hadn't been on his way up to the house. She didn't want another encounter.

She sighed. It was considerate of Jack to visit his ailing father so often, to talk with him, play cards, and perhaps laugh over wicked, manly jokes. Laura would have done the same — even the latter, but Lord Caldfort didn't care for the conversation of women. He also believed women should never gamble, and he enjoyed playing cards only for money.

She straightened, tightening the draw-string of the bag. Lord Caldfort was not an easy man to live with but she tried to be understanding. He'd been an active man for most of his life, and becoming an invalid had turned him sour. It had been particularly bitter that his health had failed just as his fortune turned, just as he had inherited a title and estates from his brother.

An unlucky family, the Gardeynes. Her father-in-law had come into the title because his brother's only son had drowned in the Mediterranean. Now his own older son, her husband, Hal, was dead at thirty-two.

Any ill luck wouldn't carry on to her son. Laura made a vow of it. She picked up her newspaper, checked that nothing else was left, and led the way back up the slope toward the house.

She had once thought Caldfort House delightful. It wasn't large, which was part of its charm for her, since she'd grown up in a modest house. Built only fifty-two years ago, it was perfectly designed for a private family home and occasional gracious hospitality. Its proportions were elegant and it had plenty of long windows to let in the light.

Yes, she'd liked it when visits had been an occasional respite from life in the fashionable whirl. Being stuck here forever with bitter Lord Caldfort and peculiar Lady Caldfort was another matter entirely. Add in Jack and her macabre suspicions, and the house was as appealing as a cell in the Tower of London.

Needing the comfort of her son in her arms, Laura exchanged burdens with Nan. Harry had his thumb stuck in his mouth but she didn't try to remove it. He only did that when he was upset and tired.

He was a sweet, trusting weight, the most precious thing in the world. Hers to raise. Hers to protect. Even if her fears seemed insane at times, she couldn't afford to ignore them. She'd never forgive herself if anything that she could prevent happened to Harry.

The closer they came to the house, the slower she walked. She didn't permit herself pointless regrets, but they settled on her now. She'd felt blessed by the gods on her wedding day, but she'd not found true happiness in her marriage and now her future was bleak.

She was only twenty-four years old, but she was a prisoner as surely as if she was in the Tower.

Lord Caldfort insisted, with some justification, that his heir be raised here. She was allowed to take him away, but only for short visits to her family. Her movements were not restricted, but how could she leave Harry, even for days, when she worried about his safety?

She straightened her shoulders and walked into Caldfort House. Her prison until her son was of an age to take care of himself.

# Chapter 2

As they entered the marble-tiled hall, Harry gave a little *hic* as if he might be crying. Laura moved him slightly to see, but he was fast asleep. She brushed a kiss across his forehead.

Had he detected something bad about Jack? They said children and animals were sensitive, and Harry had never taken to his uncle. She mustn't build monsters out of nothing, though. A snarling dog would upset any small child.

"What's the matter with him now?"

Laura started and saw Lord Caldfort, wheezing, bloated, and leaning on his cane, at the open door of his study.

"Nothing, sir. He's just tired."

"Jack said he ran screaming from his dog."

"The dog growled at him, sir."

"You mollycoddle him! Jack's right. The lad should spend some time with him. Learn manly ways."

Laura hoped her dread didn't show on her face. "What a good idea," she said cheerfully. "He's a little young yet, though, don't you think? He would benefit from your attention, sir, if you feel able to give it. You have raised two fine sons, so you know the way of it."

It was blatant flattery but he nodded, even preened a little.

"Might be something in what you say, m'dear. Not up to outdoor stuff these days, but I'll spend a bit of time with the lad. Get him in the way of things."

Laura thanked him, dropping a curtsy, then headed upstairs, hoping that her suggestion blunted the impression of Jack's. The trouble was that it was perfectly reasonable for an uncle to take his brother's place in guiding his son. In other circumstances she would have suggested it herself.

Laura climbed the stairs, praying that all went well with Jack's wife. She had offered to attend the birth, but Emma had pleasantly refused. Remembering her own confinement, Laura hadn't been surprised. She and Emma were always cordial but they were too different to be close. At such a time, a woman wanted harmonious companions.

She knew Emma longed for a son as much as Jack did, but as she entered the nursery and passed the sleeping child to Nan, Laura prayed that this child be another girl. If there was anything to her suspicions, then Jack having a son could be disastrous.

That prayer wasn't answered. When she went downstairs for dinner, she found Jack with her father-in-law, and both men were beaming.

Jack pressed a glass of claret into her hand, and Lord Caldfort raised his. "A toast, m'dear! To Henry Jack Gardeyne!"

Laura froze, glass at her lips. It was family tradition to call first sons Henry, but it was as if a replacement for her Harry was being prepared.

Jack smiled at her. "If you don't object, Laura, we mean to call him Hal."

"Of course not," she said, and found a smile. "Congratulations."

She was about to ask about Emma when Lady Caldfort wandered in, thin and vague as usual. She stared when given the news, as if she'd forgotten that her daughter-in-law was confined, then said, "How convenient. An heir in case the other one dies."

Even the two men seemed taken aback at this blunt statement of fact, but they were all accustomed to Lady Caldfort's ways. She tended to say exactly the words that others were too discreet to let out.

Laura wished she'd been watching Jack. She might have learned something from his reaction.

Lady Caldfort was a cold, angular woman who had little interest in other people and no facility for dealing with them. Apparently Major John Gardeyne, as Lord Caldfort had been then, had married her for her money.

Her only interest in life seemed to be insects, which she collected and arranged in display boxes. That wasn't unusual, but Lady Caldfort kept the boxes stacked in a spare room, never on display. Laura worried that one day her mother-in-law would become completely insane — and that she'd have to take care of her.

"Isn't it time to eat?" Lady Caldfort said, and headed for the dining room, even though the meal hadn't been announced. With a shared look, Laura and the two men followed.

As soon as they were seated, Lord Caldfort and Jack began a discussion of estate matters. As Harry's mother, Laura had an interest in his future property, but that was a battle not worth the powder at this point. She listened, as she always did, gathering knowledge. Eventually their talk turned to sporting details, and she looked away.

Lady Caldfort was frowning at the nearest candle. She might be angry because the food wasn't in front of her, but she could as easily be pondering some problem of entomology. Laura knew that an attempt to start conversation there was hopeless. She was a veteran of hundreds of dinners exactly like this, except that if Jack was not here, there was often no conversation at all. Even so, she was expected to attend.

How many such dinners?

Eleven months since Hal died. That would be about 330.

Since Harry's birth, she'd spent at least half the year here, because both Hal and his father had objected to her taking him away much, and she liked being with her son. She'd enjoyed visits to London, Brighton, and other fashionable spots, but happily sacrificed time at hunting house parties.

Hal had probably been here with her about half the time — a quarter of the year. Sitting opposite her. Looking at her with that look in his eyes that said he was already thinking of an early retreat to their bedchamber and his other favorite sport.

At thought of that sport, her body clenched like a hungry stomach. She pulled her mind back from those lost pleasures.

Calculations. Her antidote to lust.

Two years and five months from Harry's birth to Hal's death. Two times 365 plus about 150 equals 880. She had been here without Hal about a quarter of that time: 220.

Add the 330 since Hal's death: 550.

No, more, because Hal had left her alone here through much of her pregnancy. It had overlapped prime hunting season, after all. She hadn't minded. Her sister Juliet had been with her during the last months, and then her mother had come. Watcombes were powerful medicine against sourness and gloom.

She could add perhaps 50 to make it a round 600.

Six hundred of these dinners, with thousands still to come. Perhaps she would become as eccentric as Lady Caldfort, except in her case it would take the form of eating in her room with a good book or the newspapers. How crazy would she have to appear to get away with that?

Lady Caldfort suddenly banged her spoon on the table. "Where's the food? Why is there no service in this house? Lazy slovens, the lot of them!"

Thomas the footman dashed in. "It's coming, milady. Just a few minutes more." Then he dashed out again.

Lady Caldfort kept rapping the spoon on the table, such a grim look on her face that Laura feared she was contemplating violence.

"Take that damned spoon off her," Lord Caldfort growled.

Laura did so, grateful that at the same time he snapped, "Stop your folly, Cecy!"

Lady Caldfort gave up the spoon but scowled.

"Pour the wine, Jack," Lord Caldfort ordered, and Jack rose to fill all their glasses with red wine. Lady Caldfort took a deep draft and it seemed to pacify her. Laura tried to feel sorry for the woman, who had endured the Gardeynes far longer than she had, but it was hard. She was so totally selfish.

*Like mother, like son?* Laura wondered, for Hal had been selfish at bottom. Unlike his mother, he'd been blessed with good looks and a kind of jollity that passed for generous charm, but underneath . . . Fortunately, he'd had a kind of generosity in bed, for he took pride in pleasing a woman. A gentleman's duty, he would declare, but she'd suspected that if she were hard to please, he'd have neglected her. Fortunate for their marriage that she had not been at all hard to please.

The strangest thing was that she'd only quickened once.

*No, don't think about the pleasures of marriage. Multiply the number of glasses by the number of plates. Add the number of candles in the chandelier. . . .* At last, thank heavens, the servants hurried in with dishes.

"And about time, too!" Lady Caldfort snapped, lifting the lid off the nearest dish herself and spooning soup into her plate.

Laura smiled at the maid placing a tureen in front of her and thanked her. How lucky they were that Caldfort had a competent and forbearing housekeeper in Mrs. Moorside, who came to Laura rather than Lady Caldfort if any troubles arose. The soup, as always, was excellent. A good cook was another blessing, and Laura made sure to count them all.

She believed in people accepting responsibility for their actions. She had married Hal Gardeyne by choice, thinking herself the most fortunate young woman in Dorset. In the first years of her marriage she would have described herself as a happy bride.

She had made this bed and must lie in it, and she would do so with as good a grace as possible. She could even be content if she could only be sure that Harry was safe.

*A gun,* she suddenly thought. *A gun would be very useful.*

With that in mind, she welcomed Lady Caldfort's early and abrupt exit from the dining room and followed her, even though there was no question of the ladies taking tea together. Lady Caldfort marched upstairs. Laura picked up one of the spare candles, lit it at the hall fire, and headed toward the back of the house. Toward the gun room.

Hal had taught her to shoot. It had been amusement for him while living quietly here, and had amused her until he'd tried to get her to target a rabbit. She'd refused, and in disgust he'd given up the lessons.

She knew how to load and prime a gun, however, and Hal's were stored in the gun room, waiting for the day when Harry would be old enough to use them. Splendid hunting pieces, ornate dueling pistols, practical, deadly horse pistols. Her interest, however, was a smaller pistol that he'd carried in a pocket when out at night.

She went into the room and made a face. The former Lord Caldfort had dabbled in the new art of taxidermy in order to preserve his hunting triumphs. A stag's head loomed over the door, three foxes, one with a chicken in its mouth, ran along the tops of cabinets, and various predatory birds eyed her. She supposed they were all properly preserved, but to her the room always smelled of decay.

She hurried past the racks of big guns and put her flickering candle down to open the drawer where Hal's pistols were kept.

It was empty.

She frowned and opened the one to the left, but it held Lord Caldfort's pistols. The drawer to the right contained old ones, kept only for curiosity value. She slowly closed that drawer, guessing where Hal's pistols were.

Jack had taken them.

She stared at a beady-eyed hawk. Again, it was not unquestionably suspicious. Hal's guns were the best money could buy, and if his brother wanted to use them until his son was old enough, why not?

But it felt like a deepening of the threat. She considered Lord Caldfort's pistols, but shook her head. If she was discovered, what excuse could she make? With Hal's guns she had intended to say she wanted Harry to get used to one — unloaded, of course.

The bigger guns wouldn't be of much use to her, anyway. Her hands were small and she'd never really been able to handle Hal's ordinary pistols. Only the smaller one.

She picked up her candle and left the room, as weaponless as before.

# Chapter 3

Laura didn't sleep well that night, despite trying to persuade herself that any threats were in her imagination. The next day brought a blessing in the form of a long letter from Juliet. After making sure that Harry was safe in the nursery, Laura took the letter to her boudoir to enjoy.

One benefit of marriage to Hal had been her ability to introduce her younger sister to London society. Their own family were county gentry of the most minor sort. Their grandfather had been a yeoman farmer until he made the transition to gentleman farmer. Hal Gardeyne, heir to a viscountcy, had been a brilliant match.

In London, Juliet's good looks and loving nature had won her, too, a man of excellent family. She'd had to wait two years for Robert Fancourt to rise high enough in the Home Office to afford a wife, but she hadn't seemed to mind. That thought troubled Laura now and then, but things in the past were past worrying over.

Juliet was certainly happy now. She adored her Robert and thrived on living most of the year in London.

Lines of social gossip and stories of comings and goings soon had Laura relaxed and smiling. Here at Caldfort, it was easy to forget that elsewhere life went on its merry way, even in October.

Fashionable London would be quiet, but Juliet clearly found much to keep her busy. The bustle and hum almost rose from the page like an aroma, catching Laura's breath with longing.

She looked up from the letter and out at the tranquil countryside. It was doubtless shallow of her, but oh, to be in town, too. Walks in the parks, shopping, the theater, exhibitions, lively company, and the sheer fun of being with her favorite sister.

She shook off wistfulness and turned to the next sheet. Juliet never tried to economize by crossing her writing.

*Can you imagine whom Robert brought to dinner not long ago? Sir Stephen Ball! He asked after you.*

Oh? Laura felt a strange sensation, as if

something had tugged at her insides.

*I know he was only your friend's brother,
but I did think you and he might make a
match of it. Before Hal, of course.*

Laura wondered how many other people
had thought that. The idea had never
crossed her mind — until the day Stephen
had so inappropriately proposed. She'd already been betrothed to Hal. What had she
been supposed to do?
But she shouldn't have laughed. . . .
She looked back at the slightly blurred
writing.

*I was somewhat taken by him myself. Do
you remember him as Valancourt when you
made a play of Udolpho? Blond and heroic. Fuel for romantic dreams. He could
have been no more than seventeen, but at
thirteen, seventeen is a great age.*

Laura had achieved the grand age of fifteen when they'd performed that play, but
to her, too, seventeen had seemed a great
age. Stephen had been one of those young
men who mature early, perhaps because of
his serious attention to his studies and to
issues of politics and law. He'd never been

dull, though. She remembered working with him for weeks during his summer holiday from Harrow, turning the dramatic novel into a short play. The taste of it in her mind now was of challenge and pure, thrilling excitement, yet she'd not thought of it for years.

How strange. Had she deliberately wiped it from her memory?

Staging the play had been pure, thrilling excitement of another sort. She'd had the role of Emily and he Valancourt. Daringly they'd written in a kiss, and she'd come close to swooning with embarrassment at that stiff and awkward press of lips to lips in front of an audience of his and her families.

She laughed a little now at that, but what business did Stephen have of asking after her? Their friendship had faltered after his proposal, and died when he'd maliciously pinned her with the name Lady Skylark. They'd hardly met or spoken in six years.

Lady Skylark. She still didn't understand how he could have been so cruel.

She'd gone straight from her wedding to London, and instantly become a toast. She'd loved being the beautiful Mrs. Hal Gardeyne, which had soon become La Belle Laura. Heady stuff at eighteen, but she didn't think she'd been insufferable.

Then someone — rumor said it was Brummell himself — had turned that into Labellelle. It simply meant the "beautiful *L*," but the unique construction had seemed mysterious and sophisticated, everything Laura longed to be.

But then, overnight, she'd become Lady Skylark.

Everyone thought it charming and a perfect fit, and so it had stuck.

She'd hated it.

People assumed she had a lovely singing voice, and she didn't, but the real problem was the other meaning. Overnight, she'd transformed from mysterious, sophisticated Labellelle into a feckless and immature child, because *skylarking* was a term used in the navy for lads who played dangerous games high in the rigging.

When she'd heard a rumor that Stephen had christened her that at some drunken, manly gathering, she'd known it was true and known it was malicious because *Skylark* had special meaning for them. A meaning connected to his absurd and embarrassing proposal.

She'd known immediately that she shouldn't have laughed, known that she'd hurt him, which she'd never wanted to do.

He'd abruptly walked away from her and left the area until after her marriage, so she'd had no chance to make amends. She understood his pain, but there had been no call for such a cruel retaliation.

It was all in the past, all in the past, but if Stephen was asking about her now, she worried about his motives. Did Juliet have anything to say about that?

*He's making quite a name for himself in Parliament, you know. A brilliant speaker, Robert says, though I have not heard him. Sitting in the visitors' gallery, no matter how fashionable it may be, is not my choice of entertainment. Robert says he may be offered a position in the ministry. At only twenty-six. That will be quite a stir at home, won't it? He's still unmarried. Perhaps not surprising when he's still young.*

*He's two years older than I am,* Laura thought, and skimmed over Stephen's noble causes, Stephen's pithy quotes, Stephen's prospects of becoming Prime Minister, for heaven's sake.

*Imagine that! Of course Pitt was a Member of Parliament at twenty-two and Prime Minister at twenty-four, which makes Stephen quite a sluggard. From my mature perspective, I'm not surprised that you didn't marry him. He's frighteningly clever, of course, and he can be terribly witty, but I find him daunting. I found myself in danger of being tongue-tied all through dinner. Me! Can you imagine it?*

No.

*Speaking of political advantage, which I was, dearest, if you will only look back up the page a little, Robert has gone on some mission to Denmark, which he says will have that effect, so I am returning home for a few weeks. Is it possible that you could join me there? I long to see you and little Harry again. I would come to you, but in all honesty, Caldfort makes me shudder!*

Laura let the letter sag.
Go home?
Immediately she thought, *Why not?*
She hadn't seen Juliet since the wedding six months ago. She hadn't been home since then, either. She rose to her feet, folding the letter, a smile already tugging at her lips.
A week away! It felt like paradise and would restore her perspective. Perhaps she

would see that her fears about Jack were gothic, and most important, in her bustling home in another county, Harry would be completely safe.

Eager to have it settled, she hurried downstairs and knocked at the door to her father-in-law's study. Silence. She knocked again, thinking that if she started preparations immediately, they could even leave tomorrow.

Tomorrow!

No reply.

She frowned at the door panels. Lord Caldfort lived between this room and his bedchamber across the hall. He preferred the study during the day, but he retired to bed if he suffered one of his bad spells. She couldn't pursue him there.

She turned away, but then heard a faint, "Come in."

She went in quickly, thinking he might be ill. Indeed, though he was sitting behind his desk with the postbag and letters still in front of him, he looked even pastier than usual.

"Is anything wrong, sir? Do you need your tonic?"

"Nothing more than the ordinary. What d'ye want? Disturbing m'peace. Everyone's always cutting up m'peace."

Laura abandoned concern. He wouldn't hesitate to summon the doctor if he felt worse. She made her request, hoping his mood wouldn't turn him difficult.

He surprised her. "Back to Merrymead, eh? Well, why not? It's a six month or more since you've been there. When do you want to go?"

This was a little more enthusiasm than Laura was used to, but she wouldn't complain. "I see no reason to delay, sir. We seem to be in a spell of dry weather. I would like to be off tomorrow, if that is agreeable."

Again, he made no objection. "Of course, m'dear. And why not make a nice long stay this time? A month or so, eh?"

Laura blinked at him, almost protesting out of shock. She conquered that insanity and quickly agreed. "Thank you, sir," she said, and curtsied and left before he could change his mind.

She paused in the hall, wondering if she should send for the doctor, anyway. Lord Caldfort was not his usual self. She reminded herself to never look a gift horse in the mouth and hurried upstairs to give instructions for the journey. Only when that was done did she let herself return to the puzzle.

She retired to her boudoir, frowning over Lord Caldfort's suggestion that she and Harry be away for a whole month.

Did he want nothing to do with Harry now there was another Gardeyne to inherit? That made no sense. Harry was a Gardeyne, too. Why should Lord Caldfort favor one grandson over the other? He'd always been fond of Harry, in his careless way.

Was it simply that the existence of an alternate heir meant that the other one could be let out of sight? She'd welcome that, but it wasn't rational. Babies were delicate creatures, especially in the early days. The longer a child lived, the more likely it was to survive.

That reminded her that she'd not visited her sister-in-law and should do so before she left. She put on a warm spencer, but then thought of Harry.

Jack could sneak into the house and . . .

Oh, rubbish! She'd end up in an asylum at this rate. He'd be safe with Nan.

She put on a bonnet, gloves, and sturdy leather half-boots, then set off for the mile walk to the village, enjoying the exercise and fresh air.

She tried to put her worries out of her head, but her mind kept returning to Lord

Caldfort's strange behavior. He had looked decidedly unwell. But he'd not sent for the doctor.

He'd been dealing with the day's post.

Had he just received bad news?

The instant she thought of it, she knew it was true. Lord Caldfort had looked as if he had just received very bad news.

The explanation should soothe her, for she couldn't imagine how such news would affect Harry and herself. But then, it was as if the bad news had made him eager to have Laura and Harry away from Caldfort.

Disease in the area?

No. That news wouldn't arrive by letter, and the alarm would be more general.

She realized that she'd stopped and was staring blindly at a rambler covered with scarlet rose hips, and set off again. A lawsuit? Debts? Scandal?

In the months after Hal's death there had been awkward letters. Creditors had emerged like maggots, and two women had claimed to be carrying Hal's child. In view of her own difficulty in quickening, Laura had been skeptical, though she didn't doubt that Hal had been with many women when away from her. He'd been a lusty man.

Eleven months after his death was late for a new child to turn up, and in any case, another Gardeyne bastard would not upset Lord Caldfort. He seemed to see them as a mark of virility.

Scandal or lawsuit involving Jack? Even if he was a villainous uncle, that seemed unlikely.

Yet something had happened.

Wild investments failing, leaving them all penniless?

From what little she knew of the Gardeyne finances, they were managed cautiously. Lord Caldfort, to his credit, was satisfied with the wealth he had unexpectedly inherited.

Laura entered the village of Cald St. Edwin's having come up with no plausible cause for alarm. That was more worrying rather than less. Something strange had arrived in this morning's post. She was sure of it.

By the time she approached the green door of the red brick vicarage, she knew she had to try to find out what it was. She didn't want to leave Caldfort for a month ignorant of a possible threat behind her.

# Chapter 4

Laura went up to her sister-in-law's bedchamber thinking that it wouldn't be surprising if Jack lusted after Caldfort House. The vicarage was small for his growing family, and it also lacked charm. It hadn't been built by the Lord Caldfort who'd commissioned Caldfort House, but by the previous one, who looked to have done it on the cheap.

She found Emma Gardeyne glowing, however, especially with the satisfaction of finally producing a son. Laura admired the sleeping baby, who was as mysterious and entrancing as all newborns, then sat to take tea and listen to an account of the birth.

Perhaps even there she'd been unjust to Jack. Emma claimed to have had an easy time of it and to have driven her husband out of the house.

"He would keep popping in to see if all was well, which is very distracting, as I'm sure you know."

Hal had never popped in, but Laura made vague noises of agreement.

The midwife came to check on the health of mother and baby and stayed to chat. Mrs. Finch was wife to the local blacksmith and had attended Laura's confinement, too.

Everything seemed perfect, but Laura thought she detected some strain in Emma's manner. Was she imagining that?

She must be. It was just barely possible to imagine that Jack was plotting infanticide, but never that Emma was part of it. Emma's gentle goodness and firm moral beliefs frequently put Laura to shame, which was part of the reason they hadn't become close. Laura had to bite her tongue too often in order not to challenge Emma's conventional beliefs, and if she relaxed and spoke naturally of subjects that interested her, Emma was shocked.

And didn't hesitate to comment on it.

But Emma was truly *good*. Laura had never heard her say an unkind word about anyone, and she would not gossip. Which was a shame, since there was a delicious rumor circulating about the innkeeper of the Red Hen and Dr. Trumper's housekeeper.

When Mrs. Finch left, Laura broke her

news, unable to stop herself from watching closely for any reaction.

"And Lord Caldfort says Harry and I may stay for a month."

Emma's eyes widened, but only in natural surprise.

"How lovely for you, Laura. I long to visit my family, but it is so far to Durham and would cost a great deal for a private carriage. Anyway, I'm sure Jack is right that days on the road with young children would be very difficult. And, of course, he has his duties to the parish."

"You should persuade him to take on a curate."

Emma's face tightened. Was all not perfect here after all? "It would be an expense, and there are so many calls on his purse."

*Not least his horses and dogs,* Laura thought, but didn't say it. Jack was no worse than any other man in that respect. Perhaps it was unfair to think that a vicar should be willing to economize on his own pleasures to provide his wife with a visit to her family.

Laura wanted to know if Emma had an explanation for their father-in-law's strange behavior, so she said, "I am puzzled to be allowed to take Harry away for a whole month."

"Perhaps Father Caldfort is becoming more moderate." Lord Caldfort hated to be referred to like that. "After all, there is little Harry can learn here at such a young age." But then Emma fixed Laura with an intent look. "Jack does hope to take a father's place with Harry, Laura. It hurts him when you don't agree."

Laura's mouth dried and she sipped more tea. "Harry's too young yet."

"Would you say the same if Hal were alive?"

"That would be different."

"It's as if you don't trust Jack with Harry, Laura, but you must know he would be as careful of Harry as Hal."

What could she say? "I'm sure he would."

"Don't mind his way of talking. He doesn't mean what he says."

Laura stared. "What can you mean?"

Emma's color rose. She was pretty, with soft blond hair, and seeing her blush like that, no one would believe that she was a matron of thirty with four children in her nursery.

"It's just the thrill of a son. You know how men are about such things. Jack has said once or twice that if . . . if anything were to happen to Harry, little Hal would one day be Lord Caldfort, but it doesn't mean anything."

Laura found a light laugh. "Of course it doesn't! It's a simple truth, as if I were to say that if Lord Caldfort took a turn for the worse, Harry could end up being an infant viscount."

Emma's smile showed relief. "Yes, that's it. It wouldn't mean you were *wishing* for his death." But then she flushed a deeper red at the implication of her words.

"Of course not." Laura brushed over the moment. "I wish Lord Caldfort a very long life so that Harry can grow up without burdens. I fear it will not be. He seemed particularly unwell this morning. I think he may have received bad news in the postbag. Jack hasn't mentioned any concerns about the estate, has he?"

Emma was clearly grateful for a change of subject. "No. Well, there are the usual problems due to the depressed state of the economy and the atrocious weather. The harvest was sadly off, and many will feel the pinch. We intend to take a special collection to provide winter food for the desperate. I hope you will contribute."

"Yes, of course."

Emma could be guarding marital confidences, but Laura didn't think so. Emma lied no more than she gossiped. "You don't think the estate could be in debt?" she tried.

"I shouldn't think so. Jack would know, wouldn't he? And I'm sure he would tell me something like that. But if Father is unwell, has Dr. Trumper been sent for?"

Laura rose. There was nothing to learn here. "He never hesitates to summon Trumper if he feels the need, but I'll check his condition again when I return to the house."

She kissed her sister-in-law's cheek and left the room, feeling as she always did after time with Emma — like a lower form of womanhood.

As she arrived at the hall, the front door opened and Jack came in bringing brisk fresh air.

Laura searched him for any sign of evil and found none. "I've been visiting Emma and the baby. Congratulations, Jack. A fine, robust boy. A true Gardeyne."

"Aye. Nothing frail about *him*."

She kept her smile in place. "Emma seems well, too."

"Birthing's no trouble to her."

"Even an easy birth is a considerable challenge, Jack."

Perhaps he flushed. "Aye, well . . . Father says you're going to Merrymead for a week or two."

She caught a strange tone and braced for trouble. Would he try to stop it? "Harry should know his other family."

"True enough."

Laura was sure she heard a silent *but*. Her attention, however, was on the fact that he must have visited his father in the past hour. "Has Lord Caldfort sent for Dr. Trumper yet?"

He frowned. "Not that I know of. Why?"

"He seemed to have a funny spell, though he denied it."

His frown deepened. "I thought he looked a bit the worse for wear. His heart?"

"I don't know." She considered for a moment, then added, "It might have been something to do with a letter, since he was reading his correspondence at the time. He didn't say anything to you?"

He stiffened, doubtless at the notion that he would discuss estate business with her. "No. Therefore there can't have been anything of import. Summon Dr. Trumper anyway, Laura."

Laura bit back a sarcastic, *Yes, sir.* "I must be on my way. There's much to be done if we're to leave tomorrow."

"You'll bring Harry to visit his father's grave before you go?" It was phrased as a question, but sounded like a command. Laura was tempted to refuse for that reason, but Jack was right. She and Harry visited the grave every Sunday, taking fresh flowers, so they should do that before going away for weeks.

"We'll drive over later in the gig," she said, but then came to a resolution. "Do you have Hal's guns, Jack?"

Perhaps his ruddy cheeks grew a little redder. "Aye, why not? Don't want them rusting away up there."

"Of course not, but I was thinking of what you said about manly ways. If Harry had the little pistol — unloaded, of course — it would be a memento of his father and get him in the way of such things."

She was sure she saw hesitation, but then Jack said, "Not a bad idea. I'll get it."

He strode off and returned with the case. Laura opened it. She tried to make her scrutiny look like fondness, but she was making sure that all the essentials were inside. "Sad memories," she said, and it was true. Poor Hal, who'd enjoyed life so much and was no more.

She closed the case. "Thank you, Jack."

"Be sure to keep the balls and powder hidden. Boys get the hang of that sort of thing more quickly than you'd think."

"Of course."

Laura left and set off back to Caldfort, considering Jack's last words. She'd swear his concern for safety had been genuine. Thank heavens she was going to Merrymead. It could straighten the brain of a Bedlamite.

Once back at Caldfort, she plunged into the arrangements for travel. She sent a groom to order a chaise for the morrow, then supervised the packing, letting the excited Harry help with his.

"No, Minnow. You can't take flowers to Grandmama. They'd be dead before we arrived. Come to my jewelry box and you can choose something to take as a present."

Her valuable jewelry was in the safe, so she let him look through her box, which amused him for quite some time, as she wrote instructions for Mrs. Moorside.

In the end, he chose a pretty rose pin that her mother would like. It had been a gift from Charlotte Ball, she remembered. For her eighteenth birthday. Stephen had remarked that pink roses were a strange choice.

From the depths of memory came a clear recollection.

She'd asked what flowers would suit her.

He'd said, "Poppies."

"Poppies? Weeds of the field?"

"Vibrant, beautiful, and a great deal more resilient than they appear. And then, of course, there's the type that provides a powerful drug that turns men mad."

She'd been startled and unsure whether she was being teased, flattered, or insulted. His gift, she remembered with a snort, had been a copy of William Wordsworth's "Ode: Intimations of Immortality."

"Mama?"

She started and looked down at a worried Harry. "Yes, dear. I was just thinking about when I received that brooch. Grandmama will be very pleased with it. Come along and we'll wrap it up prettily and tie it with a ribbon."

Where, she wondered, had that slim volume gone? It was a reminder, however, that Stephen had disapproved of her even then, before Hal Gardeyne had visited the area and changed everything.

# Chapter 5

Harry chattered about his grandparents, his uncles and aunts and cousins. He seemed to remember them all remarkably well, when it had been six months since their last short visit. Laura couldn't help thinking that he could have a happier, healthier childhood at Merrymead but she was powerless to change his home.

Powerless.

In a right and just world, a mother should have more power, but in this one, Lord Caldfort was Harry's guardian. When he died, the power would transfer to Jack.

She stilled in the midst of tying a pink ribbon. She truly wished Lord Caldfort a long life.

She managed to eat enough lunch that Harry didn't notice anything wrong, then took him into the flower garden, which was not much cherished. He chose some

Michaelmas daisies and stocks and some delicate grayish foliage. Laura gazed around, thinking that perhaps she should dedicate her life to gardening. But surely if that had been her calling, she would have felt it before now.

Her mood was certainly suitable for a visit to her husband's grave, but she didn't want Harry to be sad, so as they walked to the stables, she started a song he enjoyed. By the time she lifted him into the one-horse gig, her heart was lighter, which proved her belief that people could mostly be as happy as they tried to be. To have Harry to herself was certainly a delight, and soon she'd have him to herself for a whole month.

She never took Nan to Merrymead. There wasn't much free space there, and there were always plenty of people happy to look after a child. She didn't take her maid, either, for the same reason.

"Just you and me, Harry," she said as they rolled along the lane toward the village, the bells on Nutmeg's harness jingling.

"Just you and me!" he echoed, bouncing on his seat.

He was so excited — and at tomorrow's journey, not this one — that Laura drove slowly. They were in no hurry and she didn't want him to fall out. In truth, she'd rather not spoil his or her bright spirits by this visit to Hal's grave, but that was an unworthy thought. Poor Hal deserved to be remembered.

Harry pointed to cows, horses, sheep, and trees. They paused by Figgers Farm to watch some ducks. When she lifted him out by the churchyard, he beamed at her. Was there anything so magical as an excited, happy child? She planted a big kiss on his cheek before putting him down.

When the horse was securely tethered, she took Harry's hand. "Come along, Minnow. Hold tight to those flowers."

They walked through the gate and up the path.

"Church?" he asked, pulling toward the ancient building.

"Not today, sweetling. Today we're going to put the flowers near your father's grave because we won't be at church next Sunday. We'll attend St. Michael's near Merrymead."

"Merrymead!" he caroled, making her laugh.

She hastily controlled that. It was hardly appropriate for a widow visiting her husband's grave. Instead, she began to talk about Hal, as she did during every visit, to try to keep his memory alive for Harry. She knew it couldn't work, though. Poor Hal would end up as only a grave and a stranger in some portraits.

She couldn't even tell Harry the whole truth. Hal Gardeyne had not been a particularly clever man, and he'd inherited all his father and mother's selfishness. There were positive aspects, too, however, or she would never have married him.

"Your father was a strong man, Harry. Over six feet tall and broad shouldered. I think that one day you'll be the same. He had such energy it almost sparkled around him, and he was generous."

In bed. Judging from the way some women found their husbands' attentions a burden, she supposed other husbands were not. She recognized, too, that if she'd been highly fertile she might have been wary of her husband's approaches herself.

She fought a smile. What would the world be like if secret thoughts were heard by others?

"Here we are." Laura halted before the handsome marble stone upon which Hal Gardeyne's life was recorded. Eldest son of John, Lord Caldfort of this parish, beloved brother of the Reverend John Gardeyne, vicar of St. Edwin's. Sorely missed by his loving wife, Laura, and his son, Harry.

Beneath was carved the phrase that Jack had insisted on. HE LEFT LIFE LEAPINGS⋆.

The alliteration had always made it sound slightly humorous to Laura, but she knew the words came from a brother's understanding. Hal had indeed been full of vibrant energy and had died doing one of the things he loved most — flying over a jump in the hunting field.

Laura hoped there were horses and hedges in heaven.

She looked down to see that Harry had already taken out last Sunday's wilting flowers and was trying to shove the new ones in. She went to help him. "Now we need to get water from the pump, love. Come on."

Harry had sat down, however, and started to pick a new bouquet of buttercups with the intensity typical of a three-year-old. Laura shook her head and left him to his work. The Gardeyne plot was close to the pump.

She worked the pump handle, keeping an eye on Harry to make sure he didn't wander. Thin sunlight lit the scene, but the wind was soughing through the tall elms that shadowed the plot, creating a melancholy air. It seemed they were more sorrowful than she.

She did grieve for Hal, but it was unselfish sorrow. He'd been snatched from vibrant life so soon, and that was tragic.

She recognized that her own sorrows were entirely selfish. She resented being abandoned in this constrained and tedious situation, barred from both her family and the fashionable world she'd enjoyed. She grieved — had grieved for years — for the marriage she'd dreamed of at eighteen.

Dazzled by an energetic, worldly man, she'd expected his courting attention to continue. Instead, he'd drifted back to his manly sporting world. He'd seem to enjoy her company when with her, but his heart had been solidly elsewhere. Time tends to flow to where the heart dwells.

She'd come to realize that they had nothing in common, not even their fashionable life. He'd preened to be husband of Labellelle, but he'd liked being the husband of Lady Skylark even more. He'd thought Labellelle too highfalutin and suspect.

"Brummell," he'd said once. "Funny sort of fellow, Brummell. Don't like to hunt because he gets mud on his clothes. Lady Skylark, that's you, my dear. Happy as a lark."

They'd been in bed then, relaxed and sweaty. . . .

How fortunate that an observer would not be able to read her thoughts. In all the sympathy about her widowed state, no one mentioned bed. She supposed they couldn't, but no wonder there were so many wicked widows.

Even that relief was not open to her. She couldn't imagine taking casual lovers, but she certainly couldn't risk scandal. A scandalous mother could be cut off from her children. If Jack was as evil as she thought, her misbehavior could seal Harry's death warrant.

He was still sitting by his father's grave, surrounded by massacred buttercups. She picked up the wooden bucket and set off back toward the grave, being careful not to splash her skirts.

Harry looked at something in his hand, then shoved it in his mouth.

"Harry, no!"

Laura started to hurry, and the water splashed. She dropped the bucket and ran. Buttercups weren't poisonous, but still . . . She grabbed his hand. It was covered with something brown.

"*Harry!* Don't eat that. Spit it out!"

He was chewing, looking mutinous, so at

least it couldn't be dung.

"Open!" she commanded in her sternest voice.

Glowering, he obeyed, revealing a mess of brown and white. It looked like some kind of sticky bun.

"Harry, you know better than this!" she scolded as she scooped out as much as she could with her fingers. "You don't eat things you find on the ground. Spit out the rest. Immediately!"

Face crumpling, he did as she said, and she wiped his mouth with her handkerchief. Then she towed him over to the pump, grabbing the empty bucket as she went.

"Never, never, never eat something you find on the ground! It could make you ill." She began to pump. "Drink from the water as it comes out and then spit. Try not to swallow."

She wasn't sure he could follow her instructions, but he did, even though he got drenched in the process.

Laura's panicked heart began to settle, and she felt dizzy and had to lean against the pump for a moment. It had only been a sticky bun that someone had dropped. At his age, Harry probably wouldn't put something vile in his mouth, and if he did he would spit it out.

She knelt and gathered him into her arms, wet though he was. "I'm sorry if I frightened you, Minnow, but you frightened me. You must never eat things you find lying around, no matter how tasty they look."

Some of the wet on his face was tears. "I'm sorry, Mama."

She kissed his temple. "I know, sweetling, and all's well that ends well. Let's finish the flowers and get you home and dry."

They completed the business quickly, then Laura said, "Come along, now."

Harry dragged on her arm, so she picked him up again, sorry to have alarmed and upset him. She definitely needed to get away from Caldfort and be restored to her usual sunny nature. She gave him a special hug before putting him into the gig, and promised him another cake when they arrived home.

Evening was settling and the air was turning sharp. Laura stripped off Harry's wet jacket and helped him into his coat, which she'd brought in case. Then she wrapped a shawl around herself, winding the ends country-fashion behind her and knotting them there.

Harry leaned against her so she kept one arm around him, but that meant she couldn't drive fast. She wanted him home and into dry clothes, but she couldn't deny him a hug. They had entered the parkland around Caldfort when he whined, "Mama . . ."

A moment later, he threw up over the side of the gig.

She halted the horse and wiped Harry's mouth. "It must have been that bun, Minnow. Heaven knows how long it had been there. You'll feel all the better for getting rid of it."

She gathered the reins again, but he was crying now and clutching his stomach. Suddenly full of dread, Laura gripped his coat and urged the horse to speed.

They were in the stables in minutes.

She abandoned the gig, gathered her screaming child into her arms, and raced for the house, for her stillroom, where she kept her medicinal supplies.

The vomiting and pain could just be from excitement, but she must rid his stomach of any trace of that bun. She put him down and grabbed the infusion of ipecacuanha. Her hands were almost shaking too much to pour some into a glass and force it down his throat.

61

He fought her but she made him swallow. In moments, he hurled up all the contents of his little stomach, then burst into sobs again. She held him close, trying to soothe him, but ecstatic to see bits of bun among the vomit.

By then, the housekeeper and a maid were hovering.

"Whatever is it, ma'am?" Mrs. Moorside exclaimed.

"Harry picked up something from the ground and ate it. Could you make some lemonade for him, please, with lots of honey and a little brandy?"

Harry was hiccupping with tears and sucking his thumb as she carried him up to his room, where Nan cried out with alarm. Laura told the story again as they worked together to strip off his damp and messy clothing, wash him, and dress him in his nightshirt. Then they tucked him into a warm bed and Laura sat beside, watching for any further ill effects.

Mrs. Moorside herself came up with the lemonade, and Laura coaxed Harry into sipping it. It was one of his favorite drinks, and soon half of it was gone. The brandy made his lids droop, and in a moment he was fast asleep.

Laura checked again to see that his brow

was cool and his pulse normal. His tummy wasn't hard or showing any sign of distress, and her boiling panic settled to a simmer. If there had been danger it was probably over. Probably. It took great willpower to leave the room, to leave her son in Nan's hands even for a while, but she was wet and foul.

It was only when she reached her room that she faced her deepest fear. She leaned against the wall, legs shaking so much that they gave way and she sank to the ground.

Someone might have tried to poison her son.

Jack Gardeyne might have tried to poison her son.

Laura crawled to a chair and got into it, dirty as she was.

A bun, even if it was days old, shouldn't have such an effect. On the other hand, vomiting and pain could just be a nervous reaction. She might have caused it herself.

She couldn't make herself believe that. She couldn't afford to believe that. Thank heavens they were leaving tomorrow; otherwise she'd go mad from fear.

Her maid rushed in to take care of her and she had to pull herself together, to pretend to be only an upset mother as she stood to undress, to wash, to put on fresh

63

clothing. As she sat to have her hair tidied, to be restored to perfect Laura Gardeyne.

By then a message had come up from Lord Caldfort demanding a report on what had happened to his heir. Laura collected the last disordered scraps of herself and went down to his study. He was in his big chair by the window, swollen legs raised on a footstool, looking distressed and haggard again.

"Harry's fine now, sir," Laura said quickly. "He's in no danger."

"But what danger was he in, eh?" Lord Caldfort demanded. "What were you doing to let him eat poison?"

"Poison?" she gasped, wondering what he knew.

"I hear you forced an emetic down him. Was that for amusement, woman?"

Laura sat down before her legs betrayed her again. "No, sir, of course not. But it may not have been necessary. I couldn't afford to take any risk. Harry ate something he found on the ground. A bun, probably."

"Rat poison, was it?"

She shuddered. Such deaths from poisoned bait were unfortunately common. "Who would put out rat poison in a graveyard, sir? Doubtless someone dropped the bun and there was nothing wrong with it, until my panic excited his stomach."

He narrowed his eyes at her. "But you don't think so."

She licked her lips and repeated what she'd said. "I couldn't afford to take the risk, sir."

He scowled, looking like a dyspeptic bulldog. "You're a good mother. Thought you were nothing but a pretty flibberti-gibbet when Hal married you. Didn't the *ton* used to call you skylark?" He snorted. "Not for your singing, either. For your larking around. But you've turned out to have all your wits about you. Hal was fortunate."

It was the first time he'd said anything like that to her.

"Thank you, sir. I do grieve for him."

"Aye." He sighed. "He lived for hunting, though."

"He would have chosen that way," she agreed. He certainly wou[ld] wanted to outlive his abilit[y to] hunt, as his father had.

"I suppose you'll w[ant] departure," he sai[d]

Laura's stomach that's necessary," s[he] she could manage. these things quickly. [U] worse, we will leave tomorrow as planned."

She braced for resistance, but he nodded. "Aye, that would be best."

Laura curtsied and left, relieved in one way but not in another. Did Lord Caldfort share her suspicions? Could his distress this morning have been due not to a letter, but to something Jack had said?

She paused in the hall to go over everything, and she couldn't make it fit. She was almost certain Jack hadn't visited that early, and everything pointed to Lord Caldfort being alone, reading his correspondence when the shock occurred. . . .

"Laura? Is something the matter?"

She started and whirled, hand to chest, to find that she hadn't imagined that distinctive, slightly drawling voice.

"Stephen! What on earth are you doing here?"

# Chapter 6

Elegant, blond, lean, and quizzical, Sir Stephen Ball was indeed standing across the hall from her, though her stunned mind couldn't imagine how. It was as if he'd appeared in a puff of theatrical smoke.

"What am I doing?" he asked, strolling toward her. "Attempting to speak to Lord Caldfort on a political matter, but I gather there's a problem in the house. Cook's burned the sauce? A rat's invaded the larder?"

Stephen, here, sardonic as always. Wishing to speak to Lord Caldfort . . . ?

Her dazed mind suddenly sharpened. Was his arrival connected to Lord Caldfort's earlier shock? Had a letter heralded political scandal or disaster?

"Laura?" His brows had risen, and his lazy eyes were now sharp. As her shock faded, she realized that he hadn't appeared in a puff of smoke, but simply walked out of the reception room.

She gathered scraps of information. He'd come here to speak to Lord Caldfort and been shown to the reception room. Her drama had distracted all the servants and he'd been forgotten.

She managed a light laugh. "Stephen, I'm so sorry! As you say, we have all been distracted by a domestic matter, but how shameful that you've been neglected. You're here to see my father-in-law? I'll go and let him know —"

She began to turn, but he caught her arm, shocking her. As she turned back, she knew it wasn't just the outrageousness of it. It was a man's touch. It had been so long since she'd felt a man's touch like this.

But Stephen . . . ?

"Take a moment to settle your nerves," he said, letting her go. "I don't wish to intrude, but is there anything I can do to help? I'm quite a hand at catching rats."

To spill every detail to him now was perhaps the strongest temptation Laura had ever experienced, but she stopped herself. Once they had been as close as sister and brother, but once long ago. For six years, he had avoided her as deliberately as she had avoided him.

"Thank you, but the drama is over. My son ate something noxious and I had to give him an emetic. Lord Caldfort is upset because, of course, Harry is his heir."

"What did he eat?"

"A bun of some sort, dropped in the churchyard."

She managed to speak lightly, but shocked thoughts rushed in anyway. *And possibly deliberately laced with poison.*

An arm came around her and she needed it, needed assistance into the reception room and onto the sofa there. She couldn't afford to be so weak, but muscles and sinews don't always obey will.

"I'm all right. . . ." she tried.

"Going sheet-white and swaying is Lady Skylark's latest party trick, is it?" He went to the fireplace and rang the bell.

"All the rage in these parts." She managed to say it lightly, but was relieved to be sitting down. She even closed her eyes and leaned her head against the back of the sofa for a moment, listening as if from a distance as Thomas arrived, apologizing fervently for having forgotten the visitor.

"Never mind that," Stephen said with cool authority. "Mrs. Gardeyne needs a restorative. Sweet tea and brandy. Immediately."

Thomas left and Laura opened her eyes. Despite everything, she even found herself smiling. "How typical of you, Stephen, to be giving orders in someone else's house."

"Playing lord of creation. Do you mind?"

"Of course not."

But what if he'd come to tear her bit of creation apart?

A final act of revenge? No, she couldn't imagine Stephen sinking so low. They had been friends once, good friends.

He came to sit beside her on the sofa and she noted a new grace in him. He had grown into his height and strength, but that shouldn't surprise her. They had met now and then over the past six years.

He was in boots and leather breeches. Country wear, but London made, she noted. After all, they called him the Political Dandy. A riding crop lay with his hat and gloves on a table.

He'd ridden here. From where? People rarely chose to ride long distances — off the hunting field, that was.

His lips twitched. "As readable as ever, Laura. What am I doing here? I stopped by to speak to Caldfort about some Parliamentary matters."

She straightened and gathered her wits.

"Yes, you said. But stopped by? Berkshire is hardly next door to Devon or London."

"A little out of the way. Am I unwelcome?"

*Yes.* But she couldn't say that.

"Of course not. It's only that I'm still shaken by the incident with Harry. I fear you've wasted a journey, however. I doubt Lord Caldfort will appear in Parliament again. He can hardly leave the house." She lowered her voice. "He may not last long."

"Unfortunate. He's always been a supporter of military reform, which is the issue in hand."

She tried to read his expression, but he'd always been skilled at concealing thoughts and feelings. Was the explanation of his presence that simple? No connection to her father-in-law's distress? She distrusted coincidence, but she supposed it did happen.

The tea arrived with the brandy decanter on the side. Stephen would have poured, but Laura insisted, even though the pot felt heavy in her still-unsteady hands. She stirred more sugar into her cup than she normally took, and let Stephen add some brandy. As soon as she sipped, her nerves began to calm and she smiled at him.

"This is exactly the thing. You must have

thought me demented."

"Just distressed. A threat to your son is explanation enough."

She froze with her cup halfway to her lips. "Threat?"

His brows rose. "Possible poison is a threat, is it not?"

She forced a laugh. "Yes, of course. It's just that *threat* sounds deliberate, and of course it was not. An accident, that's all."

She was babbling, so she occupied her mouth with tea again.

When he didn't say anything, she grimaced at him. "This has not been a good day, but there's no mystery, so don't turn your gimlet mind to it."

"You know the source of the tainted bun?"

She should have known she wouldn't deflect him.

She gestured it away. "Oh, it probably wasn't tainted at all. Children's stomachs are upset by the slightest thing, including excitement. If I'm distressed, it's that I fear I forced the emetic on Harry for no reason, and he's wrung out, poor mite. If not, I'd take you up to meet him. So," she said, forcing the conversation back to his affairs, "what journey brings you past Caldfort?"

She thought he might reject the change

of subject, but he relaxed. "I've been in Oxford — a neighboring county at least — and I'm on my way home."

That route would bring him close. Relief unsteadied her almost as much as fear had, but she still had to deal with him.

Even in normal circumstances, Stephen's arrival would be a strain. Today it was close to intolerable. How quickly could she speed him on his way? Not until he'd spoken with Lord Caldfort. She would arrange that now. . . .

But then the clock chimed five.

"So late?" The words unfortunately escaped her.

He put down his cup and rose. "I've kept you with this idle chatter when you have a sick child. Forgive me. I'll put up at the local inn and return tomorrow to talk to Caldfort."

She rose, too, and acted as she must. "Of course, you will stay the night here, and I'm sure Lord Caldfort will be happy to speak to you now if he is able. He misses involvement in the world's affairs. I'll go and see."

This time he made no attempt to stop her, and Laura could escape.

She paused halfway across the hall, struck by a sickening new realization. Stephen did nothing without thought. He'd arrived here late in the day and then, yes, he had kept her talking when she had a sick child in the nursery. He'd made an invitation to stay impossible to avoid.

He and she had avoided each other for six years. He would never come to her home for a trivial purpose. Whatever the purpose was, however, she could see no way to prevent it.

She carried on to Lord Caldfort's study and watched his reaction to news of the guest. Pure delight. She took Stephen to him and would have loved to linger and find out more, but Lord Caldfort would never stand for that.

In the hall again, she shrugged. If a sword was to fall on the Gardeyne family, it would fall. She summoned Mrs. Moorside and gave instructions for the preparation of a room.

"And tell Cook there'll be one extra for dinner. A gentleman likely to eat more than the rest of us together."

Despite Stephen's slim build, he'd always had a healthy appetite, especially after riding. She remembered —

She blocked that. "Oh, and as there's no sign of a valet, tell King to be ready to assist Sir Stephen if needed."

King was Lord Caldfort's man and might enjoy attending to a man of fashion.

Laura wanted to check on Harry, but she took a moment to be sure that she'd done all that was necessary. There was one more task. She went to Lady Caldfort's room to inform her that they had a guest. Laura had taken over the running of the house, but she tried not to ignore the older woman.

"A *young* man?" Lady Caldfort asked, turning to face Laura, brandishing a beetle on a pin.

"Yes, I suppose so."

"Good. You should marry again. Get away from here."

Lady Caldfort turned back to her work and Laura left, wondering if that was a warning, but no one was less likely than her mother-in-law to know of secret plans. After all, she was clearly blind to the fact that Laura was pinned here like a beetle in a box.

Now, thank heavens, she could go up to the nursery. When she saw how much Harry was recovered, most of the knot of tension in her unraveled. He was awake from his nap and demanding his supper. Laura checked again for fever or pain, but no one would guess he'd been so unwell.

"Very well, but just soup with bread in it. And then some stewed apples and cream if you feel like them."

His bright eyes said he did. She played with him a while, but couldn't stay with him all evening when they had a guest and Harry was clearly recovered. She kissed his brow and went downstairs, but her mind wouldn't stop circling the events of the day.

Had she imagined Lord Caldfort's distress?

Had that bun really been poisoned, or had that been her own unbalanced interpretation?

Was Stephen's arrival an innocent coincidence?

One shock after another after another had caused a turmoil inside her that was almost as violent as the one caused in Harry by that bun. She could no longer tell truth from fiction.

She entered her boudoir and leaned back against the door, trying to reason away her fears.

Lord Caldfort's problem probably had nothing to do with her.

If Jack wanted Harry dead, why try such a clumsy way when better occasions would turn up in time? Boys will be boys, and in a few years Harry would be climbing trees, boating on the river, learning to ride, and even to jump fences. A fatal accident could literally be child's play.

As to Stephen's arrival, at least it must mean that he'd put old rancor aside. It might be time for her to forgive and forget, too. They were close to strangers now.

Laura's maid bustled in. "With a guest for dinner, ma'am, you need to change."

"Not for Sir Stephen, Catherine. We're old . . ." Laura sought the right word and in the end settled on "acquaintances."

"And that dress is likely older, ma'am! I only chose it because I thought you might need to do more sickroom duty."

Laura looked down and saw that she was indeed in one of her oldest, simplest dresses. It had been a favorite once and that was probably why she'd kept it, but only for the messiest household tasks.

Not one she'd have chosen for greeting any guests, let alone Stephen.

She spread the skirt. "You'd never know, but it was lovely once. A leaf-green stripe on white." And now the stripes were faded like tired leaves, the white yellowed. "I do believe this dates from before my marriage."

Before her marriage, indeed.

She'd been wearing this gown — the green fresh, the white pure — when Stephen had proposed.

Had he recognized it? What had he thought?

# Chapter 7

"Come along, do, ma'am, or you'll be late!"

Laura went into her bedchamber but she couldn't stop memories breaking through the barriers she'd erected around them.

A June picnic at Ancross, hosted by Stephen's parents up on the hill that was crowned by the ruin of ancient Ancross Castle. Her whole family there and most of Stephen's, along with Hal and his hosts, the Oxholmes, and some other local families.

Most of the party had still been eating in a sheltered, sunny spot, but she, Charlotte, and Stephen had taken Hal on a tour of the ruins.

Charlotte had teased Hal to help her climb the crumbling stone steps to the tower. Had Charlotte been jealous that such an eligible gentleman had asked for Laura's hand? Laura had never considered that before, but it was probably the case.

She and Stephen had dallied on the ground. The ruins were familiar and held no great interest anymore, and perhaps she'd been thinking that she didn't want to risk her lovely new gown in the climb.

But they'd stopped while the other two had gone on.

Why . . . ?

Because they'd been caught by the song of a skylark.

It was as if she could hear the beautiful tune now. They were not so common around lush Caldfort, so it was a sound she associated with her home.

The bird had shot up not far from their feet, perhaps because they'd come too close to its nest. As skylarks do, it had soared up, singing to distract them, climbing and climbing. There was only one way to watch a skylark, so they'd sunk to the ground and lain back, eyes on the pristine blue sky as the bird became a dot too small to distinguish.

As presented by her memory, it had been one of those perfect moments when nature seems heavenly, with no hint of predators, blight, or storms.

Once a skylark was out of sight, the only thing to do was to wait for it to descend in the mad plunge that always seemed suicidal but never was.

She had never seen the bird return.

Stephen had sat up, then pulled her up to sitting. Then he'd asked her to change her mind, to marry him, not Hal. To wait a few years until he finished his legal studies . . .

Catherine began to undo buttons, pulling Laura out of the past. She swallowed and managed not to shudder.

Stephen could not possibly think she'd worn this dress to torment him. Coincidence again, which meant his arrival here was the same, and there was no particular significance to it. She had only to survive dinner. Tomorrow he would leave.

She washed, then put on her one silk mourning dress. A dull weave, as was appropriate, and an equally dull lilac color. She was suddenly desperately tired of these mourning shades. Even the bilious old dress was preferable.

For a moment she considered her wardrobe of rich colors, but then put that aside. She would give Hal his full twelve-month due, and she certainly could not feed Lady Caldfort's twisted mind by appearing for dinner in fine feathers. Heaven knows what she would say.

She could wear pearls instead of jet and

steel, however, and so she did so. That raised her spirits a little, but the lilac-trimmed cap that matched the gown made them plummet. Purple shades had never suited her, but she'd given the matter no thought before tonight.

She glanced at the clock. She must go down to make sure all was in order for a guest. Not too soon, however. She always calculated her arrival in Lord Caldfort's study so that she would have to spend as little time as possible there before dinner was announced.

On the other hand, she suddenly thought being early might provide an opportunity to look for the cause of Lord Caldfort's distress. He always made the laborious journey across to his bedchamber to change, and he'd take especial care for a guest. If she hurried down now, the room might be empty and she could . . .

What?

Poke around in the desk? Read Lord Caldfort's correspondence? The very idea appalled her, but she steeled herself. She'd break into the Tower of London if it was necessary to protect Harry.

She glanced at the clock and hurried downstairs. The study door was open, as it always was from the time Lord Caldfort went to his bedchamber until they went in to dinner. She braced herself, feeling as if her wicked intent must be obvious, and walked in. Her struggle was for nothing. Lord Caldfort was there, in his chair by the fire.

He scowled at her. "Isn't it time for you to be in colors? That tired old thing you had on earlier was more cheerful than that."

How very peculiar that he was echoing her own earlier thoughts. It was hardly sympathy, however. He was complaining as usual, which was why she always avoided these moments.

"It is not yet a year, sir."

"Damn near enough. If I don't care, why should you?"

She met his pouched eyes. "I will give Hal his due." Before he could jab at her anymore she asked, "How are you, sir? I hope the day's alarms haven't weakened you."

"Alarms?" He stiffened as if he'd try to rise from his chair. "There's been more than one? And I haven't been told?"

"An exaggeration," she said quickly. "Sir Stephen's arrival was not an alarm, but it was unexpected."

He sank back down. "That it was. Pack of trouble, guests are, but he's a sensible man, for a youngster. Old friend of your family, I gather."

She was surprised Stephen had mentioned it. "His family estate lies three miles from Merrymead, yes. And, of course, he's member for our local town, Barham."

They talked of her home area without much interest on either side until Stephen and Lady Caldfort came in together. Not arm in arm, Laura noted, though she was sure Stephen had offered.

Lady Caldfort halted near the door to wait in her usual impatient silence, but at least she seemed willing to wait. Stephen shrugged slightly and came forward to converse with Lord Caldfort.

Since they spoke of military pensions, Laura seized the chance to stroll about the modest, book-lined room. She looked for letters, though she didn't expect to find any lying out in the open. More to the point, she studied the desk. Though shocked at herself, she faced the fact that she was going to try to search it in order to read the letters that had arrived today.

The inlaid, walnut, bowfront desk had seven drawers, three in each pedestal and one in the center. All had brass lock plates, and none had a key sitting in it. She assumed the desk would follow the normal pattern and one key would fit all the locks, but without that one key she would be at a loss. She could hardly force open the drawers. It would leave marks.

She looked casually over the top of the desk. No key was obvious. There were two small boxes — one of inlaid wood and another carved from onyx — but she couldn't poke around in them. Not now, at least.

Later tonight, when the house was quiet, she was going to have to return here and do just that.

It was possible that Lord Caldfort kept the key on him, but he frequently complained that getting anything out of his pockets with his swollen hands was a "plaguey nuisance." She strolled back to his side and confirmed at a glance that he didn't wear a watch chain or any fobs where a key could be hung.

He might give the key to his valet for safekeeping, but why? She didn't think he kept anything of value in the desk, and having to send for King to lock and unlock would amount to another plaguey nuisance. So where would it be . . . ?

"Laura?"

She started and found Lord Caldfort standing, braced by a hand on his chair and another on his cane.

"We are summoned to table," Stephen said, extending his arm.

She blushed as she took it, and they followed Lord and Lady Caldfort. For once, Lady Caldfort was keeping pace with her husband's slow progress.

Laura's blush wasn't just embarrassment at her distraction. There had been a question in Stephen's eye and she didn't want him alerted to mysteries. To distract him, she said, "I've been trying to remember when we last met. Some social occasion in London. A glittering one."

"The Arden wedding ball."

"Oh, yes!" She in red; he looking splendid in dark evening clothes. "The social event of last year."

"And a successful one. The Ardens are now blessed with a son."

"It was in all the papers. I gather the christening was magnificent, too."

"But of course. The next heir to Belcraven. Though Beth Arden seems determined to raise the child in as normal a manner as possible for a future duke."

She glanced at him, surprised that he seemed intimate with such an aristocratic family when his circle was more that of the political reformers. But then she remembered.

"The Rogues," she said. "Arden is one of the Company of Rogues, your group of friends at Harrow. You're all still close?"

Too late, she recognized danger. Talking of youthful matters, of more intimate days, felt like stepping near the edge of an unreliable cliff.

"Did I really bore you with stories of them that much?" he asked wryly. "But yes, Arden is a Rogue, and we keep in touch."

"Lord Darius Debenham was one, too, wasn't he? I thought of that when I read the news of his miraculous return. You must all be delighted."

They had reached the table and he merely said, "Yes," as he seated her, then went around to his place opposite.

"How is Lord Darius?" She glanced to either side. "We are speaking of the Duke of Yeovil's younger son, who was thought lost at Waterloo, but who was discovered recently, still suffering from his wounds."

"Fishy business," Lord Caldfort muttered. "Gone a year?"

"A head wound, sir," Stephen said. "That plus the effect of opium for the pain."

"Mad, is he?"

"No, sir."

Stephen's face and tone were equable,

but Laura could tell he was angry. Before Lord Caldfort could speak again, he said, "The treatment of soldiers maddened by war is one of the matters under discussion. . . ."

The conversation became safely impersonal.

Deft, but that didn't surprise Laura. Even when young, Stephen had been tactful and skilled at manipulating people. Which was why his awkward proposal had been particularly shocking . . .

She blocked that.

The conversation was now firmly political, however, which meant that Lord Caldfort was acting as if the women at the table didn't exist. Stephen glanced at Laura, and she sent him a reassuring smile.

Lady Caldfort was frowning, but at least she wasn't beating her spoon on the table or screaming for the meal. There was no need, anyway. Thomas entered with the soup. As it was served, Laura allowed herself to study Stephen.

The Political Dandy. When she'd first heard him called that, it had amused her, for he'd given no thought to clothes when young. But then she'd realized that he'd always made the simplest garments look their best.

When she'd next seen him in London she'd noted that his clothes were elegant in the subtle way made fashionable by Brummell. He wasn't precisely a dandy, even so, but it had become the thing to designate men who dressed well that way. The Racing Dandy. The Hunting Dandy. The Golden Dandy.

She chose stewed eels and surveyed Stephen's current style.

He was all muted colors, but there was no suggestion of mourning. His coat and pantaloons were plain black, his waistcoat a beautiful damask of beige, black, and silver. His cravat was tied in one of the com- plicated knots men prided themselves on and held in place with one touch of color, a swirling jeweled pin. Emeralds, sapphires, and diamonds, alive in the candlelight.

She suddenly remembered that pin. He'd been wearing it at the Arden ball. Wasn't something grand enough for that occasion out of place here?

As she ate, ignoring the conversation as easily as it ignored her, Laura considered that event.

Hal had been cock-a-hoop at being invited. He and Arden were hunting-field acquaintances, but no more than that. He'd wanted to show her off and urged her to order a new gown.

She'd chosen a gown of daring red, wide on the shoulders and low on her back, which was veiled only by a lattice of ribbons. Hal had given her rubies to wear with it. The gown had been a huge success, and she'd enjoyed the event until they'd encountered Stephen.

Hal had called him over, mentioning something about Melton. She'd been surprised that Stephen stole time from politics for sport.

Stephen, she remembered, had been perfectly polite. But he'd given them the courtesy a gentleman reserved for strangers or for those he did not like. She'd thought it was directed at her, but then she'd become aware that Hal had forgotten that he was in a ballroom in London rather than in the Old Club in Melton.

She'd steered him away from Stephen and guided him through the evening so that there'd been no disaster. But she remembered wishing that she'd not attended, even when Hal had crowned the event later with particularly vigorous lovemaking. That had been the first time that she'd felt ashamed of Hal, and she'd known then that it was because of that encounter with Stephen.

She'd not returned to London again that year, and in November, Hal had died.

This simple evening was beginning to resemble an estate riddled with gin traps to catch poachers. An idle question about where she and Stephen had last met had bitten her with steel-toothed jaws.

# Chapter 8

At least Stephen could be trusted to manage conversation throughout the long meal. At first he tried to include Laura or Lady Caldfort, but was enough of a realist to give up. Laura confronted a pork chop without any appetite and wished Lady Caldfort would make one of her abrupt departures so she could leave, too.

"Do you have an opinion on electoral reform, Laura?"

So Stephen hadn't given up. Laura pulled a face at him, but replied, "It does seem wrong that some members are elected by a handful of people and others by thousands."

"Tradition," snapped Lord Caldfort. "Can't play ducks and drakes with tradition."

Laura took braised turnips and held her tongue.

Stephen took the same, but said, "Tradition had schoolboys holding the rank of colonel in the army, sir, and you approved of that reform."

Laura smiled as Lord Caldfort grunted and attacked his food. He liked to think of himself as a reformer, but it stopped short of anything that would damage his own interests. As Viscount Caldfort he controlled a so-called pocket borough, where the thirty voters elected whom he wished.

Stephen cut into his meat. "And tradition says that all property owners should have the vote. What, then, of women who hold property?"

Laura watched in horror as her father-in-law turned puce. *"Women? Voting?"*

"Don't bellow, John," snapped Lady Caldfort. "You know it upsets my digestion."

"To perdition with your digestion!"

"Don't distress yourself, sir," Laura said, shooting Stephen a chiding look.

Lord Caldfort turned his glare on her. "Would *you* want the vote, woman?"

Laura was pinned like one of Lady Caldfort's insects, unwilling to lie but not wanting to tell the truth and distress him further.

"See?" he said, turning to Stephen. "She can't even make up her mind on a simple question! Women don't have the brains for these things, Ball, and if they do, they're unnatural. World would go to rack and ruin."

"Strange," Stephen said, looking at Laura from beneath his heavy lids. "As I remember, Laura could give me a good game of chess."

Lord. How long was it since she'd played chess?

"Games." Lord Caldfort dismissed that with a wave of his fork. "Anyway, how many women own enough property to qualify for a vote? Besides tavern keepers and such."

"Perhaps that's another area of the law that needs examination, sir. Women's control over their own property."

Though Stephen's expression was innocent, from long practice Laura recognized that he was deliberately stirring trouble. She wished the table was narrower and she could kick him.

Lord Caldfort let his fork fall. "Damme, sir, but you're a radical!"

"I fear I am." Stephen glanced at Laura and perhaps understood the look she was firing at him. "But I am firmly in favor of law and order," he added. "Wouldn't you agree, sir, that the mob must be controlled for the good of sober citizens?"

Lord Caldfort returned to his meal. "Aye, there you speak sense. Bring in the military. Shoot a few."

Laura doubted Stephen had meant that, but he let it go and soon Lord Caldfort was comfortable again, especially when Stephen moved talk to sporting matters. But then that took a strange turn. From hunting to riding, and the old king's belief in riding for vigor, which hadn't kept him sane, poor man, and then on to other sorts of races.

"Running races," Stephen said as the main courses were removed and the sweets brought to the table.

"For footmen." Lord Caldfort's attention was on a damson pie. He shouldn't eat such things, but there was no stopping him.

"And occasionally for wagers. Lieutenant Naismith recently won five hundred guineas in a footrace over five miles. I assume that running would be as healthful an exercise as riding. Or swimming," Stephen added, glancing at Laura before turning to inspect the pie being offered.

Laura almost spilled wine down her gown.

He'd known that she and Charlotte had

gone swimming, but something in his eyes suggested that he knew about the other.

"Swimming!" Lord Caldfort sneered. "Amusement for lads, but nothing more than that. Don't hold with that sea dipping, either. The king used to do that, and look at where it's led. Stark, staring mad! A gentleman should stick to riding and walking. I'd be a happy man to be able to do either."

Silence settled. Laura could have started a new topic but she was too distracted by wondering what Stephen knew.

One particularly hot summer's day when she'd been about fifteen, she, Charlotte, and some other girls had daringly cooled themselves in the River Bar near to Ancross, in a spot where Charlotte said the boys swam. They'd carefully posted a maid to keep watch and only frolicked in the shallows in their shifts, but it had been both wonderful and wicked.

The next day Stephen had let slip — which amounted to a tactful warning — that the spot could be seen from the upper floors at Ancross. Doubtless he'd thought to deter such folly, but it hadn't worked. What's more, it had sparked something even more wicked.

She and Charlotte had kept watch, with

the added weaponry of Sir Arthur Ball's spyglass. She had to struggle not to smile at how deliciously shocked they'd been to discover that the males swam naked! How intrigued to be able to study their mysterious bodies through the telescope.

An ache jolted inside her along with a sudden rush of embarrassing heat. She kept her head down as if damson pie fascinated her, but even the swirl of purple juice in rich cream seemed arousing. It was so long since she'd seen a man's naked body, since she'd pressed against one in her bed.

Hal's familiar body. Heavily muscled but lean in the hip, furred on the chest.

Stephen's body had been different back then. Even among other young men he'd looked slender, but he'd been swift as a fish through the water. Mostly he'd been in the water and hardly visible, but he'd stood once in the shallows, laughing, pushing wet hair back off his face, caught in a sunbeam, looking like a young water god.

Then she'd thought her reaction to be shock and embarrassment. Now she recognized that it had been arousal, prickling like heat across her skin, tingling in her swelling breasts, beating like a pulse between her thighs.

She picked up her wineglass and sipped from it, looking at Stephen through her lashes. If he were Hal . . .

Lady Caldfort stood, startling Laura out of her shocking thoughts. Without a word, her mother-in-law left the room, and Laura seized the excuse. She stood, murmured, "Gentlemen," and escaped.

She fled upstairs. Was she really as pitiable as that? Would her hungers surge every time a virile man sat opposite her at table? She heard a noise below and turned to look back. Jack was striding across the hall toward the dining room. He'd heard about the guest and come to enjoy a bit of company.

His arrival was as sobering as cold water.

She rushed up to the nursery to be sure Harry was safe.

# Chapter 9

Harry was fast asleep, of course, with no evidence of the day's dramas. He was unguarded, however. Laura hadn't thought to tell Nan not to leave Harry alone. It wouldn't even be fair. Nan deserved a little time with the other servants.

Laura couldn't bear to leave until Nan returned, however, so she sat by his bed to keep watch, smiling at him.

He was so beautiful lying there in sleep that he could model for a dark-curled angel. He wasn't, and in time he would become as troublesome as most men. What fretted her was that he was already adventurous. He was Hal Gardeyne's son, after all — and hers. In her youth, she'd not been famous for being cautious.

That swimming expedition had been her idea, as had been the watch kept with the telescope —

No, she wouldn't let her mind return

there. She had best cultivate the mind of a nun and concentrate on keeping Harry safe through a normal, adventurous youth. But how? To try to wrap him in flannel would be a disaster of its own.

Perhaps when she was home she could talk about this with her father and oldest brother, Ned. They were such bluff, honest people, though. They'd think her mad, or even worse, come straight to Lord Caldfort about it.

There was always Stephen. . . .

He had a complex mind, which her father and brother did not. He knew the law. She pulled a face. The time was long past when she could ask Stephen for help, but she could help herself by finding out what had disturbed Lord Caldfort.

The door opened and Nan looked in. "Oh, ma'am," she whispered, "is everything all right?"

Laura stood and went out into the corridor. "Yes, of course. I came up to check on Harry and decided to sit a little. Sleeping children are delightful, aren't they?"

"That they are, ma'am."

"Is everything ready for departure tomorrow?"

"Yes, ma'am."

Laura felt reluctant to leave, but that was

carrying concern too far, so she went back down to her room. She couldn't resist pausing at the banister overlooking the hall and listening for Jack's booming voice.

There it was. He was in the dining room.

Laura retreated to her room and had her maid prepare her for bed. It was early, but she had the excuse of today's alarms, and travel the next. Once she was ready, she sent Catherine to bed.

She would sit up to make sure Jack didn't come upstairs, but also, when everyone was asleep, she would invade the study. She paced the room, watching the ticking clock, but then made herself sit and read the day's newspapers.

Her eyes read lines of print without taking in much of the meaning, but her attention was caught by a story in the paper about army officers whose minds had been turned by the horrors of war. Stephen had mentioned that.

They were now to be treated in their regiments for a year before being sent to an asylum, which would give a chance of recovery. Asylums for the insane were horrible places, likely to turn someone mad if they weren't so already.

As Caldfort House seemed to be deranging her?

She looked at the clock. Nearly half past nine. Lord Caldfort was often in bed by ten. Why wouldn't Jack go home! She opened her door a crack, but even from here she could hear his voice.

She sat again and moved on to a hair-raising account of the captivity of the English consul in Algiers during the confrontation there in August. The consul and his family, along with some naval officers who had tried to rescue them, had been chained, locked in a pit, and marched over long distances with only bread and water.

Another story of imprisonment, and one that put her own resentments to shame.

The prisoners' release was due to the efforts of the American consul, though the dey of Algiers had been humane enough to send the ambassador's child back to the safety of a British ship.

Wasn't it a universal rule to try to avoid harm to children?

Only if they were irrelevant to the issue. Other children had not fared well. The Princes in the Tower. Prince Arthur, who had stood between King John and the throne of England.

She forced her mind back to the paper. Two coaches had come to grief while racing to be first into Brighton. She shook her head. One of Hal's friends had died in a similar accident. Men seemed to need no reason to kill one another. Improve the roads so they were safer, and madmen raced on them.

She finished the paper and again looked at the clock. Though she felt it was an age since she'd left the dining room, it was only quarter past ten.

There was no point to sitting here watching the hands of the clock, so Laura settled to writing a letter to her sister, Olivia, who was wife to a naval captain.

Was that movement below?

She opened her door and — praise be — heard Jack call his good nights. A little later, footsteps came up the stairs. She closed her door and listened as someone, surely Stephen, passed and another door closed down the corridor.

At last.

Lord Caldfort would be settling for the night in his bedchamber. The servants would be clearing the dining room, then washing the last dishes before taking to their beds. Lady Caldfort had been in her rooms for hours. Laura didn't know when her mother-in-law went to bed or went to sleep, but she'd never been known to emerge after dinner.

As the house settled into silence, she itched to set off, but she had the whole night. Though she fidgeted and paced, Laura waited until the clock showed eleven thirty before she would let herself leave her room. Then, senses screwed for any sign of life, she carried her candle downstairs and across the hall to her father-in-law's study.

She had a story prepared, though it didn't stop her heart from pounding. Lord Caldfort kept road guides in his study. Her excuse would be that she wished to study tomorrow's route. It was flimsy because she knew the way well, but it would do.

She was, after all, an idiot woman.

When she arrived at the door, Laura paused once more, ears pricked for any sound, but then she entered the room without further hesitation. If someone was watching, she must not look furtive, even if she felt it. She couldn't believe that she was intruding into someone's study intent on reading his private correspondence.

She crept to the desk, put her candlestick down there, and surveyed the surface again. Nothing had changed since before dinner, except that now she could open the two small containers on top of the desk. The box held small coins; the bowl was empty.

She hadn't expected it to be so easy, but it would have been a pleasant surprise.

Aware that she was passing from excusable to inexcusable, she went around and sat in her father-in-law's chair. If anyone came in here now, she was sunk.

She tugged on the handle of the central drawer — and it slid out. She almost laughed with surprise. It didn't hold letters, however, but only the necessities for writing them. There were sheets of paper, pens, and some open boxes holding sticks of sealing wax, sand, a penknife and such.

She closed that and tried the top one on the left.

Locked.

That was to be expected, but the center one had given her hope. She quickly tried the others, but all were locked. She muttered the sort of word that ladies were not supposed to know and considered again whether it would be possible to force the drawers open. The locks did not look sturdy, but she couldn't see how to do it without leaving marks.

She glared at the desk. Expecting difficulties didn't make them any the less disappointing, but she regrouped and put her mind to work. If the key was here, where would it be?

She lifted and examined every object on the top of the desk, even peering into the inkwell. At that insanity, she reminded herself that the key wasn't hidden in that sense. Lord Caldfort presumably used it every day. He wouldn't fish it out of ink.

She felt under the kneehole and down the inner sides. She was about to crawl under when she realized that her father-in-law was incapable of that.

So where?

She looked around the room at a daunting array of bookshelves and objets d'art. The key could be anywhere, but the more she thought about it, the more sure she was that Lord Caldfort would not want to be heaving himself up out of his chair to get the key or to hide it.

So where?

It seemed too careless a place, but she opened the center drawer again and explored it all the way to the back. Nothing but dust. She poked through the box of sand — nothing — then tipped out the box of sealing wax into her lap.

A small ornate key glinted in the light of her candle.

Hardly able to believe it, she tried the key in the lock of the top drawer on the left. It clicked sweetly. Could she take this as divine approval? No. This intrusion was wicked, but she had to do it. She put back the sealing wax and closed the center drawer, then settled to her search.

The top left drawer contained ledgers and estate portfolios. No letters. She closed that drawer and locked it, then opened the next one down. A few more ledgers. The bottom one was empty. Of course, bending so low would be difficult.

She opened the top one on the right. Letters!

They were all folded, but the seals she could see were broken. Ones received, not ones waiting to be sent. This was what she was looking for.

There was more than a day's worth, however. Laura tried to remember how many had been on the desk this morning when Lord Caldfort had given her the letter from Juliet. Perhaps six? She counted quickly. Eleven.

Did he keep the letters in order of arrival? She wanted to intrude as little as possible in this search, but she might have to at least glance at them all.

She picked up the top one and unfolded it, the rustle of paper sounding loud in the quiet house. A quick glance showed it was about a purchase of a bull. She couldn't see how that could be a cause for alarm.

The next was about a case before the courts in London, but nothing dangerous or controversial. Then a letter from France from an old friend. She read it all the way through, but saw nothing strange.

She continued opening and glancing at letters, trying not to read any more than she had to. Then she picked up one that was clearly on cheaper paper — thinner and less white. She tensed with excitement. Unlike the others, it had been sealed with a wafer rather than with sealing wax. It was addressed to Lord Caldfort, and the only indication of sender was the place of origin.

Draycombe in Dorset.

That startled her. She came from Dorset. Draycombe was on the coast near the western edge of the county and she'd never been there, but could this alarm have something to do with her?

# Chapter 10

She unfolded the paper with unsteady hands, terrified of tearing it or doing anything else to show that it had been disturbed.

She expected uneducated writing to match the paper, but the contents were neatly written, though there was something a little strange about the handwriting. An angularity, perhaps. A weight in the use of the pen.

She looked first to the bottom, seeking the sender's name.

Azir Al Farouk.

What sort of name was that?

*Great Lord,*

*I have information of interest to you about a certain HG, connected to Mary Woodside. Having been for some years a guest of Oscar Ris, HG has now changed course and might trouble you. You will find enclosed an item of relevance.*

*I would be happy to assist you in the avoidance of this trouble for payment of ten thousand guineas.*

*I can be reached through Captain Egan Dyer, care of the Compass Inn, Draycombe, Dorset. I am in hopes of being your most humble servant, great lord,*

*Azir Al Farouk*

Ten thousand guineas! That was certainly enough to give Lord Caldfort a nasty shock, but apart from the figure, the letter mystified her. This had to be the letter she was looking for, however.

HG. Henry Gardeyne?

Her Harry? Surely not. He'd not been anywhere for "some years" and certainly not with Oscar Ris, whomever that might be. The Gardeyne family tree was full of Henrys, however, in one form of the name or another.

She started to run through the recent ones in her mind, but stopped herself. She could think in a safer place. Fearing that she would forget some detail, she took out a sheet of paper, dipped the pen, and made a precise copy. When she was sure it was exact, she refolded and replaced the original.

She looked around the desk for the item of relevance. There was nothing there except letters, and she was sure there was nothing unusual in the central drawer.

She couldn't search further now. She had no idea what she might be looking for. A scrap of fabric, a button, a lock of hair, a picture. She might not know it even if she saw it. She was sure she'd found the troubling letter, but she glanced at the remaining three, just in case. They were all ordinary correspondence.

After checking that the pile of letters looked as it had before, she locked the drawer and replaced the key. Once she was sure that the center drawer was in order, she closed it with sweating hands, picked up her candle — and froze.

Was that a sound?

She stopped breathing to listen, but the house seemed dead around her. She was tempted to race up to the safety of her room, but she must appear innocent to the end.

She went to the shelf of road guides, found the one that included the road to Merrymead, and slipped her copy of the letter inside it. With her excuse in hand, she left the room feeling as if guilt were stamped on her forehead.

If it was, there was no one to see it. The house slept except for the ticking of clocks. Even her slippered footsteps sounded loud.

She went up to the nursery again, compelled to check that Harry was still safe. He was sound asleep, but she realized that her arrival here had not woken Nan.

Just as easily, Jack could have returned to the house, come quietly upstairs, and smothered Harry with a pillow. Or thrown him out of the window with the explanation of sleepwalking. There were so many ways to kill a child without it clearly being murder.

She hated to leave, but she must. She would be thought unbalanced if she slept up here, and she needed to study the letter. She couldn't stop thinking that there was a connection between it and Lord Caldfort's insistence that she take Harry away for a month, and thus a connection to Harry's safety.

She slipped downstairs and was at the door to her room when a soft voice said, "Is something amiss?"

She turned, heart jolting. Stephen stood outside his room, dressed for the night in a blue banyan over his nightshirt. He looked fully alert, however, not roused from sleep. Laura felt as if he could see into the book she was clutching and identify the letter.

"I've just been up to check on Harry," she said quietly, astonished by the calm of her own voice.

"He's all right, I assume."

"Yes. Fast asleep. Good night."

She turned back to her room, but he said, "You went down earlier. To get that book in your hand."

She looked back at him. "Pray, what concern is that of yours? I wanted a road guide. We leave tomorrow for Merrymead."

A flicker of amusement spoke of skepticism. "And you don't know the way?"

"I wanted to remind myself of details along the way so I can amuse Harry with them."

He strolled closer, and she made herself not draw back as if afraid. She was not used to thinking of Stephen as so tall, however, or so formidable.

"You travel home?" he said. "I wish I'd known. I would have accompanied you. I'm on my way there, but I'm promised to a meeting in Winchester tomorrow."

"Alas," she said, but thought, *Thank heaven!* The pressure of his company for days would be intolerable. For some reason, she couldn't think clearly when Stephen, clever Stephen, was observing her. As he was now.

"So there is nothing amiss in the house? Nothing wrong with your son?"

She matched calm with calm. "No, nothing. I'm sorry to have disturbed you, Stephen. Good night."

She went into her room and closed the door.

Stephen regarded the closed door thoughtfully and then returned to his room. It was a perfectly adequate room with all that a guest could require, and yet it spoke in subtle ways of a place unused to visitors.

Caldfort House was architecturally elegant and efficiently run, but it was not welcoming. It was not a home. He wouldn't like to live here, and he couldn't imagine Laura liked living here, either. Did that explain her tension, her . . . fear?

No, that was because of the threat to her son. He didn't believe that she'd overreacted, and the only rational murderer was the boy's uncle, the hale and hearty Reverend Gardeyne. Thus Stephen had spent the after-dinner session evaluating the man.

Sporting mad, clever enough but not brilliant, and the sort of man who put enormous stock in siring a son, as if it proved his virility.

Wanting a son was rational when a title

was at stake, or any other inheritance that must go in the male line. But it would make no practical difference to Reverend Gardeyne.

Unless his little nephew died.

Despite hours of observation, Stephen had no certainty that Gardeyne was a potential murderer, but he was relieved to hear that Laura and her son would be leaving in the morning. It was only a respite, however, so no wonder she was wound tight with worry.

He smiled wryly. A fine time he'd chosen to come courting.

He'd planned it so carefully, too. Not earlier in her mourning, which would have been inappropriate, but before the end, just in case she moved back into society and the other men flocked to Lady Skylark.

To make his excuse ironclad, he'd arranged meetings with reformers in Oxford and Winchester, and devised a valid excuse to stop here. Pathetic cowardice, really. If she still regarded him as a brother, she need never know his intent.

So now what should he do?

Brother or lover, he could not abandon Laura when she was worried, perhaps terrified, especially when she'd been sneaking around the house in the night for some purpose.

The hospitality here didn't run to decanters of spirits for the guests, but he kept a small flask of brandy in his bag and he sipped from it.

Laura.

He'd expected the brilliantly fashionable Mrs. Hal Gardeyne, and come prepared to entice. Or Lady Skylark, who would appreciate wit and high spirits. Instead, he'd found Laura, in a dress he remembered all too well, her hair disordered almost to a girlish state, almost at point of collapse from fear.

It had almost unmasked him. Threat to her or hers enraged him. He'd tear the world apart to make it right for her, but . . .

He laughed again and drank more brandy. But he had clearly been nothing to her but an inconvenient guest. Not even a friend, dammit. Merely someone to be taken care of in the name of hospitality. He hadn't missed her exclamation at the time, or that she'd offered a bed at Caldfort House with reluctance.

Tempting, so tempting, to hurl the brandy flask at the wall, but the damn thing was metal and wouldn't even smash.

Just because he'd never forgotten her, because he had loved and desired her longer than he'd known and shamefully taken the news of her husband's death as a second chance, didn't mean she felt the same way.

And clearly she didn't.

He wanted to flee and lick his wounds as he had six years ago. To plunge into work, trying to persuade himself that Laura was no loss. That he didn't need a skylark for his wife, a social flutterer who would drag him from ball to rout to frivolous house party.

It seemed that common sense was being reinforced by reality. She felt nothing for him at all.

He eyed the brandy flask, capped it, and put it away. Even if Laura didn't regard him as a friend anymore, he couldn't abandon her.

If Reverend Gardeyne was a Wicked Uncle, there had to be ways to keep her son safe. If she was leaving to visit Merrymead, that gave him time to investigate the situation. He had a feeling there was more going on, however.

After coming up to bed, he'd stayed alert in case Reverend Gardeyne returned to the house. Instead he'd heard Laura leave her room. From the upper landing he'd watched her go into her father-in-law's study. A slight hesitation at the door had suggested that she wasn't entirely at ease.

A road guide? She'd remained there a lot longer than it would take to find that, and he thought she'd emerged even more tense than when she'd entered. She'd gone to the upper floor, presumably to look in on her son. When she'd come back down he'd decided to interrupt her, hoping she'd share her problem as once she surely would have done. Instead, again he'd been an intrusive nuisance. But she needed a friend, needed help. He was sure of it.

Six years ago he'd tried to rescue Laura Watcombe from folly and made a complete fool of himself. He'd been wrong, as well. He'd thought she was making a mistake, but she'd been happy as Mrs. Hal Gardeyne. Happy as a damn lark.

Now he was going to do it again.

With the same sickening sense of being about to make a fool of himself, and the same awareness that he had to try, he left his room. If Laura's room was dark, if she'd gone to bed, it could wait until the morning, at least.

But a light shone out from beneath her door.

# Chapter 11

He knocked, not expecting the door to open instantly, but it did. Laura was wide-eyed, but when she saw him, fear turned to exasperation. "Is something the matter?"

He was nothing but a bother, but he was here. He might as well go through with it.

"I'm sorry. Did you think it was something to do with your son?" He moved forward and she stepped back. She was still frowning, but at least he didn't have to fight his way in.

Perhaps because this was not her bedchamber, but her boudoir.

Probably as well, though it whispered of her delicate, sophisticated perfume. Nothing from her girlhood about that. He'd heard that the famous perfumiers, Lascelles and Brun, had created a unique fragrance for Labellelle. The men were geniuses.

"This is an intolerable intrusion," he said, closing the door behind himself, "but we were friends once, and friends don't turn their backs on one another in need. Something's going on, Laura. Something that sent you down to your father-in-law's study —"

"The road guide."

He glanced at the desk behind her. "And a letter?"

She seemed frozen, so he moved around her to where the sheet of paper lay open on the desk, bright beneath the candle. "May I?"

She didn't say yes but she didn't say no, so he picked it up and read it with increasing astonishment and — yes — interest. He delighted in puzzles.

"Clearly not a normal piece of correspondence." He turned it and saw no address or sealing wax. "A copy?"

"Yes." She came to life and gave him a look that reminded him of the Laura of old. "I suppose I do need help, if you promise to keep this confidential."

"I'm offended." He spoke lightly but was hurt.

Perhaps she colored. "I'm sorry, but it's a long time since we were friends."

He considered how to respond to that

and settled on the truth. "I never stopped being your friend."

"Lady Skylark?"

His heart missed a beat. He hadn't thought she would know, or care, who had suggested that name.

"That offended?"

She shrugged. "I preferred Labellelle. More intriguing."

There was more to this than appeared on the surface, but now was not the time to delve into it.

"Then I apologize. But I stand your friend, I assure you. Tell me about this letter."

After a moment, to his immense relief, she sat down at her desk.

Of course, it would be better if she showed awareness of their being in her boudoir in their nightwear. It would be better, much better, if she weren't wearing an ugly nightcap over her lovely hair, but at least her robe was a pretty rose. The colors of mourning didn't suit her at all.

"I spoke to Lord Caldfort this morning," she said, "as he was dealing with the morning postbag, and he seemed distressed. With everything else that's happened today, and because I'm leaving tomorrow, I decided to try to find out what had disturbed him."

She met his eyes, chin set defensively. "Matters of importance to the estate are of importance to Harry."

"I agree." He picked up another chair, put it close her hers, and sat. "What do you make of it?"

Being this close by candlelight was a crumb to the starving.

"Thus far, little." She touched the letter. "Azir Al Farouk is an Arab name, I believe."

Stephen looked at the letter again, commanding his brain to his lady's cause. "It sounds like it. The English is good, though. Was it addressed to Lord Caldfort? This only addresses 'Great Lord.'"

She grimaced. "I should have copied both sides, shouldn't I? But I'm sure it was addressed to the Right Honorable the Viscount Caldfort."

"An Arab with a nice understanding of English protocol. Most intriguing."

Like her scent, which made it damn hard to think.

"Let's be orderly," he said. *Yes, do let's.* "HG. We assume that's your husband, Hal Gardeyne?"

She shook her head. "How could he return to trouble anyone? You may not know, but first sons in this family are always called variants of Henry."

"Ah. So Lord Caldfort is a Henry, too?"

"No, because he was a second son, so his name is John. He inherited when his older brother, Henry, died. That Lord Caldfort had a son — Henry, of course — who died at sea."

"Navy?"

"A scholar of some sort. He was traveling to Greece. But poke around the Gardeyne family tree and there are dead Henry Gardeynes by the bushel."

"But how many alive?" he asked.

Fear flickered in her eyes. "Only the two infants. My Harry, and Jack's newborn Hal."

He wanted to take her in his arms, and only to comfort. "HG can't be them, then, can he? *Having been for some years a guest of Oscar Ris . . .*' So it must be something to do with a dead Henry Gardeyne."

He had his reward when she relaxed, even smiled a little. "Old debts? Old scandals?"

"Connected to a woman called Mary Woodside. Could she have been a mistress to any of the dead Henrys? Perhaps turning up with a bastard child in tow?"

Too late he realized that could embarrass. He knew Hal Gardeyne had been a notorious womanizer, but did Laura?

She didn't even seem conscious of it being a delicate subject. "A bastard wouldn't shock Lord Caldfort. He regards them as proof of manly virility. Do you know what nationality a man called Oscar Ris might be?"

"Spanish? Portuguese?" He looked at the letter again. "What about Captain Dyer?"

"Lord Caldfort has many military friends, but I've never heard the name."

"With a military man involved, it might be something to do with the war."

She sat back, shaking her head. "Lord Caldfort retired from the army nine years ago, and even then he'd been behind a desk for a decade. There've been no other military men for generations. The Gardeynes like the comforts of England. The only one I know of who's gone traveling was the old viscount's son, and see what came of it. A watery grave."

But then she came alert like a pointer sensing game. "Could it be? His ship went down in the Mediterranean, close to Arab countries. He was on his way to Greece. Could Oscar Ris be a Greek name?"

Suddenly, delightfully, she was the Laura

of his youth — quick, bright, and soaring above reality.

"Not obviously," he said.

As always, she wasn't daunted. "But his return would certainly be a shock, wouldn't it? Because then Lord Caldfort wouldn't be Lord Caldfort anymore."

As always, her enthusiasm was infectious. "It's an idea. And this Farouk is offering to remove the inconvenience. Astonishing."

But then, unlike the Laura of old, she came back to earth. "It is, isn't it? Astonishing. Unbelievably so. How could anyone come back from the dead?"

"Lord Darius did so."

"But that was one year, not ten."

"True." Stephen looked back at the letter to focus his mind. "What do you know about this Henry Gardeyne?"

"Very little. He died — or whatever — long before I married Hal."

Her voice was enough to make thought difficult. Voices didn't change, and it was almost as if they were back in Ancross, working on a puzzle.

"There's a memorial to him in the Gardeyne plot," she said. "I think it says he was twenty-one. And a portrait of him hangs in the hall."

"Ah, I saw that and wondered if it was the vicar as a younger man, but there's something too dreamy about it."

"In his eyes, I think."

He made the mistake of looking up and was caught by *her* eyes. There was nothing dreamy about them, alas, but poets had praised Laura Gardeyne's brilliant sapphire eyes.

He'd known them all his life, but not like this, by intimate candlelight; she an experienced woman, he a desirous man. *Desirous.* What a pretty word for burning hunger that threatened his sanity, his reason, and his control over this situation. If he tried to move his hand, he feared it would shake. If he tried to speak, he could not possibly make sense.

"I've always thought that picture shows a romantic zest for adventure rather than dreaminess," she said, seemingly unaware of the effect she was having. "It makes his early death so sad. I'd like him to be alive, but where could he have been all these years?"

He grasped the simple question like a lifeline. "With Oscar Ris, apparently." *Think. Think.* "But as you say, that makes no sense. Why would he linger abroad when a title awaited him in England?" He sought a suggestion as a courting bird might seek a worm to tempt his mate. "What if Henry sired a son before he died? A legitimate one."

Her lips parted in a delighted smile. "And the wicked Farouk is offering to kill the child for money? Brilliant, Stephen!" But then she sobered. "We have to prevent that."

*We.* What towers of hope a man could build on one word.

"Even if it deprives your son of his inheritance?"

Those eyes could spit fire, as he well knew. "You imagine I would blindfold myself to another child's death in that cause? What sort of monster do you think I am?"

He raised his hands. "I'm sorry. Of course I don't think that, but I'm a man of law, Laura. I'm accustomed to pointing out the legal consequences of decisions. As long as you understand."

"I do." Now she was cold, but it was a passionate cold. Everything she did was passionate. "So, a child, and the object enclosed must have been proof of his legitimacy. I looked, but I didn't see anything. Certainly not a document." She fixed him with her gaze, and even cold it burned him. "We have to do something."

*We* again. *If you insist,* he thought, as a

worm of an idea uncurled, an idea he knew he should resist.

She was looking into nowhere now. "You're going to think me mad."

*I know I am.* He sucked in the vision of her, the delicate perfume, the movements of her breasts with every breath. He should speak. "Why?"

"Because, I'm looking with hope at the thought of Harry *not* being the heir to a title." She turned those eyes on him again. "Stephen, if Henry Gardeyne is alive, or his legitimate son is alive, they are the key to Harry's safety." She reached out and grasped his hand. "If Harry isn't heir to anything, he's *safe.*"

It took the strength of Hercules to keep his hand passive in hers, and his heart was thundering. "Many would think you mad."

She laughed. "So he won't have a title and he'll have to make his own fortune, but he won't have to grow up at Caldfort, and he will *live!*"

He turned her hand then, held it in both of his, longing to raise it, kiss it. "As your legal adviser, no matter how informally, I have to ask you to think before you act on this."

She snatched her hand back. "What became of Stephen the warrior for justice?

How can I possibly permit a murder, even by inaction?"

Words escaped him for a moment, then he managed, "I don't mean that. This could all be a hoax, however, an attempt at extortion. Do you want to succumb to that for your own advantage?"

Yes, she did, he saw. Her angry frown came of guilt. "With so much evidence?" she demanded.

Now that this had become a legal matter of sorts, he regained some sanity. Her legal adviser. God have mercy.

"How much evidence is there?" he asked. "Someone knows that Henry Gardeyne existed. That could be anyone. He has sent some supposed proof of something, we know not what. Mary Woodside eludes us, as does Oscar Ris and any explanation of a ten-year absence."

"You're being coolly analytical again," she complained with a pout. Yes, definitely a pout that made him want to hug her, it was so part of their youth. Perhaps she recognized it, too, for her expression softened and she suddenly looked away.

Was that the first sign that she saw him as a man?

"My virtue and my flaw," he agreed. "Shall I attempt to awe you with my brilliance to compensate? I'd be willing to gamble that Mary Woodside is the name of the ship Henry Gardeyne traveled on. The one that sank."

She looked back at him, eyes bright again. "Oh, brilliant, indeed!"

"That's public knowledge, too," he pointed out. "A villain could have discovered it."

"But a villain would have to have a reason to look it up. Hence," she declared triumphantly, "contact with Henry."

He had to smile. This followed the pattern of so many debates of their youth. "A point, I grant you."

She smiled back, and he'd swear it was unrestrained, a smile she might have given him in the past, before Hal Gardeyne had come into their lives. No, before he had made a mess of everything while a skylark sang.

"I'm glad you happened to come here today, Stephen, and that you invaded this room. I think I'd be going mad without your steadiness."

*Steadiness?*

"Do you see that as aging?" she asked. Damn, she'd always been too good at reading him. "We're both past being wild, I think."

"Are we?" Quickly he added, "Yes, of course we are. I'm a responsible Member of Parliament, supporter of worthy causes, and you're a respectable matron and mother. Wearing caps, no less."

That bloody cap — plain, encompassing, and tied beneath her chin — should be illegal. She touched it as if suddenly conscious of it. And blushed. What the devil about her damn cap made her blush?

She grabbed the letter and read it again, though they'd sucked it dry. Oh, the deuce, he'd as good as said she was an aged antidote.

"I'm sorry. You're still a young, beautiful woman, Laura. If you return to society, you'll be a toast again."

"Toast?" she echoed, still hectic with color. "Thank you, but I can't leave Harry as long as there's any hint of danger."

"Take him with you when you marry."

Her bright color faded. "Lord Caldfort will never permit that. He says his heir should grow up here, and he's right."

"Ah. But only as long as he is the heir. I understand better now."

"I'm not doing this for selfish reasons."

"Of course not." But it was certainly additional motive for him. If Laura needed to find a new heir for Caldfort before she

131

could marry, he was heart and soul for the cause. What's more, it fit in with his plan.

"What we need is the truth," he said, "and that can only be found in Draycombe."

She smiled brilliantly at him. "You would go there and find out for me?"

"No."

Color rushed beautifully into her cheeks. "Stephen, I'm so sorry! Why should I assume that you have time to do that? You must be very busy —"

He raised a hand and stopped her. "I'm never too busy to help a friend." He couldn't help adding, "Especially you, Laura. I can certainly go and uncover some facts, but once we have them there may be decisions to make. Decisions only you can make."

"What decisions?"

He was telling the truth, he realized, which certainly made this easier. "I don't know, but I can imagine dilemmas. What if HG is Henry Gardeyne's son, but an idiot or impossibly corrupt? Do we inflict such an owner on Caldfort?"

"The law . . ."

". . . must always be tempered by common sense."

"Stephen, I'm shocked!"

He waited and she added, "I can't decide that."

"Who else? Your Harry is too young, and Lord Caldfort's desires might not be the same as yours. He could well pay Farouk's price. That's why you must travel to Draycombe and judge for yourself."

She stared at him. "How? It's impossible without explanation, and how could I explain?"

"You're about to visit your family, which is halfway there."

"But I can hardly arrive at Merrymead, then immediately leave."

She was right, but he thought he saw a solution. He needed to tighten and tidy his plans, but he thought they would work. In more ways that one.

"It's late," he said, standing, "and our minds are buzzing with tiredness and tangles. Let's sleep on it. I'll travel part of the way with you tomorrow, which will give us time to talk far from prying ears."

She stood, too. "I suppose I'll have to do something. Perhaps Father or Ned could go to Draycombe."

"I've always thought them rather conventional. Salt of the earth, et cetera, but if matters become . . . irregular?"

She winced. "You're right. But I don't

like to impose on you, Stephen."

"Sleep on it," he said, suppressing all reaction.

But he could not resist taking her hand
and kissing it. Lightly, but even that was
more than he'd ever done before. Holding
her hand, he said, "I stand your friend,
Laura, and I will help you sort this out. It
will be no imposition."

Her fingers tightened on his. "Then I
think heaven did send you here today."

"There's an Eastern philosophy that says
that nothing happens by chance. That we
are ruled by destiny, which cannot be
fought. Good night, Laura."

He made himself leave, having found less
than he longed for but more than he'd
hoped. And probably a great deal more
than he deserved.

# Chapter 12

Laura watched the door close, then sank into her chair. Stephen's last words hung in the air as if they had import, but that must be exhaustion speaking. She needed sleep, but it felt impossible. How could she sleep with her mind and her body in turmoil?

They'd been together in her boudoir in their nightwear!

That awareness had prickled over and through her, so it had been a miracle that she'd spoken a word of sense. It sizzled in her still, making even the movement of her cotton nightgown against her skin scarcely bearable.

She stood and went into her bedroom, stripping off her clothes, then scrubbed with cold water. Disgusting — that's what it was when carnal lust distracted her from matters of life and death. Life and death for Harry. She clasped a dripping cloth to her breasts and the cold water trickled down, gathering on her thighs.

The first unmarried, virile man to enter her orbit, and she had become a would-be whore.

She tossed the useless cloth back in the bowl, but the madness was cooling. When she was dry and back in her nightgown, it no longer tormented her skin. She looked in the mirror, fearing to see a slack-mouthed slut, but she was Laura Gardeyne, lady.

In her cap. She put her hand to it. Oh, Lord, her cap!

That had almost been her ruin.

Hal had made a game of her nightcaps. He liked taking them off, which was largely why she'd worn them. He'd saunter into her bedchamber saying, "Off with that cap, wench. . . ."

Her body clenched at the memory of the words, at the memory of what always followed. She pressed her hand over her mouth, then bit it. She missed it so much, so *much*.

She could relieve herself and she would, but it wasn't the same. It was more than a year since a man's strong body had pleasured hers, and it would be many more before one would again, and her tears marked a tragedy fierce enough for the Greeks.

She climbed into bed but it took a long time to fall asleep, and she woke twice in the night. The second time, unable to settle, she went up to the nursery to reassure herself that Harry was still all right. He was fast asleep and she stood there looking at him, wondering if he'd hate her one day if she managed to free him of a viscountcy.

That, not lust, had stolen sleep, but it wasn't as if she had any choice. If Henry senior or junior existed, Caldfort must be theirs. She couldn't try to prevent that.

But she would rejoice if Harry became safe and she became free. No lying about that. She wanted to be free to leave, to live, to love.

She returned to her bedchamber. As she passed Stephen's room she only allowed herself to think about important matters — the journey and the letter from Azir Al Farouk. Because she was concentrating on that so fiercely, she realized there was something useful she could do. She could sketch a copy of Henry Gardeyne's portrait.

Her drawing portfolio was already

packed in her coach bag, but she dug it out and slipped into the dim corridor again, candlestick in hand. What would be her excuse if she was caught now? She was almost beyond caring. She'd announce that she was as eccentric as Lady Caldfort, but devoted to nighttime portraiture.

She went down to the hall and copied the picture as best she could by the light of one candle. She paid particular attention to the bones of the young man's face, the line of his nose, and the shape of his one visible ear. Those things didn't change much over time.

She would have made a more finished job of it, but the clock struck six and she heard a rattle from the kitchen area. The staff was stirring. She hurried back to her room and closed the door with a shudder of relief. She almost felt as if her own life was in danger. Perhaps it was. What would the Gardeynes do if they learned that she knew this secret?

She wouldn't feel safe until she and Harry drove away. With Stephen as escort. Thank God for that. She could even imagine Jack riding after to kill them both. She wasn't sure what Lord Caldfort would do about the letter, but she felt certain Jack would not accept the return of his cousin.

After acquiring Hal's small pistol, she'd not done anything with it. Now she carefully cleaned, checked, and loaded it. She paused, thinking that if Hal was looking down from heaven, he'd approve.

"You're an unlikely guardian angel, Hal," she whispered, "but keep our son safe."

She packed the case in her trunk but put the pistol in her coach bag, feeling considerably more secure.

No chance of getting back to sleep now, but too early to ring for breakfast. She worked a little on the drawing, but then realized it was a mistake. Anything she added now might make a better picture, but would be less like the original. She put it in her portfolio and returned that to her bag.

She read over the letter again, but it gave up no more wisdom. Oscar Ris. They'd come up with possible explanations for everything else, but not that. Perhaps it had a private meaning for Lord Caldfort.

Dear heaven! Could Lord Caldfort have had a hand in his nephew's disappearance all those years ago? Consigned him to imprisonment with Oscar Ris?

She'd try the suggestion on Stephen, but she could see the main objection. If the then Colonel John Gardeyne had decided to get rid of his nephew, he would have killed him, not locked him away somewhere. And only in fairy tales did hired killers turn softhearted and spare the victim.

The clock struck half past six. The sun was up, so she could be, too. She rang for Catherine, and by seven was taking breakfast with a fidgety, excited Harry. Waiting until eight for the post chaise to arrive was clearly going to be a torment for him. She and Nan occupied him with last-minute packing and with the important choice of toys to take in the coach.

With half an hour still to go, Nan said, "Will I take him down to the stables, ma'am, to wait there? The horses and cats will amuse him."

It was an excellent idea, but with escape so close Laura didn't dare let him out of her sight. She felt as if Jack could be lurking, ready to pounce, and she couldn't warn Nan.

"No, I'll take him down to my room. You make sure everything goes down to be ready, then wait there to say good-bye."

Her bedchamber and boudoir did distract Harry a little, especially her mechanical singing bird in a cage — a favorite

140

treat. She thought for a moment of taking it with them, but recognized in time that the winding and playing would weary her long before it wearied a child.

Even now it was making her sad. Hal had given it to her for her twentieth birthday, saying he'd bought it because she was Lady Skylark. Even then, when he could do no wrong, she'd recognized that it didn't fit. No one caged a skylark. What point, when it sang only when on the wing?

"The coach is here, ma'am!"

"Thank heavens," she said to Catherine, and they shared a smile. "Come on, Minnow."

He was already at the door and would have rushed down the stairs if allowed. She had no intention of risking a fall now, and made him go at a decorous pace.

Mrs. Moorside and Rimmer, the butler, were waiting to bid her farewell. She went first with Harry to Lord Caldfort.

If she needed proof that Lord Caldfort was not his usual self, she found it. He seemed paler and weary, as if weighed down by something. Or as if he'd not slept. Hardly surprising if he thought he was about to lose everything.

*Or,* she wondered, *is he burdened by the decision? Is he thinking of paying Farouk to remove the problem?*

He kissed Harry's forehead, holding him too close. Harry squirmed as he always did, and Laura didn't blame him. His grandfather smelled of snuff and camphor at the best of times, and today he smelled worse. Sour.

She did feel sorry for the old man. However he was thinking about it, Azir's letter must have been a shock, and it laid a terrible burden on him.

"You enjoy a good long holiday," Lord Caldfort said again to Laura as he let Harry escape. "No need to hurry back. Lad's too young to be learning estate management yet, you know."

Just how far would this stretch? "My sister Juliet is at Merrymead at the moment, sir. Perhaps I might travel back to London with her."

She saw the struggle, but then he said, "Good idea, good idea. Just for a few weeks, though."

Why had that letter caused this peculiar behavior? If they found Henry Gardeyne's legitimate son, perhaps it would be a kindness to the old man, as well. His dilemma would be over and it might be possible for him to live out his life here.

She and Harry said farewell to the senior

staff, then went outside. Laura sucked in the crisp autumn air as if it were freedom itself and let Harry run down ahead to the horses. He knew not to go too close.

The four horses looked fresh and healthy, jingling the traces as they shifted, ready to be off. The last trunk was being loaded into the boot, and in a moment the lid was slammed shut.

Stephen was already there, but a handsome bay horse was saddled and waiting for him. How were they to talk if he was riding? Mind you, how were they to talk with an excited Harry along?

Laura remembered that he hadn't met Harry and collected her son. "Come and make your bow to Sir Stephen, Harry. He's an old friend of mine who's going to travel with us a little way."

Stephen came to meet them halfway. Harry did bow and say, "Pleased to meet you, sir," in proper manner, but then added, "May I ride with you, sir?"

Stephen looked startled and Laura said, "He must remember doing that with Hal. No, Harry, not today. When we get to Merrymead, your grandfather and Uncle Ned will take you riding."

"May I get in the coach, Mama?"

"Of course. Off you go."

He raced to the coach as if speed would make the journey start sooner.

"A charming lad," Stephen said.

"Yes, but the next two days will take fortitude."

"No nursemaid?"

"I never take her. She's not needed at Merrymead. How far can you come with us?"

She meant, *When can we talk?*

"To Andover."

About twenty miles and two changes. It would do.

Harry was hanging out of the carriage and calling for her to hurry, so she did. She was as keen to be away as he. Nan took a tearful farewell, Stephen mounted, and they were off.

Laura looked back at Caldfort House as long as she could, but that was only for the relief she felt when it finally slid out of sight with no sign of Jack Gardeyne in hot pursuit. Harry was now safe.

# Chapter 13

The novelty of the carriage and the passing scenery held Harry's interest for quite some time, and then the changing of the horses at the first stage fascinated him. Laura let down the window so he could lean out and watch.

Stephen rode over to chat, but this stop would be too brief for much. "All went well, I assume?" he asked.

"Yes, though Lord Caldfort is definitely in a strange state of mind." Laura kept a grip on the back of Harry's jacket as he leaned out, and spoke softly. As they say, little pitchers have big ears. "He even agreed to let us spend some time in London if we wished. Why would this matter of HG make him do that?"

"To be sure that you don't catch wind of anything he does about it?"

She nodded at him. "That could be it."

The new horses were in the shafts, their

postilions in the saddles. Laura pulled Harry back into the coach, and Stephen said, "Call a halt at Andover and we'll talk properly."

She agreed and they set off again, fast enough to keep Harry glued to the window. Stephen rode beside them at a canter, and Laura was glued to watching him.

She'd always thought of him as a thinker more than a sportsman. He'd certainly never been as sporting mad as her brothers and the other young men of the area. Or like Hal, but Hal had been an extreme case. A blood, a buck, a Corinthian.

Being married to a Corinthian gave a woman an appreciation of a fine rider, and to her surprise, Stephen was one. He was clearly riding because he enjoyed it, and she enjoyed watching him. There was something sensual about a good rider on a good horse. She'd never thought that before.

Not even with Hal.

Something was changing, as if the strange events of yesterday had cracked a seal. If Harry was not the heir to Caldfort, she could marry again. It would no longer be wicked to view men as potential husbands.

Men like Stephen?

She grimaced. After the debacle six years ago, he was the last man to be interested in marrying her. Last night had proved it. Not a hint of interest in anything but the letter and the mystery.

Despite the riding, he was clearly still a man of the mind — and besides, she remembered Lady Skylark. That showed what he thought of her. A foolish player in the riggings of life.

There would be suitors, however. She'd been the toast of Dorset before her marriage and a toast of London after it. She was older now, but it would be coy to deny that she still had charms enough to attract a new husband.

She wouldn't pursue those thoughts yet. It would make disappointment too sharp. But they lingered like a distant but pleasant melody.

In Andover she told the postilions that she wanted tea, and took Harry into the White Hart. Stephen soon joined them, but Laura pulled an apologetic face at him, because Harry was eager for refreshments and wanted to chatter about everything he'd seen.

She'd brought his bag of carved animals, however, and once he'd drunk his milky tea, eaten a cake, and talked for a while, he scrambled off his chair to play on the floor.

It seemed a minor miracle, and Laura thanked heaven for it.

She shared with Stephen her thought about Lord Caldfort having a hand in his nephew's disappearance.

Stephen saw all the problems she did. "I suppose it's possible to imagine that Oscar Ris, hired assassin, had a daughter who managed to marry Henry before her father carried out his wicked work. . . ." Eyes laughing, he shook his head. "No, it isn't."

"But I do think HG must be a child rather than a man," she said. "It explains the delay. His legitimate origins may not have been clear until recently."

"If true, it might be hard to prove his claim."

"There's whatever evidence was sent. I wish I'd found that."

"Caldfort may have destroyed it."

"I suppose so. I do have something, though."

She showed him her copy of the portrait.

"Clever woman. I tried to commit it to memory, but this is much better. I'd forgotten how skilled you are at drawing. You were always sketching us." He glanced at her. "What happened to those pictures?

They must be a record of a misspent youth."

There'd been one, drawn from memory, of the swimming. "I don't know," she said honestly, "but they must be around somewhere. I would never throw them away."

"Ah," he said. "I wondered." After a silence he went on. "So if we come face-to-face with someone claiming to be Henry Gardeyne, we can check for resemblance to this, but if the claimant is his son it becomes harder. Resemblance to fathers is a chancy thing — for which, I'm sure, many women are grateful."

"Cynic!"

"Realist."

They smiled at each other, but then Laura sighed. "I still don't see how I can go to Draycombe, Stephen. Not, at least, in the next few days. I can't arrive home and immediately leave —"

Harry put an animal on the table by Stephen. "Cow!"

"Definitely," Stephen said, which fortunately seemed an adequate response as Harry returned to managing his farmyard.

"He'll be back with another one," Laura warned.

"If a similar response is all that's required, I believe I can cope. I can get you to Draycombe, too, if you're willing."

"How?"

"Definitely," he said in response to a presented "Hen!" Then he continued their conversation. "We have a little breathing room. Caldfort will have to investigate this Azir Al Farouk. Do we assume that he'll send the vicar?" He glanced down. "A baa-lamb. Assuredly, sir."

This slightly more complicated response caused Harry to frown, but he went back to his animals for a while.

"You could always make the appropriate sounds," Laura said, fighting to keep a straight face.

"*Baa?*" Stephen responded with horror. Feigned, she thought, though she wasn't sure. She couldn't interpret him as she once had. It shouldn't surprise her, but it did.

"He'd have to send Jack," she agreed. "Whom else can he trust? And that certainly gives us breathing room."

"Why?"

"Today is Thursday. On Sunday, Jack has two services to lead. He could get down to Draycombe and back in time if he pushed, but he'd have no time to investigate there."

"Curate?"

"He doesn't have one."

"Then you're right." He looked at the animal presented, glanced at Laura with a mischief that was familiar, and did a creditable imitation of a turkey gobbling.

Harry broke into giggles and turned back to his animals.

"Now you've done it."

"It was your idea."

"I never thought you would!"

*"Oink, oink,"* Stephen said to a pig, but caught Harry's hand. "Your mother and I need to talk a little without interruption. Then I will play barnyard animals with you. Yes, sir?"

Harry frowned mutinously, but if a battle of wills waged, Stephen won. "Yes, sir," Harry said, and wandered back to his toys.

"Well done."

"A short respite, I'm sure. Now, getting you to Draycombe. Would your family be suspicious if you claimed friendship with a Mrs. Delaney, living near Yeovil in Somerset?"

"Perhaps not. They don't know every detail of my life. But I don't know this Mrs. Delaney."

"You do now. Eleanor Delaney is the wife of a friend of mine —"

"I know. King Rogue!"

He winced. "I really did bore on about the Rogues, didn't I?"

"We were fascinated. Nicholas Delaney. King Rogue. Leader of your merry band. So he's married now?"

"Yes, and in the right place, but most of all, in a matter like this we can trust him."

Laura didn't like to express doubts, but she must. "This is a delicate matter, Stephen. Complex and private. I don't think it's suitable for . . . for schoolboy nonsense."

Instead of offense, he seemed to fight a laugh. "Oh, I assure you we're past that. Trust me, Laura, in matters delicate and complex, the Rogues are your men, and in totally adult ways."

"Rogues? Plural? This can't be broadcast around England!"

Any amusement faded. "You can trust all the Rogues, but if you don't wish to, so be it. I still recommend trusting Nicholas. I pledge my life that you can."

How could she respond to that other than by agreement, even though doubts lurked?

"His home is only a few hours' journey from Draycombe. More to the point, Nicholas and Eleanor will accept us as guests, lie for our cause, and if it comes to trouble, be useful support."

"Trouble?"

"We don't know how violent and desperate this Farouk is, or how many people he has with him."

The situation shifted. "I never thought of that. How foolish I am. I'm embroiling you in danger."

"You think me too delicate for it?" It was phrased almost as a joke, but Laura detected affront. She wasn't sure why he would feel that way, but she hastily re- assured him.

"Of course not. But this is only your concern by accident."

That didn't seem to help, so she tried to smooth his ruffled feathers. "I don't know what I would have done if you hadn't turned up, Stephen. And I value your help in more ways than the practical. I know you'll advise me well. You know the law, and I trust your judgment. You've always followed the highest principles."

"Have I? It has cost me greatly at times."

What was that wry tone supposed to convey? He was an enigma, but she had no time for delicate male feelings just now. "I still can't leave Merrymead as soon as I arrive."

"No? What if you receive a letter explaining that your friend is about to travel elsewhere. That it's then or never. Given that you have a month at home, that should do."

She supposed it would, but his strange mood had her on edge. "Harry will have to come," she pointed out. "He won't be happy to be left for days, and I wouldn't want to leave him."

"The Delaneys won't mind. They have a daughter. She's younger, but they're accustomed to children."

"You seem very sure."

"I am."

She shrugged. "Very well, then, and we need to be on our way. If we travel to the Delaneys together —"

"That could cause talk. I will arrive separately."

"You could always pretend to be courting me." The words slipped out and her cheeks burned. "I'm sorry."

He smiled. "A useful excuse if we need it."

He seemed to feel no awkwardness about it, for which she was grateful. But his response proved that he no longer felt like that about her. For which she should also be grateful.

"Anyway," she said, "I wouldn't do anything so deceitful."

"Laura, Laura! We're going to have to lie, and possibly cheat and steal, too, for this cause."

She looked at him. "You're right, beginning with lying to my parents. I'm going to hate that."

"If you insist on perfect virtue, our enterprise stops here."

Virtue. That made her rethink everything. "Then it must stop here. I can't afford scandal, Stephen, and my being in Draycombe with you would be a terrible one. It would give the Gardeynes an excuse to cut me off from Harry, and if I'm right about Jack, that could cost him his life."

He frowned in thought. "Disguise, then. I should be myself. My position might be useful if we need to call in the authorities, and I'm also fairly well known to some gentlemen of the area. But you can be a distant relative. One in poor health, whom I'm escorting to try the sea air. Nicholas will arrange it. He's good at that sort of thing."

Laura felt as if he was dragging her into danger. "You're forcing this. *If* I agree to this plan, then I agree to the disguise. But I think I should stay at the Delaneys'." She saw his resistance and put a hand on his arm. "If it's only a few hours away, I can make decisions from there. And then I can stay with Harry. We can't take him to Draycombe if I'm in disguise, and I can't leave him with strangers."

His arm was tense beneath her touch. "You used to trust me more than this, Laura."

"We were children then. The consequences were minor."

"Were they? They seem to have brought us here. But come along. You'd best be on your way. You have two days to think over your decision."

Harry sensed liberation and ran over to them. "Horsey!"

Stephen whinnied, causing a peal of delight.

Laura knew there was no point in arguing further now and went to help Harry gather up his toys. He kept out a duck and ran to present it to Stephen.

"*Quack.*" Then Stephen swung Harry into his arms, and for a wonder, Harry didn't object to that, or to being carried out and placed in the chaise.

Strangely close to tears over many things, not least of them Stephen's animal noises and the sight of Harry in his arms, Laura hurried after.

Stephen handed her into the vehicle. "I'll send a messenger so that a letter from Eleanor will await you at Merrymead or arrive soon after you. I'll also reserve rooms at the Compass for three days hence."

"Stephen, I can't go!"

"If you can come up with a better plan, I will rejoice with you." A smile twitched his lips. "Don't pout."

"A look of resolve is not a pout. You're pressing me."

"Because there's need. Caldfort will probably take some time to consider his actions, but he might even now be dispatching Jack to investigate. You say his church duties will constrain him, but in the face of this disaster can you be sure?"

"No," she admitted. "I should be used to you winning every argument."

"That's not as I remember it."

She brushed that aside. "This is no time for the past. What if Jack arrives in the Draycombe area before me? I'll have to stop frequently on the way to Merrymead to give Harry a chance to run around."

She had the window down and was leaning out, one hand on the top. He covered it with his. "Am I not the efficient one? I intend to ride back and check on Gardeyne's movements. If he's still at home, we can assume you have at least the day's grace you need. If not, I'll go direct to Draycombe."

"My, my," he said to Harry, who was presenting a lion. He managed a ferocious roar that had Harry pealing with laughter and crying, "Again! Again!"

"Next time," Stephen said with a smile that seemed to encompass more than a child's games. Then he mounted and rode away.

# Chapter 14

When Jack walked into Lord Caldfort's study without knocking, the old man quickly slid another letter on top of the one from Azir Al Farouk. "What is it?" he grumbled. His legs were swollen, he hadn't slept, and he felt as if he could hear his weary heart laboring in his breast.

And here was Jack, taunting him with life and vigor. Jack wouldn't feel so cocky if he knew what was going on. Tempting to tell him, but not yet, not yet. Not until he decided what to do.

"Just dropped by to see how you are, Father."

"Piss awful, but that's no news."

Jack paced the room as if demonstrating health in the face of illness, complaining about him letting Laura take little Harry away for so long. Preaching a damn sermon, but Jack was no saint.

Lord Caldfort knew he hadn't been a

perfect father, but he'd always understood his sons because they were a lot like him. There was something cold about Jack, however, and he'd never been a cold man himself. Nor had Hal.

The boy probably got it from his mother. Thirty-five years ago it hadn't seemed to matter that Cecily was a bit strange. Her dowry had been twenty thousand pounds, and she'd been plain and peculiar enough for her family to be grateful for a younger son. He should have remembered that you didn't breed a bad hound.

"A month at her home'll do Laura good," he said when the sermon ended. "She's been looking a bit worn."

"A bit demented, if you ask me. She'll smother the boy with her cosseting! All that fuss because he picked something up off the ground and ate it. I'm not sure she's a fit mother, Father."

So that was how it went. "Who would take care of the lad if not her?"

"Emma and I," said Jack, every inch the charitable vicar. "He'd be better off in the midst of a family, and he'd still be close enough to Caldfort to know the place. Or," he added, "we could all move here."

Ah. Jack would like that, but Lord Caldfort wasn't having a pack of noisy brats all over the place. One quiet one was bad enough.

"It'd be better for Laura, too," Jack went on. "She's still a young woman, and must be hot to marry again. She'd be free to take up residence in some lively spot. Heaven knows, her jointure's rich enough. Hal was besotted to increase it like that."

"I approved it," Lord Caldfort growled.

Jack looked at him sharply, but didn't let go of his bone. "Then you should let her enjoy it. She'd be welcome to visit Harry here as often as she wished."

So cogent. Lord Caldfort admired his younger son's way with words. He preached well to his parishioners, too. Not too long, livened with a bit of earthy humor, and making a worthy point. What he said about Laura made sense, too. She'd find another husband in no time, but Jack, typically, hadn't thought it through.

"She's still a beautiful woman, Jack, so she'd probably marry well. If a powerful man becomes Harry's stepfather, we'd find it hard to keep him here, where he belongs."

Jack's eyes narrowed, but then he shrugged. "We can face that fence when we come to it."

What fence? That was the question.

Keeping Harry here, or getting rid of him altogether? But Jack wouldn't go that far. Not that far.

"This isn't the hunting field," Lord Caldfort growled. "Law be damned, a powerful stepfather for Harry would be a plaguey nuisance. Then there'd be no way to stop Laura mollycoddling the boy to disaster."

Jack smiled. "He's a Gardeyne, Father, and boys will be boys."

Lord Caldfort was sure then. As sure as he could be until the day Hal's boy lay dead, dead of some boyish enterprise gone wrong. But what was he to do? Dr. Trumper warned he could go at any time, and then Jack would be Harry's guardian.

Time to change that, but to whom? You didn't leave a woman as guardian to a peer of the realm. Laura's father? The man was little better than a farmer and lived days away. . . .

"Father? Are you all right?"

Lord Caldfort looked up into Jack's ruddy, healthy face. Did he see a glint of anticipation? If he died and then Harry died, Jack would have it all. Except that Henry Gardeyne might be alive. He felt a touch of glee at maybe having Jack's plans scuppered like that, but mostly he wished everyone would leave him alone.

" 'Course I'm all right. Or I was before you barged in here haranguing me. Go away!"

Jack pulled a saintly, forbearing face and took his leave.

Lord Caldfort pulled out the plaguey letter. Pain in the bloody arse, but it needed handling. How, how? If he put it in Jack's hands, he knew what would happen.

But perhaps he should. It would all be taken care of then, and he could have some peace.

# Chapter 15

When the chaise rolled into Barham, Laura remembered that Friday was market day. Streets full of stalls and animals slowed their progress, but made her smile. Despite the noise and smell, she'd always loved the town in the market-day bustle, and loved exploring the wares of itinerant merchants.

Moreover, she and Harry would soon be home, where she could take action about HG. She'd had two days to think, and Stephen's rationale was inescapable. She had to go to Draycombe. Now her chief concern was to get there before Jack.

A post chaise with regular changes travels as fast as humanly possible, but she'd stopped last night when the light went and not started again until the sun was up. Someone on an urgent mission might not do that. Her hopes were pinned to Lord Caldfort's innate caution and Jack's parish responsibilities, but most of all to the fact that neither man could guess that anyone else knew about Farouk and HG. They had no reason at all to think there was urgency.

She hoped the letter from Redoaks awaited her at Merrymead, but even so, it was already late afternoon, so she could not leave until tomorrow. More delays. More danger for HG.

"A cock, Mama! *Cock-a-doodle-dooooo!*"

Laura looked. They were leaving the town, and a cock paced in male arrogance among his harem of hens.

Stephen's animal noises had made a lasting impression on Harry, which hadn't made the journey any easier. They'd passed all too many cows, horses, sheep, and pigs, not to mention ducks and chickens. No lions, thank heavens, but that hadn't stopped Harry from practicing his roar.

"Are we there yet?"

Laura laughed and hugged him. "Very, very soon, Minnow. Just around the next bend. Do you remember the lions at the gates?"

He nodded and pressed to the window, letting out his best roar. Oh, dear. Was he going to do that throughout their visit?

Stone lions guarded the entrance to

Merrymead House, and on their last visit, they'd fascinated Harry. That was why she'd bought him the inappropriate lion for his farmyard animals.

The lions had been her father's contribution to the family's rise into the gentry. Merrymead Farm — three hundred years old — had become Merrymead House in her grandfather's time, masked by a new facade that included a pillared entrance. Her father had transformed the paddock between the house and the road into a garden and marked the entrance with low stone pillars topped with crouching lions.

Having been designed by her father, the lions did not snarl a warning. They grinned merrily, welcoming all, and seemed designed for children to pretend to ride. They probably had been.

Harry's nose was squashed to the glass, so she let down the window so he could hang out a little. "See the tower of St. Michael's? Merrymead's very close to there."

Laura was almost as excited as he was, and tempted to hang wildly out of the window to catch a first glimpse. The chaise turned the bend and Harry pointed. "Happy lions! Happy lions! *Roar!*"

Laura laughed as the postilions guided the horses carefully between the smiling guardians and up the short drive to the door.

Her mother and Juliet rushed out to stand under the classical portico, grinning and waving. Her mother was unchanged — round, gray, and beaming. Juliet looked to have reverted to younger years. She was wearing her brown hair tied back and a simple blue dress, and was bouncing with excitement like a mere girl. No one would imagine she was the wife of an important servant of His Majesty.

As soon as the coach door was opened, her mother swept Harry into her arms. Laura climbed out and into Juliet's arms.

"Oh, it's so good to see you, Laura! And for a whole month. We could hardly believe the message you sent ahead. And Harry's grown so much."

Juliet took Harry's face and planted a kiss on his nose.

Harry didn't squirm away, but he was looking overwhelmed, so Laura took him in her arms. "Where's Father?"

"In town for market day, of course," Laura's mother said, shepherding everyone inside and to the drawing room.

The so-called drawing room was large and part of a new extension, but despite the name it was as comfortable and informal as the old parlor next to the kitchen.

"Him and Ned both," her mother went on. "Aggie! Here's Laura home. Come and take their coats and such and find George to deal with the luggage. And they've taken Tom and Arthur," she added to Laura as the middle-aged maid rushed in smiling to take away the clothing.

"That explains the quiet," Laura said, putting down Harry and stripping off his warm coat.

Tom and Arthur were her brother Ned's seven- and ten-year-old sons. There was a thirteen-year-old, too — Edward, who was off at Winchester School. Merrymead was usually bursting with noisy life, and even with only the women at home, it completely lacked the chilly calm of Caldfort.

Dogs circled, and the two indoor cats leapt up from in front of the drawing room fire, possibly with an eye to escaping Harry. Laura watched for a moment, but they seemed willing to be stroked.

Her mother was ordering tea and chattering at the same time, as if she'd give all the news of the family and gossip of the county in a minute.

Laura sat down on the familiar red-striped sofa, feeling very, very happy. Even the smells were familiar. Wood smoke, baking, rose potpourri, and a hundred others that told her she was home.

"Laura!"

Her sister-in-law, Margaret, came in smiling, with her baby in her arms. Her four-year-old daughter, Megsy, was at her side, cradling a doll in solemn imitation. Mother and daughter looked so alike that it made Laura smile — both were sturdy, forthright, with bubbling brown curls, and dimpled smiles.

Megsy and Harry had played well together on their last visit, and he talked about her sometimes. She hoped it would work out now.

Megsy marched over and offered her doll to Harry. "But she's only to lend!"

Harry took it, nodding solemnly, and arranged it in his arms as Megsy had. Laura gave thanks the Gardeyne men weren't here to see Harry cradling a doll. She'd brought his bag of toys from the coach and wondered if she'd have to prompt him to share in turn. He sat down on the carpet, however, and tumbled out his animals with one hand.

After a hesitation, he chose the lion and offered it. "Only to lend. It's a lion, and it roars."

He demonstrated, which made the adults laugh.

Negotiations over, the two children settled to playing with the animals, the doll, and the cats when the cats allowed.

Laura turned to Margaret, who was beside her on the sofa. "She's becoming quite the little lady."

"Only when it suits her, I assure you. You're looking well, Laura."

"It's good to be home."

It was, but Laura saw her mother's flicker of alertness at the word *home*. She'd forgotten the other thing about home. Everyone had their nose in everyone else's business, and her mother knew all her children too well. Telling lies might be even more difficult than she'd imagined. Besides, having arrived, the last thing she wanted to do was leave.

For the moment she settled to enjoying a normal homecoming, including holding and admiring darling four-month-old Ruthie. Tears suddenly pricked her eyes. Why hadn't she realized how much she wanted more babies? Perhaps because she wasn't the sort to pine for impossibilities. As long as Hal had been alive it had been in God's hands, and since his death, it had seemed impossible. If HG was the true

Viscount Caldfort, however, things could change there, too.

Escape from Caldfort.

A new home, one much more like Merrymead.

More children.

She tried not to hope, but it swirled in her as she tried to follow six months of news.

The baby stirred and demanded food, so Margaret took her and put her to the breast. Laura rose. "Come along, Harry. You must help unpack your trunk."

Anyone would think she'd suggested a penance. "Can't I stay with Megsy?"

"Leave him here," her mother said. "I'll keep an eye on him."

Juliet bounced to her feet. "I'll come with you. We're in our old room."

"He'll be indulged to death," Laura said as they went upstairs.

"Of course. It won't hurt him any more than it hurt us. He won't get away with brattiness."

Juliet led the way into the room they'd shared as girls and young women. It had been papered with red roses after Laura had left home, but otherwise looked just the same.

"I was so unhappy when I couldn't go

abroad with Robert," Juliet said, "but this almost makes up for it. We'll be like girls again!"

"Except that we're now wicked women of the world."

Juliet grinned. "And isn't it lovely? Do you remember our whispered speculations about what happened between husbands and wives?"

Laura turned away to unlock her trunk. "I remember that book you got your hands on."

"Oh yes. It mystified us rather than enlightened. It makes more sense now."

"Yes." Laura lifted out a neat pile of shifts and passed them to her irrepressible sister.

"It is rather wonderful, isn't it?"

Laura caught her breath. "Yes."

"Oh, poor Laura. You must miss Hal dreadfully."

"Really, Ju!" Laura laughed, but she knew she was blushing.

"For more than bed," her sister protested. "But for that, too."

Laura abandoned stoical pretense. "I'm certainly young to enter a nunnery."

"Don't be silly. You'll marry again."

Laura took out a gray dress and laid it in a drawer, wondering what to say. For now she might as well stick to the unchanged situation. "I doubt it. I can't leave Harry, and Lord Caldfort won't let Harry live away from Caldfort House."

"That's horribly unfair." Juliet was putting away stockings. "Don't you have any pretty ones?"

"I'm still in mourning, remember."

"Oh yes. I still think it unfair that they're trying to trap you at Caldfort House until you're as gray as your wardrobe. No lilac, even?"

"Voilà!" Laura took out her lilac dress. "If you'll remember, purples never suited me. Black does better, but lurking in black for twelve months would have been excessive."

"Lurking at Caldfort House for decades would be even more so."

"Ju, I have no choice. And Lord Caldfort is correct. Harry should grow up there. He could even be viscount soon. Lord Caldfort isn't well."

"Then perhaps you could marry a man who'd be happy to live at Caldfort. A scholar, or even a gentleman with no significant property of his own."

Laura stared at her. Juliet had always liked to find solutions to every problem. "A possibility, I suppose. I don't see how the Gardeynes could make any objection. But I'm not sure I'd want to marry a penniless man."

Juliet put away the lilac dress, looking pleased with herself. "He doesn't have to be penniless, just without a property. A nabob from the East, even. There, see. Now, what other problem can I waft away?"

Laura smiled at her, close to tears. "Oh, Ju, I have missed you. Do you solve all Robert's problems, too?"

"Whenever I can. So?" Juliet cocked her head. "I have the impression that something is weighing on you."

"Is it as obvious as that?" Laura closed the lid of the empty trunk, realizing that her words admitted there was something. "I can't tell you at the moment. Perhaps later."

"Is it a man?"

"No!"

"It's a reasonable assumption. The Gardeynes don't want you to marry, but you've fallen in love. Romeo and Juliet . . ."

"I'm Laura, remember? Petrarch's beloved, adored from afar. No balcony kisses, but no death, either."

"To avoid death is to avoid life," Juliet

stated, reverting to their lifelong debate about their namesakes. Their sisters, Beatrice and Olivia, both some years older, had claimed smugly to have more normal fates; Beatrice with her Benedick in *Much Ado About Nothing* and Olivia with her Orsino from *Twelfth Night*, a duke, no less.

Laura was in no mood to play, especially when the fate of saintly Laura seemed to fit her all too well these days.

"Let's unpack for Harry," she said to escape, and led the way to the smaller nursery bedroom where he'd sleep with Megsy. His things were soon put away there and Laura went to find him.

He was in the kitchen with Megsy and his grandmother, happily covered in flour and shaping dough into rolls, adored by the servants preparing dinner. He smiled at her, but he didn't seem to have missed her at all.

It hurt.

Her mother said, "He's no trouble, love. Go into the drawing room and have a nice chat with Juliet."

It was as good as a command, but Laura said, "Let's stroll around outside, Ju. Sitting in a carriage for two days leaves my legs feeling neglected."

They rambled the garden and orchard

and then into the farm proper.

"There are kittens," Juliet said as they strolled by the stables. "Harry will like that."

"He'd like a cat, but Lord Caldfort doesn't like them."

"He's a sour old despot, if you ask me."

"He's a sick and bitter old man, but it is his home."

"It's yours, too."

"Not really." It came out because she was relaxed, and because she was tired of saying the right thing all the time. "Where's your home?" she asked Juliet as they passed through a gate to walk along the edge of a stubbled field.

"Wherever Robert is." Then Juliet pulled a face. "Well, not Denmark. Or at sea, which is probably where he still is. But yes, our London house is home. Perhaps it's because it's ours, not his father's."

"That would make a difference." Laura picked a rose hip from the hedge and broke it open to look at the seeds. "As it is, I feel . . . transient. The vessel for the next Lord Caldfort, but no more than that. Of course, when Hal was alive we didn't spend much time at Caldfort House. Or before Harry was born, at least." She shrugged. "Hal was not rooted anywhere.

Home was where his horses were."

Too late she realized that sounded as if he loved his horses more than her.

"I always thought it a love match," Juliet said.

"It was, but love . . . changes."

She saw a protest form on her sister's lips and be suppressed.

"Not for everyone," Laura said quickly. "I believe in true love, lasting love. But I think it's hard to detect at the beginning. Like knowing gold from gilding. It has to be tested. Scratched —"

A bird burst up out of the nearby stubble and shot into the air, singing.

"A skylark!" Juliet said, shielding her eyes to watch it climb.

Laura did the same. "It can't have a nest at this time of year."

Memory stirred despite her effort to suppress it. Poor Stephen, but at least they were friends again now. She and Stephen had lain down to watch. They couldn't do that —

Then Juliet did. Right there on the rough ground. "Come on. Let's watch it return." She looked at Laura. "Come on! One advantage of wearing dismal clothes has to be that you don't care if they're stained."

With a laugh, Laura sat. "I've never thought of mourning clothes like that before."

She lay down, shifting away from some stubble that was digging into her back. The sky wasn't a perfect blue today. It was mostly cloudy, but the clouds were high. The ground was chilly beneath her, but at least it was dry.

When had she last lain back to look up into the infinity of the sky? Perhaps that last time with Stephen. It was a shame. Everyone should do this and be aware of . . . She contemplated it. Of the grandeur of the universe, in which mere mortals moved.

"That bird sees more of the world than we ever will," she said. "Perhaps that's why it flies so high."

"I think it flies and sings because it can. Out of sheer joie de vivre. Here it comes!"

First as a dot, then growing larger, the bird plummeted down, wings tucked, only spreading them at the end to circle around. It was as if the bird knew they were watching him.

Laura sat up, hugging her knees. "Can you imagine doing that? Deliberately falling from the sky, knowing you'll be safe?"

Juliet sat up, too. "Sounds rather like you-know-what."

"Ju!"

"Or the appeal of danger. People do take risks just for the thrill."

"Like hunting," Laura said softly, and quoted, "He left life leaping," perhaps understanding it for the first time.

Juliet reached over and took her hand, but Laura's doubtless grim expression was for another reason. The same passion that sent men into battle and over fences could drive a man to kill.

# Chapter 16

The letter arrived the next morning. Laura's father came into the breakfast parlor with the postbag and sorted through the correspondence.

"One for you, Laury-love," he said, studying a letter before passing it on. "From Somerset. Didn't know you knew anyone in Somerset."

Laura managed her part, even though she felt as if *liar* must be written all over her. "It must be from my friend, Eleanor Delaney. I wrote to her hoping we could meet while I was here. We haven't seen each other since we became mothers."

Was she explaining too much too soon?

She read through the letter, expecting to have to lie about the contents, too, but it was a clever imitation of a letter between old friends, including bits about supposed shared acquaintances and their two children.

It made it easier to produce her next lines in the play. Better to think of it as a play rather than as lying to her parents.

"Oh, dear. Eleanor says they're to travel north soon." After a moment of supposed thought, she suggested, "If I'm to see her, I must go soon. Will you mind, Papa, Mama? Harry and I are here for a month."

Her father's bushy gray brows rose, but he said, "No, no, love. If now's the only time to visit your friend, now it must be. You're thinking to go for a few days, then?"

"If you don't mind. I can't make it there and back in a day and have time for a proper visit."

"Of course we don't mind, dear," said her mother, passing around a platter of eggs and urging more on everyone. "It's such a treat to have you here for so long that we can afford to share. I don't think I've heard you mention this lady, though, have I?"

Squirming inside, Laura gave the story she'd prepared of a London friend who was now mostly a friend by correspondence.

"How nice to meet again, then," her mother said. "I'm sure it must have been dull for you at Caldfort after dear Hal died, so letters will have been a solace. But a real meeting is so much better. And Mrs. Delaney has a child, too, you said?"

"Yes. Arabel. But she's over a year younger than Harry."

"Still, someone for him to play with."

"I'll arrange a chaise for you?" her father asked.

"Yes, thank you, Papa."

Talk moved on to the best road to take, and Laura thought it all done. She hoped she was imagining a speculative look on Juliet's face.

After breakfast she packed again, but only a valise, since they would be away for a short time. When the post chaise arrived from the George in Barham, she went to find Harry. He was in the stables with his uncle and Megsy.

She took his hand. "Come along, Minnow. We're going for another little journey."

He stared at her, then ripped his hand free. "No. I'm not going!"

"Harry! Don't be foolish. Of course you're coming. You can't stay here."

"Well, he can," said her brother. "He's no trouble."

Laura glared at the traitor, took a breath, and knelt to explain. "It won't be a long journey, Minnow, and the Delaneys have a

182

little girl to play with."

Harry's face set in mutiny and he shook his head.

"There'll be plenty of animals along the way."

He just scowled.

She couldn't believe it. He'd never behaved like this before.

Laura glared at her brother again, but as usual he was dense as a rock. "Leave him here, Laury. The traveling'll be easier alone and you can enjoy a holiday."

*Holiday!* She didn't need a holiday from Harry. Of course, Ned didn't know that Harry's life was in danger. She stood and grabbed Harry's arm. "Harry, you are coming. We'll be back in a few days."

He didn't protest, but he became a dead weight and she saw tears trickling out of his screwed-up eyes.

She let him go. "Harry, what's the matter with you?"

If Harry wouldn't come, she couldn't go, yet she had to. She had to find out the truth in Draycombe and make sure everything was done properly, but she couldn't explain to him or to anyone else.

Laura glared at her brother. "Ned," she mouthed. "Do something."

He shrugged. "He probably thinks

you're dragging him off home. Every other time he's been here, he's climbed into a coach to go back to that house. Leave him. We're happy to have him here."

Laura went back on her knees, finding a bright smile. "Sweetling, we're not going back to Caldfort! We're going on to another house."

But Harry had reached a state of mutiny that was impervious to reason. "I'm staying *here*. You stay here, too."

Laura recognized a crucial moment. Apart from her need to go, she couldn't let Harry dictate her movements to suit himself.

She got to her feet. "Very well. If you really don't want to come, you can stay here."

He grabbed her skirt. "No, you *stay!*" He even stamped his foot.

Controlling an urge to return temper for temper, she said, "That can't be, Harry, but you can stay here."

He glared at her in a way that could break her heart, but she didn't waver. In the end he let go of her skirt. "Stay here. Stay with Megsy and Uncle Ned and Aunt Margaret and Grandma and Grandpa."

Laura fought not to show her shocked betrayal. She'd never believed that in the

184

end he would choose others over her. When she could speak through her tight throat, she said, "Very well, love. I won't be gone many days, and I'll write you a letter every day."

Perhaps he, too, had thought he'd win, for his lips trembled. "With drawings?"

Laura blinked away tears as she hugged him. "With drawings. You'll be good, yes?"

He nodded.

Laura realized that she was still waiting for him to change his mind, to declare, now he saw that she wouldn't falter, that he'd come with her. But he didn't. Instead he wriggled free, said, "Bye-bye, Mama," and ran back into the stables.

After a moment her brother said, "There's kittens."

Laura couldn't find anything to say to the traitor, so she turned and stalked back into the house, wavering, wondering if she shouldn't go after all. Stephen would go in her place. He could report back.

But a letter would be two days to and from, and matters could turn urgent.

Her parents and Juliet were waiting by the door to wave her off, and she had to explain the change of plan.

"That's no problem," her father said heartily. "In fact, it's a treat for us." He and Ned were very alike.

Her mother understood. "They all go in the end, love. Particularly the boys."

"But he's so young."

"And he'll miss you dearly. But they become dictators if we let them, and it never serves. You go and have your little visit. It'll do you both good."

Laura hugged her mother, who meant well and was probably right, but — Lord! — it crashed in on her that she would be leaving Harry unprotected. She believed he would be safe here, but even so, she had to warn someone.

Her parents? Ned? But she knew them too well to think that would work.

Juliet.

"Oh," she said, "I have all Harry's things packed. I must undo that."

She commanded the valise unloaded and carried back into the house, then dug through it to extract Harry's clothing. When Juliet came to help, Laura looked for condemnation but saw none.

Even so, she said, "I have to go."

"So I gather. Don't worry about Harry. He'll be fine."

*Perhaps I don't want him to be,* Laura thought, then was ashamed of herself, but his content with the separation was a knife in her heart. He wasn't even here to see her off.

She grabbed the pile of Harry's clothes. "I'll take these back upstairs."

"No need. I'll do it."

Laura shook her head and Juliet caught the hint. She took half of the small pile, and they went upstairs together. Once in the room, Laura dropped the clothing on the bed and explained the essentials as succinctly as she could. She wanted to tell Juliet only about Jack, but she had to say something about Draycombe to explain leaving at all.

Juliet frowned as she followed it. "You truly think Reverend Gardeyne might come here to try to kill Harry?"

Laura put a hand to her mouth. "No. If I did, I'd never go. If Jack's doing anything other than writing his sermon, he'll be heading for Draycombe. That's why I have to get there first, but I couldn't bear to leave Harry here with no one alert for problems. I don't *expect* any, but I need you to promise that if Jack Gardeyne comes here, you won't let him be alone with Harry for a moment, no matter what pretext he comes up with."

Still looking skeptical, Juliet nodded. "I promise."

"And don't let him take Harry any-where. Not even to church."

"Very well. But in that case, you know, I might have to tell Papa or Ned." After a moment, she asked, "Don't you think you should tell them now?"

From downstairs, Laura's father called, "Laura? Are you all right, love? Don't keep the horses standing."

She opened the door. "Coming, Papa! No," she whispered to Juliet. "They'd think I was mad, and you know what they'd be like! They'd want to go to the magistrates. I don't have time for that, and in the end I have no proof. Oh, if only Harry would come with me!"

"Into danger?" Juliet asked.

That caught Laura. "Heavens, you're right. I'd rather leave him here than with strangers at Redoaks."

"But what about you? Are you going into danger? Who is this Mrs. Delaney? Laura . . ."

At any moment, Juliet was going to decide that she had to tell their parents herself.

Laura had left out one detail.

"Stephen is helping me. Stephen Ball. The Delaneys are friends of his. He's meeting me there, and we're going to investigate this together."

Juliet's eyes went wide, but now with mischievous delight. "I *knew* there was a man involved! Go, go, and have a wonderful time!"

# Chapter 17

It took three hours to travel to Redoaks, and three hours gives ample time for worry. Laura worried that Harry would already be missing her. She worried that he wasn't. It still hurt that he seemed able to wave good-bye to her without a care in the world. It hurt, simply, that each turn of the wheel separated them more. They had been so little apart.

Perhaps everyone was right. Perhaps even Jack was right that she clung too closely to her child. She would try to do better, but only when Harry was safe. She prayed that HG was Henry Gardeyne's legitimate child, and that she and Stephen would be in time to save him.

When the post chaise rolled up to the elegant brick house called Redoaks, she was ready to leap out and go on immediately to Draycombe. She knew that couldn't be. They would have to plan a little, and she would need some disguise.

Because what she was about to do was scandalous.

That awareness had grown in her. She and Stephen were old friends, once as close as brother and sister, but that wouldn't count for anything if they were caught together at an inn. It would ruin her.

The disguise had better be excellent.

The door opened and a couple came out, the man carrying a pretty infant in a pink dress. Eleanor Delaney, a handsome woman with auburn hair, came forward. "Laura! How lovely to see you again."

Laura missed her cue by a heartbeat, then realized that indeed they should act their parts, even before the indifferent postilions. She went into the other woman's arms. "It's been so long." Pulling free, she turned to the man and child. "And this must be Arabel."

She would have kissed the child, but the girl shrank back, face puckering as if she'd cry.

"She's shy," Nicholas Delaney said with an easy smile.

King Rogue. He didn't look regal or wicked, though there was something unusual about him — apart, that was, from the fact that his shirt was open-necked beneath a loose jacket. Informal, to say the least. Perhaps the uncommon impression came from his coloring, for unlike most fashionable gentlemen his face was tanned by the sun to a shade that almost matched his dusky gold hair.

"A pleasure to see you again, Laura," he said. "I'll attend to your luggage and the carriage. You go into the house. You must be ready for refreshment."

Laura went, but she couldn't help finding it strange that Delaney kept the little girl with him rather than passing her to his wife.

Eleanor Delaney didn't seem to mind. "No Harry?" she asked as they went upstairs. "Arabel will be disappointed."

"I'm sorry. He's enjoying his cousins, and there are kittens in the barn. No Stephen?"

"Not yet, but we expect him shortly."

Eleanor Delaney took her into an airy bedchamber with blue-and-white curtains and bed hangings. In this house Laura had an impression of casual elegance that made her long to settle in and enjoy. But there was also something as unusual as its owner.

Perhaps it was the colors, or even the scents. She detected potpourri, but perhaps incense, as well. On the landing, she'd recognized a large pale statue of a laughing fat man as a representation of Buddha. She remembered Stephen saying once that King Rogue had gone traveling instead of to university.

So it would seem.

"I'll go and get some hot water for you," her hostess said.

She left, which was tactful, as Laura did need to use the chamber pot. She hadn't anticipated, however, how very strange it would feel to be foisted upon strangers with Stephen not here. Was she to carry on chatting as if they were old friends? When would she be allowed to stop lying?

She took off her black bonnet and gloves and her gray spencer, then relieved herself. As she waited for her washing water, she looked out at a pleasant, unpretentious garden, an orchard, and placid scenery beyond. A lovely spot, but not the setting she'd expected for daredevil Nicholas Delaney.

Stephen put great faith in him, but was he really able to help them? People changed. *Yes,* she thought, considering the past few days, *indeed, people do.*

Eleanor returned, carrying the jug of hot water herself.

"This is a lovely house," Laura said.

"We like it. May I call you Laura all the time? It's best to act a part completely — I have that from a master of deception. And you must call me Eleanor."

It would feel awkward, but Laura said, "Of course."

"And do call Nicholas, Nicholas. No one who knows him would believe that an old friend of mine wouldn't."

That would feel even stranger, but pouring water into the bowl, Laura agreed. As she washed her hands and face, she asked, "Is there need to pretend in front of the servants?"

"It's best to be thorough. Did you have a smooth journey?"

Laura followed that lead. She wouldn't be here long, after all, but she wished she knew how much Stephen had told his friends.

"I gather that you and Stephen intend a further journey," Eleanor said.

So he'd told them that much. "There's nothing improper about it. Well, there is, of course, but we do it only from necessity."

Eleanor's eyes twinkled. "Exciting necessity, I'm sure, Stephen being a Rogue."

Did it seem she was engaged in this for

194

*amusement?* "Perhaps I should explain . . ."

But Eleanor waved a hand. "Oh, no, it will be more efficient to do it all at once. Now, would you like tea? We will have a lunch when Stephen arrives."

"Tea would be lovely."

Laura realized that what she really wanted was to be alone, to be free of pretending friendship and guarding what she said. She remembered a good reason.

"I promised my son letters. Deceptive, I know, but if I write them, will you send them each day?"

"Of course," Eleanor said, without a hint of disapproval. "I'll get you some of our stationery."

She left, and returned in moments with a portable desk containing everything Laura needed. "I'll send up tea and let you know as soon as Stephen arrives."

Laura sat at the table by the window, aware of feeling disgruntled and it being unreasonable. Eleanor Delaney was so very amiable and even tempered that it was irritating. Of course, Eleanor had not married a man like Hal Gardeyne. She was the type to have more sense.

Laura winced. She wouldn't be reduced to thinking mean thoughts about Hal. She'd made that choice and would live with it. He hadn't changed; she had. Or perhaps sim-ply come to know herself better.

It wasn't even as if she wanted a life like this for herself. It struck her as much too placid.

She liked the bustle of Merrymead, and she loved London.

Thinking of that was a waste of time. She uncapped the inkwell and chose a pen. Stephen would be here shortly, and these letters must be written.

Tea came and she sipped it as she wrote. Soon she had five simple letters written, dated today and subsequent days, except that one was for both tomorrow and Monday. Neither people nor letters trav-eled on Sunday.

On Monday, Jack might set off for Draycombe, but it would take him at least two days to make the journey and by then surely she and Stephen would have dealt with the situation. She had four days. Four days that might solve her problems or land her in disaster.

She enjoyed gambling, but only for trivial stakes.

A clock somewhere began an interesting harmonious chime. Laura counted, but she knew it had to be noon. Where was Ste-phen?

She didn't want to join her hosts until he arrived. She remembered promising Harry drawings, so she began to illustrate the letters. On the first one, she drew a post chaise across the top, with herself at the window, waving. On the next one, she drew a church with her coming out with the Delaneys and little Arabel.

Such a pity the child was so shy. She gave thanks that Harry had a robust, sunny temperament. It made him trusting, however. Too trusting.

Juliet would keep him safe.

She drew the view from her window on Tuesday's letter, then, her imagination failing her, a meaningless border of flowers on the last. By the time Harry got Wednesday's letter, she might be home again.

There was a tap on the door, and Eleanor came in. "Stephen's here, and lunch is ready."

*At last.* Laura quickly folded her letters and sealed them. Sadness poked at her. "Harry usually does this. He loves it."

"Arabel, too."

They shared a smile and Laura felt more comfortable. Children were children and mothers mothers. It would not be long before Harry was sealing her letters for her again. She stacked the letters and gave them to Eleanor, then they both went downstairs.

Stephen was in the drawing room, seated on the sofa with little Arabel leaning trustingly on his knee, apparently showing him her doll. It was quite a plain one. A stick-and-rag doll. Stephen was smiling, and the little girl was smiling, too. He liked children and they liked him, even shy Arabel.

He would make a good father.

Then Arabel saw Laura and ran to her father.

He picked her up as if this were normal, but said, "Mrs. Gardeyne is a friend of Uncle Stephen's and thus a friend of ours. Make your curtsy, poppet."

He put the girl down. The child's look was so distrustful that Laura thought she might refuse, but she dropped a curtsy. Immediately afterward, however, she scrambled back into her father's arms.

Laura felt mortified to be terrifying a child so, but why? Harry had been terrified of one of his great-aunts, who wore red circles of rouge on her cheeks in the old style. She, however, was without face paint and wearing a simple dark gray gown and white cap.

She caught a flicker of something on Eleanor Delaney's face. Perhaps it was embarrassment at the way her child was behaving, or even unhappiness that Arabel so clearly preferred her father. All was not well in this house, after all.

Stephen greeted Laura in a casual sort of way. "Did everything go smoothly?"

"Perfectly. Our plans are in place."

"Yes, and when I left the Caldfort area a second time, the vicar was making no unusual moves."

Laura had thought that Stephen's arrival would make everything easier, but it was quite the opposite. She realized that she'd expected Stephen to be more struck by their reunion.

As she was?

Talk became general, then Stephen asked Nicholas, "How's Dare?"

"Coming along."

"Fit for visitors?"

"For you, of course." Nicholas glanced at Laura. "Lord Darius Debenham, a friend of ours who is still suffering the effects of a war wound."

"All England talks of the miracle. And, of course, Lord Darius is one of the Rogues."

Nicholas grinned. "Ah, you know all."

"I'm sure I don't, but I heard many

schoolboy tales. Is there hope of full recovery?"

"Excellent hope, yes. I see lunch is ready.
I'll take Arabel upstairs and join you in a
moment."

At least he carried the child over for a
mother's kiss before taking her away, but as
Laura went to the dining room with Stephen and their hostess she felt uncomfortable about the whole situation. It was none
of her business, but she couldn't help
thinking that King Rogue indulged his
daughter too much. As with letting Harry
dictate to her, it would prove disastrous in
the end.

# Chapter 18

Servants placed dishes on the table and then left. By the time Eleanor was finishing the serving of the soup, Nicholas joined them. "So, who's going to dish up the story?" he asked.

Laura exchanged a look with Stephen. "You're the one with the gift for words."

He pulled a face at her, but then gave a succinct account that was over by the time the Delaneys cleared the soup plates and uncovered the next course.

"I can imagine your concern," Eleanor said to Laura. "It must have been so hard to leave your son behind in these circumstances."

Laura flinched from that reminder. "I'm sure Jack Gardeyne will not go to Merrymead, and my sister knows the dangers."

She explained that, and Stephen said, "Excellent. Juliet always had a clever mind and quick wits."

More so than herself? Laura wondered.

Nicholas ignored his pork. "Let's look at that letter."

Laura produced it, but Stephen said, "I don't think even you can squeeze more out of it. The answers lie in Draycombe. I did confirm that the ship that went down, supposedly taking Henry Gardeyne to the deeps, was the *Mary Woodside*."

"Well done!" Laura declared.

"And achieved in a couple of days on the road," Nicholas said. "Brilliant as always."

Stephen didn't seem particularly pleased by the accolade.

"You don't have a clue about Oscar Ris?" Nicholas asked. "Heaven knows there are strange names around the world, but it doesn't fit with any nationality I know." He passed the letter to Eleanor. "And how could he keep someone prisoner for ten years?"

"What if it were voluntary?" Eleanor suggested. "A flight from disgrace or scandal? Perhaps Henry's father cast him off and it was made to look as if he'd died."

Nicholas raised his brows. "I never knew you had such a gothic imagination, love. But if he wasn't disinherited, why not rise from his watery grave once his father was dead? The key question I see is, Why *now?*"

Laura was making an attempt to eat. "We think this HG might be his son. Raised by Oscar Ris, but newly discovered to be legitimate."

"Now that makes a fragment of sense," Nicholas said. "Azir Al Farouk is entrusted with the task of bringing the child to England to claim his inheritance — perhaps because of his excellent command of English. But the villain has recognized a chance to make his fortune."

"In league with Captain Dyer?" Eleanor suggested. "Could there be a band of ruffians involved?"

Stephen put down his knife and fork. "That's what worries me. I don't want to take Laura into danger."

"Then you shouldn't take her at all," Nicholas said. "Whenever there's villainy, there's the possibility of danger. Desperate people will do desperate things."

The words seemed to have a meaning that shadowed the room. Whatever that meaning was, they cleared Laura's mind. She couldn't send Stephen alone into danger.

"I want to go, and I won't be in danger. I'll simply be visiting a respectable seaside resort. I have no intention of skulking around in the dark or doing anything foolish."

Stephen gave her a look. "I believe I've heard that before."

She looked right back. "When we were children. You were right when you argued that any decisions are mine to make."

Nicholas finally cut into his meat. "I think we should involve Captain Drake."

"Oh, good idea," Eleanor said.

Laura looked between them. "Whoever he is, no. We can't involve any more people. Not when things might become illegal."

"She's right, Nick," Stephen said. "Who the devil is Captain Drake, anyway?"

Laura recognized Nicholas's smile as mischievous, which seemed horribly inappropriate. "He's the smuggling master who controls the coast round about Draycombe."

"Smuggling!" Laura gasped.

Stephen groaned. "Trust you to know the local criminals."

"It wasn't me. It was Con." Nicholas glanced at Laura. "Con Somerford, Viscount Amleigh, briefly Earl of Wyvern. Have you heard of the affair?"

"He inherited the earldom earlier this year and then someone else claimed it. It's being fought in the courts, isn't it?"

"It's being arranged amicably, but the

stamping and sealing takes time. Crag Wyvern, seat of the Earl of Wyvern, is about three miles from Draycombe."

"But how does Con connect to the smuggler, Captain Drake?" Stephen asked.

Nicholas shared a look with his wife. "He's going to be upset with me."

"You always knew that," Eleanor replied.

Stephen put down his cutlery. "You've been up to something illegal again."

It was said levelly, but Laura tensed. Stephen was angry? Because of illegalities? Did he try to keep his irresponsible friends in line? If so, why had he involved them in her serious affairs?

"Not I," Nicholas protested.

"But as usual, you protected me from any dirt."

"Stephen," said Nicholas, suddenly serious, "you're the Rogues' secret weapon within the legal and political system. We can't have you tainted."

"For pity's sake —"

Eleanor stopped Stephen with a raised hand. "Before you two have a Roguish fight, you're going to have to decide how much to tell Laura. Private matters in public are not polite."

"I've had my knuckles rapped." Nicholas turned to Laura. "My apologies. Since you've told us your secrets, I have no problem with telling you ours, but I need your assurance that you will keep them in confidence."

"Illegal matters? I'm not sure. If I were to find them wrong, wicked . . . I'm not sure."

"Excellent. Honor should rule. How strongly do you feel about smuggling?"

"Not strongly at all. The taxes are iniquitous."

"Then you should have no difficulty. I've been wondering how Al Farouk and HG arrived in England, you see. There are formalities at official entry points. My guess is that they came ashore on a smuggling boat. If it was anywhere near Draycombe, Captain Drake will know all about that."

"I see, but can we get the information without telling him why?"

"Possibly, but I think we should involve him more. It's his business to be informed about any unusual people visiting his territory. In addition, he commands most of the people along that stretch of coast and can even summon an army if required. If Farouk is part of a vicious gang, Captain Drake can keep you and Stephen safe."

A noise came from Stephen that sounded like a stifled protest.

Nicholas looked at him. "Steve, you know I don't approve of courting danger. It comes on its own easily enough."

"Not to me."

"Now that," his friend said, "is idiotic. As well ask to break a bone."

Laura noted that Eleanor looked resigned, as if this was an old battle. The Rogues tried to keep Stephen out of dangerous activities because he was more useful to them as a sober, respectable citizen? Clearly Stephen objected.

How much danger could a group of English gentlemen get into in the normal run of things?

Stephen turned to her. "It appears that this Captain Drake might be of use, though I share your concerns. He is a criminal, after all."

Nicholas said, "And before I say more, I must have your word that you will keep this secret. I promise there are no worse crimes to reveal."

After a moment, Laura said, "Very well. You have my word."

"Captain Drake is also David Kerslake-Somerford, soon to be Earl of Wyvern."

Laura knew her jaw had dropped.

Stephen exclaimed, "Good Lord!" But then he said, "Yes, I am upset. I assume the Rogues had a part in the rearrangement of the earldom and all know about this but me."

"No. Con knows, of course. It was his affair —"

"And his wife is Kerslake's sister! I was at the wedding. I met the man. He's a gentleman."

"It's a long and complex story."

"When is it not?"

"And not surprising if no one wanted to burden your conscience with it unnecessarily, Steve."

Stephen went silent, but Laura saw that he took this matter of being protected hard. She remembered when she'd worried that she was dragging him into danger. No wonder he'd turned frosty.

Nicholas said, "Miles, Francis, Lee, and Luce are as much in the dark as you, I promise. And note, I *have* told you now that there's a purpose."

There was apology there, but the cool voice of command, too. Laura looked down at her plate, wondering why nothing could be simple anymore. She'd thought the Rogues were a close-knit, endlessly supportive group. She'd thought the same of her family, but in this extreme, she'd not confided in them.

"Let's return to Laura's problem," Stephen said. "So, Captain Drake might know when Farouk arrived, and what companions he brought. Perhaps even their whereabouts. You're right. That will be useful. I'm not sure, however, about making open contact. Smugglers have a rough way of keeping their secrets."

"You and Laura have agreed to keep the secrets, and David is a Rogue by association now."

"Ah, is he?"

"Too useful to be ignored."

"And," said Eleanor dryly, "now owner of a truly astonishing collection of strange books and artifacts."

"Are you ascribing base motives to me, my love?"

She grinned. "Just practical ones." She looked at Laura. "I know David quite well now, and he can be trusted. Because of his responsibilities he cannot always act legally, but he will always act honorably. Once he understands this situation, I'm sure he will feel about it just as you do, and he's perfectly placed to rescue HG and deal with trouble."

Laura felt a strange pang of disappointment, as if a daring adventure had been snatched from her, and she understood

Stephen's mood. How silly. Safety and a quick resolution were what they needed.

"Then I agree. How will it be managed?"

"I'll send a discreet note," Nicholas said, "asking him to contact you at the Compass."

The sonorous clock struck one.

Laura pushed back slightly from the table, ashamed of how little she'd eaten, but eager to be off. "We've done all we can here, I think."

She realized that it sounded rude, but with talk of armed gangs and smugglers, she couldn't linger. Not when there was a child at risk.

Everyone stood, but Stephen said, "There is one thing. We can't risk Laura's reputation. If she were to meet anyone she knows, it would be disastrous. I was hoping for a disguise."

Nicholas turned to eye her. "As what?"

"An older, sickly cousin."

Humor sparked in Nicholas's eyes. "A pity to cloud such beauty, but I think it can be done."

# Chapter 19

Not long afterward, Laura looked in the mirror, still disconcerted by her appearance. She knew she'd need something, but she hadn't imagined a change as thorough as this.

Nicholas had produced a faded blond wig as if it were the kind of thing every house contained. The wiry curls bubbled excessively around her face, which was rendered sallow with a tinted cream. A darker cream around her eyes made her look dismally unwell. As the coup de grâce, a large mole now squatted on the edge of her upper lip. She'd heard such marks called "beauty spots" but there was nothing beautiful about this one. There were even a few hairs sticking out of it.

She'd lived with her beauty for so long that it was unsettling to have it gone. She could tell, however, that anyone meeting her would see only mousy curls, ill health, and mole.

She'd thought her mourning clothes dull enough, but Nicholas had decreed they were too stylish. She and Eleanor were stripping off some trimming, but Laura thought half the work had already been done when she'd abandoned her corset.

They'd realized that she couldn't use a maid to help her undress, because there was no way to make her body fit her face and hair. Eleanor had lent her a kind of bodice that hooked up the front. It was decent, Laura supposed, but didn't raise and support the breasts as she was used to.

A glance at her hostess suggested she was wearing such a garment herself. Comfortable, Laura granted, but . . . well, it was a good thing Eleanor's dress made no attempt at fashion.

*All in the cause,* she told herself, and sat to rip off a belt of ruched gray silk. "It's as well I'll soon be out of mourning. I'll be able to give these to my maid, except that I doubt she'll want them."

"They'll bring her a little in the secondhand shops." Eleanor was unpicking a white lace ruffle from around a neckline. She glanced up with a twinkle in her eye. "So wickedly frivolous, ruffles."

"And I thought I'd been dressing so plainly."

"You're used to high fashion. I was green with envy of the gown you wore at the Arden wedding. Low in the back with crisscross ribbons. Rubies, and red feathers swirling through your hair."

Laura was surprised to feel embarrassed. "I don't remember meeting you, I'm afraid."

"Oh, you didn't. But you were one of the bright lights. I haven't offered my condolences on your husband's death, have I? It must be especially hard when a husband is taken so young and suddenly."

"Yes," Laura said, unwilling to even look at her increasingly muddled feelings about Hal. "Do you visit London often?" she asked, to steer talk to safer channels.

Stephen had been left alone for a while. Nicholas had decreed that he must not witness the transformation so that he could give an honest first impression.

Time to think.

Time to doubt.

Looking out at the plain but pleasant garden, he tried to decide whether his recent actions had been heroic or villainous. They certainly hadn't been wise — or unavoidable. There were other ways of dealing with this mystery. He had framed this plan to get Laura to Draycombe, to create time together and alone. Perhaps even to compromise her.

He wasn't consciously planning that, but he couldn't ignore the fact that if they were caught, if the world discovered them together at Draycombe, they would have little choice but to wed. The damnable thing was, as a man, he wouldn't suffer much from the scandal, but her reputation would be smirched forever.

When Nicholas came in, Stephen wasn't sure how much time had passed. He turned from the view. "Beauty transformed?"

"Excellently. It's an insubstantial quality, isn't it?"

"I don't think so."

Nicholas smiled. "Nor do I. But we're speaking of deeper beauty, I assume. A saber through the face has ruined many a man's beauty. Laura and Eleanor are attacking her clothes."

Nicholas sat, so Stephen did, too. "They're devilish dull as they are."

"But far too stylish for Mrs. Priscilla Penfold. Mrs. Hal Gardeyne has always had an unerring instinct for style."

"I didn't know you knew her."

"I don't, but we do visit London. I was

there extensively in 1814, if you remember."

"I could hardly forget." That was the year Nicholas had played a dangerous game of counterespionage, married Eleanor, and almost died. "But Laura wasn't there as often after her child was born."

"One only has to see Olympus once. She's a rare specimen. I assume you wish to collect her?"

Stephen reacted to the hint of disapproval. "I'm helping an old friend." When Nicholas raised his eyebrows, he said, "Devil take you. Very well. I want her, but I don't like the word *collect*."

"Nor do I, but I think it's what women like that stir in some men. A desire to own, to bask in reflected glory. No, not even that, alas, but to bask in pride of possession. Hal Gardeyne was like that. Puffed up like a cock to own her."

Stephen found himself driven to defend the man. "What's the difference between that and being an adoring husband?"

Nicholas thought. "What is valued, I suppose. What did Gardeyne truly value?"

"His hunters."

Nicholas nodded. "In the end our true love will rule. His was sport. They were destined to drift apart. A man with a passionate avocation should be careful where he weds."

Stephen tensed. "You refer to me?"

"I would claim it to be a universal truth, but yes. If you are not passionately devoted to the political life and noble causes, you've been doing a remarkable imitation of it."

"I should give up my life upon marriage, as you have given up yours?" Stephen flinched at the sharpness of his own attack, but didn't retract it.

"I've given up nothing. Once I traveled, but I'd already wearied of it when circumstances brought me home. You can hardly think that London enthralled me."

Stephen was suddenly angry at being advised. "You and Eleanor are not markedly alike."

"Lock and key don't have to be identical. In fact, it would defeat the purpose. I'm a mental magpie. She's interested in some of the treasures I bring to the nest. She's a practical countrywoman, and I'm learning the joys of being in one place. She is restful, which I find a blessing. She enjoys being excited now and then. We can be as silent as a starlit night and blessed by it."

"You're saying I should *not* marry a

woman who is interested in politics and reform?"

"Steve! You're a cleverer man than I am, so don't sink to that level. You should marry a woman who will bring joy to your life in many ways, because if she's of value to you in only one way, what when that changes? What if Laura's beauty is ravaged by smallpox?"

"She's been inoculated." Stephen recognized that as irrelevant, however. "I don't know."

"Find out. And be sure that you can give joy to her, and without sacrifice. Sacrifice is a galling burden."

"How very unchristian."

"I didn't say it isn't good for us to be galled sometimes."

Stephen rose and walked to the window, trying to sort through what Nicholas had said. Did he simply want to possess Laura's beauty, as if she were a vase or a painting?

"Do you know her?" Nicholas asked.

He turned to stare. "She was my sister's closest friend. We were almost like brother and sister."

"Are you the man you were six years ago? If not, why assume she is that woman? My advice . . . Damnation, I took a vow to

217

stop giving advice."

"As well tell Coleridge to give up opium."

It was a sharp enough cut to draw blood, but Nicholas merely smiled. "I would if I thought it would do any good. He's too far gone, poor man."

"And Dare is not?" Stephen asked, to change the subject.

"No. He was never dependent on it for escape, you see." But Nicholas wasn't deflected. "I've wondered what was amiss with you. I think I know now, but old passions can prove poisonous when stirred. My advice is to try to forget the past and to discover Laura as if you were meeting her now. Perhaps her new appearance will help. I think I hear them coming."

They went into the hall, and Stephen was glad to have that encounter over, even if he felt he carried it with him like splinters buried in his skin.

He didn't know Laura?

Once prompted, he recognized truth.

Vibrant Laura Watcombe. Brilliant Mrs. Hal Gardeyne. Labellelle, toast of society. Even Lady Skylark, which he knew now hadn't been fitting even five years ago. . . .

He looked up the stairs and saw a sallow, sickly woman.

The dress was the same, he thought, though it had somehow become frumpy. Beneath the plain black bonnet, a close cap was tied beneath her chin by ribbons as narrow as string. It hid all of a faded blond wig except for a frame of tight curls that created the impression of a low forehead. A disfiguring mole ruined her lovely mouth. She was even wearing beige net gloves to hide her elegant hands.

The whole effect was sealed by a remarkably ugly shawl in yellows and browns that managed to clash even with the gray spencer.

"Where do you find these things?" he said to Nicholas.

"Oh, Nicholas collects like a magpie," Eleanor remarked as she and Laura arrived in the hall.

Stephen flicked a glance at his friend, but Nicholas merely said, "It is the virtue of the magpie to be undiscriminating."

"Virtue?" Laura asked, and at least her voice was the same.

Eleanor laughed. "Don't encourage him to expound on the virtues and dangers of discrimination. He says you never know when his indiscriminate collections will be of use. And as usual, he's right."

Stephen was still trying to absorb

Laura's appearance. "That mole . . . What we will do for the cause."

She stiffened. "Do you think I wouldn't give up all my looks for this cause? To save two young Henry Gardeynes?" Then she winced. "I'm sorry. I'm on edge."

"So am I. But it was only a joke, Laura."

They might have apologized back and forth, but Nicholas interrupted. "Don't forget to move and speak like a plain woman, Laura. Be uncertain in your speech, and don't expect people to pay attention to you. Efface yourself. It will be useful anyway if people hardly notice you. Such a light disguise is an illusion rather than a perfect concealment."

"I've never thought of these things before."

"Do. I've sent word to Kerslake, Steve. We're sticking as close to the truth as possible, so if you need to explain the connection, you're a friend of a friend. Con's friend, of course."

"Right."

Discover the real Laura. Nicholas was right. He held out his arm. "Come along. It's a game, an adventure. Don't I remember a time when you put blue streaks on your face and stuck feathers in your hair in order to be a Red Indian?"

That brought back a smile that was pure Laura. "With a bow and arrow. I shot your hat off."

"Damn near killed me. Thank heavens you're not armed now."

"Ah," she said as they left the house. "Did I forget to mention my pistol?"

He looked at her, about to object, but remembered Nicholas's advice. Learn about her now. "Can I assume Mrs. Hal Gardeyne knows how to use it?"

"Of course you can."

As he handed her into the curricle, Stephen reckoned he deserved a medal for self-control. Speaking the man's name had almost choked him.

# Chapter 20

Laura thought her cheerful manner deserved a medal.

She looked awful, but she'd hoped that in some way Stephen would be able to ignore it. Clearly not, but the pain of that had made it dawn on her — literally, like the crack of dawn opening in the dark sky — that she was attracted to him.

Perhaps just physically.

Perhaps not.

Whatever her feelings were, they demanded that he look at her with appreciation and admiration.

This made her newly unsure about this enterprise. She didn't understand her own emotions, and she didn't have time to ponder them, but she knew they made this journey doubly, triply hazardous. Yet she must go, not just to uncover the truth and possibly rescue a child, but to explore these mysteries. Her life teetered on a balance point, and the issues at hand extended beyond the future of the viscountcy of Caldfort.

They were using Nicholas's curricle, which made transport to Draycombe simple. As Laura and Stephen drove away, they waved back at the three Delaneys. Little Arabel had reappeared and was again in her father's arms.

"He's a devoted father," Laura remarked.

"Yes."

"Unusually so."

They swung into the road at speed, showing impressive skill. "You disapprove?" he asked.

Her thoughts had shown and she grimaced. "I'm sorry, but having recently forced myself not to cling to Harry, I'm sensitive to such things. It can't be wise to encourage a child to cling like that, particularly to a father."

"Do you really find a devoted father so unusual?"

She almost said a blunt yes, but then considered the question. "Hal certainly wasn't, but he might have become so when Harry was of an age to share his interests. I suppose Ned dotes, but he leaves most of the care of the little ones to Margaret, particularly the girls. It's the usual way."

He negotiated another bend and then they were on a straight stretch and he could give the horses their heads. "Nicholas is unusual in nearly everything he does, but there's a special reason. I don't think they'll mind me telling you. Arabel was kidnapped not long ago."

Shock hit like a fist. "No! How?"

"By a woman who hated Nicholas and wanted money. It's left Arabel shy and anxious when she used to be the most cheerful, trusting child. Ah, I should have realized."

"What?"

He glanced at her. "She's particularly wary of strange women in dark clothing. That must be why she shrank from you. As for her clinging to Nicholas, he was the one to rescue her. Unfair to Eleanor, of course, but a child's view of the world is simple."

As Harry's was. Coaches meant change, so having arrived at a place he liked, he refused to get in one again. Harry was safe, but Laura had to ask, "How was she taken?" What had she forgotten to guard against? What might lure him into danger? "Tempted away by a stranger offering a treat?"

"She was snatched from her bed."

"In her own *home?*"

Stephen halted his horses and turned to her. "Laura, what is it? She was rescued."

"Harry!" She clutched his arm. "I'm sorry. I can't do this, Stephen. Turn around. You must go to Draycombe to rescue this other child, but I have to get back to Merrymead. I never thought to warn anyone about that. About him being taken from his bed . . ."

He freed his sleeve from her hands and gripped them. "Laura, this was nothing like Harry's situation. Arabel was held for ransom. If Jack Gardeyne tries to harm Harry, he has to make it look like an accident. How could a child being stolen from his bed be that?"

"Sleepwalking?"

He shook his head. "At Merrymead, and no one will notice?"

"That's true. Mothers have an extra sense for children stirring in the night."

"And remember, Gardeyne isn't a lunatic. He has to know there'll be better opportunities."

"He tried with that bun. If I didn't imagine that."

"Perhaps he panicked when he heard you were going away for a month. I doubt he'll do that again."

Laura began to settle, aware of great comfort from Stephen's hands around hers, from his steady eyes.

He smiled slightly, which eased her heart even more. "And he'll not have a chance to harm Harry with Juliet on guard."

"That sounds as if you admire her more than me."

The smile deepened. "Don't be a goose."

She found herself laughing. *"Honk?"*

"In my experience, they hiss and then attack. Nasty creatures, geese."

"But they end up on our dinner tables. Perhaps they have reason for anger."

"Perhaps they do, at that. All right now?"

She nodded and slipped her hands free. "I'm sorry for panicking, but the poor Delaneys. I feel for them."

"As do I. Especially as I wasn't around to help or even support." He put the horses into motion again.

She could use that as an opening to ask about his grievance with the Rogues, to discuss the allure of adventure and the wisdom of avoiding it, but she was wound too tight for a serious topic.

"Tell me more tales of the Rogues, Stephen. I assumed it all ended with school days."

He amused her with stories, though she suspected most of them were carefully edited. A horse race at Melton seemed innocuous enough, but clearly some espionage in 1814 had not been. Even when there was no need for action, the Company of Rogues seemed to have regular gatherings, mostly in London or Melton, but apparently marriage and progeny were making such meetings more difficult.

"It's doubtless time for me to marry," Stephen said, eyes on the road, for they'd passed the one-mile marker to Draycombe and the way was now rough and narrow.

His words caught at her heart in a way that was a warning. She watched him as she said, "I hope this business of mine isn't interfering with your plans."

"Plans?"

"To marry."

Was that a smile? "How could it?" he asked.

They might as well be talking of the weather. "You could be courting someone," she pointed out, "instead of squiring a quiz of a relative to a watering place."

He seemed to find that amusing. "Don't concern yourself. This doesn't interfere with my plans."

"What if we end up in a scandal? That

might cause difficulties."

"Hold on." He slowed the horses for the descent down a long, steep hill into the small town strung along a bay. "If we end up in a scandal, we can always marry."

She could read nothing at all from tone or expression. "All the more reason to be quick and careful."

"As you say."

Aware of something that might be annoyance, Laura welcomed their first glimpse of the sea and of their target, Draycombe.

It looked to be more of a large village strung along a bay and hemmed in on both sides by headlands. It had probably been a simple fishing village before seaside visits became fashionable. Boats were still drawn up on the pebbly beach and whitewashed fishermen's cottages clustered where this steep road met the sea.

Newer buildings had spread in both directions. To the left, Laura saw a church spire, and to the right, the tiled roofs of modern houses mingled with the thatched ones of the past.

When they reached the cottages, the road split. Stephen halted and asked directions to the Compass Inn. He was pointed to the right and they turned that way, past a row of shops that must mostly serve the visitors, and a square, modern inn, the King's Arms.

Laura took it all in, searching for an obvious foreigner, a military man, or a stray child with Gardeyne features. "There seem to be many invalids, even this late in the year," she said, seeing two blanket-swathed elderly people being pushed along the seafront in long wheeled chairs.

"Draycombe's noted for its sheltered climate and healthy air." Stephen flicked her a look. "Yes, I read up about it. My fatal flaw."

"It's not a flaw. Look. Two military men — one navy, one army. We don't know which Captain Dyer is, do we?"

"We know nothing but his name. No turbans?"

"Do you really think Farouk will be so obvious?"

"From his name, I doubt he can pass as an Englishman, and foreign servants, especially from India, are not unheard of."

"In Draycombe?"

He grinned at her. "It does seem to be a sleepy backwater, doesn't it? Speaking of which, the Compass looks ancient. But decent."

The inn's long and wavering two-story

front held only small windows, but they were plentiful and clean, and one on the ground floor was bowed.

Stephen steered his team through open gates into a large coach yard. Stables and other such buildings formed three sides of the square, and there were few windows on the back of the inn. Laura deduced that the Compass had a single line of rooms on the upper story, all facing the front.

No sign of a military uniform or anyone who looked foreign in the coach yard. So tempting to immediately ask about their quarry, but they must seem merely guests. In such a small inn, however, they should soon encounter Dyer and Farouk.

# Chapter 21

As Stephen helped her down, he murmured, "Frail antidote," and Laura remembered to move like a woman of uncertain health with no high opinion of herself.

They entered the inn and were greeted by the innkeeper, Mr. Topham, who immediately produced a letter for Stephen. "From Mr. Kerslake-Somerford of Crag Wyvern, sir. A gentleman very much in the public eye these days."

He was clearly bursting to tell the extraordinary story, but Stephen quelled him. "Yes, we know of his situation."

The innkeeper deflated and led them up to three adjoining rooms. They were pleasant and already warmed by fires, though this being an old building, the rooms were small, with only one modest window in each. Those windows looked out at the bay, however. Laura chose the bedchamber on the left of the central parlor, thinking that she might enjoy a visit here if so much wasn't at stake.

Laura had tried to count doors, but as their rooms were close to the stairs she couldn't be certain of the number of rooms up here. Eight, she thought, so if Farouk, Dyer, and a child were here, they must be close.

The innkeeper was about to leave so she asked, in the manner of a perpetual worrier, "What other guests are there here, sir? My nerves cannot take disturbances."

"Only one, ma'am," the innkeeper assured her. "A military gentleman and his servant. Both very quiet."

As soon as the door closed, Laura turned to Stephen. "They're here!"

"It would seem so, but we can hardly pelt anyone with questions immediately. Not without raising suspicions."

She sighed. "You're right, and there was no mention of a child. But it should be simple enough to stage an encounter, and then nosy Mrs. Penfold can quiz the servants to her heart's content. What's in the letter? When can we meet the smuggler?"

Stephen had already broken the seal and was reading. "He'll call tomorrow, for lunch."

"Tomorrow!"

"A smuggler-earl must be a busy man."

"But now we're here, I want to *do* something." Then she laughed. "I'm flapping, aren't I?"

"Like a skylark."

It was said with dry humor so she really couldn't take offense, but it made her resolve to be calmer.

"As for doing something," he said, "I suggest a stroll to learn more about this place and stretch our legs."

Laura had been thinking more of knocking on doors in order to meet their fellow guests, but she knew he was right. "Very well, but we should delay long enough to unpack. Dashing straight out might look strange."

He smiled at her. "I should have known you'd be an effective criminal colleague."

Laura returned to her room better pleased with that response. Skylark, indeed. Was that how he saw her, even now? It stung particularly sharply when she was beginning to feel differently about him.

Was this fluttering inside her the same excitement she'd felt when she'd first met Hal? Or was it solely because of this risky adventure? Or was it because she'd been stuck at Caldfort like a nun in a convent and was giddy at being with any handsome man again?

Had she felt anything for Nicholas Delaney? She didn't think so, but she'd always had a disciplined nature. She didn't think she'd allow herself to feel anything for another woman's husband.

"Oh, perish it," she muttered, and tugged on the bellpull.

A sharp-faced but smiling young woman arrived with washing water. She curtsied, gave her name as Jean, then quickly set to deal with Laura's valise. Laura gave occasional instructions and decided she could safely ask some general questions.

"Such a pretty place," she fluttered. "I hear the air is healthy here."

"Very bracing, ma'am. We've had invalids come here and leave again dancing."

"Remarkable. I don't suppose there are many here so late in the year, however."

The maid hung Laura's dull gowns on hooks in the armoire. "Oh, not so bad, ma'am. We get mild winters here, you see, so some stay all year round."

"Really? Do you have any notable visitors?"

But the maid pulled a face. "Not to speak of, ma'am. I reckon they all go to

Lyme Regis, see, it having a royal connection."

Laura thanked the maid and gave her a tip, though she hadn't revealed anything useful.

Laura hadn't taken off her outdoor clothing, so she had only to pull on gloves over her tiresome net ones before being ready to go out. A habitual last glance in the mirror almost made her yelp. She'd forgotten what an antidote she looked. No fear of anything amorous happening as long as she looked like this.

When she joined Stephen, he instantly asked, "What's the matter?"

She must remember that he was ferociously observant.

All the same, his question sparked a laugh. "What's the matter? Until a few days ago, my main complaint was boredom. I was afraid for Harry, but I thought it was probably in my imagination. I was mainly in the doldrums because Caldfort House did not present an exciting future.

"Now I seem to be teetering on the edge of danger and disaster. Even the Delaneys turn out to be not just allies but a lesson in the vulnerability of children. And here I am, pretending to be someone else — an

235

ugly someone else — and if I'm recognized, my reputation will be in shreds, my access to Harry might be threatened —"

"Laura." He reached for her.

"And soon I'm going to be lunching with a smuggler!"

The absurdity struck her as it did him, and she collapsed into a chair, laughing. He was grinning at her, looking so much like the Stephen of the past. She held out her hands to him and he pulled her up.

"I'm sorry," she said.

"For laughing? Certainly not in character for Cousin Priscilla . . ."

Did he remember at exactly the same moment as she did?

It had to be spoken of. "I'm sorry for laughing all those years ago — when you asked me to marry you."

His laughter died, but perhaps it lingered a little in his eyes. "It was all those years ago, Laura, and we were both very young."

"I was old enough to marry."

"And I wasn't."

But Juliet had waited for her Robert.

"I suppose you weren't, but truly, I never meant to hurt you. I never . . ." — she sought the right words — "I never thought your offer ridiculous. I want you to know that."

They were still holding hands, and looking into each other's eyes.

"I won't say it was pleasant," he said. "I was young, every emotion raw. But I knew you hadn't meant to be cruel. I knew, even when 'screwing my courage to the sticking point' that it was an idiotic thing to do. . . ."

"Not idiotic."

He let go of her hands and stepped back. "Yes, it was. I thought you didn't know your mind, but Gardeyne was exactly what you wanted."

Laura shocked herself by almost denying it. She fussed with her gloves. "If we're going, we should go."

"Yes."

He extended his arm. She was tempted to continue the conversation, but she knew it would be unwise. They left the room and descended the stairs with no sight of any other guest and walked out of the inn into the damp, sea-tanged air. The sky was overcast now, however, and the wind cut.

"Bracing, the maid called it," Laura said with a shiver.

"Blows the cobwebs away."

"I am not inhabited by spiders. Do let's walk, and briskly."

"You forget. You're frail Mrs. Penfold."

"Oh, a plague on it."

He chuckled. "Tut-tut."

"Don't make me laugh. I'm sure it's not in character."

They walked back as far as the steep road into the village and then retraced their way. No one in a turban, and both military men had disappeared. Everyone was probably heading home for their evening meal.

They dawdled past the windows of the shops, for Laura hadn't seen any even as minor as these for months. There was a promising bookshop and an apothecary advertising ALL MODERN CONVENIENCES FOR THE FRAIL AND INVALIDS⋆.

"I'm sure I should be interested in that establishment," she said, "but this is much more to my taste." She stopped to study the dressed dolls in the window of a mantua maker. "Are skirts really being worn shorter in London?"

"To the gentlemen's delight, yes."

She gave him a look. "There have always been ways to display an ankle, and it's more effective when they're normally veiled."

To demonstrate, she eased up her skirt slightly as she raised a foot onto a step.

He looked down and smiled. "I see —

but not perhaps the behavior of my sickly Cousin Priscilla?"

She pulled a face at him but dropped her skirt. "Do you have a cousin called Priscilla Penfold?"

"No, but then your name would have been different before marriage. You must have married into the Penfolds of Warwickshire. A sober, studious bunch."

Where she would have once thought he fit perfectly, but now she was too aware of the ready laughter in his eyes, not to mention his remarkably fine looks and what she was coming to see was a strong, athletic body. A few days ago she would have said she knew Stephen very well. Now she was not so sure.

"I'm not sure I can play that part," she said. "Sober and studious."

"Look absentminded and mutter something about empiricism and Hume."

He clearly thought she wouldn't understand, so as they walked on toward the inn, she said, "Oh, that I can do. I've read Hume's essays."

His look of surprise was not unexpected, but it stung. She didn't confess that boredom had led her to read nearly everything in the limited Caldfort library except the sporting almanacs. "I have interests beyond the length of skirts, you know."

"Do you support Hume, then?"

Was he testing her? "He has many interesting ideas, but I cannot agree with his attacks on God and religion."

"Religion can sometimes be a vehicle for evil. Look at Reverend Jack."

"His evil, if true, has nothing to do with him being a vicar. True religion is virtuous by definition."

"Even if it demands that a widow throw herself on her husband's funeral pyre?"

She frowned at him. "No, but is that truly a religious belief or a social one?"

"You're trying to define religion to fit your premise. . . ."

When they neared the inn, Laura realized that she was enjoying a spirited philosophical debate. Her first instinct was to flutter and protest that these subjects were of no interest to her, but it was obvious Stephen didn't dislike her for it.

But really, anyone would think her a bluestocking!

Because of that, she did explain about boredom and the Caldfort library. "I didn't think the works had made such an impression on my mind. Perhaps one day I'll join your sister Fanny's philosophical circle."

She meant it to be flippant, but he said, "Why not?" But then added, "Cousin Priscilla."

With a suppressed exclamation, she remembered to be dull and awkward, which was probably helped by a feeling of depression. Was that the sort of woman he admired — a bluestocking?

Lady Skylark's only accomplishments had been high spirits, beauty, and charm.

Perhaps — and the thought was truly depressing — becoming physically plain changed everything, including Stephen's impression of her. Was it worse to be assumed feckless when beautiful, or to only be taken seriously when plain?

She paused to frown at him. "I don't see why an interest in philosophy should require being unfashionable."

"Nor do I," he drawled, and she had to fight a laugh. Of course he didn't. He was the Political Dandy. Even his plain traveling clothes were the height of fashion and beautifully made.

"Thank heavens for that, for I do enjoy pretty clothes."

"You'll be back in them soon."

"Will you still talk philosophy with me then?"

His brows quirked. "Now, what do you

mean by that? I will talk anything with you, Laura, whatever you're wearing." As he opened the door for her, however, his smile was merely polite. The connection that had spun during their discussion had disappeared.

Laura moved to enter the inn, but a man was about to come out. A man in a long black robe, a three-quarter-length coat of sorts, and a bright blue turban. He stepped back to make way for her.

Laura felt her effort not to stare should be palpable — but then she realized that she *should* stare, at least a little.

She slid a glance to the side as she passed and took in the strange clothes, mahogany skin, strong, austere features, and impassive brown eyes.

And yet she felt that he had studied her just as keenly as she had studied him.

# Chapter 22

She had to almost bite her lips until they were in their parlor with the door shut. Then she could exclaim, "Farouk. Now we have our excuse to gossip!"

"So we do," Stephen said, pulling the bell, but Laura sat, suddenly unsteady.

"He's real. I wasn't sure until now."

"Nor was I. Or at least, that Azir Al Farouk was the Arab he sounded like, not a strange device."

"And staying here. There aren't many rooms —"

She broke off as the door opened and Jean came in to curtsy.

"We'll order our dinner now," Stephen said with unusual coolness.

The maid curtsied again and listed the various dishes available. Stephen gestured for Laura to select and she did so, wondering if he was going to ignore this opportunity for questions.

Of course not. "We encountered a foreign gentleman on our way in," he said. "Is he a guest here?"

His tone had shifted from cool to icy, and the maid's eyes turned wary. "He is, sir, yes. But he's no trouble. Farouk's his name. From Egypt. Servant companion to a sickly gentleman, Captain Dyer."

"Does Captain Dyer have a number of such servants?" Stephen asked with an astonished hauteur that made Laura want to giggle. She'd never heard him put on such an intolerably superior manner.

"Oh, no, sir! Just the one. Farouk does everything for his gentleman. Won't even let us in to change the sheets or build the fire."

Excitement began to fizz. Because they had a child confined in their rooms?

"Are they staying long?" Stephen asked. "I am not pleased to be sharing a roof with a *heathen*."

The maid's fingers were tugging at her apron now. "I'm sure I don't know, sir. They've been here only a week and show no sign of leaving. The climate here is very healthy, you know."

Perhaps Stephen sniffed. Searching for a heathen odor? Laura pursed her lips, praying not to laugh. Surely Priscilla

Penfold would purse her lips at this horror.

"Do these people have rooms near us?" Stephen asked at last.

The poor maid turned pale. "Well, sir, the captain's parlor lies next to your bedchamber, sir, but there's no adjoining door! There's no other way, sir, for Captain Dyer's taken the center rooms, you see, and we only have the eight up here and two down below, but an elderly couple has those on account of him needing a chair to go out." She ran out of breath and asked desperately, "Shall I get Mr. Topham, sir?"

Stephen appeared to consider it. "That will not be necessary at this time. At least assure me that there are no children around. My cousin cannot abide a childish racket."

"Oh, no, sir! No children other than the boot boy."

Laura longed to soothe the maid, but suspicion and affront gave a better basis for curiosity. She was relieved when Stephen, radiating disapproval, sent the maid off to get their dinner.

As soon as the door closed, she laughed. "You were insufferable."

His eyes twinkled. "Yes, wasn't I? But we know our men are here and nicely close."

"But where's the child?"

"There may not be one, Laura. That was only supposition."

She realized she'd built young Henry Gardeyne in her mind to point of reality. "Then who is HG? I know, I know, this could all be a hoax, but it may not be."

"Perhaps HG is hidden somewhere else. This is all speculation. We need more facts, and we'll find them in time."

She almost spit back, "Time!" but suppressed it. Stephen seemed to bring out the child in her.

He turned to look toward his room. "So, we share a wall."

That was more like it. Laura rose. "You think we might be able to hear something. Do let's try!"

But he raised a hand. "Patience. Dinner will be here soon, and you can hardly be found in my bedchamber."

"We could switch. I don't think it's fair that you have that one."

"What? Would I let my frail cousin sleep next door to a heathen savage? I'll go and listen while you wait for the meal." When she would have protested, he added, "There's doubtless no point yet, Laura. Farouk has just left, so who would Dyer be talking to?"

Accepting that, Laura only pulled a face at his back, then went into her own bedchamber to remove her outer clothes. She really must stop acting like a girl — and yet it was as amusing as sharing a bedroom with Juliet at home and chattering as they once had.

She turned, smiling, for her habitual check in the mirror, and remembered. She snarled at Priscilla Penfold and returned to the parlor. Stephen was already there.

"Silent, as expected." He eyed the door to the corridor. "I wonder if their doors are locked."

She grabbed his arm. "Now who's being rash?"

"I will merely be checking out these suspicious characters for fear that they might attack my poor cousin in the night." His smile was boyish as he slipped free and left the room.

He was back in moments. "Locked, which is certainly suspicious if Farouk is merely a servant."

Laura frowned in the direction of the next room. "I'm not normally impulsive, but I wish we could break in."

"Not impulsive? Don't I remember a prizefight you attended, dressed as a lad?"

"I was twelve. And you took me!"

"Even so. And the time when you and Charlotte went swimming in the river without thought to the view from Ancross."

"A gentleman wouldn't have looked. I could remember some of your childish scrapes, you know."

*I could remember watching you swimming in the river, too.*

"I indulged in no scrapes to match yours," he said, strolling to the window to look out. "What about the time you bribed the gypsy at the Barham fair to let you take her place so you could give most peculiar predictions to your friends and neighbors?"

Laura covered her mouth. "I thought no one but Charlotte knew about that. Did she tell you?"

He looked back. "No, but when I heard some of the fortunes I kept watch, so I saw you slipping out of the back of the tent. So don't tell me, Laura Watcombe, that you are not impulsive."

"That, sir, was a carefully thought-out plan."

But he'd called her by her maiden name, as if he, too, were back in the past.

He didn't seem to notice. He was looking out of the window again, and said, "Farouk!"

She ran over to look. "Now can we

listen? If dinner arrives, you can emerge to deal with it."

To look out at Farouk, she had pressed close to Stephen's body. A tingling awareness washed through her, almost causing her to gasp. She slid away, trying to make it look natural.

"You always get your way," he said, but his voice sounded strange. She glanced at him and saw a tight expression. Disapproval of her impulsive manner, probably. Or disgust at her appearance. Or both. She couldn't tell. It was most peculiar to inhabit a different skin, to make different ripples in the world around.

They turned together and hurried into the adjoining room, past his nightshirt hanging on a rack before the fire to warm. Through a faint aroma of spicy soap, and him . . .

The shared wall was mostly taken up by the head of the bed and a chest of drawers. He moved into the available space and beckoned her to join him. She could hardly refuse. Or perhaps she didn't want to, even though she had to squeeze against him there. That frisson dazed her again, and now she was aware of his scent.

She knew about the arousing smell of men, but Stephen's was both new and familiar. She wanted to press closer to his chest and inhale, but had willpower enough to instead press her ear to the rough plaster wall.

# Chapter 23

Stephen pressed his right ear to the wall, but his mind could not escape Laura. She was facing him, and they were squeezed into the small space available, her back to the bed. She was almost where he wanted her.

In his arms.

In his bed.

Had she just looked at him with awareness that he was a man, not just her old friend? He was used to assessing situations and making quick decisions, but now, in the midst of the most important situation of his life, his brain seemed like a soggy pudding.

"Can you hear anything?"

Laura's soft question pulled him out of the pit and he concentrated. "Only a faint murmur."

"Me, too."

So hard not to press his body against hers, hard to look anywhere except at her breasts, swelling softly beneath her dull, high-necked gown. Impossible to avoid that perfume.

The one created for Labellelle.

Careless, that. It wasn't at all the scent for Priscilla Penfold, but he wouldn't ask her to change it. He tried to remember what scent she'd used as a girl. Something light and flowery, he thought, probably made in the Merrymead stillroom from garden flowers. This was a complex masterpiece.

As she was.

Nicholas had been right.

To all the other Lauras he was aware of, he must now add philosopher and quick-witted partner. He shouldn't be surprised — Laura had never been stupid or silly.

Something about her appearance was twisting his mind, as well. Would he have even mentioned philosophy to her without her sallow skin and faded hair? On the other hand, the way he was reacting now had nothing to do with Priscilla Penfold.

He swallowed and concentrated again on the voices beyond the wall. Frustratingly, they were almost distinct, so he felt that if he concentrated hard enough he would be able to distinguish words. Either that was untrue or concentration was beyond him.

"Well?" he asked.

She shook her head.

That gave him an excuse to move away. He didn't want to, but for sanity's sake, he must.

When they were safely back in the parlor — people could make love in a parlor — she said, "It sounded like a normal conversation, though, didn't it? No anger or fear? And adult voices."

He tried to recollect and couldn't. Devil take it, being squeezed close like that had clearly had no effect on her. Would he have to watch as she again married another man?

"Stephen?"

He pulled his wits together. "Probably."

She spun away and took a tempestuous turn around the parlor. "How frustrating this is. Is there *nothing* we can do?"

His hungry mind put a different interpretation on her words, and her sizzling energy burned him.

"Stephen? What is *wrong* with you?" She'd stopped and was frowning at him, hands on hips.

"I was thinking. Wait a minute."

He fled into his room to collect himself, taking a deep breath to try to sort out his wits. Now he needed an excuse for his abrupt departure. Some result of his brilliant thoughts. Some action.

He opened his valise, took out the long leather case, and returned briskly to the parlor to show it to her. "A telescope. Nicholas lent it to me. Tomorrow, if nothing else avails, we can spy on the windows from the beach."

"What a clever idea!" She glanced out of the window. "We could do it now."

"Impatient again."

"Do stop throwing my heedless youth in my face."

"I liked it."

He had, too. It occurred to him that his love was rooted in the Laura he'd known until her marriage. That he hadn't disapproved of her then, even if he'd teased.

She frowned slightly. "Do you like me less now?"

"Devil take it, Laura, don't take me up on every word. I like you now. I liked you then."

*I didn't like you when you were married to Gardeyne.* But he managed not to say that.

"Good. And," she added, "there's no reason not to go out now to look for boats through a telescope. Dinner can be held."

"It's almost dark."

She grinned at him. "We're impractical landlubbers. The local people will only laugh at us."

He found himself smiling back. It was exactly what the Laura of his youth would have said. "Then let's go and amuse them."

They headed out again, pausing to tell a servant that they would dine in fifteen minutes. Stephen could feel Laura's excitement bubbling beside him. Unfortunately, his baser nature translated it into another context.

As they headed into the wind, down onto the pebbly beach, he knew she would be a magnificent lover. That bit like shark's teeth, because she must have been a magnificent lover to Hal Gardeyne.

As they crunched close to the rippling waves, she held her bonnet in place and raised her face to the wind, reveling in the sensual elements.

"I don't think Cousin Priscilla would do that," he warned.

"It's the latest medical advice. To inhale the vigor of the wind off the sea." She turned an invigorated smile on him. "It's wonderful here, isn't it? I've only been to the sea at Brighton, and it's so busy there. Here it's more elemental."

The breeze pressed her clothing against her body. He didn't need that to know that it was lovely. Her breasts looked soft, as if she wasn't wearing a corset. The sight didn't help his sanity. Her mind was on nature, however, not on him, so he tuned his senses to hers. "The sound of the sea on the shore is a complex music, isn't it?"

She was back to inhaling, eyes closed. "Exciting and soothing at the same time. It's as if nothing terrible could happen by the sound of the sea."

*People die in the sound of the sea,* he thought, but he didn't want to spoil her pleasure.

"Yet the sea can be brutal," she continued. "It can smash and kill, as with the *Mary Woodside.* I wonder how many died then."

It was as if she'd picked up his feelings. Or, he thought with hope, as if their minds were more in tune than he'd thought.

She turned to him. "You're very quiet, my friend."

*Friend.*

"Appreciating everything around."

She looked around, missing his meaning. "Some of the inn windows are lit. We might see something. Where's the spyglass?"

He took the telescope out of its case, wondering if the damn woman really felt nothing but the magic of the sea and the intensity of her purpose. "To have an excuse to look at the inn, we'd better pretend to admire the ships out there first. Here, you can be the idiot."

Her laughter danced on the wind. "Very well. Give it to me."

She dutifully studied the distant bobbing lights. "Do you think we could see France in daylight?"

"I doubt it. My turn." He took the spyglass and turned it on the inn.

"That's not fair. I thought we were supposed to pretend."

"We've pretended."

"Cheat. So what do you see?" She pressed close, as if she could share the view piece.

Devil take it. He could hardly keep the telescope steady as he scanned across windows. "That's one of their rooms, but the curtains are down." He could feel her warm breath on his jaw. "Ah!"

"What?"

"Their parlor curtains are open."

"So what do you see? Talk, Stephen, talk! Or let me have the glass."

He couldn't help but grin. "I see Farouk

257

in his blue turban, standing, bowing slightly over the other man, who is sitting down."

"Dyer is described as sickly. What does he look like?"

"His back's to the window. Lightish brown hair."

"Let me see."

She gripped his wrist and tugged. Her touch, even through gloves, sent such a jolt of raw desire through him that he froze. It was that or grab her into his arms, tumble her down onto the beach, even.

Damnation, he'd never expected this to be so challenging. He'd never expected the fire to burn so fiercely. He was a man of the mind, wasn't he?

Not the slightest damn bit.

She seized the glass from his hand, stepped apart, and put it to her eye. He watched her. He couldn't not do so, but at the moment she was unlikely to catch him at it.

A hint of light from the inn and other buildings sketched in her perfect profile, which curls and cream could not distort. Straight nose, but just a little short. Lips full and slightly parted with concentration. Neat, determined chin.

"Farouk's moving around," she said.

"There could be a child there, out of sight. . . . Oh, no, he's lowering the curtain."

She turned to give him the spyglass. "I had quite a good view of Farouk, but we've seen him, so we achieved nothing."

"To solve everything within hours is too much to expect."

"But we can hope." He heard a smile in it as she turned back to face the wind and sea.

Over time, the most wrought emotions have to mellow. As Stephen slid the glass back into its case, he felt surprisingly content to be here in the clean wind, soothed by sea music, with Laura at his side.

"If Dyer is a cripple, he can't be a henchman," she said. "So we have only Farouk to deal with."

"We?"

She turned to him. "I will have my part in this."

"It could turn dangerous."

"I gave you no permission to protect me."

"I need none. A gentleman does not let a lady fall into danger."

"So a gentleman automatically takes command?"

"Yes."

He could sense rather than see her frown. "You forget our past."

"I remember it all too well. You were always recklessly impulsive."

"And you have become intolerably stuffy!"

"Adult."

"Timid with age!"

Something snapped. He pulled her close and kissed her, quickly, but hard. When he let her go, he said, "I am not so aged as that."

Her eyes were huge, but in the darkness, he couldn't read her reaction at all. He had probably just destroyed any chance he had.

"So I see," she said, and turned to walk back to the inn.

# Chapter 24

Darkness, Laura thought, was a friend to the embarrassed and the confused. In daylight, who knows what Stephen might have seen? She certainly didn't. She didn't know her own feelings.

She didn't know whether to laugh or weep. What did it mean when a man kissed a woman in anger? What would have happened if she'd kissed him back?

To the music of the sea rolling rhythmically against the beach and the crunch of feet — his and hers — through pebbles, she made herself accept that to kiss him back would have been disaster. She didn't even know this man. She hardly knew herself. She'd thought the young, wild Laura past and done with, but now she danced inside her like a possessing imp.

By the time they arrived at the sanctuary of the inn, she could face the light. She had no idea what to say, but as she hoped,

Stephen didn't refer to what had happened. All the same, when Topham popped out of a room, it was a huge relief.

"Sir Stephen, Mrs. Penfold, I want to assure you that Mr. Farouk has created no problems in the week he has been here."

"It was something of a shock to my poor cousin," Stephen said haughtily. "Her nerves are not of the best."

Laura tried to look frail and fearful when at this moment, fresh from sea air and that kiss, she felt anything but.

Topham wrung his hands at her. "I assure you, ma'am, that you have nothing to worry about."

"So alarming. After all," she added, dropping her voice to a whisper, "Mr. Farouk cannot be a Christian."

"Alas, I fear you are correct, ma'am, but I assure you he behaves like one."

As they seemed to have a perfect opportunity for more questions, Laura asked, "And his employer? What sort of man is he?"

"An English officer!" Topham said triumphantly. "Sadly frail, but an Englishman born and bred. Been in the India service, I gather."

"Frail, you say? Elderly, then?"

"Oh, no, ma'am. Quite young. Very sad.

A war injury, I suppose. His man had to carry him up to his rooms, our ground-floor ones being already taken."

"Oh, the poor man. I do hope Mr. Farouk takes him out to enjoy the sea air. After just two short strolls, I am feeling much restored."

"I rejoice, ma'am," said Topham, beaming. "I'm sure Captain Dyer would be well advised to do the same, but thus far he has remained in his room."

Laura hid dismay. That would make things much more difficult.

"And doctors?" she asked, deciding that it would be useful to establish Mrs. Penfold as intolerably nosy. "Does he see excellent doctors?"

"Again, ma'am, not so far."

Laura couldn't resist a glance at Stephen. Surely a genuinely sick man would consult a doctor.

"But if you need medical advice," the innkeeper went on, "permit me to suggest Dr. Nesbitt. A most excellent physician and a particular favorite of the ladies."

"Thank you. So kind," Laura fluttered, then added, "Do you think poor Captain Dyer might want company? My cousin and I would be happy to take tea with him."

Topham bowed. "You are the soul of

kindness, Mrs. Penfold. I will suggest it to Mr. Farouk, though I must warn you that Captain Dyer has not entertained whilst he's been here. Your dinner is ready, sir, ma'am, as soon as you wish it."

"Serve it, then," Stephen said, and offered Laura his arm.

She placed her gloved hand on his sleeve and they went up the stairs. For the first time, she was nervous to be going into a private room with Stephen, but he acted as if that kiss had never happened.

Very well. If he could act that way, so could she.

"It may be harder to encounter Dyer than we thought," she said as she stripped off her leather gloves.

"But his staying in his rooms fits with him being a prisoner."

"So he could be HG! Or if there is a child, someone must stay with him."

"I doubt they could have a child here with no one aware of it."

"I suppose you're right."

He said nothing else so she escaped to her bedchamber, where she tore off her dull bonnet with a degree of rage. She didn't understand him, she hardly understood herself, and this matter of HG was likely to be a great deal more difficult than they'd thought. What were they going to do if Dyer remained closeted in his room? How were they to compare him to the portrait?

She puffed out a breath and commanded herself to be sensible. Or at least patient. They'd only been here a matter of hours. She checked her appearance —

Perish it! Perhaps she'd stop looking in mirrors for the duration.

Laura returned to the parlor, where Stephen was leaning on the mantelpiece, staring into the fire. He looked up with a slight, impersonal smile. Some lingering hopes she'd not really been aware of popped like soap bubbles.

"I've been considering what we know," he said. "Dyer's apparent frailty might be because he was drugged or bound."

"But unless he's kept drugged at all times, wouldn't he cry for help?"

"Then perhaps he's kept drugged at all times."

She considered it. "That might make rescue difficult. Someone will have to carry him."

"As Farouk apparently carried him up to his room, I should be able to do the same. He and I are of a similar build, I think."

She considered his physique, which was

no penance. "Yes, so do I." Both men were lithe but strong. Farouk was probably wider in the shoulders, but not by much.

She began to pace the room. "Do you think there's any chance they'll accept the invitation to meet? It would solve everything. Probably not," she answered herself.

"Especially," he said dryly, "if Dyer is HG tied to his chair."

He was looking at her strangely.

"Was that a bad idea?" she asked. "To suggest tea? They have no reason to suspect us."

He moved away from the fireplace. "It was an excellent idea. Just what a kind-hearted lady would do, not to mention a nosy one. But be careful. Keep in mind that Dyer could be both confined to a chair and part of the plot, which is a simple attempt to fleece money from Lord Caldfort." After a moment, he added, "I don't want you taking risks, Laura, or letting your hopes rise too high."

She bit back an instinctive protest. "I know."

Their dinner arrived then, which was a relief. When the servants left and they sat to the meal, Laura became aware of a new discomfort.

A meal for two, she thought, serving oxtail soup. How very matrimonial — except that she couldn't remember ever sitting to such a meal with Hal. Whenever they were at Caldfort, his parents, and often others, ate with them. Elsewhere, they'd rarely eaten at home. Only when they were playing host to others, in fact. It made this simple meal at a small table awkward, especially with that fierce yet impersonal kiss still ignored between them.

"So," she said, when she'd consumed half her soup, "what do we do tomorrow?"

He smiled. "Tomorrow is Sunday, so as a Member of Parliament and a respectable widow, we go to church. It's always possible that Captain Dyer will be God-fearing, too, but if not, there should be opportunity to gossip."

She found herself smiling back. "Of course! Draycombe is bound to be in a ferment about a heathen in their midst. And the smuggler is coming to lunch. He will have much to tell us."

Her smile faded. He was looking at her in a way that did not seem connected to church or smuggler.

"You surprised me with your knowledge of philosophy," he said.

"I being a mere woman?"

He laughed dryly. "Remember my sister Fanny."

"Then why assume I'm a feather wit?" But she knew. "Because I never showed great interest in such matters when we were young, I suppose. That's probably more truly me than what happened today. I told you, there's not much to read at Caldfort."

He put aside his soup plate and uncovered a meat pie. "I assume you could have ordered novels if you'd wished to."

"And I did. But one cannot read novels all the time."

"Charlotte manages to."

He served her pie. She served him vegetables. "Charlotte and I are much alike."

"You were. But you and I rubbed along pretty well, too, I think."

Laura picked up her knife and fork, considering his sister. "Perhaps Charlotte and I are quite different now. Perhaps that's why we're no longer close."

"We drift apart from people over time. It's a natural force."

"And drift toward others."

"I would say you hurtled toward Gardeyne."

"He was a very attractive man."

"Wealthy and heir to a title."

She speared a carrot. "There was more to him than that."

So much for matrimonial, or even friendly, harmony. They abandoned conversation by agreement, and finished the meal quickly. That was easy for Laura, as she'd lost her appetite. To her surprise, Stephen ate little, too.

Surely they could do better than this. She pushed away most of a pear tart. "Why are we fighting?"

"I was not aware that we were."

"I know you never liked Hal."

"I would prefer not to talk of him. It seems disrespectful to the dead."

"Only if you say disrespectful things."

His brows quirked in a way that suggested that there was nothing else to say.

"You can't deny that he was a brilliant rider."

"So are most jockeys."

She pushed away from the table and stood. "You're right. We shouldn't talk about Hal. We should talk about our plans."

"We're here and have gathered some information. Any further discussion would be repetitive."

*Let's talk about that kiss, then.*

She almost said it, but knew it would be

disastrous. If it had meant so little to him, what was there to say? If it had meant more, she wasn't ready to explore those depths.

She tugged angrily at the bellpull and soon Jean arrived to clear away their dinner. Perhaps the picked-at meal would confirm her sickly status. She wanted to question the maid further about Dyer, but couldn't think of a reasonable question. Patience was probably best, but what were they going to do now? It was only eight o'clock, a ridiculously early hour to go to bed, and she didn't want to. She wanted to explore Stephen, infuriating as he was.

When the maid left, she suggested, "Cards?"

"By all means. What?"

"Bezique. Piquet?" She tossed out the gambling games deliberately, and added, "I was married to Hal Gardeyne, remember?"

His lips tightened. "Piquet, then. Do you have a pack? If not, I'm sure Topham can provide."

"I do, as it happens. Sometimes I play simple games with Harry." She went to get them, then sat at the table and opened the wooden box. "How good are you?"

He sat opposite. "Good enough. I was raised among Rogues."

"Excellent." She sorted out the lower cards, aware of a simmering annoyance that lent edge to the game, and of enjoying it. "Do we play for paper points?"

"Not at all. I want you in my debt."

A shiver went through her that was surely not what he intended, though if she were willing to permit herself fantasy, she could imagine a vivid scenario.

She passed the reduced pack to him. "You want to use my poor widow's mite to fund some reform, I assume."

He shuffled with those promising, long-fingered hands. "Certainly to bring about a significant change." He put the cards in front of her. "Cut."

She did so, exposing a ten. He cut to show a six.

"Your deal," he said, and they settled to the game.

# Chapter 25

Guttering candles forced the end of play. When they'd completed the last *partie,* Laura leaned back, aware that anger had transmuted into a peculiar and unexpected pleasure. For the past hours everything had disappeared except the game. Stephen had simply been Stephen, the sharp-witted player she wanted to beat.

Now he was more than that, as if the hours of intense play had burned away dross, leaving clarity.

"Who won?" she asked, without great interest. They'd been evenly matched and the points had gone backward and forward.

He was calculating on a piece of paper. "You," he said, looking up. "By one hundred and fifteen. Guineas?"

"Lord, no. I'd never play for guinea points. Shillings."

"Five pounds fifteen, then. I assume

you'll take my word for it?"

It was an idle pleasantry of a conversation and the strange idea came to her that it was like the words spoken after coupling, contented and dreamy.

"Of course, and I'll give you time to pay."

He passed the paper to her, but she didn't bother to check it. "That was an excellent game."

"You're very good."

"As are you."

With her mind stuck in bed, it was . . . stimulating.

He rolled the paper and threw it accurately into the fire. "Too late for more, I assume."

She bit her inner cheek to control a smile. "Could you rise to the occasion?"

"It's past ten, but I'm not exhausted. I was merely thinking that we should be up with the larks to spy on our neighbors."

*Up* amused, but *lark* sobered. She looked down for a moment, then met his eyes again. "I forgive you for Lady Skylark."

He stilled. "I never thought you'd mind."

"You didn't mean it to be a constant reproach?"

"Ah . . . Perhaps I did. What I meant was that I didn't think you'd mind being Lady Skylark."

She wished he hadn't misjudged her so, but she only said, "It was too light. It doesn't matter anymore. Thank you for coming, Stephen. For helping. For being you."

"And who is that?"

He pinched out one wallowing candle, which turned his features shadowy. In childish competition, she licked her fingers and did the same to the other. Now only firelight lit the room.

"Stephen the thoughtful, the observant," she said, but then saw a flicker of distaste. "Stephen the fighter for those who cannot fight."

It was the right thing to say. He took her hand. "I will fight for you, Laura. You have my promise on that."

"Thank you." Her heart pounded deeply, a beat that seemed to pulse through her body. *Will you also kiss me again?*

But he held her left hand, and Hal's wedding ring glinted in the candlelight. It no longer bound her, but it gave her strength not to speak her thought.

She didn't want to go, didn't want to break this moment, but she made herself free her hand, rise, and say good night. In the privacy of her bedchamber, she closed the door then leant against it, breathing deeply and trying to sober her heated mind.

When she realized that she was rubbing her hands over her body, over her breasts, she stopped, but she couldn't stop desiring Stephen in a direct and feverish way.

If he were Hal, she could go to him, touch him, kiss him, and get exactly what she wanted. If he were Hal, she wouldn't feel quite this way.

She puzzled over that as she took off her cap. When she looked in the mirror, however, she saw the sallow skin, the ugly mousy curls, and the mole. She tore off the wig so roughly it hurt, then sat, head in hands. What was she *doing?* What had become of her orderly life? She'd always coped, always created a way to be content. Why this turmoil now?

Because of Stephen. Her feelings now were nothing like feelings she'd ever had with Hal, but Stephen was Stephen. She was no suitable match for a future Prime Minister!

She took out the remaining pins and shook her own curls free, then realized she still had to ring for her washing water. She did so and put the wig back on, stuffing her own hair roughly under it.

To put distance between herself and the

door, she stood by the window, realizing that she hadn't lowered the curtain. If someone was out there with a spyglass they could have seen everything. She let down the balloon curtain, then went to her empty valise.

When the maid knocked and entered with her hot water, Laura said "Thank you" without looking up.

"Was there anything else, ma'am?"

"No, thank you. I can undress myself."

When the door closed, she straightened and began to undress. The substitute corset was very comfortable. As her fashionable days were over, perhaps she'd have some made.

Rational clothing. Rational actions.

Somewhere inside, the old Laura laughed.

# Chapter 26

Laura awoke from a restless night overhung by inconvenient hungers and an awareness of just how perilous her situation was. Urgency had carried her to Draycombe, but now it seemed like a headlong, heedless rush into danger and temptation.

Last night she'd scraped and washed off her disguise — except the mole, which was glued so firmly she wondered how she'd eventually get rid of it. Putting her disguise on again was tiresome, but she tried to take reassurance from it. Priscilla Penfold would never do anything scandalous.

When she ventured into the parlor, she found Stephen already there, eating his breakfast. He'd ordered enough for two, and immediately poured her coffee. Laura surreptitiously studied him, wondering if he, too, had suffered a restless night, but she could see no sign of it.

Abandoning hope that he, too, was

seething with restless and confused desires, she turned her attention to food. The delicious smell of warm rolls was already reminding her that she'd picked at her dinner last night. She remembered why, but all the same, a body must eat.

She buttered a roll, and the first delicious bite settled her nerves somewhat. "Do we know what time the service is?"

"Am I not the epitome of efficiency? The church is St. Peter's, and the service is at ten."

"Bravo, but I assume you simply asked the servants."

His smile acknowledged it.

"If Dyer attends, we could rescue him then. Claim sanctuary, even."

"That's protection from the authorities, not villains." He was still smiling. It was strangely comforting to be back to friendly ease.

"But in the midst of a staunch English congregation, Farouk would be powerless," she pointed out, then sighed. "Which almost certainly means Dyer won't be there."

"Remember, we don't know that Dyer is a prisoner, or that he is Henry Gardeyne. We need more information before we act."

He sounded apologetic, but as Laura ate

another bite of roll, she recognized that she was pleased. It was wicked of her, but she didn't want this adventure over just yet. It was as if she'd turned the first few pages of a fascinating book — about Stephen and about herself. She couldn't bear to abandon it.

Once they'd finished breakfast, they both dressed for the cool weather and set out to walk to the church at the other end of town. It was small, simple, and quite full. Three worshippers arrived in wheeled chairs pushed by servants. None, however, was a young man, and, of course, there was no turban.

The vicar preached a sermon that mentioned the holy duty to be hospitable to visitors, then touched more delicately on the need to convert the heathen by showing Christian charity. They'd been right to think that some of the local people were uneasy about, or even hostile to, Azir Al Farouk.

As she and Stephen filed out of church, Laura murmured, "It would have been more politic of him to wear normal dress."

"I believe the turban is part of the religion."

"Even so, with a normal jacket and trousers, he wouldn't stand out quite so much."

They had to break off then to speak to the vicar, who confirmed that some of his parishioners were angry about Farouk, especially with the news not long ago being full of the horrors of Algerian slavery.

"Fear for the honor of their womenfolk is also good excuse for deep drinking," remarked the worldly vicar. "May I invite you and your cousin to dine with us, Sir Stephen?"

Stephen extricated them from that, then had to do the same with the rotund, jowly squire, Mr. Bartholomew Ryall, who knew him from London. Next, a Mr. Frobisher wanted to shake his hand. Of course, Laura had to be introduced — a problem she hadn't foreseen. She blessed her concealing bonnet, and used her sickliness as excuse to keep her head and voice low.

She was part of each encounter, however, and realized that a great many people here knew Stephen, or knew of him. He was a Member of Parliament from Dorset, even if his constituency was on the eastern edge, but that didn't account for the attention. He was a well-known, and well- admired, man.

It was no surprise to her that Stephen had a flourishing political career and that, as Juliet had written, he was even spoken of as a potential Prime Minister, but she'd not understood the extent of his reputation until now. In her mind, he'd remained the childhood friend with too deep an interest in books.

The military captain, Trainor, shook Stephen's hand and thanked him for his support of better treatment for injured officers. Mrs. Ryall praised his work to reform the Poor Laws. A frail elderly gentleman in a chair turned out to be the Dr. Grantleigh who with his wife had the ground-floor rooms at the Compass. Unfortunately, he had been one of Stephen's tutors at Cambridge and went on and on about how he'd always predicted a brilliant future.

"Not like the rest of them," the old man said, "Arden, Cavanagh, Debenham. Using an ancient college as a club for drinking, gaming, and worse. You, sir, used the opportunity to learn!"

Laura sucked in her cheeks to stifle laughter, for Stephen was looking uncomfortable. No gentleman, no matter how clever, wants to be known as an ink-nose.

As the Grantleighs were staying at the Compass, there was nothing for it but to walk back with them and the manservant pushing the chair. The road was rough in places, so progress was slow. Stephen walked beside the chair, apparently amusing the old man. Laura was paired with Mrs. Grantleigh, who said not a word.

"I do hope Dr. Grantleigh is finding benefit in the sea air," Laura said, to break the silence.

Mrs. Grantleigh sighed. "I'm not sure how, as the weather is generally too inclement for him to enjoy it. But our doctor insisted, and my husband chooses to do what his doctor says. Dr. Nesbitt here is encouraging. But after all, time cannot be halted, nor age reversed."

Laura approved of stoicism, but only to a point. She wanted to suggest that if the case was hopeless, the couple should move to a place where they would find the setting and company more congenial. Instead, she tried for information about Dyer and Farouk.

"Such a shame that there are so few guests at the Compass. Only ourselves and Captain Dyer, whom the innkeeper says never leaves his rooms and never entertains."

"A sad case," Mrs. Grantleigh agreed. "I saw him arrive, you know, but not a glimpse of him since. I must say that I didn't think him quite so unwell as that.

No worse than my husband, I'm sure, and yet Captain Dyer did not attend church."

The older woman had pursed her lips, so Laura did the same. "I noticed that, Mrs. Grantleigh, and I could not help wondering if that *heathen* in some way prevented him."

Mrs. Grantleigh looked startled. "I don't see how he could."

"Sometimes servants can gain an unhealthy power over their employers, my dear lady."

"Why yes, I have known such cases. . . . But alas, there is nothing to be done."

Stoicism could definitely be carried to extremes, and Laura had seen a way to use this situation. "I believe I might mention the matter to the vicar when next I see him. If he were to pay a visit, I don't think he could be denied."

"What a good idea." Mrs. Grantleigh seemed truly admiring, and rather surprised that anyone — or perhaps just a woman — might come up with an idea at all.

Laura feared Mrs. Grantleigh was the sort of woman who had depended all her life on her husband for guidance — which is what most people would think right and proper. But see the result. With her husband failing in body and mind, she was adrift, unable to form firm decisions and unused to considering what was truly best for them both.

Laura couldn't help seeing that her situation had been somewhat the same. She had felt lost and powerless after Hal died, but she had recovered, even if it had needed an emergency to shock her. She decided that when her current problems were dealt with, she would find some way to help the Grantleighs. Stephen was acquainted with them, so it must be possible.

"Sir Stephen is an admirable young man," Mrs. Grantleigh suddenly said, and went on to tell some stories of his virtues as a student. Again, it was probably the sort of praise that he would blush over, but it alerted Laura to a completely new aspect of their situation.

She'd thought that if this deception were uncovered, it would only be disastrous for her. But Stephen was at risk, too. He wouldn't be ruined but he would lose some of the respect of these people.

Most men of fashion, even MPs, wouldn't care about being discovered in an assignation with a widow, but Stephen might. He was held in high respect not because of rank or wealth, though he had a modicum of both, but because of who he was. She searched for the best word and settled on a Biblical one. He was a *righteous* man.

He worked hard, and not only for selfish ends. Most MPs were in Parliament to increase the power of family or faction. Stephen, it would seem, was working to make life better for people of all sorts. Once she might have made a joke about anyone in her circle being "righteous." Now the realization weighted her with a sense of inadequacy.

What place did Lady Skylark have in the life of Sir Stephen Ball? She could win him votes at the hustings by lively charm, but she'd lose him as many from those who disapproved. He didn't even need that kind of help. Barham wasn't a rotten borough, but the voters there would return him to Parliament as long as he was willing to stand.

She could run his household and throw glittering parties that might sway important people he wanted to influence, but she suspected that wasn't Stephen's way. She had only rarely seen him at *ton* affairs.

Could she fit into the mold of his life? Live quietly, helping him with his research and arranging occasional dinners for groups of serious-minded men who would regard any woman at the table as a distraction. She supposed, with a sigh, that she could chair committees of ladies working to support worthy goals.

She'd been on such committees — it was expected of any lady of fashion — and she'd liked being useful, but she knew she couldn't dedicate her life to that. She liked parties and balls and musical soireés. She liked laughing and flirting and charming men. She liked being at the center of the fashionable world.

If she had to live quietly at Caldfort in order to take care of Harry, then she would, but she couldn't imagine choosing to live a sober, serious life in London, not even with Stephen. It would be like forcing a gourmet to live on gruel within sight of fine cuisine. That made her a despicable, shallow woman, but it was better to know it now than too late.

The Grantleighs invited them to lunch, but they could plead their other engagement.

Laura entered their parlor and studied Stephen, trying to blend the handsome man of fashion with righteousness. "Perhaps you should be in disguise, too," she said.

"I certainly didn't anticipate Grantleigh. Are you all right?" Was that question because he knew holding to her character had been a strain or because he detected something?

She turned away, fussing with her gloves. "Yes, of course. I don't like to live a lie, however."

"Nor do I. We should be able to be done with this soon."

He sounded eager to escape. So, in a way, was she. She turned back and related Mrs. Grantleigh's remarks about Dyer. "If he wasn't particularly ill, it lends weight to him being a prisoner."

He frowned. "Yes, it does. Damnation, but this is frustrating. I'll go and check the wall."

He strode into his room, and Laura smiled wryly. He must be driven crazy by this situation to swear in front of her. Or perhaps he was simply relaxing back into friendship. That was better.

He was back in moments. "Mumble, mumble, mumble. If only they'd fall into a shouting match, I might be able to understand something."

He paced restlessly to look out at the street. That provided an opportunity for Laura to study him some more, but to do so would be folly so she broke the silence. "Were you nervous the first time you stood to speak in the House?"

He turned his head toward her. "No, but only because of the brash arrogance of youth. I'm more nervous now sometimes because I want to make my arguments in a way that'll carry others with me."

"I'm sure you do."

A smile expressed wryness. "I am a good orator, but not golden-tongued. I haven't yet reduced the house to tears as Sheridan and Fox did. In any case, I prefer to make my arguments to reason rather than emotions." After a moment, he added, "For that I am doubtless a fool."

"Reason is gold, whereas emotion is gilding, soon worn away."

"A strange observation from Labellelle."

She met his eyes. "Beauty and reason being antagonists?"

"Unfair, wasn't it? I'm sorry."

They had no time to progress from there, for a knock at the door brought Topham. "Sir Stephen, here is your guest, Mr. Kerslake-Somerford!"

The innkeeper spoke as if he could take credit, and certainly the new arrival was someone to take credit for. Laura couldn't have said what she expected of a smuggling master, but it was not this handsome young man with glowing vigor and an open, unguarded smile.

Topham bowed again. "I'll have your lunch brought up, shall I, Sir Stephen?"

Stephen agreed, and the man left with yet another bow, seemingly directed to the smuggler-earl.

"You're an important person, sir," Stephen said, shaking hands. "May I present Mrs. Gardeyne, currently masquerading as my cousin, Mrs. Penfold."

"Ma'am." Kerslake-Somerford bowed to her. "I gather the Rogues are up to something again. I must say, association with them is enlivening my life."

More boyish enthusiasm. "I wouldn't have thought your life short of livening, Mr. Kerslake-Somerford."

"Different kinds, Mrs. Gardeyne. Most of my . . . professional activity is no more exciting than bookkeeping. The whole point, in fact, is to keep enlivenment to a minimum."

"Ah, I think Mr. Delaney said something similar. That danger comes of its own."

"Precisely. It's those who lead dull lives who seek it out."

Laura made sure not to look at Stephen. A dull life? Surely not. "Excitement comes in many forms," she said. "I'm sure politics can be hazardous."

"Not anymore," Stephen said dryly, perhaps guessing her intent to soothe his feelings. "No one's been beheaded for opposing the monarch in generations."

"Prime Minister Perceval was shot," Kerslake-Somerford pointed out cheerfully.

"By a madman," Stephen said. "That sort of thing could happen to anyone."

"Not just anyone. Perceval was shot because the assassin thought the Prime Minister the creator of all his problems. The danger of being a figurehead."

Foolish to fear for Stephen, but Laura couldn't help it. "You are a figurehead, too, Mr. Kerslake-Somerford."

"For my sins. Please call me Mr. Kerslake, ma'am. It's how I've been known all my life. I've only adopted the other as part of my claim to the earldom."

Their lunch arrived and was spread on the table. Once the servants left, they sat and got down to business.

"What's amiss?" Kerslake demanded. "And how may I assist you?"

# Chapter 27

Kerslake had drunk two cups of tea, eaten bread, ham, pie, and fruit, interspersed with pertinent questions before all was clear. Laura was uncertain at times about telling this man everything, but he had been vouched for by Nicholas Delaney, and they needed his help.

"I've known about Azir Al Farouk since he landed. Drew Chideock brought him in from France on the *Long Jane*. Now we're at peace, we don't get many such passengers, so we were all curious. But" — he shrugged — "as long as a man pays we don't ask questions. In fact, it's easier now. During the war we tried not to carry spies."

"Just Al Farouk?" Laura asked.

"Him and Captain Dyer."

"No child?"

"None was mentioned. You expected one?"

She shook her head. "Please, tell us what you know about the arrival."

Kerslake took a plum. "Despite the rank, Dyer wears no uniform. He's some sort of invalid. Can walk a few steps with a cane, but Farouk had to carry him from the boat to the cart that stood ready to take away the cargo."

"Carried him upstairs here, too, apparently," Stephen said.

"So it wasn't temporary. Chideock took them to Lyme Regis and fixed them up with Paul Wey's coach, which brought them here. All part of the price." Kerslake looked at Laura. "What about the child?"

Laura shared a look with Stephen. "He might have come separately. A boy, perhaps nine years old."

"I've heard of none, but I'll ask."

"What about a party of men?" Stephen asked. "Or no. Nicholas would flay me for assuming the villains are all men, especially with a child involved. It could appear to be a family group."

"That would certainly make them harder to detect, but we don't have many visitors this late in the year. Do you mean a group arriving normally, or by a smuggling vessel? I'm almost certain no child has arrived here recently that way."

Laura shared another look with Stephen as she tried to fit these new pieces into the puzzle. "If there was a reason Farouk and Dyer came in surreptitiously, why would they send HG openly?" It struck her like a loss, a death. "I suppose I must accept that there is no child. He's become so real in my mind, I'm loath to let him go. It's as if he's imprisoned without anyone even knowing about it, and I must set him free."

"I'll make enquiries, Mrs. Gardeyne," Kerslake said kindly. "I can find out what strange children are in the area, too. I mean ones not connected with local families. There probably won't be many this time of year, but it will take a few days to have the tally."

"Thank you."

Stephen took her hand. "It's better not to have a child at risk, Laura. What's more, this means that if anyone is Henry Gardeyne, it must be Captain Dyer himself."

That revived her. "Yes, of course. Tied up. Behind locked doors."

"We still have the puzzle of a ten-year absence," Stephen warned, "and as Nicholas asked, why now?"

"I know, but if it's true, it's better. If it is Henry, he'll be able to prove his identity without any difficulty, and we have his portrait to match him with." She turned to Kerslake. "I have a drawing of Henry Gardeyne. Do you think Mr. Chideock and his men might recognize whether he's Captain Dyer?"

He pulled a face. "It all happened by night, and their attention was probably more on their cargo. I could ask them, but to be frank, I'm not sure it would be wise. I trust them to a point, but only to a point. They'd likely let something slip, and then it would snake around the area and reach the people here. After all, you're here, next door. It shouldn't be hard to get a look at the man."

"You'd think so," said Stephen, "but it's proving tricky for law-abiding citizens."

Kerslake laughed. "I'm no dab hand at breaking and entering, but if you can't manage it legally, I'll have someone help you. Shame old Elsie Musbury's dead. She owned this place before Topham and had been hand in glove with smugglers all her life. Topham's a new man from Exmouth way. He knows what's what, but I can't trust him as I would Elsie."

Stephen nodded. "What if Farouk has supporters standing by? Would you know of unexplained bullyboys in the area?"

"Certainly, but would they be that? As you said, they could masquerade as a family or as other orderly visitors."

"You mean they could be anyone?" Laura asked, thinking of the various people they'd met today.

"Not anyone. Most people here now are local or long-term visitors, but sensible villains announce their identity no more than smuggling masters do. In fact, it seems strange to me that this Farouk is creating such a stir."

"He could never pass for an English gentleman," Stephen said.

"True, but from what I hear, he's almost making a point of being peculiar."

"That bears thinking on. But who in this area could be called suspicious?"

"No one," Kerslake said. "It's my business to know of possible preventive men."

"Do the forces of law and order sometimes prowl around in disguise?" Laura asked.

"They do anything they can to catch us."

"I saw two military men as we arrived," Laura said. "One army, one navy."

"Captain Sillitoe, RN, cousin of a local family. Captain Trainor of the Buffs, attending his grandmother. We're keeping an eye on both just in case, but neither has acted out of character."

"I'm impressed," Stephen said.

"I told you, knowing these things is my business. I keep the trade going because it's the main means of support for many along the coast, especially this year, with the poor harvest and the economy going to hell with the peace. My main intent, however, is to avoid violence and keep my people out of jail."

Laura was beginning to have considerable respect for young Captain Drake.

Kerslake rose. "I need to be off. I'll find out about children and other unexplained strangers, but I suspect the action is all here. Do you have a plan? If you want to break the prisoner out now, I can arrange it."

Stephen smiled. "Not yet. You see, we don't know what we should do. Even if Dyer is Henry Gardeyne, we have an unexplained decade of absence. We also have a cripple. In body only, or in mind? He might not be the sort of man who should be given control of an English estate and all the people dependent on it."

"Ah."

Laura studied the man. "You don't seem shocked, Mr. Kerslake."

He turned to her. "My predecessor as

Earl of Wyvern was insane, Mrs. Gardeyne, but not enough to be confined, which was unfortunate. He did considerable damage. If someone had prevented his reign, it would have been a blessing."

"Then you understand why we have to try to find out more before taking any action. Because . . ."

"Because when you liberate him, you might wish to cage him elsewhere. I'd offer Crag Wyvern except that it might tip a delicate mind into madness all by itself. I do know some safe places, however."

"Why am I not surprised?" Stephen murmured.

Kerslake's lips twitched. "There's a farm not far inland from here where the people are completely trustworthy. If you liberate Gardeyne but don't want him on the loose, take him to Stonewell Farm. I'll draw a map."

He took out a tablet of paper and drew roads and signs. On the back he scribbled a note of introduction. "I'll stop by Stonewell on my way home and warn the Huddlers. No details, just that they might need to keep a man confined for a day or two."

Laura found herself again feeling that she'd landed in an unreal world where these shocking things were taken as normal.

He passed the paper to Stephen. "They'll be happy it's not smuggling business. That's getting risky. That's one problem about the end of the war," he said, putting away his tablet and picking up his riding cloak. "Too many ex-officers willing to become preventive men, and the navy with not enough to do, creating trouble all over the place. That's the only reason the slaves of Algiers were liberated, you know. A fighting navy with nothing else to do."

"And that expedition cost a shocking number of lives for little direct value to Britain."

"Freedom," Laura protested. "Thousands of Christian slaves were freed, and one was from Berkshire."

"A handful were English, yes. But only a handful."

"So we should care less about foreigners?"

"Resources are never infinite, Laura, so they must be used with discrimination."

Kerslake swung on his cloak. "I'll leave you to the ethical debate and pursue the practical." But he added to Stephen, "The key to ending smuggling is to lower taxes

298

to reasonable levels. I intend to apply myself to that when I'm in the House of Lords. Will I have your support in the Commons?"

"Certainly." The two men shook hands. "And now you're associated with the Rogues, there'll be others."

"So I gather. Life takes strange turns, doesn't it? Less than a year ago I was an estate manager with no weightier responsibility than that."

He turned to bow to Laura, and she thought of one more thing.

"Could you alert us if the Reverend Jack Gardeyne arrives in the area? Lord Caldfort will probably send him here at some point."

"Of course."

He left, and Laura said, "A very impressive man."

"I certainly look forward to working with him in London. So, what do we do now?"

"I'm puzzling over something," she said. "Something about Kerslake . . ."

"What?"

But she'd realized what, and it wasn't something she wished to speak about. The oddness was that the young man had never once looked at her with the interest, or just the acknowledgement of beauty, that she'd

299

come to accept as her due. How terrible that she was so accustomed to it. Perhaps this time in disguise would be good for her. Like a penitential fast.

She moved on to other matters. "So we have only Farouk and Dyer to deal with, and our hypothesis, that Dyer is Henry Gardeyne. I was thinking about that during the sermon."

"Tut-tut."

She grinned at him. "I was thinking that if Henry is alive, he must have changed. I'm going to reproduce my copy of his portrait and try to age him."

"An excellent idea."

Did he seem surprised?

She went to get her drawing portfolio and returned to find Stephen gone. He reappeared from his room. "Just checking the wall, but I think that's hopeless. They'd have to bellow for us to hear what they're saying."

"We might hear more through the doors."

"I thought of that, but didn't you notice how the boards in the corridor squeak? Embarrassing to be caught out there. More to the point, it might make them suspicious. We don't want them to make a run for it before we've sorted it all out."

She sighed and sat in a chair that caught the light. "It seems such a simple problem, doesn't it? But it has us stumped." She took out a clean sheet of paper and set to work. "When I've done this, we still have to find a way to compare it to Dyer. Perhaps when Farouk goes out . . ."

"Locked doors," he reminded her.

"They could be locked from the inside."

"Why?"

"Ah-ha! So you do think he's a prisoner. Thus, he's Henry Gardeyne!"

He laughed. "Checkmate. But I'm not willing to make any assumptions."

"Nor am I . . ." An idea occurred. "I think what I need to do is 'accidentally' leave the altered picture where people can see it. Mrs. Grantleigh, Topham, the servants."

"An excellent idea!" He leaned closer to look at her work. "What would ten years do to a man? Surely they can't have been comfortable ones. Adventuring. Imprisonment?"

Laura looked up from the light outline she'd drawn. "Didn't the maid say Captain Dyer is pale? Some English people were imprisoned in France."

"But they were all released in 1814."

"Perhaps he was badly injured and has

only just made it home."

"With an Egyptian servant? That is damned peculiar."

"It all is," she complained. "But I won't give up hope. Sit for me, Stephen. I need to see how a man's face changes."

He obliged, moving a chair opposite, but said, "I must point out that I'm not Gardeyne's age. I'm only twenty-six."

She smiled as she studied him. "I promise you, I do not see you as aged. Or," she added, "stuffy."

Their eyes met in wary acknowledgement of that kiss, but they weren't ready to talk about it yet.

Laura seized the excuse to make a quick sketch of Stephen, capturing the elegant lines that his body seemed to fall into so naturally, his long hands, and his high, intelligent forehead. She conveyed his features with a few strokes, unwilling to linger there. Long, straight nose, high cheekbones, flared brows, and clever lips.

She wasn't sure why that word came to mind, but it did. He'd always had expressive lips. When he saw her studying him, they turned up slightly in a guarded question.

"How do you see me, then?" he asked.

*As the man I want naked in my bed.*

That thought startled her with its brutal honesty, but Stephen — any man — deserved better than to be used to slake a widow's hunger. She returned to the drawing of Gardeyne and chose a safe response. "As a very good friend."

When she looked up again it seemed to her that Stephen's lips had hardened. Did he want to be more? Would a quiet life with Stephen not be so dull after all?

Later. There would be time enough later to work through all of this. She blinkered her mind on the task of creating a picture of an older Henry Gardeyne. That youthful roundness would have gone. Would he be as lean as Stephen? Frail, someone had said. She thinned the face close to the bone, hinted at sunken eyes, then turned the happy smile bitter. The hair?

Men wore their hair shorter now, so she removed most of the poetical locks. She fiddled with it, then passed it to Stephen. "I think he looks too old now. It's all guesswork."

"Older, but perhaps not too much so if he's had a hard time of it. He's even slightly familiar. More of a resemblance to Reverend Gardeyne, perhaps."

Laura moved the drawing so they could

both see it. "I don't see that except in the general Gardeyne features. Jack is fleshy. A bit more like Hal, perhaps." But then she pulled a face. "It feels lifeless to me. I've never tried to do an imaginary portrait before. I don't know how."

"It'll do. We know what we're looking for now, and perhaps a glimpse in a window will be enough. Let's get you out for another dose of sea air, spyglass in hand. Sooner or later the man must obligingly sit at his window."

"It will be more difficult to study the inn during daylight."

He rose and rang the bell. "Heroes relish a challenge."

"Heroes?" she queried.

"We are equal in this enterprise, I think."

That warmed her, a warmth that lingered as she put on her outer clothing. Equals. For much of her life she'd not even considered that. She'd accepted that women, for all their qualities and abilities, were not the equals of men.

When had that changed? Perhaps some time in the past year when she'd had no husband, and when his substitute, Lord Caldfort, had been so obviously frail in mind and body. But perhaps the final straw had been Jack.

Jack was the sort of man who expected to command women by right, but she'd never felt any inclination to bow down. Once she'd suspected that he wanted to harm Harry, he'd become her enemy. One could not feel subservient to an enemy.

# Chapter 28

When they left the inn, Stephen kept his mind fixed on their purpose, but it was an effort. Moment by moment, Laura was shredding his sanity. He was even beginning to read wicked interest in her friendly glances.

"Let's move behind that wooden rig," he said. "We can probably study the Compass from there without being too obvious."

She agreed and they ambled down onto the beach in that direction.

"What is this?" she asked as they moved into position.

He looked at the tall timbers. "Perhaps something to support a boat in the building?"

From within the ugly, concealing bonnet, framed by faded curls and dark circles, her blue eyes sparkled. "Does it hurt to admit to ignorance about something?"

He smiled back. "Of course not. There

are vast fields of human knowledge that have escaped me."

"Really? I've always been in awe of your knowledge."

A rational man would appreciate being admired for his mind.

He turned toward the Compass and focused the lens. "The curtains are up, but I see no one." He turned the telescope back out to sea. "Plenty of ships."

He passed the glass to her and she scanned the waves. After a while, she swung the spyglass around, pausing on one building after another until she could settle on the inn.

"You're right. Nothing to see." She lowered the glass and gave it to him. "We can't stay here doing this for long without being thought peculiar."

"Let's do one brisk walk along the front," he said, putting away the telescope. "That will be expected."

"Not too brisk," she reminded him as they walked back up to the road. "I'm frail."

"Perhaps I should hire a chair. I could wheel you up and down."

She grinned at him. "That might be fun."

"Cousin Priscilla," he said with a

quelling look, "does not enjoy fun."

"Yes, she does. She finds her fun in gossip and nosiness."

Laura found it was hard to be Cousin Priscilla while strolling in the autumn sunshine arm in arm with Stephen, especially when the rustle of the waves seemed to whisper of wickedness.

"I'm not at all surprised that seaside visits have become so popular."

"Invigorating, isn't it?"

*That's one way of putting it.*

She'd expected to be comfortable with Stephen, especially once they'd dealt with the embarrassment of his proposal and her unfortunate reaction. They'd even cleared the lingering sourness of Lady Skylark. She'd expected a return to before, when they'd been living in the remains of youth, still like brother and sister.

Now, despite occasional teasing, they were man and woman, and this — a stroll, arm in arm — was the sort of thing a man and woman, not a youthful pair of friends, would do. It had the same effect as eating a meal together had, just the two of them.

They passed a notice about an upcoming assembly, a sight that reminded Laura of how she'd used to avoid dancing with Stephen. She'd not disliked it, but it had seemed too like dancing with a brother. Everyone knew that no young lady would do that if she could obtain a real partner.

How very, very strange.

They arrived back at the inn and were snared by Topham bearing an invitation to take tea with the Grantleighs. It was impossible to completely refuse, but Laura made the excuse of tiredness and sent Stephen down alone. She spent the time migrating between listening at the wall and watching through the window, and achieved precisely nothing except even more tangled thoughts.

By the time Stephen returned, she'd abandoned vigilance and was reading a book. "Did the Grantleighs know anything about the other guests?" she asked.

"Nothing new. As you said, Mrs. Grantleigh saw them arrive. Dyer was pale and swathed in blankets, and Farouk carried him upstairs." He looked over her shoulder. "Ah-ha! A novel."

"I never denied reading them."

"*Guy Mannering*. It's good."

She cast him a look of exaggerated astonishment. "Sir Stephen Ball reads novels!"

"We took turns reading from *The Mysteries of Udolpho* once."

"When we were very young." But she smiled. She was coming to love these returns to the past. "We even made a play of it, remember? You were noble Valancourt, and I was Emily because you refused to act love scenes with your sister."

"It would have been most unnatural."

"You could have romanced Juliet."

"She was too young for such things." But he was smiling in an interesting manner. " 'Ah, Emily!' " he quoted. " 'I have then little cause to hope. When you ceased to esteem me, you ceased also to love me!' "

"You remember that? Wait, wait . . ." The words popped into her memory. " 'And if you had valued my esteem, you would not have given me this new occasion for uneasiness!' Said, as I remember, turned away, with pale and faltering hand stretched back to dissuade insistence." She stood and took the pose.

"Exactly. 'Is it then true, Emily, that I have lost your regard forever?' "

"I turn, hands clasped to trembling bosom. 'Oh, sir, explain yourself.' "

" 'Can any explanation be necessary?' I demand imperiously. 'Oh, Emily, how could you so degrade me in your opinion, even for a moment!' "

"I believe you skipped some there," she

complained. "It was a long speech."

"He did prose on a bit. That was the crux of it. She should have trusted. If these feather-witted heroines would only trust their heroes, all would be simple."

"If men were not so pestilential, it would be easier for heroines to trust despite the evidence!"

"On with your part, wench."

"I'm not sure I remember it." But she knew her lips were twitching. "Oh, very well. 'Valancourt!'" She stretched out her hand to him. "'I was ignorant of all the circumstances you have mentioned —'"

"'All,' note. Even she thought he went on a bit."

"'The emotion I now suffer,'" she quoted sternly, "'may assure you of the truth of this. Though I had ceased to esteem —'"

"Fickle . . ."

"'— I had not taught myself entirely to forget you.'"

"Weak willed . . ."

"Say your next line, sir."

He laughed. "'Am I dear to you, then, still dear to you, my Emily?'"

"Dense dolt. Well might she demand, 'Is it necessary that I should tell you so?' And then she says, 'These are the first moments of joy I have experienced since your departure. . . .' "

Though there were no similarities between the dire tale of Emily and her Valancourt, those words drew special meaning from the air.

"And then," he said softly, taking her hand, "we kissed, as I remember."

"As tentatively as if our lips were flame to gunpowder."

He drew her closer. "We could do better now."

She saw all the dangers, but said, "I would hope so," and cooperated as he lowered his lips to hers.

It was as chaste a kiss as that they'd dared all those years ago, on a stage in front of their families and a few guests, but it was not tentative. They both knew kisses now, and their lips brushed and played with delicate experience.

The effect rippled down through Laura like warm wine, pooling as desire, then flaring into intoxicating fever. Though it took all the strength she possessed, she did not press closer, did not tighten her hand on his arm, did not open her mouth to taste him fully. But her heart pounded and her legs began to tremble . . .

He broke the kiss and stepped back.

"Ah, youth. Ah, drama."

His lids were lowered, concealing his expression, but color had risen in his cheeks. She thought to check what else might have risen, but he turned away to look out at the restless sea. "Astonishing what lurks in our memories."

"Yes." She tried for a light tone to match his, but how could she manage that when aware of his body as if he wore no clothes at all? Her hand itched to explore his long back and taut buttocks, his chest, his muscled abdomen, and more. . . .

"I might as well go out again," he said, "being healthy and restless. I should check at the King's Arms to see if they know anything there. I can use the excuse of considering a move from this heathen enclave."

Sanity was returning and his absence would make self-control easier. "What do I do? I tell you, I'm tempted to break down HG's door."

*In lieu of other passions.*

"Patience. This is only our first day."

He meant only the first day of their enquiries here, but Laura's body clenched as if that were a promise. Considering the changes in the day since they'd arrived, what could happen in two or three more?

What should she allow to happen? Flame

to gunpowder, which could destroy them both.

He walked to his bedchamber door but paused there and turned. If there had been any physical reaction, it had been controlled. "Promise me you won't rush into action while I'm gone."

"Rush into action?"

"I know you. If Farouk goes out, you'll be tempted to act on your own and try to see Dyer. Don't. It's too dangerous."

Laura sighed. "Very well, sir. I will try to restrain my mad passions."

If he caught the double entendre, he gave no sign of it as he left.

# Chapter 29

Laura settled back to her book, promising herself that she would indeed practice restraint. Matters were too important for self-indulgence. The novel could no longer hold her interest, however, when thoughts of Stephen dazzled her mind.

Three times they'd kissed, now. First awkwardly, then angrily, then . . . truly. Yes, though nothing had been said, that had been a true kiss, one that in any other circumstance could have led to more.

She put the book aside but saw the dangers of sitting here sunk in such thoughts. She had to be sensible and in control. There must be something useful to do, something distracting. She went into Stephen's bedchamber and listened at the wall.

A murmur of voices as indistinguishable as the murmur of the sea. No sign of fear, anger, or pain.

She glared at the wall and even checked it for a crack at the top, bottom, or sides. The Compass Inn was in unfortunately good repair. She turned to go back into the parlor, but instead she drifted to the bed as if pulled there by a magnet.

She trailed her hand over the rough wool of the blue coverlet, inhaling, finding Stephen in the air. She couldn't resist pulling the coverlet down from the pillows so she could touch the place where his head had rested.

Maudlin nonsense.

Yet she picked up the pillow and inhaled, pressing her face into it. She'd not been aware before of knowing Stephen's smell like this, but she did. It was as distinctively his as his signature, and it trickled into her body, exciting every part of her.

She held the pillow closer, sinking to sit on the bed, igniting at the thought of being here with him, of breathing in his skin, licking his sweat. . . .

With a gasp, she scrambled off the bed. What did she think she was *doing?* Desperately she put back the pillow and tidied the covers, smoothing them over and over to erase any trace of her idiocy. Then she fled back through the parlor to the privacy of her own room, feeling, when she closed the door, as if she'd shut out the devil.

After a minute or so, she peeled herself away from the door and went to the mirror. She didn't look deranged — but then she saw a smudge of the dark around her eyes and realized she must have left some trace of her face paint on Stephen's pillow.

"Perish it!" she muttered, ripping the cover off her own pillow. She raced back to Stephen's room and dashed to the window to check for his approach. No sign. *Please heaven, keep him out for a while longer!*

As she'd feared, smears of brown marked the pillowcase. Heart thundering with urgency, she stripped it off and replaced it with hers, then straightened the bed again. Would he notice any difference? She'd normally think not, but Stephen was infernally perceptive.

She hurried back and put his pillowcase on her pillow. Only then did she feel safe.

The feverish energy lingered and she paced her room, multiplying the miles to Redoaks by the year, 1816, by her age, by the time. . . .

It didn't help. She was tempted to clutch and inhale her own pillow now. She forced herself away from her bed. In fact, this would be an excellent time to go down to the public parlor and exhibit her picture. She might learn other gossip there, too.

She wrapped her virulent shawl around herself, picked up her drawing portfolio, and left the room, assembling her persona of Priscilla Penfold. In fact, Priscilla Penfold would venture down the creaking corridor, just in case she might overhear something. It did her no good, however. The adjacent rooms could be uninhabited for all she could tell.

She headed downstairs, trying to appear timid. However, as she descended the stairs she decided Priscilla Penfold wasn't timid at all. She was the sort of woman who pretended uncertainty as a disguise. She would flutter and hesitate in order to hide the fact that she was a weasel in search of eggs of gossip.

She would worry out loud that she was bothering people so that everyone would have to assure her that she wasn't. She would timidly declare that she was just a silly woman so that everyone would have to pay attention to what she said.

Laura struggled not to laugh. She was describing a particular person she knew, someone who had exasperated her for years.

She crossed the hall and entered the

small, bow-windowed parlor. It was painted a pleasant yellow, perhaps to suggest sunshine even on a dull day, and warmed by a large fire. It even seemed free of drafts. The only occupant, however, was a sinewy gentleman in a chair to the left of the fire who was drinking tea and reading a newspaper, pince-nez on his long nose.

He rose when she entered, but then resumed his seat and occupation.

Laura sat by the window and looked out, but the wind was rising and few were taking the air. The sea was steel gray and choppy, and she wondered if they were in for a serious storm. She opened her portfolio on a small table and took out a clean sheet of paper, leaving her aged sketch of Henry Gardeyne exposed.

The gentleman was engrossed in his newspaper.

Laura began to sketch, trying to catch the feel of the gathering clouds as she waited for someone else to come into the room. A lad came in with a bobbing bow and put more wood on the fire. He hardly raised his eyes and certainly didn't look at her drawing.

Laura drew boats tossed by the growing waves, and did a quick sketch of a man chasing after his tumbling hat. She silently cheered when he caught it just short of the sea. But it was becoming clear that she was unlikely to encounter anyone here except the newspaper reader.

To speak to a strange man was somewhat improper, but she was a dull widow, not a brash flirt.

She started with a timid clearing of the throat. When he looked up, she said — hesitantly, of course, "I fear we are in for a storm, sir. Are you, too, staying here for your health?"

He lowered his paper and looked at her over his glasses. "Only in a manner of speaking, ma'am. I am Dr. Nesbitt of this town, and I have been visiting a patient here."

She remembered Topham mentioning him. This could be exactly what she'd hoped for!

"Poor Captain Dyer?" she asked.

"No, ma'am." His look had become alert. "The captain requires medical care?"

Laura suppressed disappointment and fluttered. "Oh, I'm sure I don't know, sir. But the innkeeper said he is an invalid, and it seems he never leaves his rooms. They're next to ours, you see. Those taken by my cousin, Sir Stephen Ball."

"Ah. Sir Stephen." He beamed. Clearly

her status had immediately risen.

"So kind of him," she simpered. "For my health, you see. But Captain Dyer has only the one servant, it would appear, and he is a foreigner." She lowered her voice as such people often do when about to criticize. "He wears a *turban* — the servant, sir — and I fear he is dosing the poor captain with *foreign nostrums*."

The doctor removed his spectacles. "My, my. That certainly raises alarms, ma'am." He rose, putting his newspaper on a table. "I shall have a word with Topham and see if I may tender my services."

With a bow, he left. Laura supposed it was too much to expect that if he attended Dyer he'd return and report to her, but if she remained here, she might learn something. She eyed Dr. Nesbitt's newspaper, tempted to read it, but it would be out of character for Mrs. Penfold. In her experience, nosy gossips were never interested in important matters.

She returned to her sketching but heard returning footsteps and turned to the door, wearing an anxious, questioning look.

"It is as you described, ma'am," Dr. Nesbitt said, shaking his head. "But from what Topham says, Captain Dyer is in a chronic rather than an acute state. Sad to say, medicine often has little to offer such cases other than rest and fresh air. Bleeding and cupping sometimes, but I am not in favor of those when the patient appears pale, which is as Topham describes him. I will, however, send over a bottle of my patent restorative, which might assist his return to health."

He had come over and now looked at her drawing. "Why, ma'am, you are quite an artist!"

Laura realized that her artistic ability was out of character with Priscilla Penfold, too, but there was no help for it now. She simpered. "So kind. Just my little hobby."

He had turned to the sketch of Henry. "Now there's a man who looks in need of my services, ma'am. Consumption?"

Laura was caught unawares, and any fluster was completely natural. "Oh, dear, I do hope not, sir. That is my brother. He . . . er . . . suffered a serious accident in the hunting field, but is recovering well now."

"I'm glad to hear it, Mrs. Penfold, but if he were my patient, I would want him to take my restorative draught. For now, however, I must take my leave. Another patient awaits."

With that, he drained his teacup, tucked

his paper under his arm, bowed, and left. In a few minutes she watched him struggle against the wind down the road until he turned into a nearby house.

She waited. A young couple came in, windblown and laughing, to take tea. It turned out that they had driven from Seaton with no care for the weather. Laura suspected that they were on their honeymoon, and that perhaps wind and wild sea was exactly what they wanted, which made them positively irritating.

They left, rapt in one another, and Laura hoped the young man could manage to keep his mind on the road. She was about to give up and return to her room when Mrs. Grantleigh came in. What good fortune that she hadn't yet put away the picture.

The elderly woman paused. "Mrs. Penfold. Do you mind if I join you? My husband is dozing, and I like a change of scene but cannot go too far."

"Not at all." Laura pointed encouragingly to a nearby chair, remembering to be Priscilla Penfold when she would much rather befriend this poor woman. "I fear a storm is rising."

"I fear so, too," the older woman said, sitting by the picture but looking out at the sea. "So dismal."

Laura liked storms, but she fervently agreed. "I just met Dr. Nesbitt. He seemed an excellent man."

That set Mrs. Grantleigh off on an account of the doctor's kind but ineffectual treatment of her husband, along with the other doctors consulted back home in Cambridge, and in Bath.

Then, at last, she looked down and started. "My, that is an excellent portrait, Mrs. Penfold." She glanced around, clearly not believing what she saw. "Your work?"

Laura simpered again. "Just my little hobby."

Mrs. Grantleigh's glance was shrewd, and perhaps even suspicious. No fool after all. "A talent, Mrs. Penfold," she said firmly. "You should not hide it under a bushel."

Laura felt herself flush beneath her sallow cream. It was partly because she was caught in a lie, but also because she hadn't done anything in particular with her talent.

Mrs. Grantleigh was studying the picture, however. "There is something slightly familiar about this man," she said, "and yet I do not know. . . . Perhaps I might have known him before he was so unwell?"

She looked up, demanding an answer.

Laura had to tell the same story. "My brother, Reginald," she said, cheeks so hot she feared they'd melt the paint. "He suffered an accident in the hunting field. We . . . er . . . feared we might lose him, so I did that sketch. But he is much recovered now. I don't think he has ever visited Cambridge, however. He lives year round in the Shires."

Mrs. Grantleigh pushed the picture away with a moue of distaste. "Then you are doubtless correct, Mrs. Penfold. I have no patience with men who use their lives for nothing but sport. How refreshing to know a man like Sir Stephen . . ."

Laura let her sing Stephen's praises and slid away the picture. What was she to make of that moment of recognition, however? Did the picture look like Dyer, but too frail? After some thought, she tidied her portfolio and let the original copy of Henry's portrait flutter to the floor.

"Oh!" she exclaimed and grabbed for it. Then she turned it toward Mrs. Grantleigh. "My dear younger brother, Cedric. So scholarly."

The older lady smiled. "And he looks more robust and happy for it, Mrs. Penfold. May he be saved from the ways of dissipation and vice. Oh, my, look at the time!" She rose. "But it has been most pleasant to chat with you, Mrs. Penfold. I hope we can do so again."

She left the room, and Laura frowned at her pictures. Mrs. Grantleigh had shown no recognition of the picture of young Henry. None at all. If only she'd been able to ask if the familiarity with the aged one had anything to do with Captain Egan Dyer.

Topham. He was the other person most likely to have seen Dyer. Laura thought up and discarded a number of cunning ways of getting the man in here, but then shrugged and pulled the bellpull. A maid — a young, plump one she did not know — bustled in. "May I help you, ma'am?"

Laura willed her to come over to the table where the drawings still lay, but she stayed by the door.

"I wish to speak to Mr. Topham," she said.

In moments, the innkeeper was there, bowing. Laura stayed seated by the window and the man did come over. "What may I do for you, Mrs. Penfold."

"Oh, dear, oh, dear," said Laura with a hand to her chest, "I have been watching the storm rise. Are we safe, sir? Are we safe?"

He put on a beaming smile. "Safe? As houses!" He chuckled at his own joke. "Certainly a little storm is rising, but the Compass has weathered a hundred such."

She gave him an uncertain smile. "If you are quite sure. I was thinking that the King's Arms . . . it being constructed out of stone . . ."

He bridled. "Not at all, ma'am. Only been there ten years. Not stood the test of time."

"Oh, I see. Thank you. That does make me feel safer. Perhaps you could help me gather my papers, Mr. Topham. My hands are quite unsteady."

He quickly did so, flattering her artistic abilities but showing no recognition. Then he tenderly escorted her upstairs and left to arrange a steadying brew of brandied tea.

Laura sat at the table and spread the two portraits in front of her. "Did Mrs. Grantleigh recognize you, Henry, or was it some other fleeting resemblance? Are you dead, or are you Dyer?"

She frowned over that, wondering if the name Dyer was some complicated play on *die.* They had never solved the puzzle of the name Oscar Ris.

A gust of wind rattled the windows and

she rose to look out, wishing Stephen would return. The light was going now and she wanted him here, safe. She smiled wryly at that, knowing her feelings flowed deeper and deeper by the moment.

She started at a knock, and called for the person to enter. It was Jean with the brandied tea. She watched carefully as the maid went to the table and put her tray down there, carefully away from the drawings. The maid paused, looking at them for a moment.

Laura hurried over. "My little hobby," she said.

"They're very cleverly done, ma'am."

Laura tittered. "People keep saying they recognize them, but they are my brothers who have never been here. I do find, however, that sometimes strangers look like people we know."

"That's the truth, ma'am. I went right up to someone in Seaton who I thought was a woman who used to live next door. And I must say that one" — she nodded to the aged one — "does put me in mind of someone."

"A guest, perhaps?" Laura prompted.

The maid shrugged. "I can't bring one to mind, ma'am. Likely it's just as you say and he reminds me of someone else. Folks aren't so different in the end, are they? Now, shall I pour your tea? And do you want to order your dinner, ma'am?"

Laura sighed. "No, thank you."

When the maid had left, she sat and poured herself tea. She could smell the brandy already. She supposed smuggling country had an ample supply. She sweetened it and sipped, enjoying the strong taste and the warmth, then carried the cup over to the window to watch the storm grow.

She drained the cup and found clean paper to do rapid sketches of wind and weather, reveling in the raw energy of the storm as shown in roiling clouds, whipping waves, and people fighting to make their way to their homes.

A blue turban caught her eye. Farouk! He was striding down the street away from the inn, robe flapping around his legs in the wind. Where could he be going? Because she had her pencil in her hand, she sketched him.

He was a fine figure of a man — tall, straight, and vigorous. What was he doing here, writing letters to an English lord, offering to kill for pay? She drew in palm trees behind him, bent in the wind, trying to imagine going to Egypt and attempting such a crime. Impossible. She and Stephen must be missing pieces of this puzzle, but she couldn't even imagine what they were.

If Jack wished to kill Harry, that was evil, but she understood why. An Egyptian coming to England to offer out of the blue to kill Henry Gardeyne, a man supposedly dead ten years ago? It was a fairy tale.

Then she saw Stephen emerge from the King's Arms, spot Farouk, and plot a course that would intersect. She sketched him, too. Merely the sight of him flushed heat through her body. How was she to cope with this?

The two men met and exchanged a few words, before Stephen turned toward the Compass and Farouk walked on, past the King's Arms. Where on earth was he going?

At least Stephen would know how good Farouk's English was. Every scrap of information could be useful. As she thought this, she drew Stephen walking back toward the inn, clutching at his hat. Suddenly he gave up, and she saw his grin as he took it off and let the wind whip through his hair.

She smiled in sympathy, wanting to run out and let the same wind blow her hair and clothes, down by the edge of the wild sea. Alas, alas, that she was Priscilla Penfold and not Lady Skylark.

When he came in, bringing crisp, salty air with him, she said, "The windblown, I assume," referring to the fashionable hair-style.

He grinned. "Definitely."

"I saw you speak to Farouk. Is his English good?"

"Fair, though heavily accented. He confirms he's from Egypt. His master is not well but improving. They plan to stay here indefinitely. That's it."

"I tried the pictures on the visiting Dr. Nesbitt, Mrs. Grantleigh, Topham, and Jean, the maid. Jean and Mrs. Grantleigh thought they might vaguely recognize the older picture, but surely if it looked like Dyer, whom they saw recently, it would be more than that. Nothing at the King's Arms, I assume."

"Just the expected rumbles about heathen savages."

"Then there's nothing for it but invasion. Farouk's out, though where on earth is he going?"

"Not far in this weather. It's too risky," he added. "Invasion, I mean."

Laura twitched her shawl into place. "Nonsense. I can try sociability. Priscilla

Penfold would do that as a cover for her nosiness. Should I send a message through a servant? No" — she headed for the door — "simply knock."

"Laura." He caught her on the way to the door, as he had in Caldfort. His hand sizzled on her arm.

Perhaps he'd meant to stop her, but he let go and stepped back. "Very well. But be careful. I'll be on guard. Don't hesitate to scream."

"I am the best one to do this," she said, understanding. "Priscilla is precisely that sort of curious meddler."

"I know."

She smiled her thanks, then, correct manner in place, ventured into the corridor. As there seemed to be no other guests up here, she wasn't surprised to find it deserted. All the same, she stayed in character and minced along to tap on the door next to Stephen's.

Hearing nothing, she knocked harder. Ear to the door, she thought she heard a faint movement. "Captain Dyer?" she called in a fussy voice. "It's Mrs. Penfold, a fellow guest. I wondered if you would like some company, sir."

Silence.

She'd expected that.

"Are you all right, sir?" Having given reason for her concern, she turned the knob.

Again, the door was locked. Disappointing, but it supported her hopes. If Farouk locked the doors when he left, Dyer was a prisoner. If Dyer was a prisoner, he must be Henry Gardeyne, Harry's savior.

She glanced behind and saw Stephen watching her. She waved him back. If this was the parlor, then the next door must be the bedchamber. She walked along and tried that one.

It, too, was locked.

She returned to the parlor door and tried another knock, but heard nothing to indicate anyone was there at all.

She returned to Stephen. "He made one slight noise."

"If he wanted to be rescued, don't you think he'd make more? And you're only just in time. Farouk only walked down to the sea, as if wanting air. He's almost back."

# Chapter 30

Stephen was sure he would be a lunatic soon. Enacting a stage kiss, when he wanted Laura in his arms with passion. Letting her go into danger, no matter how slight. Sharing these rooms, assailed by her perfume and her body.

Even his bedroom now seemed to carry a ghostly hint of her fragrance. He was going to have to spend another night in that bed, surrounded by it, aware of Laura so close with nothing between them — except honor.

A sane man would want to be free of this torture as quickly as possible, but he dreaded the end of the brief adventure. It was clear that Laura, however, was desperate to be done with it.

"They might be becoming suspicious," he said. "That was the second time we've tried the doors."

"They don't know who it was the first

time, and since I gave my name, I should seem innocent. Anyway, if Dyer is a prisoner, he may not tell Farouk. But we're getting nowhere! Let's go out again with the spyglass."

"Out? The light's going and I think a storm is rising."

She turned to the window as if doubting his words, but surely she could hear the wind, feel it beat against the windows? Outside, dark clouds were pouring into the bay and the storm whipped the sea into white-edged blades. Anchored boats were tossing so wildly some of them might break free in the night.

"Oh, perish it," she muttered, but then moved closer to the window. "I love storms."

"I remember."

He remembered her habit of running out to dance in torrents of rain, hair and clothes plastered to her. Strangely, he didn't remember being aroused by it, only concerned that she'd catch her death of cold. Perhaps he had been a dull dog.

"I've only been close to the sea in a storm once before," she said. "At Brighton. I danced at the edge of it, flirting with the crashing waves."

"I know. It was written about in the newspapers."

He'd been furious. Furious that she was still so foolish, that she might have been in danger, that Gardeyne had probably egged her on. That she'd frolicked as good as naked before the world.

She turned to him with a sane and rueful smile. "So they did. They disguised me as 'a wild-spirited Thetis of fashionable society,' with sly hints about the way the spray plastered my gown to my body. Hal was angry for some reason."

"Perhaps he feared you'd put yourself in danger." For the first time he felt some fellowship with the man.

She seemed surprised. "Perhaps he did. At least Thetis was famed as a good mother. Dipping Achilles into the River Styx to make him immortal. Of course she botched it, missing the heel she was holding him by."

Was she thinking of her own son, worrying that she'd not done enough to safeguard him?

"I believe the oracle said that if any part of her touched the water it would blacken and die."

"That shouldn't have weighed with her. Or she should have used a rope."

"But what if the rope dissolved? The gods never make things easy for humans."

" 'As flies to wanton boys are we to the gods,' " she quoted. " 'They kill us for their sport.' The Christian God is supposed to be more thoughtful and kind, yet Shakespeare was a Christian."

"Perhaps we all have times when we doubt the benevolence of God. As during any war." But then he grimaced. "This is too weighty a matter for a stormy night."

"Especially when I'm out of sorts because we've done a paltry day's work. Jack could be on his way tomorrow."

"But is not likely to be. Remember, he and Lord Caldfort have no reason to think there's urgency. Caldfort may not have told him yet. He may never tell him. Tomorrow the town will be busier. I'll go around and see what I can find out. And if necessary, we'll enlist the smugglers and invade."

He was rewarded with a smile, but then a powerful gust shook the whole house, making Laura look around anxiously. "It won't be so hard to play nervous Priscilla Penfold tonight. I love storms, but I have no taste for having a building blow down around me."

He wanted to take her into his arms, to comfort and protect her, but that would raise a different kind of storm. "Look on the bright side. If the walls come tumbling down, presumably we'll finally see Captain Dyer."

"At the gates of heaven."

She was truly anxious, and he might have gone to her, but with a knock the maid entered with wood for their fire.

Having built up the fire and filled the box with logs, she asked, "What will you like for your dinner, sir? We have a Flemish soup, and cock-a-leekie, and good fresh sole, poached or fried. There's the capon as was cooked with the leeks and a kidney pudding, and to follow, a ratafia dish and a bullace pie."

"Not the kidneys, please," Laura murmured, and he remembered that she'd always disliked them. He also thought he heard her stomach rumble. He could at least feed his lady.

He ordered the leek soup, fried sole, capon, and both pastries. She had a sweet tooth. "And Topham's best claret," he added, "with port and brandy to follow with cheese."

When the maid had left, he smiled at Laura. "I trust that will do."

She laughed. "You heard my stomach's demands. Perhaps a storm stimulates the appetite." She gave him a strange look and hurried on, "Shall we read *Guy Mannering* aloud? We can take turns."

"If you wish."

She went to her bedchamber to get the book.

An occupation that would bar any personal conversation, Stephen thought. That kiss had clearly alarmed her, though he thought he'd controlled himself heroically. If he'd managed any true heroics, she might be more impressed, but she was right; it had been a paltry day's work. He was at a loss how to better it without resorting to crude measures, such as breaking down a door. Under cover of the storm, perhaps?

Laura took a moment to collect herself. Stormy appetites, both for food and for a man. The wind rattled the building but it was the deep-throated roar of the sea that shook her, and the pounding beat of it that she felt from her feet up.

She remembered that time in Brighton. Hal had run out to her and swathed her in a cloak, berating her. But when they'd reached her bedchamber, their loving had been some of the best and fiercest ever. She almost felt it now, a fierce, pounding pleasure to the rhythm of the sea.

She swallowed, straightened, and returned to the parlor.

Stephen was sitting in one of the two chairs that bracketed the fireplace. She took the other.

*Like a married couple,* she thought, but again, she and Hal had rarely if ever spent quiet, domestic evenings. If Hal was sitting opposite her with nothing to do, he'd already have that look in his eye. . . .

She hastily opened the book and began to read, doing her best to slide away to Sir Walter Scott's Scotland. The plight of orphaned Lucy and the return of Guy Mannering from India seemed to meld with the storm, however, whispering of forbidden desire.

After a while, she passed the book to Stephen, hoping listening would be more calming, but she'd forgotten how well he read. He put on no airs and didn't try to act out the parts as if on the stage. He simply read the words, letting them spin out the story in her mind, though soon she was hearing him rather than the drama. Simply him.

The arrival of the meal was a relief, though Laura wasn't sure she could eat. As soon as they sat at the table, she realized that they needed a safe topic of conversation. Safe. Was anything safe tonight? Politics! A dry enough topic for a convent.

"Tell me about your adventures in Parliament."

"Adventures?" he said, serving her soup. "Hardly that."

"They must excite you at times."

"But they would bore you."

She halted her spoon between bowl and mouth. Moments ago she'd thought the subject dry, but she was hurt by that.

Perhaps he colored slightly. "Let's say that I don't know how to make amusing stories out of it."

He thought her nothing, a mindless *skylark*. "Why don't we talk about military reform?" she said briskly. "I know that many of our brave soldiers are now left in a sorry state."

"Yes, but that's a separate issue except in the matter of pensions. They are inadequate and often hard to obtain."

"Can't that be changed?"

"It's all tied in to the purchase system. . . ."

By the time they moved on to the main dishes, they were talking back and forth about issues of importance and Laura was no longer trying to prove a point. She was fascinated. When Stephen said, "We have to do something about the situation of children in factories and mines," she heard the *we* as acknowledgement that they were talking as equals.

Not lovers, and she was weak enough to feel a pang at that, but mental equals. "Factories are certainly terrible places."

"Yet industry is beneficial," he said, taking more meat. "It creates wealth and employment and leaves workers less dependent on the elements for survival. Consider this storm. Such a wanton act of nature ruins crops and blows away winter fodder."

She pushed aside her plate, frowning at him. "You think factories are better? People work such long hours and are often injured in the machinery. Even children."

"You are surprisingly well informed."

It was like a shock of cold water. "Surprisingly? Why do you persist in seeing me as having a head full of feathers? I beat you at chess, remember."

He suddenly smiled. "Yes. But can you claim to have been an eager consumer of information about social hardships and legislation back then?"

She wanted to, but it would be a lie. "I am truly interested now. Children not much older than Harry are put to work.

That cannot be right."

He nodded. "That's why we need legislation. We've brought in laws to control the cotton factories somewhat. They're the worst offenders. Little fingers, they say, are nimbler. But there are so many others. Pudding?"

Laura was not much interested in more food, but she took a little ratafia pudding as he served himself to bullace pie and thick cream.

She ate a spoonful, smiling at him. "So you're charging in there, lance lowered."

"I hope you're not seeing me as Don Quixote, tilting at windmills."

"Sir Galahad, at least." She abandoned the pudding. "So what other Grails do you pursue?"

"Nothing so insubstantial, I hope." He, too, put aside his plate. "Port? Brandy?"

"Port, please."

Laura accepted the glass of ruby red liquid, recognizing, with a deep beat of her heart, that he was about to speak of the things most important to him.

He poured himself brandy and cut a piece of Stilton cheese. "My prime interest," he said, "is legal reform. Did you know that there are hundreds of capital offenses on the books? It's a hanging matter to damage London Bridge, or to destroy any tree not one's own. A man was executed for that only two years ago."

She stared at him. "How is that possible?"

"Because it's the law. I gather he was a petty criminal of long standing, but the authorities hadn't managed to catch him. When they snagged him on this one, they used it as a means to get rid of him."

"Good lord. But is it wicked of me to see the temptation?"

He pulled a face at her. "Honest, as always."

"But I do see your point. It shouldn't be possible to use the law like that."

He nodded. "Bad and outmoded laws have to be swept from the books because they create opportunities for injustice, but there's more. They also lead to lack of respect. It's not overenforcement that's hurting us, but underenforcement. Most people don't want to see others hanged for trivial crimes, so juries let criminals off entirely."

She drank a little more port, feeling the rich wine weave dangerously into her already fevered mind. "What punishment would you ordain? Whipping?"

Even that sent a tingle through her,

though she'd never been interested in that vice.

"Barbarous," he said.

"Transportation? That seems as barbarous to me."

"But you have a good life here, Laura, with friends and a loving family. Many criminals have nothing to hold them and a taste for adventure. That makes the threat of transportation a weak deterrent. In fact," he added with a wry smile, "the army in India has a problem with men deliberately getting into trouble hoping for free transport to Australia."

Laura chuckled, aware that politics wasn't an antidote to arousal at all. In fact, this talk had stimulated her in a new and deeper way. Stephen was a Galahad, a hero, and his clarity and purpose built a hunger in her, a hunger to have him — brilliant mind, generous heart, and virile, handsome body — for her own.

She recognized what had turned sour in her marriage, what had made even passion unsatisfying in the end. Hal's idle, self- indulgent life had drained her respect.

Though her mouth was dry, she had to say something. "So, what do you suggest?"

He sipped his brandy, his eyes on hers,

shadowed in the candlelight as if he was wondering what she was thinking. She hoped he didn't know.

"Criminals must be deprived of liberty and idleness."

"In prisons? They are rife with sin and scandal."

"Reformed prisons, where they're kept in separate cells and obliged to work. Meaningful work, too, not tow picking or the treadwheel."

She rested her elbow on the table and her chin on her hand. "It's a shame to have to confine people at all. Can we not rid the world of crime? So much of it arises out of poverty and unemployment. We see that now. Hard times have pushed even respectable people to vagrancy and theft."

"Thus," he said, with a warning glint of triumph, "we need industry and prosperity. Give a man hope of a better future for himself and his family and he won't risk it through crime. Give him property and he will support the laws that protect property."

She relaxed back, laughing. "I should have known you'd win a debate in the end."

The low candles showed how long they'd talked. They'd never rung for the dishes to be cleared, but Stephen had risen a couple of times to build up the fire. It seemed to her to have been the most perfect evening of her life.

"This has been wonderful," she said.

"Talk about Parliamentary committees and social reform?"

"Talk about something important. I don't know when I've last done that."

"When you were in London, did you not take part in some of the more serious female salons?"

She felt her cheeks color and laughed to cover it. "Heavens, no. There were too many other things to do. Oh, dear." She seized on her abandoned port and sipped. "That sounds as if I only discussed serious matters here out of boredom. I assure you that isn't true."

"I never thought that."

She put aside her port again, needing him to understand. "What I mean, Stephen, is that I was not serious-minded then. I *was* Lady Skylark. For me, the term *haute volée* was appropriate. I loved flying high. But we all change, and now my interests and occupations are different."

"You now prefer the quiet of the country?"

She grimaced. "Are you deliberately

misunderstanding me? It was the tedium of the country that stirred an interest in politics and the issues of the day." She shook her head, seeking honesty because suddenly honesty was all-important.

"Why do we grow as we do, change as we do? If I had not had Harry, if Hal had not died, perhaps I would have continued on course to be a fashionable matron all my life. A patroness of Almack's, even, believing that who is let in and who is excluded is important. I was not unhappy before. You know I have never been as serious-minded as you."

"Yet you've just held your own in a challenging discussion." He rose and rang the bell. "Do you want tea or coffee now?"

She stared at him, shocked by his indifferent tone. She'd thought they were sharing thoughts and ideals, coming together on a deeply intimate level, but clearly he'd just been passing the time.

"Tea," she managed.

Two maids came to clean away the dishes, and soon Jean returned with the tea tray. Stephen asked her for a chess set.

"Chess?" Laura queried, wondering if she could reasonably plead tiredness and escape to her bed. It was only minutes past eight.

"Cards being inappropriate on a Sunday, don't you know."

"I don't remember you observing that extreme propriety before. I think you want a game at which you think you can beat me."

"Can I?"

"Almost certainly. I haven't played in years." She remembered the last game, and after a moment, spoke of it. "The last person I played was you."

"In that case, the last time you played, you won."

Jean returned with the set, and Stephen moved a small table between the fireside chairs. Seared by frustration, Laura set to work to beat Stephen again, but this time she was completely outmastered.

When the game was over, she could escape, ragged by the lashings of the storm and the snarl of the hungry sea, but above all by needs and hungers she'd never expected to feel for Stephen. It was more than physical. Tonight she'd become aware that she might after all enjoy a life of quiet dinners and political discussions by the fireside, but Stephen showed no sign of feeling the same way.

Was it just her ugly appearance? She

peeled off her disguise and studied Labellelle in the mirror. Would Stephen want her again when she was beautiful? Would she want him on those terms?

She crawled into bed, still tormented by the storm that seemed to rattle the beams of the old building, and by her pillowcase, which whispered to her of the last head to lie on it — Stephen's.

No amount of calculations seemed to help, and she prayed that tomorrow they could solve the mystery of HG and escape the tortures of this jagged intimacy.

# Chapter 31

Laura rose the next morning feeling she would hardly need her disguise to look haggard. Her mirror showed her familiar face, however, except for the ugly, glued-on mole. She traced brow, nose, and lips with one finger, wondering what beauty was and what the lack of it did.

Would Stephen have talked with her about political matters if she'd been Labellelle? Even faced with sallow skin and faded curls, however, he'd thought the matters that enthralled him would bore her.

He'd kissed her in the dark the first night.

He'd kissed her again when he could see the Penfold plainness, but only after their playacting as Valancourt and Emily. She was used to more from men and she didn't know this abode.

The inn clock struck, and she counted

nine. Though she hated to do it, it was time to restore her ugliness before Jean came knocking with her water. She applied the cream and darkened around her eyes. The mole was still so firmly fixed that she was beginning to think it would be permanent, as her mother had always told them sour faces would become.

It occurred to her that it was quiet outside, and she peeped around the edge of the curtain. The sky was heavy with clouds and the sea still rippled with rough waves, but the storm had passed. Seaweed and wood littered the beach where there'd been none before, and down near the church a boat lay on its side, tossed up by the storm. She hoped no one had been aboard at the time.

It was relatively calm, however, and it was Monday. As Stephen had said, shops would be open and people about their business. Today they should be able to sort out the mystery, and if not, there was always armed force. She was in a fit state for leading the invasion herself.

She put on her wig, replaced her nightcap, then rang the bell.

Jean came promptly with the hot water. "Such a night of it, ma'am! Roof tore right off Farmer Tully's barn."

"I thought there was no danger."

"Not here, ma'am, but Joss Tully, he's a lazy man as doesn't keep his property as he should."

"I saw a boat up on the beach."

"Aye, the *Cormorant*. Broke its moorings, but it's not too badly off. Anything else, ma'am?"

"Has Sir Stephen breakfasted?"

"Not long ago, ma'am."

"Then bring my coffee and bread, please. And I'll have boiled eggs, as well, today."

"That's the spirit, ma'am! I told you as how the air here'd soon have you as right as a trivet."

When the door closed, Laura smiled. It seemed the whole town fancied itself a doctor. She dressed quickly and joined Stephen, finding him frowning at the letter from Farouk as he sipped his coffee. She sat and shared her thought about Dyer and *die*.

"Intriguing," he said with a quick, careless smile at her. "Wordplays?" He looked back at the letter. "But what does that give us for Oscar Ris? *Riz* is rice in French."

"And *ris* is part of the verb to laugh. This is all a joke?" she asked.

"In Latin, *os* means mouth. They have come to eat us all?"

His eyes were twinkling and she returned it. "The scarred mouth is eating rice?"

They laughed together, and Laura was suddenly certain that she would love to take breakfast with Stephen for the rest of her life. But that was for later, she sternly told herself. When they were safely away from here.

She took a boiled egg and a slice of toast. "You plan to wander the vast metropolis and ask questions? What am I to do?"

"As you imply, it won't take me long to squeeze Draycombe dry. You could keep watch in case any opportunity arises to see Dyer."

"Unless I walk along the outside wall like a spider to peer in the window, I doubt I'll achieve that. I think I'll station myself downstairs again with my pictures."

He rose. "Very well."

She buttered her toast. "Did you mean what you said about calling on Kerslake's men to force an entry?"

He hesitated for a moment, looking at her. "I'd prefer that to be our last resort. How long can you stay here?"

Something made her want to say *as long as you wish*, but she said, "I think I should return to Redoaks, at least, tomorrow, then return to Merrymead. To stay away longer would appear very strange, and Harry will be missing me."

She certainly hoped he was. She didn't wish him unhappy, but surely he must be missing her. "We've rarely been apart," she added, "and not at all since Hal's death."

He nodded. "Let's see what the morning brings and then make our plans."

He left, and she carried her slice of toast to the window to watch him stride away. The wind was still brisk and he had to hold on to his hat like all the other men. Women's hats with ribbons were much more practical, perhaps because the women often had baskets and children to manage. They needed both their hands.

A group of small children played on the beach, hunting among the mess left by the storm. Harry would like it here. He'd never been to the sea. An ache told her how much she was missing him.

She could write him another letter. Send him a picture of the effects of the storm. She turned to do that, but realized it was impossible. She wasn't supposed to be here. She was supposed to be at Redoaks, inland.

Tears threatened, and some of them were from shame.

She wasn't ashamed of being here trying to solve the mystery of HG. She wasn't even ashamed of her passions, as long as she didn't succumb to them. But she hated to lie to her son.

She shook herself, put her half-eaten bread back on her plate, and went to get her drawing materials. She had little hope of recognition now, but what else was there to do?

A good part of the morning passed as she'd expected, with only Dr. Nesbitt joining her in the parlor. In conversation she learned that he was a single man and liked to stop at the inn for an occasional cup of tea as a break from his house. He admired her drawings again, but his only reaction to the picture of the older Cousin Henry was to remark how fortunate the gentleman had been to recover from what had clearly been a crisis.

Laura decided to modify the picture a little and try to make Henry a little less ill.

She was startled out of her work by that sixth sense that tells us that someone is staring at us. She looked up to see Farouk just outside the parlor door. Shockingly aware of the younger picture lying on the small table, Laura tried to give him a cold, forbidding look.

Perhaps it worked, for he turned away. A moment later, she saw him striding down the street. Why had he stopped like that? Had her attempt to enter the rooms yesterday raised his suspicions?

Was she in danger? If Farouk was the villain he appeared, he might not hesitate to dispose of a meddlesome woman. When she saw Stephen approaching the inn, delight surged into her for many reasons. She gathered her papers and hurried up to their parlor. She had only put her portfolio away when he entered, carrying a small brown box and looking very pleased with himself.

"What is that?" she asked.

"A present," he said, but she recognized a tease, so she wasn't surprised when he added, "But you'll have to wait."

Because he clearly expected her to be impatient, she merely said, "Very well," and sought a completely different topic of conversation. Ah, yes.

He'd gone into his bedchamber to discard his outer clothing, but left the door open.

"Yesterday, Mrs. Grantleigh and I were clucking over the fact that Captain Dyer didn't attend church, perhaps prevented by his wicked heathen servant, and I suggested that someone should tell the vicar. Farouk can hardly bar him at the door."

He emerged smiling. "Very good! As is your patience." He gave her the box. "Not precisely a present, though I hope you'll be pleased with it."

Laura opened the box and stared at the object inside. It looked like a metal cup with a long spout, but the spout came out of the bottom.

She picked it up and peered into the cup part. She could see out through the small hole at the end of the spout, but she looked at him in puzzlement. "A different way of spying? Do we apply it to the keyhole?"

"An interesting idea, but no. Though you're close, in a way. The other way around."

She put the end of the tube to her eye and looked at him. "I'm not impressed."

"Put it to your ear. It's an Auricular Enhancer."

"That sounds risqué!"

His eyes sparkled. "Only if I whisper improper suggestions down it. If you were hard of hearing, you could hold the spout to your ear, and when I speak into the wide end, my voice would be, by some magic of science that I didn't entirely understand, loud enough for you to understand me."

"Stephen, how brilliant! Where did you find it?"

"Remember the apothecary shop with a selection of helpful devices for the sick and elderly? I was hoping for information about something bought by Farouk for Dyer, but no. By then, I had been trapped into a guided tour of his wares. He's admirably enthusiastic. The Auricular Enhancer is his latest delight. I purchased it . . ."

"Not for me, I hope. I can't be both nosy and deaf."

". . . for my grandmother."

"If you mean the Dowager Lady Ball, she wasn't deaf last time I met her."

"Don't be distracted by details." He gestured toward his room. "Shall we try it out?"

"Yes!" But then she pulled a face. "Farouk's out, so there'll be no conversation."

"Blast. You're right. Let's try it, anyway. I'll go into my bedchamber, shut the door, and orate. You listen at the wall."

He left, and by the time she had the wide end pressed to the wall, he was already into some poem.

*"Last noon beheld them full of lusty life,*
*Last eve in beauty's circle proudly gay;"*

359

It was Lord Byron's passage about the Battle of Waterloo from the latest part of his ongoing work *Childe Harold's Pilgrimage*.

> "*The midnight brought the signal-sound of*
>   strife,
> *The morn the marshalling in arms, the day*
> *Battle's magnificently stern array!*
> *The thunder-clouds pour o'er it, which*
>   when rent,
> *The earth is covered thick with other clay,*
> *Which her own clay shall cover, heaped*
>   and pent,
> *Rider and horse — friend, foe — in one red*
>   burial blent.*"

She stayed there a moment, remembering men she'd known who'd fallen in that terrible victory, then pushed straight as he returned to the parlor.

"You lost friends, too?" she asked.

"Everyone did. But one, at least, returned from the grave."

"Lord Darius."

"Yes. It worked?"

She shook off the solemn mood. "Excellently, though I think you were in orator mode. I don't know how clear an ordinary conversation would be. What a shame Farouk is out."

"We have only to wait for his return. Then we might finally discover what they're up to."

She sat and smiled at him. "I always knew you were brilliant."

He bowed. "Thank you, fair lady. Now, I intend to seek some reward in lunch." He pulled the bell.

"I'm hardly fair at the moment."

"Fair at heart."

It was an admirable sentiment, but it didn't satisfy her.

"Did you learn anything in town?" she asked.

"Everyone's aware of Farouk, of course. It's not wise of him to be so noticeable, but I've not come up with a cunning purpose for it. I suspect he simply doesn't understand the effect he has in a small English town."

"The vicar was concerned enough to mention it in his sermon."

"Let's hope it did some good. We don't want our business complicated by a riot."

"It might give us a glimpse of Dyer."

He smiled in acknowledgement. "Farouk's movements are noted, but all he seems to do is go for long walks. The only purchases I could uncover were a chess set, a pack of cards, and, believe it or not, a copy of Byron's *The Corsair*."

"Good heavens! Checking it for accuracy about the Arab world?"

Stephen shrugged, and Jean arrived then to take their order for lunch.

"And your morning?" he asked, when the maid had gone.

"Virtually nothing, though Farouk did stop and stare. My heart was in my mouth in case he came in and saw the pictures. But then," she added, "he probably wouldn't recognize them, either."

He gave her a commiserating smile. "Don't lose hope."

"I want so desperately for Dyer to be Cousin Henry. It means everything!"

"There are other ways to keep Harry safe, Laura. You can't think I would let anything happen to him."

She held out a hand and he took it. "I don't, but . . . A child cannot be kept safe, Stephen, as long as someone wants him dead. Wants it badly enough."

When he didn't argue, she knew that he saw that, too.

Their lunch arrived then, but Stephen waited by the window as the maid spread it on the table.

As soon as she left, he announced, "Here he comes."

Ignoring food, they both ran into his bedchamber. He gave her the instrument and she smiled her gratitude for his letting her go first. She pressed the wide end to the wall and put the small end in her ear, waiting for Farouk to arrive.

Stephen was over by the corridor door. "He's coming. I hear the squeaks."

"It works," she whispered. "I heard the door open and shut."

*Say something,* she thought, concentrating fiercely. *Say something that makes it clear that Captain Dyer is Henry Gardeyne.*

Then she heard another click.

She moved back from the wall. "I don't believe it. After all this, Dyer must be in the bedroom, and Farouk's gone in there."

Stephen came to take the instrument and try, but then he shook his head. "Infuriating, but they can't stay there forever. Let's eat."

"What if Captain Dyer's taken ill and is confined to bed?"

"Then we sneak into the empty room farther down the corridor."

"Of course!"

She moved toward the door, but he stopped her. "Not yet. Give them a little time, and have your lunch."

Laura had a strong urge to act like the

363

tempestuous girl she had once been, but he made sense. Sense would be easier all around if she wasn't in his bedchamber, so she went to the parlor and settled to bread and sliced ham.

Both of them, however, ate little and quickly, then Stephen rose. "I'll take first turn at the listening post."

It would be madness, besides being pointless, to crowd against him there, so she paced the parlor helplessly.

"Laura."

She started and whirled to find him at the door. "They're there." He held out the listening device.

"You're a saint!" she exclaimed as she seized it, and unthinking, she kissed him quickly on the cheek. She was halfway to the wall before she realized what she'd done. She carried on, anyway. What was there to say?

She pressed the device to the wall and applied her ear to the spout. "I can hear them!"

He came close, though not, she noticed, too close. "What are they saying?"

"They're not orating. Hush."

She and Stephen were both whispering, even though the men next door could not possibly hear what they said.

"Nine?" she guessed. "Or mine? There's so much silence."

"Only natural." He did come closer then to speak in her ear. "It's unlikely, anyway, that they'll neatly lay out their history and their plans for us. They must both know them well."

She swallowed against the effect of his voice and his breath, almost on her skin. "Except that if Dyer is Henry, he doesn't know Farouk wants to slit his throat for money."

She made herself be noble and passed the device to him. As they exchanged places, their bodies brushed together for a brief moment. He seemed not to notice.

"Anything?" she asked.

"A rattle."

"A *death* rattle?"

He grinned. "Of course not. Like dice. No, chess. He bought a set, remember. Farouk has given Dyer his choice of colors, and he has chosen white. Conversation has ceased. . . ."

Laura allowed the situation to give her permission to lean against him, one hand on his shoulder. He was so beautiful in his concentration, his features still as a classical statue, perfectly made.

In London his hair had always been

carefully arranged. Now it was windblown, and not in the elaborate artificial manner of that fashionable style. She longed to comb it with her fingers, to brush a wave from his temple.

To run her hands through his hair.

To cradle his face.

To kiss. To kiss with all the passion burning inside her.

Stephen kept his eyes closed, as if that might aid hearing, but in truth he could not let Laura glimpse his emotions. A moment ago, she'd even leant against him, her whole body brushing down his side, her hand resting lightly upon his shoulder.

Through shirt and jacket, he shouldn't have been able to even feel that light hand, but it had burned. She'd moved now. Inches, at least, separated them and the world was colder. The temptation to turn and drag her into his arms almost broke him.

He moved away from the wall, put the Auricular Enhancer on the chest of drawers, and gestured her back into the parlor.

"I don't think they're likely to say much at the moment," he said. "They have all the feel of long familiars, with no need to talk. I confess to disappointment. Despite what I said before, I did hope they would immediately reveal something to make the situation clear."

"We have to keep listening."

"I suppose so." He couldn't bear it. "Perhaps I should put your plan into action, as well." When she looked puzzled, he added, "A visit to the vicar."

"Oh. It seemed so clever at the time, but is it necessary now?"

It was necessary to escape again. At this rate, he would be rushing out every half hour.

"Do you mind keeping vigil for a while?" he asked.

"No, of course not. Dividing our forces."

"Right." He grabbed his hat and gloves. "But remember, no matter what you hear, don't do anything rash."

"Stephen."

He turned at the door, alerted by her tone. Her severe tone.

"Stephen, I'm not a girl anymore. I know that sometimes these past days I've acted it, but it was . . . a sliding into what we were, I suppose. No more than a game." After a moment, she added, "I don't want you to treat me like a girl."

What did that mean?

"I'm sorry if I have offended you," he said.

"Of course not. We're friends beyond trivial offense."

*Friends.*

"I'm merely pointing out that I must do what I think best. I'm a woman full grown, which I believe to be in all practical ways the equal of a man."

"You denied being a bluestocking. You didn't tell me you were a radical."

"I'm not sure I was aware of it myself. But here I am, shaping my fate and my son's, and unwilling to give that over to anyone else. Even you."

He had never expected this. Never expected to discover in Laura a woman like this. He hadn't thought he could love her more, but it threatened to shatter him.

He felt he should say something eloquent, but he simply escaped.

# Chapter 32

Laura bit her lip. She'd probably just destroyed any hope of happiness with Stephen, but without warning she'd come to a point of truth, a point of choice. She'd recognized herself for the first time and had to speak. And she had meant every word.

She felt as if the world had changed, but of course, it hadn't. Nothing had except her. It was as if she was settling into a new home and must make it comfortable. Whether Stephen was part of it remained to be seen. They would get nowhere useful in this hothouse of emotions, however. They needed to solve the mystery and return to normal life — ideally a life where Harry was no longer heir to Caldfort.

She headed for Stephen's room, but then thought of something. She found paper and pencil to record what was said, then went to the wall.

She paused at the end of his bed, but

more in thoughtful contemplation than in rash passion. She knew now what she was, and she knew what she wanted. As a woman full grown and responsible for her actions, she must be careful.

She put a chair by the wall, grateful that it fit in the space, then settled herself as comfortably as possible. The irritating men still said nothing except for the casual comments on the game.

She began to record the conversation anyway, though it was awkward with one hand required for the listening device. She hoped she could decipher her scribbles later.

*Dyer: Check!*
*Farouk: I should have seen that.*

Thank heavens the two voices were distinctive. Farouk's was deeper and stronger, not in volume but in character. HG's was higher and less certain. Did that fit Henry Gardeyne?

Silence settled, so she marked it with a line. She wished there was a clock here. She would note the time and length of the silences. Pointless, but it would feel as if she were doing something.

*Dyer: You devil!*

Said admiringly, warmly. If Dyer was Henry Gardeyne, he had no suspicion that his head was on the block.

She didn't like calling him Dyer. She wanted him to be Henry Gardeyne, key to Harry's safety, but she compromised on HG, who according to the letter had sailed on the *Mary Woodside* and been the guest of Oscar Ris.

*Scarred mouth rice,* she thought with a twist of the lips. She feared she was clinging to cobwebs. What could explain Cousin Henry staying away for ten years?

*Do you sometimes miss it?*

Laura started out of her thoughts. Miss what? She grabbed the pencil and tried to nudge her paper straight. That had been HG.

*F: Strangely, I do, but freedom is better.*

*Freedom!* Laura felt as if her heart was bruised. They had been *convicts?*

*HG: Yes, but I miss the sun.*
*F: I believe the sun does shine in England.*
*HG: Laughs. I think I remember* that. Faintly.

Sun. New South Wales, the penal colony,

had a hot climate, didn't it?

The men settled back to their game and Laura ignored their occasional comments. She was reading over those few, hope- destroying words.

HG had lived in England once, but was now more used to a hot climate, which was linked with imprisonment. It seemed that they'd been imprisoned together. She'd thought only British people were sent to New South Wales, but perhaps they had only to break British law.

She realized something then. Farouk had spoken perfect English, not accented at all. He must have been educated under British rule, probably in India, and Stephen had mentioned men in the Indian army committing crimes in order to be sent to New South Wales.

She pressed her hand to her head. It seemed horribly clear that the two men next door were criminals intent on extortion, but how did this link at all to Henry Gardeyne? He could not have ended up a convict, and he'd been nowhere near India!

She stilled, listening. Had that been a clink in the parlor? Their parlor!

She rose in shock. Had Farouk somehow realized what she was doing and crept around to attack? And — stupid! — she'd

372

left her pistol in her bedchamber.

She put down the hearing device and crept, heart hammering, to the door. Eased it open . . .

To find only Jean, filling the log bin. The maid saw her, however, and her eyes went wide.

Oh, Lord! Here she was, emerging from her male cousin's bedchamber.

"Sir Stephen is out," she said, fluttering. "I . . . I saw a tear in his handkerchief and thought I would repair it while he was gone."

The maid didn't look impressed, but she didn't seem much interested, either. She probably assumed that nosy Mrs. Penfold had been poking around in her cousin's belongings.

Merely to stay in character, Laura asked, "Do you take wood to Captain Dyer?"

"No, ma'am. That Farouk collects it himself, which is a blessing, for they use a lot."

"Because they come from a hot climate, I assume."

"Nothing wrong with a bit of brisk English weather. As I hear it, those hot places breed diseases."

"It seems they do."

"And it's wrong that the captain stays in

his stuffy room all the time, ma'am. Sea air is *good* for you. Everyone says so. I hope their letter comes soon."

"Letter?" Laura inquired, merely to keep the conversation going.

"Captain Dyer expects a letter, ma'am. Farouk asks about it every day. Says he's to be told as soon as it arrives."

"From family, I suppose." From Caldfort, in fact. It was good to have confirmation that Lord Caldfort had not yet responded, though if Dyer and Farouk were the villains they appeared to be, she was inclined to let Jack murder them!

The maid shrugged, indicating ignorance. "Likely they're awaiting news before traveling on. Always wise, that, ma'am. My auntie went all the way to Nottingham to visit her sister, and when she arrived her sister'd gone off to Wales!"

"What a confusion. Yes, very wise to wait."

The maid left and Laura returned to her listening post, praying to have her earlier conclusions proved wrong. She caught Farouk saying a clear, "Yes."

She hissed with annoyance. If only she'd heard the question. But they were talking again. She grabbed her paper.

*HG: I'm so tired of this, Fellow.*

*Fellow?* It sounded like a name. She put a question mark against it. Perhaps she'd heard it wrong.

*F: Not much longer.*
*HG: Then Paris?*
*F: It's no warmer there, you know.*
*HG: Greece, then, or Italy. Do you want to stay here? You said it was too danger-ous.*
*F: Yes, you're right, Des. South Carolina, perhaps. Or even Florida. I hear the Spanish are welcoming.*
*HG: Farther away from British influ-ence?*

Voices dropped and she couldn't catch words.

*Des?* Laura underlined that. Desmond? An Irish name? She didn't think HG had an Irish accent. Despard, Desford, Desalles. Certainly not short for Henry or Gardeyne. It was like the last nail in a coffin, especially with that mention of wanting to be away from British influ-ence. She hadn't thought convicts es-caped from New South Wales, but anything was possible.

*HG: I'm frightened, Fellow. This isn't*

*going to work.*

*F: It will,* nuranee. *Trust me.*

*Nuranee.* An Arabic term — or what language did they speak in Egypt? She couldn't care. These men were clearly not what she had hoped. She made herself read the words as the conversation of two petty criminals intent on a swindle. They fit all too well. Get some money from Lord Caldfort — though HG was afraid the plan wouldn't work — and then flee the country because it would be too dangerous to stay.

She tried to make the conversation fit HG being Henry, but shook her head. Close to tears, she put aside the paper. Whatever these men were up to, Henry Gardeyne was long dead and so Harry's destiny would not change. If she didn't do something, her son would soon be dead, too!

She rose, hands gripped together. She'd do *anything,* but she couldn't imagine what. She knew Stephen would help, but as she'd said, all his intelligence, influence, and legal knowledge couldn't keep a small child safe.

He would bring the Rogues with him. Her brief time with Nicholas Delaney told her that he would support her cause, but there were stronger forces. Lord Arden, heir to a dukedom, and some other titled gentleman.

Even they couldn't help, however, as long as Harry was in Jack's power.

She drew in a breath.

She had to remove Harry from Jack's power, and the only way to do that was by marriage, marriage to a man powerful enough to override Lord Caldfort's will, whether it be his purpose now or his testament when he was dead. Why hadn't she seen it before? The right stepfather for Harry was his best protection, and now she understood Stephen's reputation, the choice was clear.

How could Lord Caldfort argue that Harry would learn less by living with Stephen than by living at Caldfort? And when Lord Caldfort died, Stephen would know how to work with Harry's trustees to remove Jack from the local living. Find him a better one, but far, far away. In the north, near Emma's family. She deserved some blessings.

Then Harry would be able to visit his property without much danger. It wasn't a perfect solution, but it might work especially with the Rogues brought into play. Surely Jack would understand that once

Harry was surrounded by powerful protectors Jack would never survive murder.

All she had to do was marry Stephen.

She stirred and fidgeted about his bedroom, trembling with hopes and doubts. Once, so recently, she'd thought marriage impossible. Now it looked like a necessity, but it was also wrong — wrong to be planning to snare a man whether he wanted to wed her or not.

She could seduce him. She knew she could, and she knew that once he'd compromised her, Stephen would feel honor bound to offer her marriage. It would be easy. Whatever he felt for her, he was not immune to lust.

But she still wasn't sure that she could make a good wife for him. She wanted to. She would try. But trying was not always enough.

She'd enjoyed a political discussion with him, but she knew herself. Lady Skylark still fluttered inside her, longing to be free. She wouldn't be happy in a cage of propriety, but could he cope with her soaring flights? She thought of another political man, William Lamb, constantly embarrassed by his half-mad wife, Caroline. She wouldn't be as bad as that, but she might be a burden to Stephen. When he'd christened her Skylark, he had not meant it to be complimentary.

She considered their brief time here. At times he'd seemed loverlike, but at others only the old friend. Occasionally he'd been distant and even disapproving. She'd been hoping to explore this more when they left, to find the truth of what lay between them, but with Harry's life at stake, she could not allow Stephen any chance to escape.

She'd never had to hunt a man, and she'd never had to seduce one except in play with Hal. It was the last thing she wanted to do, especially with Stephen, because . . .

Because he was a friend, and friendship required trust. She'd come here without a thought that she might be putting herself at risk because she and Stephen were friends. She didn't think men worried about being seduced or raped, but perhaps they should.

She leaned against a bedpost and considered Stephen's bed in an entirely new way.

# Chapter 33

Laura returned to the parlor and closed the door temporarily on temptation. Now that she accepted that Henry Gardeyne was dead, she saw no point in further listening at the wall. She tried to distract herself with *Guy Mannering*, but such dramas lacked weight now. When a letter arrived from Kerslake, she didn't open it. It was addressed to Stephen, but she might have read it if she thought it carried news of importance.

She put wood on the fire from time to time, and as the light faded, lit two candles, wandering constantly from window to fireplace, trying to avoid her thoughts. Night was approaching, however, the classic time for lusty wickedness.

Stephen came in. "I'm sorry for being gone so long. Reverend Lawgood wanted to talk about the Speenhamland system." But then he asked, "What's the matter?"

Was her mood so obvious? She hoped

her thoughts and plans weren't.

At the very sight of him, she'd jolted inside. She wasn't sure if it was from guilt, lust, or both, but it shook her. She did lust, but that made her plan more wicked rather than less. She'd rather be planning a noble sacrifice to a man she did not want.

She found a slight smile and gestured to her notes on the table. "They talked somewhat. It's clear they're in this together, and both have been convicts, probably in New South Wales. Dyer can't be Henry Gardeyne."

She watched him read, praying even now that he'd find some other interpretation. But he looked soberly at her. "It does sound like that. I'm sorry, Laura." He came over and took her hand. "Don't be afraid. We can find other ways to keep Harry safe."

She knew he wasn't referring to her plan, but it felt as if he was reading her mind. "Yes, I know."

*Tonight? It might be my last night here. What excuse do I have to stay?*

She gently pulled her hands free and tried for a light tone. "I do hope that one day I will know the whole story, though. It's exasperating. Why have that unlikely pair come up with this plot? And why, as

Nicholas Delaney asked, *now?*"

"And who the devil is Oscar Ris? That really niggles at me. My impression is that nothing in that letter is meaningless."

"It doesn't relate to convicts or the antipodes?"

"Not in any way I can see, and I've studied the matter a great deal in my investigation of the legal system. Oh, to the antipodes with the lot of them. The wind's dropped. Let's go out and watch the sunset before dinner. Without a telescope. For nothing but pleasure."

It delighted her as she'd not expected to be delighted here, and perhaps she could encourage a proposal rather than forcing it. A glance in the mirror as she put on her bonnet gave her great doubts. Seduction would have to be for the night, when she was Labellelle.

It was lovely to be out, however, breathing in the fresh briny air as they walked down the beach admiring the last of a sunset that was fiery instead of gray. A sunset that turned the rippling waves bloodred.

Laura closed her eyes to that and inhaled. "Perhaps the sea air is healing."

"Now the storm's passed."

She turned to look at him. "Benign and

destructive. Two sides of the same thing."
*Like love, and desire, and two writhing bodies
in a bed.* She tried to read his every look
and word, seeking the truth of his desires — and his points of vulnerability. He
was a mystery to her, but moment by moment, she wanted him more.

They strolled on, just out of reach of
the sea's eternal lick. Like a bloodred
lover lapping at skin or at hot, secret
places. She swallowed, trying to control
the ripple of sensual awareness, but
feeling the rumble of the sea up through
her shoes, up, up . . .

Their only contact was linked arms, the
only permissible contact between a sickly
woman and her escort. She longed to turn
into his arms, to imitate the sea by kissing,
licking, and it was nothing to do with ma-
ternal purpose. . . .

"We'd best turn back," he said, doing so,
speaking as if they were only invalid and
escort.

The sun's last fire was fading, darkening
the sky and stealing passion from the sea,
but that did nothing to the way she felt. He
didn't share her desires, however. That was
obvious.

"What will you do when your mourning
is over?" he asked.

She was expected to make practical conversation? "I expected to live on at Caldfort."

"Keeping Harry safe will be easier if you live elsewhere."

"I know that." She heard her own snappish tone. "It will not be allowed."

Could she put the situation to him honestly and make a marriage of convenience? If he refused, however, it would alert him.

"Influence can be brought to bear. So, where would you choose?"

She let a silence linger, hoping he might make a suggestion, a proposal. Then she said, "At Merrymead, I suppose."

"Not London?"

"My jointure is generous, but it won't stretch to *ton* life, and Lady Skylark can't subsist on the fringes."

"You could live with Juliet until you marry again."

He was discussing it as if it were a dry matter of law.

"So I could," she said tartly. "Once I can leave Caldfort, finding a husband should be no problem at all."

*No problem at all.*

As they climbed the shallow slope up to the road, Stephen wanted to smash something or force a kiss on her, wanted to fall to his knee and beg her to marry him, him! But she wasn't following any of his leads and he didn't want to press the matter now. Not now, not here, where she had entrusted herself to him. Not when she had no easy escape if his proposal was once again an embarrassment.

Not when she might have said that she no longer cared for life in London, where his work required him to live for most of the year.

"I probably would like to live in London again," she said, making him wonder if he'd spoken his thought aloud. "If I had Harry with me and a fashionable establishment."

He couldn't give her the pinnacle of society or a peerage title, but he could manage fashionable.

Before he could put together the right response, she continued. "As for marriage, I take the matter of providing the perfect stepfather for Harry very seriously."

"And who would that be, the perfect stepfather?"

She glanced at him, but in the gathering gloom even the light from the windows of the inn couldn't reveal her expression. "Someone with enough power to overrule

Lord Caldfort, of course, and stave off any threat from Jack. Someone able to fight for Harry's welfare, but also able to love him, to be a true father. And," she added, sounding strangely rebellious, "someone with enough money to support Lady Skylark's new flight. If I go to London, it can only be to fly."

He didn't understand her tone and it unnerved him. Had she guessed his feelings and was trying to warn him away from repeated folly?

"Only a fool would want to cage a skylark," he said, and opened the inn door for her.

A few moments later, Laura swept into her room and clenched her fists. Stephen had turned cold as the sea at the mention of Lady Skylark. Why, oh, why, had she been driven to honesty? Why hadn't he taken her hints about marriage?

She felt torn into warring pieces. She was Harry's mother, who needed Sir Stephen Ball as a weapon, primed and loaded. She was Stephen's friend, who'd chase off another woman who wanted to use him as she did. She was a wicked woman who desired him — honor and sense be damned.

And tonight she must decide, and act.

# Chapter 34

She composed herself, straightened her wig, and returned to the parlor to find Stephen at the table, scribbling on a piece of paper. It reminded her of so many times in their youth that a wash of pure warmth soothed her.

She smiled and went to look over his shoulder. He had the copy of Farouk's letter open, but was writing on another piece of paper. "What are you doing?"

"Hunting for a meaning," he said tensely, pencil circling the name Oscar Ris. "The mouth of Carris. Or perhaps in distorted Latin, the mouth of love?"

"HG has been in thrall to the mouth of love?" As soon as Laura said it, a lewd image filled her mind. Quickly she added, "Backward it's Sir Racso."

He flashed her a grin. "That sounds like the villain in a farce. With a few more letters we could be looking for Scarred Boris."

She sat beside him, suddenly surprisingly happy for this lighthearted moment. "Rascal? I like rascal."

"You're missing an *a* and an *l*," he pointed out. "Osiris? An Egyptian connection."

"You're missing an *i*."

"It has to mean something," he muttered, tossing down his pencil. "I can't help thinking that it's key to everything."

Laura picked up the pencil and wrote herself. *Sir Acros. Sir Scora. Sirra Soc.*

He burst out laughing. "Sirra Soc? A buffoon in a pantomime."

"Definitely . . ." But then the letters rearranged themselves. "Stephen!" She gripped his hand. "It *is* an anagram! It's *corsairs!*"

Hope blossomed. "That explains the ten years! It explains why *now*. It explains freedom. It explains everything! Ever since the *Mary Woodside* went down, Henry Gardeyne has been a slave on the Barbary Coast, one of the ones recently freed from Algiers by the navy!"

He stared at the paper. "Good God, and look. Egan Dyer is an anagram of Gardeyne." He turned to frown at her. "But there were hardly any Britons among those slaves. And an aristocrat? He'd have been ransomed years ago. The corsairs always took ransoms if they could."

"But it has to be. It can't be coincidence."

"It must at least be the story behind it. The one supposed to trick Lord Caldfort."

She instantly saw what he meant but didn't want to think it could be true. "You're being sensible again," she complained. "It is possible, I grant, but it's equally possible that Henry Gardeyne's been a slave, isn't it? After all, why would Dyer — or whoever he is — and Farouk talk about freedom when they didn't know anyone was listening, unless it was true?"

"As you said, convicts?"

"Who have escaped from New South Wales?"

"Or served their time and returned."

"I find it hard to imagine Farouk as a convict, but I will consider it later. For now, let's assume that when the *Mary Woodside* went down, Henry Gardeyne wasn't drowned, but captured by the corsairs. Perhaps ransom was demanded and not paid."

"By his loving father?"

She frowned. "No, that's not possible. He was apparently so devastated by his son's death that it hastened his own. But there might be some explanation."

He took her hand. "I know you want to believe this, Laura, but let me play devil's advocate. If by some mischance Henry Gardeyne was enslaved in Algiers for nearly a decade, when he was freed, he could have commanded every service and comfort from the navy. He'd have been brought home on the best and fastest ship and lionized throughout the land."

She grimaced at him. "Instead he sneaks in on a smuggling boat with only an Arab servant. Farouk could be Algerian, though, rather than Egyptian."

"But it that case, Dyer — Henry, whoever — is more likely to have been servant to him. And why would an Algerian — and an educated one, since he speaks and writes English — take such efforts to bring his slave back to England? And again, why not simply deliver him to Lord Exmouth, as he was supposed to?"

Laura sighed. "The devil has an excellent advocate in you. It doesn't make sense. But it doesn't make much sense as a hoax, either. Why has educated Azir Al Farouk sneaked into England to attempt a rather feeble extortion?"

Stephen thought for a moment. "The loss of his slaves has been a financial blow.

He encountered Henry Gardeyne once. Yes," he said to her, "I'll work with the idea that Henry survived the wreck long enough to end up in the hands of the corsairs. In fact, Farouk purchased Henry, and was about to demand ransom when Henry died. He wrote it off as a loss, but in this current situation he remembered Henry and also some possession that could establish a claim. He found someone resembling Henry and brought him here to try to squeeze money out of Lord Caldfort."

"It holds together," Laura said, "but it would hold together if HG really was Henry, wouldn't it?" She answered herself. "No, because then he would have been ransomed. And besides, everyone says Dyer is pale. How could he be pale after ten years in Algiers?"

He squeezed her hand. "I'm sorry, but I think all we have discovered is the explanation behind the hoax. Perhaps there was an enclosure with the letter laying this out for your father-in-law."

"And if Lord Caldfort pays, Farouk will report the deed done, and he and his accomplice will go off to South Carolina or wherever. Oh, dear. Perhaps he really does intend to kill his dupe and leave a body for

Lord Caldfort to find."

"Perhaps drowned. That can make bodies hard to identify."

"I refuse to feel sorry for the wretch," Laura said, but she did. Farouk sounded so strong, and Dyer so weak. "Do you think he's really a cripple?"

"What? Do you want to rescue him? I doubt he'd cooperate."

Laura realized that she'd drifted to accepting the worst possibility, not the best. "I won't give up until I'm sure," she said. "Imagine if it is Henry and we leave him to Farouk's or Jack's mercies. Yes, if Dyer is Henry he should have announced himself to Lord Exmouth, et cetera, but he would have spent ten years as a slave. They were horribly punished, and he is injured in some way. Perhaps Farouk befriended him and persuaded him that this quiet return was a better idea than being, as you said, lionized."

He picked up the piece of paper and rolled it into a ball in his hands, something he'd done in the past when struggling with a decision. "You want it to be so, but the evidence doesn't point that way."

"I must be sure. I can afford to stay another day. Even if Lord Caldfort has told Jack and Jack left this morning, he can't arrive until late tomorrow."

He nodded and tossed the paper accurately into the fire. "Very well. We still need a way to compare HG to that picture. Such a seemingly simple matter to thwart us."

"We could set the inn on fire." She raised her hand. "I know. I'm not even considering it."

"You make me consider a little smoke. . . . But it's too risky. I could try to pick the lock."

"Do you know how?"

He smiled. "Yes."

"Stephen! And you never told me? Or showed me, for that matter."

"Heaven knows what you'd have done with a skill like that."

She pulled a humorous face, but inside it hurt.

"Or I could break down the door, with or without the assistance of Kerslake or Topham."

"Oh, I forgot! Kerslake sent a message." She leapt up and brought it to him. "Perhaps he has something to contribute."

He broke the seal and read, but then passed it to her. "Only confirmations."

He was right. Kerslake wrote that the details of the landing were as he'd said, and that the two men had arrived alone. He'd found no word of a likely child in the area, or of people who could be in league with the two.

"He does reiterate the offer of help," she pointed out. "I'm sure that with his help we can pop HG out of that room like a nut out of its shell."

"But once we do, the subterfuge is over. We have to be ready to take them prisoner, possibly against armed resistance. People could get hurt, and if we muff it in any way, they could escape. What do you want to do? I told you that in the end, the decisions would be yours."

That weighed on her, but at the same time she felt liberated. She wouldn't need to seduce Stephen tonight, to steal his freedom. There was still hope.

"We try patience for just a little longer," she said. "We listen at the wall in the hope of clarity. Perhaps tomorrow will be warm, and HG will sit at an open window. Perhaps, oh, perhaps something will happen. For tonight," she said, taking his hand, "let's simply enjoy this time together. We were apart too long."

His look was quick and searching, but he said, "That sounds delightful. Shall we order our dinner served now?"

She agreed and watched as he rang the bell and then gave the order. Simply watching him, listening to him, gave her such joy. And now she had hope. Some deep instinct told her that HG was Henry, so both Harry and she would be free. She would move to Merrymead for the time being, and if Stephen didn't come courting her, she would go courting him.

Not force, not seduction, but courtship, where they could both learn about each other and make the right decision.

They waited for the meal in the relaxed pleasure of old friends. "You said Farouk purchased a copy of *The Corsair*," she remembered. "That fits now. Perhaps he likes the fact that it portrays the corsairs as heroes."

"Quite possibly. It's said Byron based it on some adventures of his own, and of course he liked to dress up in the costume."

"Which was nothing like Farouk's costume."

"My money's on Farouk being authentic."

"Mine, too. He is certainly the real thing."

When the servants had spread the meal, Laura and Stephen sat and continued to talk about the famous poet and his stormy, scandalous life.

" 'Linked with one virtue and a thousand crimes,' " Stephen quoted. "Many think Byron was describing himself."

Time, talk, and perhaps wine had eased tension. "His virtue being his art?" she asked, watching the play of candlelight on her glass of claret. "Is not one great gift enough?"

He studied her across the remnants of their meal. "And what is your great gift, Laura?"

She looked at her glass, sipped from it. "Harry."

"I don't think a child, even children, can be the prime purpose of a life. Your art is above the common standard."

"I have no wish to become an artist." She met his eyes. "Perhaps my art is to be a bird."

She saw no particular reaction. "And fly high? There's nothing wrong with that. The skylark gives a great deal of innocent pleasure." He put down the glass he had been merely toying with. "I will regret this, but I must tell you something."

"Don't." It came out without thought, and she frowned over it. "I mean, don't tell me something I must keep secret. I'm not sure I'm trustworthy at this moment."

"It's not a secret. I want you to know. I did not arrive at Caldfort by accident."

She stared at him. "You are part of Farouk's plot?"

"Damn it to Hades, Laura. Of course not."

Such swearing didn't shock her, but it startled her when it was Stephen. "I'm sorry. Why, then?"

His lips tightened as if to hold back words, but then he said, "I fabricated a reason to visit Caldfort because I wanted to court you."

She realized her glass was tilting and hastily put it down. She almost said *Why?* but that would be silly. "And found me in a fuss and flurry. But you said nothing later."

She should be relieved, ecstatic. It was such a shock, however, that she felt numb. And he had given no sign until now. Or no clear sign . . .

"The fuss and flurry seemed continuous," he said. "I think I had the notion of snaring your attention through heroics, but it would seem that I'm not the heroic sort."

"Nonsense. I wouldn't have wanted anyone else by my side through this."

He smiled. "Which isn't quite the same thing."

She wasn't sure what to say. If she could believe this — and why shouldn't she? — it was everything she needed and desired.

If she could only be sure that she was the right wife for him. She didn't doubt his words, but she'd seen many men choose wives from desire and discover disaster.

"At times," she said, "I haven't been sure that you like me."

"We've talked over this. I like you."

"But do you *love* me?" She shook her head. "I shouldn't ask that."

"I don't see why not." He picked up his neglected glass and drank. "I am resolved to be nakedly honest. I'm uncertain what love is, Laura. I want you. Blunt, but there it is."

Blunt enough to hurt. "You want to possess Labellelle?"

He considered it. "Only insofar as she is the external of you."

That was better. "I'm not at all serious," she warned.

"I think you can be very serious. If not, I'm sure I can be serious enough for two."

She shook her head. "I don't think you're serious. I mean, you are, but not too serious." She rose from the table and walked away. "I can't seem to find the right words."

"A sensation I'm familiar with."

She knew he was still in his chair, which was impolite, but the right thing to do.

"You could tell me how you feel about me," he said. "I think we are friends. I think we trust each other, enjoy each other's company. But we need more than that."

Nakedly honest. She could agree that they were only friends. She could tell him that she wanted him as much as he wanted her, simply physically, his body joined to hers. She could tell him that she wanted him as husband so he would protect her son.

But she sensed that none of these things were needed here. Thank God that there was hope that HG was Henry Gardeyne, and she didn't need to betray his trust. As it was, she was too fraught at the moment to sort out her own mixture of need, desire, and fear. She'd experienced an impulsive, inadequate marriage and wanted more — especially for Stephen.

She turned and faced him. "I don't know. It's more than friendship, believe me. I don't see you as a brother. But . . ." She opened her hands helplessly. "There's no hurry, is there? I'll be at Merrymead. We can . . ."

She couldn't find the right word. *Court* did not seem to fit.

"Continue to relearn each other," he said. "No, to learn the people we are now." He rose and came to her, took the hands she still held out. "You don't mind that I went to Caldfort with intent?"

"No, of course not. Why, though? We'd spoken so rarely over six years. Why did you think you wanted to marry me?"

Slowly, he brought both her hands to his lips and kissed each one. "Because I wanted to marry you six years ago."

"When you proposed? But I thought . . ."

He smiled. "What?"

She had to give him truth. "That it was gallantry. Logic, even. You thought I was making a mistake and offered to rescue me."

His smile deepened. "Not so far off. I didn't realize myself how much I really cared. Perhaps if I had, I would have been able to persuade you."

"I doubt it," she said honestly. "Hal dazzled me, and anyway, I would have balked at the scandal of jilting him."

"Even if you'd loved me?"

She pulled free of his hands. "I'm not sure I could have recognized another love then, but the scandal would have terrified me. I was only eighteen. And," she added deliberately, "I wanted Hal."

"I know. And once you had him, you were happy. I accepted fate. I wasn't really angry at you, no. My needs were my concern, not yours."

"But that's the problem. I wasn't aware of you that way!"

"I know, but does that mean you never can be? We could test the hypothesis. . . ."

He drew her into his arms. She raised a hand between them. "Stephen, I'm not sure this is wise."

"Trust me."

She let him draw her close because she wanted this so much. Willingly, she molded to his body for their first real kiss, sliding her hand up and into his silky hair, opening her mouth to taste him, sighing with deep, revealing satisfaction.

Different, so different to Hal in every way, but right. This part, at least, was right.

And thus it was dangerous. She felt his arms tighten, his mouth demand, and clutched back at him as hunger burst into flame. She dragged free, tore away, faced him at bay.

Saw his devastation.

"No!" she cried.

Swiftly, he put his fingers to her lips, but in his eyes she saw pure pain. She clutched his hand to her lips and kissed it. "No, I'm not offended," she murmured against his skin. "No, I didn't dislike it. I liked it too much. As did you."

"God, yes. Come to my bed, Laura. I'd like it even more."

She laughed against his hand, pressing it to her cheek. "We mustn't."

"You know I want to marry you."

"That's why. If we make love, we're committed." Before he could make the obvious comment, she said, "I can't believe I'm the one preaching restraint, but I am. Desire is not enough, Stephen, even desire as powerful as this. I may not be the wife you need."

"Do I have no say in that?"

"Only half. Do you really know me?"

"I think I do."

"I'm still Lady Skylark."

"Are you?"

Strange that sadness could make her smile, but it did. She kissed his hand again and let it go. "We need time. We have time. We can bill and coo in the usual way and be sure before we make commitments."

Silence settled, marked only by the steadily ticking clock and never-ending rumble of the sea.

"You're right," he said at last. "I can't believe that you're the one preaching restraint. It probably means that you're right in other ways. That your feelings are not as deeply engaged as mine."

She could protest — it felt as if her heart was breaking — but she knew where that would lead. There was only one way to end this.

"Good night," she said and retreated to her room.

Once there, she sat in thought, but thought did no good. Goodness knows who Stephen had wanted when he'd gone to Caldfort, but now he wanted the woman who could debate philosophy and discuss laws.

He thought Lady Skylark was a person of the past.

Laura wasn't sure that was true, or that she wanted it to be, so she had to continue to be strong.

Stephen looked at the remains of the meal with disgust. Scraps, smears, and congealing fat. A good representation of his hopes. For one moment as they'd kissed, he'd thought he held heaven in his arms, but then he'd been hurtled back to earth.

She could sweeten it as she wished, but the kiss hadn't held her, her desire hadn't compelled her, and she'd retained full control of her reason.

He allowed himself a glimmer of hope. Perhaps it was this situation and all the stresses of it. He would court her in proper fashion from her parents' house, and perhaps it would all work out in the end.

He picked up his abandoned glass and drained it.

He didn't believe it.

Not for one bloody moment.

# Chapter 35

Sunshine woke Laura to her last day at the Compass. No matter what happened today, she must leave early the next. Jack might turn up, but even if he didn't, she must return home.

She didn't want to. Oh, she wanted to be back with her family and she ached for Harry, but she didn't want this special time with Stephen to end. It must, however, or they would plunge into disaster. In the middle of the night she'd had to fight the temptation to go to him, to taste him, feel him, burn with him.

And bind him.

She prepared for the day, trying to armor herself against folly, longing and fearing their next encounter, but when she went into the parlor, he wasn't there. The remains of his breakfast replaced the remains of their dinner last night, and a note lay by her place.

*Out for a walk. Back soon. S*

She picked it up, realizing that it was the first letter she'd ever received from him. It seemed absurd, but he'd never written to her from school or university. Why would he? He'd spilled all the news during holidays. Any messages from Ancross had come from Charlotte. After her marriage, there had certainly been none.

She handled the sheet of paper as if it were precious, tempted to tuck it away and treasure it. Instead she rolled it into a ball between her hands and lobbed it at the fire. It raised her spirits to see it land accurately in the flames. With a wry smile at herself, she rang for fresh coffee and settled to eat.

When she'd finished, she went to listen at the wall. Solving the anagram had given reason to believe that Dyer was Henry Gardeyne, but she wanted certainty. Proof. Did he need rescuing from Farouk or not? In fact, she'd be delighted to hear anything that clarified the situation and guided her about what to do next.

She immediately knew that being in this room was dangerous. The smell of Stephen's soap and of him was just as powerful, if not more so. The mere sight of his brush and comb stirred her longings, and she touched his book simply because he'd probably held it last night. When she looked at the title, however, she found it was the bound report of a committee investigating the country's prisons. She must not hide from what he was.

The chair was still by the wall, so she sat and listened. They were talking. She sat straighter, annoyed not to have brought paper and pencil, but then she realized it was one voice — HG's — and he was reciting.

> ". . . *But still from room to room his way* he broke,
> *They search — they find — they save:* with lusty arms
> *Each bears a prize of unregarded charms;*"

Laura recognized *The Corsair*. No doubt the copy Stephen had discovered that Farouk had bought.

She listened, enjoying the desperate battle back to the boats. There was nothing else to do, and HG read surprisingly well.

> ". . . *The Pasha wooed as if he deemed the* slave
> *Must seem delighted with the heart he* gave;

*The Corsair vowed protection, soothed*
  afright,
*As if his homage were a woman's*
  right . . ."

Those words startled her and she moved away from the wall. The first described Hal perfectly. He'd assumed he was doing her a great honor, and she'd thought the same.

It was true. He could have married higher.

Was Stephen the Corsair, wanting to protect and soothe?

She heard a noise and Stephen came into his bedchamber, halting briefly when he saw her, then continuing, stripping off his gloves.

"You look amused," he said easily, as if nothing awkward lay between them. "Are they telling jokes?"

"HG's reading *The Corsair*. Do you think a man's homage is a woman's right?"

"Hardly. Why would a woman — or man — wish to be worshipped?"

She recognized that he'd put his finger on the problem she'd sensed. "Why, indeed?"

But perhaps, she thought, she'd been as bad as Hal. She'd been gratified by his proposal, but hadn't she thought it her due? She, the beauty of her area, desired by all?

He was looking at her. "There are few things more worrying than a thoughtful woman. Are you concerned about last night? Don't be."

His calm, direct reference exasperated her, but she was also touched by his honesty. She would match it as far as she could.

"I'm concerned about many things, Stephen, but I'm not distressed. Were you out doing something useful, or simply walking?"

"Walking." He leant against a bedpost facing her. "Do you want to return to Redoaks now? It might be best."

Indeed it might, but she said, "No. I'll give it one more day. But if we have no clarity by this evening, I'd like to arrange an invasion then. Settle it once and for all."

He nodded. "I'll send a message to Kerslake. No, I should ride over. It's not far, and it's no matter to put bluntly in a letter."

Another way of avoiding her?

"No clever codes?" she teased.

"I have some and so, I'm sure, does he. Unfortunately, we neglected to coordinate."

He continually surprised her.

"Can it wait until after lunch?" she asked. "The sun's shining and I'm cooped up in here without an escort. We could have a walk, and then you might as well eat."

"By all means. We can take the telescope, in case our elusive quarry is sunning himself in the window."

The sun was pleasant, the breeze light, and the air as crisp as ever. Laura had come to love it and was hard-pressed to play her sickly part. They plied the spyglass, and she enjoyed watching a ship with full, rounded sails speeding east along the Channel.

"Coming home, probably," she said. "Soon making land at Portsmouth, or going around to London. Being on a ship like that must be almost like flying."

"One of the fishermen here could take us out." But then he added, "Sometime."

They returned to the inn, encountering people they knew. As they eluded Captain Sillitoe, Laura said, "It's definitely time for me to leave. Soon some of these people will be familiar enough with my face to perhaps remember it undisguised."

"True."

They ate a light lunch, and Laura wondered if Stephen, like she, was thinking about when next they would do the same.

Then he rose. "It's only three miles, so it shouldn't take long. I worry about leaving you here."

"I have my pistol, remember?"

"And know how to use it, yes. But don't do anything rash." He raised a hand. "I understand. But I'd prefer not to return to your corpse, you know."

"And I'd prefer not to have your corpse brought back to me, so ride carefully. I assume the route goes along the cliffs."

His lips twitched, then relaxed into a smile. "Very well, but *I* will not be in the company of villains."

"I doubt I will be, either, but if I see a chance to glimpse HG, I'll take it. But carefully. Very carefully."

He sighed. "As you will." He pulled her to him for a quick kiss. "Be safe."

Then he left through his bedroom, and shortly afterward she watched him ride away on a horse he must have hired from Topham. It wasn't as good as the one he'd ridden on the journey from Caldfort, but she still enjoyed watching him.

When he turned out of sight, she went into her room and took out her pistol. Her simple round gown had pockets beneath the skirts and she put the pistol in one, but it was heavy there. Instead she put it in her reticule and carried that with her.

She checked at the wall but it was quiet there now. She was walking away when a loud *bang!* made her jump. She looked back at the wall. A shot?

She'd only ever fired a pistol outdoors, so she'd no idea what a pistol shot in the next room would sound like, but it didn't seem likely. More like a mallet banged on a table. A chopper on a chopping block?

She couldn't ignore this. She opened the door to the corridor to peer out — and looked straight into the dark eyes of Azir Al Farouk. A quick glance showed no bloodstains.

She knew she'd started at the sight of him, so she built on that. "Oh, Mr. Farouk!" she exclaimed, hand on bosom. "I thought I heard a shot. Is everyone all right?"

"A shot, madam? I heard no shot."

"A bang, then? Most alarming! It sounded as if it came from Captain Dyer's rooms!"

"Ah. I killed a cockroach with one of my master's boots."

A likely tale.

"Oh, I see. You must excuse me."

"No, madam, you must excuse me for

disturbing you." Austerely polite, he bowed and went on his way.

Laura watched him go. His accent had definitely been stronger than when she'd heard him through the wall. Now, why would he play such games? To allay suspicion? English people were inclined to think foreigners less clever than themselves. It made her all the more determined to learn the truth.

She walked along the squeaky corridor and knocked at the first door. Not the faintest sound. Was it possible that Farouk had received his payment and that bang had been the execution?

She began to tap continuously, remembering to behave like Mrs. Penfold. "Hello? Captain Dyer? Are you all right? Hello? Oh, dear, oh, dear, what to do, what to do . . ."

She kept on tapping and twittering. Surely if he was there, if he was alive, he would have to respond.

And then she heard something. A scrape. A . . . shuffle? Was the wounded man crawling toward help?

Suddenly the lock clicked and the door opened a crack.

"What do you want?" a pale-faced man whispered.

# Chapter 36

Laura's first, crushing thought was that this was not, could never be, Henry Gardeyne.

Her next was that he *was* wounded and he'd staggered to find help.

Her third was that no, there was no blood, but the young man was truly an invalid and he'd exhausted his strength in reaching the door. He was clutching at it desperately.

She quickly put an arm around him, grateful that he was shorter than she. "My dear sir, I'm so sorry! Please, let me assist you back to your chair."

It was at the table, where cards were laid out in a game of patience.

"I apologize for causing you to rise, sir," Laura said sincerely as they reached the table and he could clutch it. "I was merely concerned because earlier, I heard such a loud noise."

The young man sank back into his chair

with a wince of pain.

The too-young man. HG couldn't be the thirty of Henry Gardeyne. If that weren't enough, he was completely the wrong type. Henry Gardeyne at twenty had possessed some fine-boned features, but not as delicate as these. Both men had brown hair, but HG's was lighter, a dark honey, and frothed in irrepressible curls.

Most impossibly of all, this man's eyes were as clear a blue as a summer sky. Gardeyne eyes were usually brown, and that portrait had shown dark eyes. An artist might take liberties, but not to this extent.

He readjusted his position in his chair with another wince. "I'm sorry if the noise disturbed you, madam. It was only F . . . Farouk killing a cockroach. He hates such things."

He sounded anxious and nervous and Laura wondered why, when he was clearly part of this plot. After all, he'd been able to unlock the door, so he hadn't been locked in. Was he afraid of punishment? Something about him summoned her protective instincts.

She made some more quick analyses.

He spoke well, but not quite well enough for the highest birth. There was the hint of an accent, but she couldn't place it. He looked an unlikely type to be a military officer, but she knew she shouldn't make that judgment. War could turn strong men weak.

Whoever he was, however, he wasn't Henry Gardeyne.

All hope died.

"Ma'am? Are you all right? I'm sorry if you were alarmed."

She supposed she should still try to find out what was going on, if only for Lord Caldfort's sake. And for Harry's. If these criminals succeeded in extorting ten thousand guineas, it would come out of his inheritance. She sat down, remembering to be Mrs. Penfold, which she feared had slipped when she'd assisted him to his chair.

"No, no, sir. Well, only a little. Much better now. So sad to be sick when so young, Captain Dyer. A war wound?"

His eyes fluttered uneasily. "Fever. And an accident. I'm getting stronger."

"I see you are playing patience. A pleasant occupation, but it becomes tedious over time. Would you care for a game? Casino, perhaps, or cribbage?"

He glanced at the door and she knew he was worried about Farouk's return. She couldn't do this to him. "I am sorry to have intruded, Captain. Would you prefer that I left?"

She began to rise, but he said, almost shyly, "No, if you don't mind. It *is* tedious here and I'd like to learn a little more of . . . things. I . . . I've been abroad for many years, you see."

She could see why Farouk kept him in his rooms. He was a terrible liar. But then she remembered that he might have been an Algerian slave, poor man.

Then brought here to pretend to be Henry Gardeyne? Whom he didn't resemble at all.

And he certainly hadn't recently done brutal physical work, or lived under a hot sun. His skin was as delicate as the most fussy beauty's, and his hands, though manly in shape, as soft.

She simply had to try to solve this conundrum.

She settled back down and put her heavy reticule on the table close by. "Foreign air can be so very insalubrious," she clucked. "But then, you cannot have been in the tropics, sir."

When he looked alarmed, she added, "You have not been browned by the sun, sir. I pride myself on my powers of observation!"

He smiled, and she wondered if it was a suppressed laugh at her idiocy. He certainly hid his eyes with lowered lids. "No, no sun."

"An icy clime! Equally harmful. England is ideal because it is *temperate,* you see. It avoids tropical and arctic extremes. Are you receiving good treatment here, Captain? I understand that there are many excellent doctors in Draycombe."

"Oh, Farouk takes care of me."

Laura pursed her lips. "Your turbaned servant, yes. But forgive me, sir, a British constitution requires a British doctor. I met a most amiable one here. I believe he sent up a restorative potion."

With another glimmer of humor, HG gestured to a dark glass bottle on a sideboard. "Farouk doesn't trust it, and when I sniffed it, it smelt awful."

Laura put on the stern expression of the Merrymead nursery governess. "The best medicines always taste the worst, sir."

"Farouk says that's why the doctors make them taste so foul."

Farouk says, Farouk says. No, this young man had never been an officer. He sounded as if he was scarcely out of the schoolroom, though he looked to be about the same age as she.

"Besides," he said, "the doctors say I need only rest and recover. It's damned boring." He flushed and apologized. "I'm so sorry, ma'am."

She waved a gloved hand. "Oh, I make allowances for a gallant soldier, sir. I don't think I introduced myself, did I? I am Mrs. Penfold, a widow, you see. We are in a similar case, for I am here for my health, though I fear I have no noble excuse for my state. Since my dear husband's death, I have been in a poor way with my nerves and so my dear cousin offered to escort me here for a little while. If it suits, I may take rooms . . ."

She burbled on in this way for a while about fictional plans for the restoration of her health and saw the man relax.

Time to pry. "So, sir, what of Mr. Farouk? Such an interesting appearance. He is Indian, you said?"

Often an error elicited truth.

It worked. "No." Then he stopped. "He's . . . er . . . Egyptian."

"Egypt! All the rage, sir. Pyramids, crocodiles, and the Sphinx. Were you posted in Egypt? Was that how he came into your service? Oh, no, you said otherwise. Russia."

She tried the error trick again, but he

said, "Perhaps we could play cards, Mrs. Penfold. I don't know the games you mentioned, but I would like to learn."

It was clearly a deflection, but his eyes were bright with interest. It presented a new puzzle, however. He didn't know casino? It was played in every household, even in schoolrooms.

Laura hesitated. If she stayed here long enough, Farouk was certain to catch her, but did it matter? HG would tell the man she'd been here, and her excuse should hold. In fact, being found here innocently playing cards with the invalid would be safer than retreating after a few questions.

She gathered the cards and shuffled, explaining the rules of casino, then dealt. To allay suspicion, she asked no questions as they played, but simply tried to understand this strange young man. He learned the game quickly, so he wasn't simple, and yet his amusement with it seemed juvenile.

Eventually she mentioned playing casino with some fictional nieces and nephews, and gained the response that his family never played cards. "Methodist," he explained, with a twitch of the lips that might be a grimace.

An explanation. There, at least, she'd constructed a mystery out of nothing.

"Well, to be sure, that is a worthy practice," she remarked, "but I cannot see any harm in a simple game of cards. One need not play casino for money, not even for farthings."

"Cards are a first step toward damnation, all the same," he said with a smile.

She saw an opening and probed. "Are you perhaps estranged from your family, Captain? Is that why you are not recovering at your home?"

"Yes, that's it." He said it too quickly, though.

"So sad when families are divided. If you have been serving abroad it is perhaps some years since you have visited your home. They might be more tolerant now."

His quick look startled her with its amused cynicism. "I doubt it."

And oh, those wicked eyes. What sturdy, Methodist home had produced this fey creature? It was hardly surprising that they'd parted ways.

"How very sad," she said. "So foolish to cling to old estrangements, but it is their loss, I'm sure. So what will you do once your health is restored? Will you return to military service or have you sold out?"

"Sold out?" he asked, as if the term was new to him.

"Sold your commission in the army. Retired."

"Oh! Of course. Er . . . yes."

"Because of your injuries." She nodded sympathetically, but wanted to roll her eyes. Army, indeed. He didn't know the term, and captains who left the army didn't use their rank thereafter.

She dealt a new hand. "Will you return to your home area to live, sir? You must have friends there. Where did you say it was? Cheshire?"

"Suffolk."

"A country estate, or in town?" she asked as if all her attention was on fanning her hand.

He didn't answer, so she looked up to smile a bland query at him.

"Er . . . Ipswich."

He mumbled it, however, and was becoming uneasy. She pretended to be puzzling over her play as pieces began to form a pattern.

A port town. A sailor? Had he run away from his stern home and gone to sea? She supposed he could be a naval captain, and naval captains didn't purchase or sell their commissions. But if it was hard to imagine him a captain in the army, it was impossible to imagine him lord and master of a ship. There was no trace of command in him.

No, if she had to lay money, she'd bet on him having run away from home as a lad to be a sailor, and a sailor could then have been captured by Barbary pirates. He could even, she realized, have served on the *Mary Woodside*. . . .

"You must have visited many fascinating foreign places, sir," she prompted, putting a three on a four. "Seven."

"No."

She glanced up politely and saw him swallow as he tried to think what to say next. "I . . . I didn't find them fascinating."

"Oh, I see. You, like me, would prefer to live at home in England."

"Or France," he said, and she remembered hearing him say the same yesterday.

She pursed her lips. "A fascinating country, I'm sure, but I cannot forget that until so recently they were our enemy and cost the lives of so many brave men."

"Or Italy," he said, somewhat desperately. "Or America. Oh, Azir! See, Mrs. Penfold has been teaching me casino."

HG's voice had risen in pitch.

Laura turned and felt a spurt of fear herself, perhaps because of the icy look on the Arab's blade-boned face.

She rose by instinct, and had no difficulty in appearing nervous and unsteady. "Mr. Farouk! I have been enjoying such a pleasant game with Captain Dyer, and he does admit to being bored alone here, so you must not hesitate to request my company whenever he wishes."

She picked up her reticule, taking comfort from the weight of the pistol inside. She thought the Arab did hesitate a moment, as if he might not let her leave, but then he stood aside.

Laura minced toward the door, and only turned back when halfway into the corridor. HG was looking like a puppy that expected a scolding. But a devoted puppy.

"Do let me know whenever you wish to play cards again, Captain Dyer."

With that she tottered to her own parlor door. Once inside, however, she raced into Stephen's room and pressed the listening device to the wall.

Farouk's voice was low and angry, but she caught bits of it.

"Foolish . . . dangerous . . ."

HG's voice was high and clear. "She's only a silly woman, and I'm so bored here. When can we leave?"

"We must hear from the Caldforts soon."

No contact yet.

"Then we can go where it's safe?"

"Yes."

"You're angry at me," HG said in a little-boy voice.

"No, no. No harm done, *nuranee*. I know this is hard for you."

"Is . . ."

The voices sank into muffled murmurs. Could HG be crying? She should think him pathetic, but instead she felt the urge to protect him. He was clearly in some sort of thrall to Azir. Perhaps he *had* been Azir's slave. Slaving underground, far from the sun . . .

But then she remembered his hands.

She growled, tired of trying to make these mismatched pieces fit. The soft voices faded even more, and then a door closed. They'd gone into the bedroom. Or HG had been sent to bed like a naughty boy.

Laura straightened and abandoned her post. She went to look out at rippling sea and sunny sky. Not a scene to match her thoughts. There was no longer any hope that HG was Henry Gardeyne.

Stephen was on a wasted journey, for there was no need to raid the room. But then she changed her mind. They'd do it in order to liberate HG from Farouk and give him a chance to live his life as he wished. She'd have to leave that in Stephen's hands, however, because she really must return home.

But then it truly sank in that Harry was as vulnerable as before. That she must return to her previous plan. It was perhaps not quite so bad now. Stephen had said he wanted to marry her, so there was no need to seduce him. She had only to say yes.

As for suitability, she would make sure it was an honest bargain. After all, she loved him, so it surely wouldn't be difficult to be what he wanted and needed — informed, concerned, serious, decorous. There would be no trace of skylarking. She'd enjoyed their quiet time here and their complex, interesting discussions . . .

She wasn't paying any attention to the scene in front of her, so it took her a moment to realize what she was seeing.

Jack Gardeyne. Riding up to the Compass!

# Chapter 37

Laura shrank back out of sight. How had Jack made it here so quickly? He must have ridden like the devil, and half through the night. She shouldn't have underestimated a sporting Gardeyne. Of course, there was nothing for him to find other than a fraud, but there'd be hell to pay if he discovered her!

She edged forward just enough to watch him. Was he planning to take rooms here? How was she going to avoid him then? She didn't believe her disguise would fool him for more than a moment.

When he turned his horse, she let out a fervent breath of relief. He'd only been checking out the Compass.

What would he do now?

She watched him ride back down the street and into the yard of the King's Arms.

Oh, thank heavens. Here came Stephen.

She waited impatiently, keeping a cautious eye on the street. As soon as Stephen walked in, she said, "Jack Gardeyne's here!"

He was instantly alert. "At the inn?"

"No, but he rode past, studying it."

He smiled. "Then things could become interesting."

"Interesting!" She sank into a chair, realizing that Stephen didn't know what she knew. "HG isn't Henry Gardeyne."

"What?"

She told her story.

He'd taken the station by the window and was looking out, so she couldn't see his expression. "Don't tell me it was too big a risk," she said at the end.

"I wouldn't dream of it." It was flat, possibly sarcastic. He turned to look at her. "You're sure? He could be very changed."

"Including the color of his eyes? What's more, I'd lay money that he was a common seaman once. It's there, even though he's been educated. And how can that have happened, when he was a slave in the Algerian mines? Which he obviously wasn't. His hands and complexion are finer than mine."

"Impossible," he said with twitching lips.

"Wait until you see him."

"Will you be jealous?"

She realized where that might take them. "*Nothing* about this makes sense. Nothing! But I want HG freed from Farouk. He . . . he dominates him, and I'm sure he can be cruel."

"Of course." He seemed lost in thought. "And we want to see what Jack Gardeyne does. We might be able to make some use of it. You'll have to stay in these rooms, though. He might recognize you."

"You're right. And when the sun is finally shining. As for Jack, what do you think he'll do?"

"Investigate, I assume. And have as much trouble seeing HG as we did."

Stephen, however, had a look she knew of old: deep thought. "What if Lord Caldfort shared his worries, and Jack decided to act on his own?"

She straightened. "Strike without warning and get rid of the problem altogether? It would be like him. And his principal target would be HG. Until he sees him. Then, I assume, he'll ride home laughing."

"Thus HG's seclusion. They could never know when an investigator would arrive, so Egan Dyer had to stay out of sight. Strange that Farouk didn't find someone a little more likely."

"Oh!" she cried in exasperation. "It *still* doesn't make sense. My brain feels like scrambled eggs. I should leave for Redoaks now."

But then she realized that would leave Stephen unbound.

"Don't you want to be here to catch Jack Gardeyne in mischief?" he asked. "It could be very useful."

"As a weapon over his head? You're like the snake with the apple."

"Hisssss."

She laughed, shaking her head, but inside she knew she was the snake, or Eve, ready to tempt him, perhaps into misery.

"What of Kerslake's men?" she asked.

"I reached Crag Wyvern — and I don't envy Kerslake that place. It's like the grimmest medieval keep. Nothing on the outside but arrow slits — to find him away at Bridport. So I left a message hinting at the situation. He probably won't get it until it's too late to come here today, but that doesn't matter now."

*No, nothing matters now.*

She found herself fretting about HG, however. He seemed so defenseless. "What if Jack's come here prepared to pay the money, and Farouk then slits HG's throat? Just because HG seems devoted to Farouk doesn't mean that Farouk isn't a deceitful villain. And the young man is strangely sweet."

Stephen gave her a look. "I approve of a tender heart, but yours is becoming mushy. What exactly do you want me to do?"

"If Farouk goes out again, can you follow him? Make sure he doesn't rendez-vous with Jack?"

"I can, but I don't like to leave you alone. I know, I know, but if Jack Gardeyne is a murderer, he'd welcome a chance to kill you, too. That would leave Harry com-pletely in his power."

A chill swept through her. "You're right. I'll lock the door while you're gone, and I do have my pistol."

She took it out of the reticule, and he came to inspect it. "A nice piece. Does it fire straight?"

"I could hit things with it. I stopped practicing when Hal wanted me to hit a rabbit."

She caught a flicker of a grimace. "Ste-phen, I cannot and will not stop talking about Hal. He was my husband for five years, and some of those years were happy. Harry is his son, and I'll do my best to keep Hal's memory alive for him."

There she was, warning him off again.

"I was simply wondering if you'll be able to fire at a man."

"Oh," she said, deflated. "Have you ever shot a man?"

"Touché. But I have shot rabbits and various other creatures."

She put the gun back in the bag. "I can only hope I'll do what I have to do."

He returned to watching through the window, and Laura paced anxiously. Though serious, this venture had not seemed truly dangerous before. She wasn't even sure where the danger came from — Jack or Farouk, or both — but she truly believed it now.

She didn't want Stephen out there, even though Jack could meet him and be not at all suspicious.

She paced into Stephen's room and listened at the wall.

Silence.

And anyway, what was the point? She knew the truth, and she knew what she had to do.

Hidden from Stephen, she leaned for a moment against one of the bedposts. She wanted him so much, in earthy ways and others, that she felt weak with longings. Only see how calm he was, though. Perhaps her warnings had taken root and he'd come to his senses. And how could she seduce her beloved out of that? Scrambled eggs, indeed.

A noise startled her, and then she knew what it was. Squeaks in the corridor. She hurried into the parlor. "I think Farouk's leaving."

Stephen picked up his gloves and hat, and Laura took his station at the window.

Stephen paused at the door. "What are you going to do if Farouk is going to the apothecary for corn plasters, and Jack sneaks in here?"

"Run out with my pistol and throw myself between HG and death . . . Don't be silly. I think I'll screech, *Fire!*"

"Do that. This is no time for skylarking. Remember, Jack might want to kill you. I'd see him in hell by tomorrow, but he may not know that until too late."

His cool intent quivered in her like desire. She couldn't resist. She went to him, cradled his face in her hands, and kissed him. "Take care. I value your safety, too."

She moved to let him go, but he pulled her to him and kissed her, a full, passionate kiss more staggering than before. Then he was gone. She touched her lips, still sensitive from his searing kiss, knowing she was smiling like an idiot.

He was not cool. Not cool at all.

What was she going to do about this? If she could believe he felt true love, she would be as carefree as a skylark, but what if he was deluded by her sober appearance? Even at Caldfort, he'd encountered Laura Gardeyne, mourning widow and devoted mother.

Within weeks she could bring out her old finery and be Labellelle. Was that who he wanted? Was that who she was — now?

She sat by the parlor window to watch for Jack and consider true honesty.

A number of people were taking advantage of the late afternoon sun, promenading to and fro for health and pleasure. Dr. Grantleigh was out there in his chair, his wife beside him, holding his hand. Captain Sillitoe was chatting to another gentleman. Jean was hurrying back from some errand.

They were all, she assumed, living relatively uncomplicated lives.

What a blessed state.

# Chapter 38

Stephen followed the blue turban, trying to concentrate on the dangers from different parties and anticipate them, but his mind seemed stuck in that kiss. He kept losing control when he was supposed to be winning Laura with care and restraint. Giving her time to think. Not pressing her. Certainly not seducing her!

He'd gone to Caldfort with the aim of stealing her freedom by courting her before anyone else had the chance. Proof of how low desperation could push a man. It had been even worse. Nicholas was right. He hadn't even recognized the nature of the prize he wanted to possess; simply been desperate to correct the old loss.

Now he knew, however, knew the remarkable complexity and strength of Laura Gardeyne, and for the first time he recognized how sane, intelligent men could be driven beyond all limits by desire, by need, of such a woman. He would not be pushed into dishonor, he vowed. He would do nothing to force her choice.

How the devil could she be expected to make any rational choice now, amid the danger and mayhem that circled her precious child?

Farouk approached the King's Arms and Stephen watched, praying that the man did not go in, for that would mean an appointment with Reverend Gardeyne. The Arab walked on and Stephen paused to think.

Farouk and Gardeyne might have already appointed a meeting elsewhere, but in so little time? If he followed Farouk, he couldn't watch for the vile vicar. He decided to stay near the King's Arms, where he could watch and guard Laura.

The vile vicar. He felt coldly certain that Gardeyne was a villain, and that his plan was to kill and leave. He could see the sense of it. As far as Gardeyne knew, no one else except his father had a hint of this affair. Eliminate any threat from a resurrected Henry Gardeyne and there'd be only one small boy to dispose of.

He didn't know that small boy had a resolute protector. No, two. Stephen was sure that Gardeyne greatly underestimated Laura.

He loitered near the Arms, buying a newssheet from a lad for an excuse, but after a couple of encounters with people who wanted to chat, he strolled down onto the beach. He could continue to observe from there.

He found his attention wandering too often to the upstairs windows of the Compass, not looking for Dyer but for a glimpse of Laura. He even wished he had the telescope. Madness, but in normal circumstances, of the sweetest kind.

He couldn't lose her. In a fair and just universe, he could not lose her again. Everything about Laura was precious to him. The turn of her hand, the line of her back, that omnipresent perfume, so subtle yet so magical. Her sparkling laugh.

She didn't laugh enough, and he didn't think it was just this situation.

He could make her merry as a lark.

He could seduce her.

Despite all his resolve, the thought returned, winding itself in false colors. He'd be saving her from another mistake, making it easier for him to protect her son.

Despite the somewhat wild reputation of Lady Skylark, he knew Laura was not the sort of woman to take intimacy lightly. She would feel she should marry a lover. She might even get with child, which would clinch it.

Unfair. Unethical. Base. But would it really matter, when it was clear she desired him, too? When they were old friends and newly delighted in one another?

"Hissss," he said, recognizing the snake in his thoughts and trying to stamp it into oblivion.

Laura had seen Stephen halt outside the King's Arms while Farouk went on. She'd watched him buy a newssheet and read it, then walk down onto the beach. She wished she were there with him, arm in arm, breathing in the sea air, walking with Stephen.

She remembered to look away, to check the wider scene for threats, to her, to him. No Jack, no Farouk.

She went to listen at the wall when there was no point, simply to be in Stephen's room.

She wouldn't let herself repeat her previous folly and disturb the bed, but she didn't seem able to control herself entirely. She wandered the room, exploring with eyes and sometimes with fingers. His valise — plain leather, well used, and with a small brass plate engraved with his name.

His greatcoat, hanging on a hook on the wall, rough to the touch, delightful to inhale, even though it mostly smelt of wool.

That book lying beside the bed, the place marked with a strip of cloth that must have been embroidered by a child. By one of Charlotte's little girls, she supposed.

The washstand containing his brush, comb, and shaving equipment. Shaving was so particular to men that it had always pleased her. She'd sometimes liked to watch Hal being shaved, which he'd indulgently thought peculiar.

The results had been predictable, which was part of the reason she'd done it, but it had made the smell of shaving soap and the sight of a razor quite stimulating.

Blond hairs were caught in his brush. She teased one free, and blushing at her own folly, tucked it down between her breasts.

If only she'd been wiser when young. Would it have been so dreadful to stay unmarried for a few years until Stephen was in a position to take a wife? As Juliet had done.

She shook her head. She understood too well the Laura Watcombe who'd thrilled to have caught the most eligible man in the area, and who'd thought she'd found a like spirit in Hal Gardeyne. They had been happy for a while. She would never let herself pretend that wasn't so.

She'd been a different person then.

She had, indeed, been Lady Skylark, immediately at home in the *haute volée*. Would that girl have been able to tolerate life in rooms in London, playing hostess to other lawyers and politicians who wanted to debate reform until the candles guttered?

Such thoughts seemed to violate some ideal, but people changed. Perhaps that was the cause of many unhappy marriages.

Ah. She went over to Stephen's window to look out at the setting sun. If she was facing hard truths, she might as well accept that in the end, she and Hal had been in an unhappy marriage.

Not miserable, not tortured, but providing none of the joy they'd shared earlier. After Harry's birth, she'd wanted a more domestic life, but he hadn't. However, the tonnish social life no longer appealed to him. He'd clearly played there to please her, but reverted to form so that he spent most of his time with his Corinthian set.

They'd lost their meeting points.

No, they'd had one. They'd both wanted more children. She wasn't sure why she'd not quickened again. Hal had sired bastards, but not that many, considering. It seemed natural that such a vigorous man would be vigorously fertile. With a wry smile, she wondered whether a lifetime spent as a "bruising rider" as they put it, had an effect.

Oh, dear, she really shouldn't think of these things or one day she'd speak of them in public. The *ton* might be amused, but the sober lawyers and reformers would not.

Backward, forward, her mind swung like a pendulum. No, like a weight on a string. She'd seen a demonstration once at the Royal Society. Something to do with the movement of the planets, she thought, but to her merely a weight on a string, set to swing in a circle but slowly falling in until it was stationary in the center.

A force of nature, which made it very like the force that kept circling her back to Stephen's bed, to touching smooth wood, rough wool, firm pillow. That sent her mind circling down to what she and Stephen could do there, and the consequences. . . .

She became aware of someone knocking on the door.

The parlor door!

She hurried into the other room, but then hesitated. "Who is it?"

"Mr. Topham, ma'am. There's a woman here wishing to speak with Sir Stephen. A woman with child."

Because of her thoughts about Hal, Laura immediately wondered if a pregnant mistress of Stephen's had arrived. What a laughable complication that would be! And the thought hurt, though she didn't imagine he'd lived like a monk.

She opened the door a crack. "Who does she say she is?"

At least the uncertainty fit Mrs. Penfold.

"A Miss Capulette, ma'am." The man looked concerned. "I'm not at all sure she's what she seems, ma'am. Arrived with Tad Whipple's vegetables. And as Sir Stephen is out . . . . But she was most insistent, and speaks like a lady."

With coins, no doubt. Now what?

But then Laura was hard put not to gasp. Montagues and Capulets? *Juliet?*

"Oh, indeed!" she twittered, opening the door. "I know just who she is. Do please bring her up. And tea. I'm sure she will want refreshment."

His brows rose, but he left. Laura would have rushed down with him, but she made herself wait. Juliet. Had she brought

Harry? What had happened? Jack was *here,* not creating danger at Merrymead.

Then Juliet came upstairs, with Harry asleep in her arms.

Laura took him, and could have wept with relief. Thank heavens he was asleep, though, or he would surely have called out "Mama!"

Juliet looked exhausted, and momentarily astonished at Laura's appearance.

"My poor dear!" Laura gushed, drawing her into the room. "You must have had such a journey." She looked back to where Topham was hovering, probably to check that everything was truly in order. "Thank you. Tea, please."

Harry stirred, but by heaven's grace he didn't let out a sleepy "Mama?" until the door closed.

Laura gave him a long, close hug. "Yes, it's me, Minnow! How wonderful to see you. As you see, I'm playing a little game and have disguised myself, but it's nothing to be afraid of."

She looked over his head at Juliet, however, her gaze asking fearful questions.

Harry was knuckling his eyes, so she carried him over to the window and put him down there. "The sea, Harry. Isn't it splendid?"

"Can I go out there?" he asked, waking up enough to press his nose to the glass.

"Perhaps tomorrow, love. It's too late now."

Oh, Lord. What would an inquisitive, restless child do to their plans?

Harry tugged at her. "We traveled on a cart, Mama."

"So I heard. I'm sure that was a splendid adventure."

"It smelt of pigs."

"Oh." Laura wrinkled her nose. "I think you smell a little bit of pigs, too. Why don't we take you into my bedchamber for a wash?"

She saw no sign of a valise or even a bundle. What had happened? She took him into the bedchamber and Juliet followed, to collapse wearily onto a chair.

"I thought we were going to have to walk the last miles, but we were taken up by a man bringing vegetables here. He was very kind, but a bit whiffy."

Laura heard the door open to the parlor and waved her to be quiet. "Let Aunt Juliet wash your face and hands, Minnow, and then there'll be cakes."

She returned to the parlor, closing the door behind her.

Jean had entered without permission —

Mrs. Penfold wasn't the only nosy one — and was placing pots, cups, plates, and cakes on the table.

"A surprise visitor, ma'am," the maid said with a smirk. "I'm sure Sir Stephen will be pleased."

Laura knew the maid, probably the whole inn, was leaping to the same conclusion that she had, except with a child, not with child.

"Very pleased," she said, "at the arrival of his sister, though it is most unfortunate that her coach lost a wheel."

A story that wouldn't hold up under the slightest scrutiny, but it was all she could think of at the moment.

The maid left with an insolent twitch, and Laura hurried back to the bedroom. She halted at the door, however, realizing that this ruined any wicked plans for the night.

Juliet and Harry would have to share her bed.

Though the results could be disastrous, it felt like salvation.

Stephen forced himself to analyze Jack Gardeyne's mind. The man was clever enough and a well-respected vicar. How could he be willing to murder an innocent nephew? How could he remain so jovial? Where was Macbeth's haggard torment? How did the man preserve his image of himself as a righteous man?

Perhaps he told himself that he was taking care of his family, especially his newborn son. How could he condemn the infant to life as a parson's son when he could so easily be heir to a title?

He might even have persuaded himself that Harry was not his brother's son. Yes, that was likely. Thus, he could see himself as correcting Laura's wickedness in foisting the child on the Gardeynes. Deceiving his poor old father.

Which put Laura even more at risk.

He must return quickly to the inn —

But perhaps he'd left it too late. The vicar had walked out of the Arms and was heading purposefully toward the Compass. *Purposefully* was exactly the word, and Stephen realized that he himself was a little farther away.

He hurried after, but the shifting pebbles fought his boots and he could hardly run without causing a commotion. He was only a few yards behind when Gardeyne reached the Compass, however, and then the vicar turned into the inn yard.

Stephen paused, letting his heart rate

calm, but then walked in after him. If he was seen, so be it. He must know what Gardeyne was up to.

Two men were unloading a cart, which gave some cover but also prevented Stephen from hearing Gardeyne's conversation with an ostler. The ostler took Gardeyne into the stables.

Stephen followed and heard what sounded like an inspection of the facilities. Was Gardeyne using moving as a reason to ask questions, just as Stephen had done at the Arms? Was he here, after all, as an honest investigator? Was he even willing to welcome his lost cousin home, if he truly lived?

Stephen retreated to a side door into the Compass and let his objective mind evaluate. It could be true. Laura could have imagined the earlier danger, and Jack Gardeyne could be an honorable man.

Soon Gardeyne emerged and walked out of the inn yard to turn left. Stephen strolled after and watched, but the vicar did nothing suspicious. He simply returned to the King's Arms.

Stephen searched the street for Farouk, but didn't see the blue turban. But then a touch of blue drew his eye up to the grassy headland beyond the bay. He wished he had the spyglass, but it would probably tell him nothing extra. The Arab had completed the steep walk and was looking out to sea, blown by the wind. An active, vigorous man who was finding the waiting irksome.

He was still waiting, however. He wouldn't be up there if he knew Jack Gardeyne was in Draycombe.

# Chapter 39

Harry and Juliet ate like the starving, but at least they both seemed none the worse for their adventure. By silent consent, Laura and Juliet said nothing of importance while Harry was with them, but eventually he abandoned the remains of a cake and wandered back to the window. Laura thought he'd fall asleep on his feet soon, poor lamb, but her immedi- ate concern was a full explanation.

"I probably acted too dramatically," Juliet said, "but there was no time to think." She glanced at Harry and lowered her voice. "Lord Caldfort sent two men to take a certain *enfant* back to his house."

"Back to Caldfort?" Laura said, astonished.

Juliet nodded, taking another scone. "They arrived with a letter, full of authority. They expected you to be there, of course, and to go with him. But your absence didn't dissuade them. Mother was in distress over it, for Father wasn't at home, but I could see she was likely to give in. I was in a dither, because you didn't tell me not to let *l'enfant* be taken there. I decided it couldn't be what you'd want, so the only thing was to come here to you, and to leave immediately. I took what money I had, but it wasn't quite enough."

"Lord above! Mother must be frantic."

"I left a note, of course, begging her to tell the men that we were out somewhere. She must have, for they didn't catch us . . . Oh, dear."

"*What?*"

"I don't think I said where I was going. Just that I was taking Harry to you. It seemed obvious, but they'll think I've gone to Mrs. Delaney's."

"Lord, what a tangle. What could Lord Caldfort have wanted? Jack's here. In Draycombe."

Juliet paled. "So I've brought Harry into danger?"

"Not particularly, but it complicates everything. But you did do the right thing, love. Thank you. I wouldn't want Harry at Caldfort House without me. But now we'll have Father or Ned here soon, and look what they'll find. We should all return to Redoaks. . . ."

But Laura looked out at the setting sun and knew it would be folly to attempt the journey now, especially with Juliet and Harry so weary.

"First thing tomorrow morning," she said.

Despite his nap on the journey, Harry's head was drooping, so Laura went over and scooped him into her arms. "Come on, Minnow. More adventures tomorrow."

She peeled him out of his grubby clothes and washed crumbs off his face and hands without much help from him, poor darling. Then she tucked him into the big bed. She snuggled with him for a while, singing the songs he liked.

He opened his eyes and frowned. "You look strange, Mama."

"I know, Minnow. But it's just a game."

He wriggled closer. "I missed you."

She fought tears. "I missed you, too. A lot."

"Go down to the sea tomorrow?"

Laura almost said yes, but she didn't make promises she couldn't keep. "Maybe, love. But if we can't, we'll come back to the sea very soon. *That's* a promise." She stroked his hair. "Go to sleep, Harry. There'll be many more adventures."

*And that's a promise, too.*

She sang some more until he was sound asleep, warm and precious in her arms. She settled his head on the pillow but her hand lingered on his hair, unwilling to break that final connection. She wanted to stay here all night but she couldn't. There were plans to make.

Especially as her bold venture had failed.

No, failed was too harsh. Chance had been against her, but Henry Gardeyne was not alive and Harry was still the Caldfort heir. Even if no one tried to force it, he would have to spend some time at Caldfort House because once Lord Caldfort died, it would be his property and his home.

Apart from all the other problems, he was too young for that. If it didn't oppress him, it could spoil him.

She could protect him from that, but the greatest threat would always be Jack. She wished she were the sort of woman who could shoot the man in cold blood.

No, no, that would be evil, and she still had no proof. Even if he'd come to Draycombe to kill HG, that was only slight evidence that he would kill Harry. Jack might be here simply to investigate the letter, in which case he, too, would eventually discover that HG was a fraud and everything would return to the way it had been.

Except that she and Harry now had Stephen on their side — especially if Stephen became Harry's stepfather.

She smiled wryly. After working herself up to settling it by seduction, she'd left it too late. Did one get credit in heaven for forced virtue?

She leaned down to brush the lightest possible kiss on her unwitting chaperon's forehead, then eased away. She locked the door into the corridor to keep him as safe as possible, then returned to the parlor.

"Dead to the world," she said, but then winced at that expression.

"What have you discovered here?" Juliet asked. "Is Henry Gardeyne alive?"

Laura sat with a bit of a thump. "Alas, no." She told the tale, which made no more sense than it usually did.

"So what will you do now?"

Laura was tempted to lay her ethical uncertainties about marrying Stephen before her sister, but they were even more complex and peculiar than the situation with HG and Farouk.

"Stephen will help. Perhaps Jack can be convinced it will be too risky to try anything."

"And you and Stephen?"

"Are living in perfect virtue."

"What a shame."

"Ju!"

"I'm sorry, but this is a perfect situation for . . . adventures."

"For follies. And look at me."

Juliet pulled a face. "I'd rather not."

"Precisely."

"I assume you take it off at night."

"Ju," Laura warned, but added, "Except for the mole. It's stuck like a barnacle."

Juliet reached over and squeezed her hand. "He'll be more enthusiastic when you look your normal self."

More enthusiastic than that searing kiss? Heaven preserve her.

# Chapter 40

Laura went to the window, searching for Stephen, but the light was going and she couldn't tell if he was still out there on the beach. Avoiding her.

"I wish he'd return," she said. "We need to sort out our plans. You, Harry, and I need to leave at first light, but I wish I could see HG safe first."

"It's the sort of thing you can leave in a man's hands."

"But I want to see this adventure through."

Stephen walked in then and stopped dead. "What on earth . . . ?" Then he closed the door. "Trouble?"

Laura, heart suddenly spinning, tried to tell him the story but her words became tangled and Juliet took over. Stephen's return seemed to have changed the air in the room. There was either too little or too much.

"Caldfort?" he said, sitting at the table and helping himself to a scone. "I don't believe he would want to harm Harry, but even so, you were right, Juliet. Though this certainly puts some extra knots in the rope."

"Especially," said Laura, coherent again, "as my father, my brother, or both are doubtless on their way now to Redoaks, expecting to find me there. I can't get there before they do."

Stephen thought for a moment, then rose. "I'll send a message to Nicholas telling him to report that you're visiting . . . Crag Wyvern, I suppose. Another message to Kerslake to cover that. You can go there first thing tomorrow."

"Goodness," Juliet said. "Instant brilliance. I *am* impressed."

So was Laura, but she told him with only a smile. "But what about Juliet?"

He'd brought his traveling desk into the parlor and was beginning to write. "Can't smooth that over entirely. You'll have to tell your father about your fears. When Juliet turned up at Redoaks, Nicholas sent . . . No, I think Nicholas had better theoretically escort Juliet to Crag Wyvern. If he can't, he'll send her with a groom. Check it over to see if it makes sense," he said, and settled to writing.

"I think so," Laura said. "So I was never here." But then she asked, "Why did I go to Crag Wyvern alone?"

"Blast. All right" — he rolled a paper and tossed it into the fire — "Nicholas, Eleanor, and Arabel will have to travel there tomorrow and have their servants say they went today. Thus you went with your hosts to visit the peculiar place. Juliet was taken on by a groom to join you."

"But Stephen," Laura protested, "that's a terrible imposition."

He looked at her. "They're Rogues."

Laura shared a look with Juliet, but she supposed if the Delaneys cooperated the plan might work. Her time here as Priscilla Penfold would never be known.

He finished the letters, then sealed them. "I'll take these down and send them by grooms."

He was soon back. "That's done, and Topham says that tomorrow, assuming the weather's fine, the best way to Crag Wyvern will be by boat. It's true that it's either a long road inland or a rough way over the top." He let out a breath. "Right. Anything happening next door?"

"Nothing. But of course, Farouk went out. HG was hardly likely to take to soliloquy. 'Oh, what a rogue and peasant slave am I,' " she quoted from *Hamlet*, but the combination of *rogue* and *slave* made her chuckle.

"What are you talking about?" Juliet asked.

Laura rose. "Come and see."

Juliet was delighted with the listening device, but soon lost interest when there was nothing to be heard. Laura led the way back into the parlor, astonished at how this latest turn had already settled into a sort of normality.

Juliet yawned. "I think I need to go to bed, too."

"We can all share my bed, Ju."

"No."

Laura stared at Stephen.

"You snore, Juliet —"

"What?" Laura exclaimed, looking between the two of them.

Stephen burst out laughing, and after a moment, Juliet joined him. Clearly they hadn't been lovers, but Laura didn't like being laughed at.

"Don't be a goose, Laura," Stephen said. "I was creating a convenient excuse. Juliet snores, and you, as Mrs. Penfold, can't abide that. Therefore Juliet and her child, which is how it must appear, will have a separate room."

"Oh, I see . . . But Harry's already asleep in mine."

"Then you can move into mine, and I will move down the corridor."

Was he, Laura wondered, attempting to make it possible for them to tryst in the night? It both tempted and shocked her. To do that with her sister and her child so close?

"That," he continued, with wicked delight in his eyes, "will mean that I will share a wall with HG's bedchamber. Perhaps they talk of secrets there."

"Oh, how clever!" Juliet declared.

*Oh, how damnably practical,* Laura thought.

"What is the point in listening?" she demanded. "We know enough."

"There's no such thing as knowing enough."

In moments, it was arranged. Juliet joined Harry in Laura's bed and was almost instantly asleep. Stephen, along with his clothing, his brush, and his shaving things, moved down the corridor.

But his essence remained. Laura had deliberately brushed aside any question of changing the sheets. At least tonight she would be able to nuzzle his pillow without need of explanation.

They ordered dinner and sat to it, just the two of them again. They ate in companionable harmony, reviewing their plans.

"At least we solved the mystery posed by the letter," she said at the end, and raised a glass to him.

He drank, but said, "Without finding a new heir to Caldfort."

"Knowing HG isn't Henry Gardeyne is important."

"Your work entirely."

She understood then that he wanted to be the dashing hero.

"You found the Auricular Enhancer."

He didn't swell with pride. "Which actually revealed little of that we didn't already know."

"It confirmed Algeria."

"Which you'd already discovered in *corsairs*." He toasted her. "You are the hero of this story, Laura."

She reached for his hand. "Heroes. We are equal. Or are you demanding the greater part by nature of being a lordly male?"

As she'd hoped, that brought a touch of humor to his eyes. "Checkmate?"

"I could have done none of this without you. Without you, I would probably have stayed at Merrymead, worrying to no purpose."

He turned his hand to hold hers. "I suggested this plan almost entirely to get you here alone with me."

She blinked at him. "That was very clever."

"Clever, I am."

"I like clever. And you know, comparisons are hardly fair. You're here as Sir Stephen Ball, MP, watched, admired, and having to take tea with the Grantleighs and the vicar. I'm infernal Mrs. Penfold, able to poke, pry, and pester. If you'd come here as a warty groom, you'd doubtless have had a lot more fun."

"I would have liked to be that kind of hero." But he stood and paced away to look down into the fire. "That is irrational. My friends — particularly Nicholas — have suffered in their heroics. It has sometimes spilled over to hurt their dearest ones, as with Arabel. I would never want that."

She was trying to think of the right thing to say when he turned to her. "But I wish they wouldn't exclude me."

She recognized a secret feeling offered to her. " 'They also serve who only stand and wait,' " she said, quoting Milton.

"That, if you remember, was a bitter commentary on his blindness."

"You are Sir Stephen Ball, MP. It must be a wearisome burden, but it's a noble calling and the Rogues recognize that."

His lips were tight. "Is that how you see me? As a saint to be preserved from taint? Would you be acting differently if I were sinful Hal Gardeyne?"

"Of course I would." Before she could continue, words spilled out of him.

"Hal Gardeyne! One among hundreds of English sporting bucks who are as much use as drones in a hive. They create a new generation, then kill themselves in one stupid activity or another."

She was speechless.

He turned away, pressing hands to his face. "I'm sorry."

All kinds of soothing words rose to her lips, but she had to remind him, "Hal was Harry's father, Stephen. He must be allowed to be proud of his father."

He lowered his hands, but stayed staring into the fire. "I know. I apologize. I would never say such things to your son, but it is probably as well that this is over."

Laura thought of arguing, but what was there to say? Walking backward, trembling slightly, she retreated to her room, his room, and closed the door.

Stephen's assessment had been cruelly

accurate, but what did that make her? A queen bee? No, just a skylark, another creature with no purpose except to sing and breed.

But what was so wrong with that? Anger stirred, and she turned to go back, to debate, but thought better of it. He was right. People were not animals and should contribute more to the world.

She knew that wasn't even the point. Stephen's uncontrolled outburst spoke of his feelings for her, feelings even more intense than she had guessed. Like a stick roll on a drum, they resonated in her, especially here where his presence lingered. She hugged herself, trying to confine a pounding desire that combined physical want with a need for everything that was Stephen.

# Chapter 41

When he heard a door open and shut, Stephen turned to confirm that Laura had gone.

That had certainly done it.

How peculiar that he'd thrown away the one thing he'd dreamed of for years. The one thing that he'd devoted a year of careful thought and planning to winning. Better his opinion of Gardeyne had spilled now rather than later, after he'd cleverly coaxed her to the altar.

He laughed. His bitter words had been accurate, but quite unwarranted. He knew dozens or more of such drones and hardly gave them a harsh thought. Sometimes he even enjoyed their company.

Hal Gardeyne's sin had not been his wasteful way of life. It had been marrying Laura Watcombe.

Stephen settled to duty, since it would seem he had nothing else left. He summoned the maid to clear away the dinner. He considered staying on guard here, but there was no need. Jack Gardeyne had no notion that Laura and his nephew were here, so he wouldn't creep in to attempt murder.

Stephen knew that he wanted to hover near Laura, but he wouldn't embarrass her by being here if she came out of the bed-chamber. He put out the candles and made sure the logs in the hearth were safe, then left the parlor. After consideration, he took the key and locked the door as an additional safeguard, but pushed the key back under the gap beneath the door.

In his new room, which totally lacked that hint of Laura that had tormented and delighted him for days, he rang for his water. When it came, he stripped and washed. Not the faintest likelihood of being disturbed tonight, so he didn't bother with a nightshirt and just put on his banyan.

Now what?

All that remained was duty, so he picked up the Auricular Enhancer, though he doubted the two extortionists would reveal anything new. The instrument worked as well from this wall, and the two men were in the bedchamber. Their voices were muffled, however. Perhaps they had the bed-curtains drawn.

They slept together?

Personal servants often shared a bed with their employers, though he'd have expected Farouk to sleep on the trundle bed. Because, he realized, Farouk was dark-skinned and therefore inferior. It was an attitude Stephen fought. Shameful to be caught by it here.

People did often reveal more in darkness in a bed than they would in daylight, so Stephen strained to hear what was said.

He only caught fragments.

". . . fair . . ."

". . . when . . ."

". . . care of you, *nuranee*." Stephen assumed that must be Arabic. A term of respect? Or how an owner addressed a slave?

Oh, what did it matter?

". . . love . . ."

Love? It was then that Stephen interpreted the pattern of what he was hearing, and it was confirmed by a gasping cry.

He stepped back, staring at the wall.

Great Zeus. HG was a *woman?* Laura had said he was delicately made, but it must be a brilliant impersonation to have convinced her, convinced everyone. It explained a lot — Captain Dyer's lack of knowledge of military matters, for example — but made other details more mystifying than ever.

An Englishwoman who'd been a slave in a harem? Had she been rescued by Farouk? It ran too close to the storyline of Byron's *Corsair*, but he supposed it was possible.

It might explain why the pair had avoided Lord Exmouth, who would want to return the lady to her proper home. No matter how heroic, Farouk would hardly be acceptable here as a husband. Especially if HG's home really had been a stern Methodist one. Stephen laughed at the thought.

Perhaps the situation wasn't so mystifying, except for this attempt to defraud the Gardeynes.

As he put away the Auricular Enhancer, he supposed this might make sorting out the situation simpler. If the lady wished to be with Farouk . . . but marriage between a Christian and a Mahometan?

Lord above.

And what would they live on, lacking Lord Caldfort's ten thousand guineas?

It wasn't his concern. He needed to cow Jack Gardeyne, then guard Laura and Harry.

From afar.

Then watch her marry another man.

He took out his brandy flask, which he'd had the foresight to have Topham refill, and took a deep drink. Damn good brandy. Not surprising, in the heart of smuggling country. He drank the next mouthful more slowly in homage. He couldn't afford to get drunk, but a little haze would be welcome.

He hadn't lit the candles, but firelight was sufficient for drinking and regrets. He sat by the window, sipping from the flask, watching the faint glimmer of waves rippling eternally to kiss the shore.

Kiss.

So few kisses he and Laura had shared . . .

The door opened and he turned, cursing the gloom, the brandy, and the fact that he was half a room away from his pistols.

*Laura?*

She must be a drunken dream.

Laura, her beauty radiantly unconcealed, her dark curls loose, wearing the rose-pink robe that had almost stolen his wits at Caldfort House. As he pushed to his feet, she closed the door and walked toward him.

Opening her robe.

Letting it slide off her shoulders and

down her arms, to reveal perfect, breath-taking nakedness.

Full breasts. The sweet curve into her waist. Flare out to her hips, thighs . . .

He quickly looked up at her face, free even of the mole.

"You need to know," she said, eyes brilliant, "that I am not at all shy."

He opened his mouth and absolutely nothing came out.

"Or hesitant."

She unfastened one, two, buttons of his banyan.

He found a word then — "Laura" — as he grabbed her hand.

"Don't be silly." She slipped free with a smile that was alarmingly like the Laura he'd known years ago. The Laura who would never have stroked him through the heavy silk as she was doing. Or continued to undo the buttons and open the robe.

"Of course, if we go too far," she said as her hand closed around his pulsing erection, "we'll have to marry. Remember that, Stephen."

*Remember* . . . His temples were throbbing and he wasn't sure he could see.

He was somehow back in the chair, and the red glow of the fire revealed her perfect face and perfect body as she straddled him.

"Are you shocked? This is who I am, Stephen."

In no more than a rasp, he said, "I have to be able to think to be shocked."

She smiled, captured his head, and kissed him, a deep, clever-tongued kiss, but when she drew back, her expression was serious. "You *have* to think. This is who I am. A lusty woman. A demanding woman. A woman who enjoys a man and knows how to pleasure him."

It was as if her words rushed straight to his penis. He gripped her hips and shifted to enter her, but she slid away and went to her knees. Her hand enclosed him and her hot mouth slid over him.

"God . . ."

Her tongue, playing games as she gently slid and sucked. Her teeth, startling him, but only teasing. He vaguely thought he should protest. Laura? But he sank his hands into her silky curls and closed his eyes. He'd never even dared dream of something like this.

But something blocked him. He looked down, then pulled her up by the hair. "I want you. In you."

Her eyes seemed impossibly full of stars. "If you come in me, we marry."

"Damn it, I *want* to marry you, remember?"

"Do you want to marry this woman? Be sure, Stephen."

He laughed. "Are you mad?"

He picked her up and carried her to the bed, tossed her there, then shed his trailing robe. He fell on her, vaguely aware that the efficient woman had pulled back the covers and was lying on the sheet.

He found the strength to halt at the brink. "Are *you* sure?"

She laughed. "Are *you* mad?"

She grasped him, guided him, and he plunged home.

Thoughts of elegance bumped at the distant edges of his mind, but he was too far gone. He slid in and out as slowly as he could bear, eyes open, every sense quivering to fix this miraculous moment so it could never be taken from him.

Laura.

His.

Even more wonderful than he could ever have imagined.

She smiled back at him, lips parted in clear ecstasy.

"At last," she gasped. "Oh, Lord, but that feels so wonderful. More, Stephen, more! Harder!"

Her hands, her nails, demanded, and he obeyed, feeling her clutch of pleasure as his mind exploded into bonfire stars.

He rolled to one side, gathering her close, kissing her hair, her neck, her shoulder, whatever part he could find. Filling his hand with a magnificent breast, assuring himself that this was real.

"Shush," she said, a hand stroking him, and he realized he was weeping.

"Oh, God . . ."

"Don't you dare be embarrassed, Stephen. I'm weeping, too."

He touched her cheek and found it wet. Licked a delicious, salty tear.

"It's been a long time for me," she whispered. "Over a year."

"Then why weep?"

"For joy. Are your tears for sorrow?"

He smiled and met her eyes. "No, but a man should weep when he experiences a miracle, shouldn't he? It's been a long time for me, too."

She looked a query.

"Since I heard you were a widow."

She raised a hand to cradle his face. "Yet you waited."

"Was I supposed to rush up to you at the graveside?"

"But later?"

"I meant to wait the full year. My will wasn't strong enough. I was afraid some other man would snatch you away."

"One might have done, and simply because I had no idea how you felt. Or," she added, tracing his brow, his nose, "how I felt. What a tragic mistake that could have been."

Did she accept that Gardeyne had been a mistake? That was irrelevant now, now that she was his at last.

Then he remembered what he'd said about Gardeyne earlier and recognized that her coming here had been an act of faith that humbled him.

"Why?" he asked.

She moved farther away, but wove her hand with his. "To capture you if I could. But fairly."

She wanted to talk seriously, but he couldn't resist tasting her breast, her full, dusky nipple. "What do you mean?"

"I wanted you. I needed you." She grasped his hair and pulled him up to look at her. "Pay attention, Stephen. I want you for myself, but also for Harry. Marrying you will be the best way to keep him safe."

"You expect me to object?" He savored her breast with his hand. "It's true."

"But I meant to tell you before you committed yourself," she protested, stopping his hand. "I wanted to explain that I'm still Lady Skylark. I'll want fine clothes and parties and light company at times. I won't be happy spending all my time on politics and philosophy —"

He caught her words in a kiss that lingered, but then he brought it to an end. "Laura, you goose, what sort of dullard do you think I am?"

"You don't like fashionable affairs."

"Don't I?"

"I hardly ever saw you at one."

"Because I worked like a nervous general to avoid you. I want to marry *you*, Laura. Are you trying to claim that I don't know you? That I don't know that you love fine clothes and dancing and parties. That you're impetuous and free-spirited? That you're beautiful, inside and out. And I've learned even more these past few days. I want to marry skylarking Laura, who has some understanding of Hume, and a lot more of social rights and justice. And who can probably beat me at chess with a little practice."

He suddenly thought to look at her left hand and found it ringless, though the mark showed. He touched it.

"It didn't seem right to wear it here, but

I'll have to put it on again."

"Until I replace it with mine." He looked up. "When?"

He recognized that it was a blunt proposal, but they were past pretty speeches.

"It's three weeks until the anniversary of Hal's death." She frowned slightly. "I'm sorry, but . . ."

"But it would look crass to marry the day after. I can wait, love. Until you're comfortable."

"I don't want to, but we must." Her hands were wandering his body, perhaps unconsciously, but with exquisite skill. "We could announce our betrothal then, perhaps. I meant what I said. I'm using you to protect Harry. Lord Caldfort won't be able to refuse to make you Harry's guardian, and then we can keep him safe."

She looked anxious, or perhaps even guilty, so he kissed her again. "Everything I am, everything I have, is yours to command."

"The balance seems unfair."

He laughed against her breast, awash in her warm, mysterious perfume. "Our pleasures here have been a little unfair. I must correct that. As for our future . . ."

He slid his hand down her body, into the hot moistness between her thighs. "My life has felt incomplete for six years. I'm no tragedy. I've lived my life well, enjoyed most of it, but I've always been aware of the missing piece. I need you. All that you are. Nicholas mentioned the lock and the key, and that's it — quite apart from any erotic connotations," he added with a smile, sliding fingers into her and seeing, feeling her quick response.

"What is a key without the lock it fits?" he went on, and tongued her nipple. "What is a lock without the key that turns it?" He rotated his fingers inside her. "Once, I would have laughed at the idea of fated partners, but we are that, Laura. It means that I can make you complete, as you complete me. Tell me what you like."

"Press harder." When he obeyed, she gasped and rose up to kiss him. "You do complete me. I've felt that ever since we arrived here, Stephen. Love. As if I was discovering the whole of me through you." Her lids lowered and she exhaled. "Ah, yes, yes . . . But your fingers aren't the true key, you know."

She grasped his erection and he let her guide it again between her thighs.

"You're a very demanding woman."

"You noticed," she said with a sultry, teasing smile as their hips joined. "Click."

# Chapter 42

"A miracle," Laura said much later, rousing out of a light sleep to sweet darkness, "cannot by definition be so substantial."

"And if we bring Kant into it, should not be so delightful."

She laughed, returning to the pleasures of licking his salty skin. "I don't want to think of stern Herr Kant. How suitable that is, that his name form a negative. I'm sure he'd say that we can't do this."

"That would be to deny reason entirely, since we are."

"No philosophy," Laura protested, tickling him.

"You started it."

"I —" But then she pushed him away. "Do you smell smoke?"

"The fire?" he said, sitting up; but she knew it was dead by now. Not even the slightest glow.

"I'm sure I smell smoke." She scrambled

out of bed in the dark and fumbled her way to the door. "It is!"

She heard the scratch as he tried to make a light, but she opened the door. The corridor had night lamps, and in their light she saw wisps of gray smoke coming up through the floorboards.

"Fire!" she cried, then gasped, "Harry! I locked the doors."

She almost ran as she was, stark naked, but took the seconds necessary to scoop up her robe from the floor. The tinder flared then, but she was already racing barefoot down the corridor, grabbing the key to her bedroom from the pocket.

Behind her, Stephen was yelling, "Fire! Fire!" and banging on doors.

No flames yet. Her hands fumbled the key, but then she got it in, turned it, and was through. Through the bedchamber, through the parlor, to her son.

Juliet was just stirring. "What . . ."

Laura grabbed Harry. "Fire! Wake up, Ju!"

Juliet came alert. "God save us!" She was out of bed and into slippers and cloak in moments. Laura had already unlocked and opened the bedchamber door, which faced the stairs. Praise God, they looked clear, though smoke swirled around there, too.

Then she heard a distant crackle of flames.

Not in this part of the building, and she was shoeless and almost naked. She thrust the crying Harry into her sister's arms. "Take Harry and get out."

"Mama!"

"You come, too!" Juliet cried.

"I'll only be a moment. I need to get shoes!"

Juliet looked as if she'd argue, but then she raced down the stairs and out of sight.

The excuse was real. There could be broken glass, anything, but Laura also couldn't bear to leave Stephen. He was still pounding on HG's door. She dashed into her dark bedchamber, shouting at him, "Leave them! Perhaps they're already outside."

But then she heard voices. So the two men were awake now, and would get to safety. She looked desperately around the room for her shoes. Where?

A bell began to clang, and she could hear yelling voices along with distant crackling flames. Then smoke made her cough.

Stephen bellowed, "Laura! Where are you? For God's sake, get out!" He appeared in the doorway. "Come on. The whole place could go up at any moment."

"I need a nightgown and the wig if I'm to escape scandal."

"To hell with scandal." He hauled her up, but she wrenched free.

"No! Only a moment."

Shoes. On. Nightdress on bed. Shed robe, pull it on. Stephen came to help her with the robe, then slammed the wig on her head, coughing. The clanging bell was a clarion of urgency.

"Come on!" he yelled. "Smoke can choke before the flames reach you."

It was danger to him as much as to herself that had her racing to the open door. So much smoke now, and a glow, as well, down the end of the corridor. The first flames, licking up from below.

Stephen's arm came around her, but they almost collided with Farouk, running out of the smoke in his robe, but turbanless, carrying a clinging, nightshirted Dyer. They let him by, then fled down the stairs after.

Laura heard a roar and thought it was a crowd or the sea, but then she realized it was another element — fire. Roaring in triumph as it began to consume the inn.

They reached the hall and she saw safety beyond the open door. Farouk raced through it, but the Grantleighs were staggering out into the hall, the old woman trying to support the coughing, hunched man. Stephen rushed to assist them.

Laura hesitated, but she wasn't needed there. She ran out into clean, fresh air in search of Harry and Juliet.

"Mama!"

She saw them then, by the ruddy light the fire was already casting over the growing crowd. She raced over to take him in her arms, to hug him close, to soothe him, to assure herself, kissing his hair, his face, that he was all right. Juliet tugged on the wig, straightening it. Heaven knows what she'd looked like.

Laura turned quickly back, seeking Stephen. Then she finally relaxed. He was safe, attending to the Grantleighs. Other people were helping. Townspeople, rushing to see what they could do.

A bucket line was forming to bring seawater to the fire. She'd run to help, but Harry was clinging. "It's all right, Minnow. It's all right."

She prayed that everyone was out of the old building, for the fire was raging now at one corner and behind, in the stable area. Men were climbing up ladders to the roofs of the neighboring buildings, ready to try to beat out new fires. The chandler's to the left had a tile roof, but the house to the right was thatched like the inn. Dangerous.

Harry was becoming excited rather than scared. She supposed the brilliant sparks flying into the air looked like a bonfire to him.

Then she realized Stephen wasn't with the Grantleighs anymore. They were being helped away, probably to some house, but where was he? Up on a roof?

She put Harry back in Juliet's arms. "Stay with Aunt Ju, Minnow. I need to find Sir Stephen."

"He might be helping with the horses," Juliet said. "Look."

Laura turned to the arch into the inn yard, which seemed only a frame for flames, and saw people and horses in there. Oh, the fool. No, the hero.

She ran forward, dodging through the crowd, seeing some horses to one side. Most of them must be out. But she couldn't see Stephen.

Then against flames and black smoke, she saw him leading out two blindfolded horses. Controlling two huge beasts that could crush him if they tried.

A scream whipped her head toward the Compass and a great gasp came from the crowd. Someone was hanging out of one of the tiny dormer windows in the thatch and screaming for help. It even sounded like a child. A kitchen maid or the boot boy?

Somewhere in the crowd, a woman screamed, "Jemmy!"

As if to frame the moment, the fire bell went silent.

Men rushed toward the burning building. One grabbed a ladder from the next-door building, propped it against the Compass, and began to climb. Other men held it, despite the growing danger. Flames could be seen, now, through the lower windows.

Laura pushed closer, as if that could somehow help. She tore her eyes away to search for Stephen and saw him handing off the horses to other men. She ran over and grabbed him before he could go back.

"The stables are hopeless!" she shouted. "The horses are all out."

They both turned to look at the rescue.

Then Laura gasped, "Stephen! It's Jack!"

She knew his shape at the top of the ladder, reaching to pull the lad out through the small window. Knew his voice as he called, "Stay calm, lad, you're strangling me!"

Jack — a hero? Had she misjudged him all along?

The lad didn't stay calm. He clung, screaming, and the ladder began to topple. As if everything slowed, Laura watched the men at the bottom try to keep it up, and it tilt inexorably sideways.

Everyone went silent, so only the roar and crackle of the flames accompanied the child's scream as the ladder crashed down.

People rushed forward. Laura would have gone, but Stephen held her back. "You have to stay out of sight. Go back to Harry. I'll take care of things here."

He was right, but she feared Jack and the child were dead. But as she backed away, someone burst out of the crowd carrying the sobbing boy to his screeching mother.

Then someone bellowed, "Watch out! It's going!"

The crowd around the ladder ran, some carrying a bulky shape, as the fire poured sideways like a burning river through the rooms at the front, the rooms where Laura and Stephen had been. Behind, it ran even faster along the stables, where the upper floor was probably full of hay.

With a roar louder than any lion, the fire caught the thatch and became one enormous bonfire. Appalled silence fell on the crowd.

But then she heard Stephen. "Get those buckets moving. Wet down the buildings to either side!"

As the bucket line swung into action, a cheer greeted men running down the road with a hose and pump on wheels. Draycombe had some provision against fire after all, and she supposed it was mere minutes since the fire bell had first rung.

But no one seemed to be in command except Stephen.

And he was magnificent.

In breeches and flapping shirt, he was organizing the buckets to soak the tile-roofed house to the left. He directed the pump to soak the thatched one to the right.

Reaction was setting in, and Laura started to shake. It was partly the cold night air, but it was so many other things, as well. She'd left her wedding ring in her room, which was now a furnace, and that seemed a terrible sin.

Jack. What had become of Jack? She should stay out of his sight, but he was Hal's brother. She moved cautiously to the huddle around someone on the ground.

She managed to push in far enough to

see. Thank heavens. He wasn't dead. He was babbling. "Sorry, so sorry. Never thought . . . Is the boy all right?"

"The boy suffered no more than a fright, thanks to you, sir." That was Dr. Nesbitt, kneeling and feeling Jack's leg. "But you have a badly broken leg, at the least. Stay still, if you please."

"So sorry, so sorry," Jack kept saying, but then he let out a scream of pain and lost consciousness.

"As well," said the doctor. "Let's move him to my house so I can attempt to save his leg."

As men grasped the blanket to carry Jack away, Laura huddled into her robe. Perhaps the others would hear Jack's babbling as meaning he was sorry the ladder had fallen, but she knew differently.

He'd started the fire, perhaps only meaning to smoke out the rats. The same plan had occurred to her once, but been instantly dismissed for exactly this reason. Fire was too dangerous to play with. Jack's had burst out of control.

She was sorry for his pain, but to her it looked like divine justice.

Speaking of justice, where were the rats? Over there.

She checked that Juliet and Harry were

all right — they both waved — and went over to the couple who were the root and cause of all her problems. And pleasures, she must confess.

HG was sitting on the ground, Farouk on guard.

"Mr. Farouk," Laura said, "I will take care of Captain Dyer if you wish to help fight the fire."

The flames cast enough light for her to see the flat rejection in the man's dark eyes. For her also to see that without his turban, he looked different. His hair was cut short. Didn't Mahometans keep their hair long beneath their turbans?

"Captain Dyer needs my support, madam."

He was speaking in that heavy accent again, but she wondered now if he was Arab at all.

Laura turned to a respectable-looking woman. "Do you live nearby, ma'am? Could you give refuge to this poor gentleman?"

"Of course, of course!" The woman seemed delighted to help and called for a man with one of the wheeled chairs to come over.

Laura was sure Farouk would have liked to protest, but HG said with surprising dignity, "I will be safe. You go."

The touch they exchanged was strange — Farouk's hand on Dyer's shoulder and Dyer's hand covering it. What was more, Laura would swear that Farouk was saying thank you for being allowed to help. She liked the man more for that.

He lifted HG into the wheeled chair and fussed the blankets around him, but then he strode off. Despite wearing what was, in effect, a dress, he climbed nimbly up a ladder to the thatched roof to help the men there beat out fires. The most dangerous job.

Another unexpected hero.

Laura wouldn't have been surprised to find Stephen at the same task, but he was still on the ground, organizing. He probably wished he had a more daring role, but he was Sir Stephen Ball, MP, and thus in charge. Many here might not know who he was, and they certainly couldn't tell from his rough appearance. They simply recognized command.

As if feeling her eyes on him, he looked away from his duties. She waved and saw his relieved smile, teeth white in a sooty face. Then he returned to his work and she knew she was out of his thoughts, as she should be now he knew her to be safe.

She, in turn, looked back toward Harry.

Thank heavens for Juliet.

Laura turned to see where she could be of most use, but then a group of horsemen thundered down the street, lanterns waving.

Laura heard "Mr. Kerslake!" but she also heard some people whispering, "Captain Drake." A new spirit of confidence surged like another fire. The leader they knew and trusted was here now. What a burden it must be to carry such authority when so young.

Kerslake swung off his horse, his five men doing the same behind him. Local men hurried to speak to him, and he gave rapid orders. Stephen joined him and the two men clasped hands, accepting and acknowledging each other's authority. They began consulting like officers on the deck of a warship and directing the action in partnership.

After consideration, Laura slipped over to join them.

Stephen's eyes kissed hers, but he didn't do or say anything revealing. Kerslake looked at her blankly a moment, then said, "Mrs. Penfold. I hope you're not hurt."

"Not at all, but I'm relieved to see you here. We need to talk when things are under control."

His look was understanding. "Where are our mysteries?"

"Farouk's up on the roof, and the other man's in a cottage. My sister and child are here, however, and Stephen made some complicated arrangements that included your Crag Wyvern."

"I received the message. That can go ahead. When things are under control here, a boat will take you all there, the two mystery men included." He flashed her a smile. "I, too, want to know the whole story."

Then he turned back to business, and Laura, suddenly exhausted, went over to take the wide-eyed Harry.

"He wants to get down," Juliet said, clearly exhausted, too, "but I neglected his shoes."

"And you're in your petticoat and cloak. It occurs to me that none of us have a stitch other than what we're wearing. How are we going to explain *that* to Father?" She kissed her son's cheek. "Another adventure, Minnow. You'll have a great deal to tell Nan when you get back, because soon you're going in a boat to a castle."

# Chapter 43

It was a while, and Harry went to sleep in Laura's arms. They were offered blankets, so Laura bundled him up. They were offered shelter, too, but she explained that they were soon to go to Crag Wyvern. A woman brought them mulled cider, and that was certainly welcome.

How were they going to explain an almost total lack of possessions? Perhaps she'd have to tell the truth. She'd prefer that, and it wouldn't matter so much now that she and Stephen were to marry.

Despite weariness and Harry's weight, she smiled.

Poor Juliet was sitting down, huddled in a blanket, clutching a pottery beaker of cider, so Laura was deeply relieved when Stephen came over.

He took Harry from her, and that was a relief, too. "We can leave now. Squire Ryall's arrived, and Captain Sillitoe.

There's a boat at the jetty. Kerslake's own, apparently. The *Buttercup*."

"Shouldn't a smuggling master's boat have a more awe-inspiring name?"

He gave an arm to help Juliet up.

"Remember, the point is not to look significant. And besides, I doubt he brings in cargo anymore than Wellington holds the line in battle."

They made their way to the wooden jetty and along to a fishing smack and a cheerful fellow called Ham Pisley, who helped them aboard. Laura looked back for a moment at the fire, hardly able to believe that it was so little time since she and Stephen had been making love in that inn.

It was mostly a blackened skeleton now, angry red in places, with flames still licking hungrily in search of new food. The adjacent buildings had been saved, thank God, and as far as she knew, no lives had been lost.

She went into a cabin that was small but comfortably appointed. There was a narrow bunk, and she encouraged Juliet to collapse onto it, Harry beside her, tucked against the wall.

Laura turned into Stephen's arms and rested against him. "You must be as tired as I am."

His arms were strong around her. "We will cope. We're alive and betrothed, yes?"

She looked up and smiled. "Yes."

"So this is perfect."

"No," she said with a chuckle, "but it will do for now."

"You lost your wig somewhere."

She put her hand to her head. "Perish it. Ah, well. I'm too tired to try to piece together a story to cover all this."

"As am I." He kissed her. "I have to get Farouk and HG, then we'll be off."

"You're a hero. I'm not sure I can keep my eyes open."

"You gave up the bed, which makes you a heroine." He opened some cupboards and found an extra mattress. It was thin, but Laura gratefully sank down onto it.

"Definitely a hero," she said, her eyes closing even as she felt him tuck an extra blanket around her.

"Jack started the fire," she managed to mumble.

"I suspected as much. He was here under a false name — Mr. John Dyer, if you can believe it — so we might be able to slither through it all without connection to the Gardeynes."

She probably should discuss it, come up with plans, consider what all this meant to

493

Harry's future, but instead she surrendered to sleep.

Laura was only blearily aware of landing and being carried to some sort of vehicle for a rather rough ride. Then she was carried again to a bed, and knew no more until opening her eyes to daylight.

She, Harry, and Juliet were in a large bed in a large bedchamber that seemed to be decorated in a pale, classical style. One wall was taken up by a mural of St. George and the dragon. Strange, but not as peculiar as she'd been led to fear. A fire burned in the massive hearth, but the room still had a chilly feel and perhaps even a touch of moldy disuse.

Laura sat up, careful not to wake the others, and smiled. Clothing! There was a small pile of boy's garments, and spread over the backs of two chairs, ladies' garments. She slipped out of the bed to inspect the treasure. Juliet would not be thrilled. Both dresses were of a severe gray and plain cut, and the shifts, stockings, and corsets, while white, matched. The housekeeper's clothes? Or was there a Puritan in the house? Laura didn't mind. She was used to mourning dullness, anyway, and any decent clothing was a treasure.

In fact, dull might be excellent today, as

her father would arrive demanding explanations. What could she tell him that would make sense of all this?

Then she remembered last night deciding to tell him the truth, or almost all of it, and her heart eased. Her dislike of lying made her a very poor conspirator, but Stephen had agreed.

And they were to marry.

She went to the window and looked down on an enclosed garden. From the season, and perhaps from neglect, it was not a thing of beauty, but it could be made pleasant. Some sort of fountain stood in the center, dry and unused.

They were to marry.

Memories of the night, of the earlier part of the night and their lovemaking, swept over her, making her smile and hug herself. She rubbed her hands up and down a body whose appetites had been stimulated rather than sated even by those intense hours of pleasure.

It had been a kind of madness to go to him. She'd known it at the time. And a kind of wickedness. But she'd lost the will to resist, the will to be restrained and sensible. Apart from any need of Harry's, she'd realized that she wanted Stephen more desperately than she'd wanted anything in her life and could not bear to part in case she might lose him.

But she'd had to warn him. After that last kiss, she'd thought she knew him, knew him to be passionate, but she'd also known that they would make a sour marriage if he preferred modest propriety in a wife, even in private. She simply couldn't do it. She'd enjoyed a lusty marriage, and the fires of desire burned fiercely in her.

She smiled, and perhaps she blushed. No doubt now that he was an equally lusty man, and skilled. More skilled than Hal in ways, because he had more control and patience. Perhaps even because he was more clever. She'd never before appreciated the wonders of a brilliant lover. . . .

She shook herself. She couldn't spend the day mooning over Stephen, and much more of this and she'd be hunting him down to leap on him in passion!

And their life would not be totally smooth. She brought trouble as her dowry. She turned to look at Harry, sleeping so innocently, sprawled on his back. Wicked to wish Jack dead of his wounds, but she did. It would make everything so much simpler.

There was no clock here, and the Crag Wyvern walls made it difficult to judge the hour from the sun, but it was not particularly early. Time to be up and about and find out what was happening. The first requirement was washing water. They were all grubby and smelt slightly of smoke.

She inspected the room. There was a door in one wall, but it was locked. Another opened into the corridor, and that did startle her.

The corridor was gloomy because the only light came from the arrow slits Stephen had mentioned. The walls appeared to be rough stone with green spots that indicated damp. When she touched one, however, she realized it was all paint. Trompe l'oeil.

Kerslake had said the previous earl was mad. If this was his work, he'd certainly been eccentric. There were even weapons hanging at regular intervals along the wall, and they weren't a trick of paint.

She retreated back to the classical setting. She'd have to keep a close eye on Harry. This place might frighten him, and heaven knows what other peculiarities it contained.

She found the bellpull and tugged on it, wondering about Stephen's complex plans. Hadn't Kerslake implied that they'd been put into effect? Could the Delaneys already be here? That would mean she could spin the story they'd prepared. . . .

She pushed the temptation aside.

A bone-thin maid with wide, pale eyes came in carrying a large, steaming jug of water. She put it on the washstand and curtsied nervously. "Will there be anything else, mum?"

She looked like a scared, emaciated sheep.

"Do you know what other guests are in the house?" Laura asked. "And where breakfast will be available?"

The young woman blinked. "Mr. Kerslake's here, mum, and Mr. Delaney, and a Sir Stephen Ball, and two other gentlemen what I don't know the names of, mum. And you, mum, and the lady and the lad in the bed there. I think that's it, and breakfast's in the breakfast room, mum!"

The maid came to the end of her recitation, looking as if she'd just attempted a test. Then she gasped, dug into a pocket, and produced a folded piece of paper.

"Mr. Kerslake said to give you this, mum! It's a map, on account of there's short ways and long ways here, see, and you'd probably better not take the short ways. And he said to say sorry if the skeleton scares your little boy."

Laura was struggling with laughter and perplexity, but she managed a sober "Thank you," and the maid left.

Shaking her head, she unfolded the paper to find a hand-drawn map of two levels of Crag Wyvern. The place was a square with the garden in the middle. The rooms all looked into the garden and corridors ran around the outside wall. A cross marked the George and the Dragon Room on the upper floor. Another marked a drawing room on the ground floor. That sounded pleasantly normal, but she'd believe it when she saw it.

Not far from the drawing room was the breakfast parlor, which also sounded normal. Perhaps the peculiarities were kept for the upper, more private floor.

There were circular staircases in each corner of the building, but she was directed by arrows past one of those to a wide, straight staircase down to the hall.

Lady Skylark stirred, suggesting that the inadvisable spiral staircase might be fun, but responsible Laura shooed her away.

"What's that?" Juliet asked sleepily. "And where are we?"

"Crag Wyvern, for which we apparently need a map." She handed over the paper.

Juliet sat up, rubbing her eyes, and took

it. She chuckled. "Extraordinary and in-triguing."

"You can explore later. For now, we'd best be up and dressed — we have clothing — and meet the others to sort all this out." She faced her sister. "I'm going to tell the truth, Ju."

"Oh, good. I don't see how I could keep a story straight that would cover all of this."

They shared a smile, then washed and helped each other to dress. Juliet, as ex-pected, grumbled about the plain gowns, but she was only teasing. Laura realized that though she'd be dressed again in plain clothes, she didn't have to wear a disguise. Tidying her hair in the mirror around her familiar features was a delight. No hairpins had been provided, however, so she had to leave her hair loose, as did Juliet.

"We look like girls again."

"From a very severe school."

Harry woke up, wide-eyed. "Where are we, Mama?"

She went to lift him out of the bed. "In the castle I told you about. It's called Crag Wyvern, and it might be a little bit fright-ening, but there's nothing here that can hurt you."

As she said that, she remembered the

weapons. Yes, Harry would have to be under someone's eye all the time.

When she put him down, he ran over to the picture. "That's a scary dragon," he said, looking not at all alarmed. *"Roar!"*

Laura laughed, delighted that he seemed no worse for his adventures.

# Chapter 44

All the same, when he was clean and dressed and they were about to leave the room, she took his hand. "This is a castle, Harry, so the corridors are dark and a little frightening, but you are safe with us."

To her surprise, from the security of her company, Harry was thrilled by the gloom and the weapons. The skeleton hanging in one corner, close to the arch into the forbidden stairs, was a particular wonder.

"A real little Gardeyne," Laura said to Juliet. "No wandering here, Harry. You must stay with an adult at all times."

The recommended wide stone staircase led down to a baronial hall full of dark oak furniture and hung with enough medieval weaponry for a small army. Harry was wide-eyed and had to be towed along to the breakfast room, which clearly disappointed him, though it was hardly in normal modern style. Instead it made

Laura think of a medieval refectory with its white walls and long oak table, but it was of moderate size and lacking blades other than table knives.

Food was clearly some compensation, however, as he ran to the table and climbed into a chair. One next to Stephen, in fact. Harry looked at him and said, "Good morning, sir. There's a dragon in my room. *Roar!*"

Everyone laughed, but Laura said, "No more animal noises at table, Harry."

She had the choice of a seat beside Harry or beside Stephen. With regret, she sat beside her son, but the smile she and Stephen shared was almost enough for now. She had to suppress another smile because though he was normally dressed, it was not to his usual standards. She suspected the clothes were Kerslake's, and he had a taste for country clothes as well as being more heavily built. All the same, Stephen gave them an elegance they'd probably not known before.

She gathered her wits and introduced the other men — Nicholas Delaney and David Kerslake — to Harry and her sister.

"My apologies about the map," Kerslake said, "but there's only a small staff here at the moment, and mostly unused to serving guests. I'm still living at my uncle's house nearby, Kerslake Manor."

As Stephen was Stephen and Nicholas Nicholas, Kerslake was soon David, even to Juliet, who looked delighted with all this informality. In fact, she was looking delighted with everything. She'd always enjoyed handsome men.

They settled to reviewing their strategies.

"Eleanor and Arabel are at Kerslake Manor," Nicholas said. "We thought the Crag might be a bit much for her yet. Perhaps Harry would like to go down there."

Laura looked at her son, who was building a tower from "logs" of toast supplied by ingenious Stephen. "You're right. He will become bored soon, but I doubt he'll want to leave me."

"He'll go with me," said Juliet, giving Laura a wry smile. "Yes, I'd like to stay, but this is your adventure, not mine." She turned to David. "Are there animals at the manor?"

"Certainly. Even ponies small enough for him to ride."

Harry looked up. "Ponies?"

Juliet came round the table. "Ponies. Come along, pet. Mama will join us soon."

Harry gave Laura a doubtful glance, and she had to admit that she was pleased he was less careless about parting from her this time. She gave him a hug. "It's not far, Minnow, and I'll join you there soon."

He hugged her back tightly. "Promise?"

"Promise, sweetheart."

With that assurance, he slid off the chair, took Juliet's hand, and towed her away, already chattering about ponies.

They all chuckled, and Laura found his happiness didn't hurt. He didn't love her less for being happy to go with others, and thanks be to God, he was in no special danger at the moment. Jack Gardeyne was not plotting harm right now.

She was about to ask about Jack when Stephen said, "We have to assume that your father and perhaps Ned will be here soon." He met her eyes. "It probably would be best to tell him the truth."

She nodded and saw his relief. "Or most of it," she amended.

A grin twitched his lips. "Indeed. Fathers will be fathers."

"But what about Jack?" she asked, unable to put into words her hope that he was dead.

"Reports from Draycombe say he'll live and probably keep his leg, but he'll never walk as easily as before and may have trouble riding."

"Oh, poor Jack." The words escaped and she looked around at the men. "Does that make me feeble? I have been thinking how much easier everything would be if he were dead."

Nicholas smiled. "It makes you compassionate, but he deserves punishment, especially as he'll doubtless escape other justice. It would be hard to prove anything, even starting the fire. And it would be inconvenient for you to have a Gardeyne on trial."

"It would probably kill his father."

"Which is why," Stephen said, "it's useful that he was in Draycombe as John Dyer. Clever move, really. It could have given him a way to get to a possible relative, Captain Egan Dyer."

A chill went down Laura's back. "He's so *cunning*. I never would have thought. How are we to keep Harry safe? I want Jack away from Caldfort. Far away."

Stephen took her hand. "That can be done, I think. Maybe not until Lord Caldfort's death, but now we're promised, I believe I can persuade your father-in-law to make me Harry's guardian."

"And perhaps he'll let me stay at

Merrymead until the wedding. I wonder if he suspected Jack, or if it was just the mysterious letter that made him want me out of the way."

"Perhaps a combination of both. He's a lazy man who likes his own way, but he's not stupid, and not without insight."

"If Caldfort proves difficult, there are many ways to exert pressure," Nicholas said in a pleasant manner at odds with the cool purpose in his eyes. "When do you plan to marry? Sooner would be better."

Stephen explained the discretions of propriety. Laura thought Nicholas had little patience with it, but he didn't argue. "Then stay at Merrymead, Laura. Even if Caldfort objects, any attempt to drag Harry away by legal force will take more than a month or two, especially with Steve handling the legal end. Why not marry on Gaudete Sunday, the third Sunday in Advent, devoted to rejoicing? An ecclesiastical calendar would give us the exact date."

David pulled a humorous face, but he rose. "I'll go and see if the library here has such a religious tome."

Nicholas rose, too. "I'll help."

"Anything to poke around in the books here again," Stephen said with a grin, but turned to Laura. "And to tactfully leave us together for a little while."

He moved to the chair next to hers and took her into his arms. It felt, thought Laura, like coming home. She opened her mouth to him and let her hands explore the body she had learned well and would learn even better, but she remembered where they were and eventually gently pushed free.

"They'll be back soon."

"I doubt it." His eyes smiled at her. "I thought you were not at all shy."

"There's a difference between shyness and propriety!" But she was smiling, too, mostly at memories stirred by his words. She ran her fingers back through his hair. "I never had the chance to tell you what a wonderful lover you are."

He colored slightly, but his eyes darkened. "Whatever I am, you are my match. It's more than that, though —"

She slid her fingers over his lips. "Yes, of course, but it's a delightful icing on the cake, isn't it?"

He laughed with her and they kissed again. She forgot propriety, and it was he who broke the kiss and moved away. "They're coming. Very noisily."

Laura was fighting laughter and blushes and knew she must look well kissed, and she saw a hint of humor on the two men's faces as they came into the room, but nothing was said.

"December fifteenth," Nicholas declared.

"And a day of rejoicing," Laura said. "I like that. We have much to rejoice for, and we can celebrate our first Christmas at Ancross and at Merrymead, Stephen. I have so missed Christmases there."

Stephen smiled, but then he looked at Nicholas. "How many Rogues do you think we can assemble for the wedding? I would open Ancross to them, of course."

"A house party!" Nicholas declared. "A splendid idea. And I take your point. If Reverend Gardeyne clings to his plans, he needs to see just how powerfully young Harry is protected. Me, of course, but I'm a mere commoner. Luce and Beth may be willing to travel. The baby will be about six months old. In fact, Luce could be your groomsman. Unsubtle to wield the heir to a dukedom like that, but there are times when a sharp battle-ax is an effective deterrent. If not, an earl will do, especially when well supported by minor titles."

"Lee? Good idea." Stephen turned to Laura. "Earl of Charrington."

"My, my."

"And," said Nicholas, "we could possibly persuade the Duke of St. Raven to grace the event."

"My, my, my! The whole Barham area will be in ferment for weeks."

Kerslake spoke. "A notorious almost-earl pales by comparison, but if my presence will add weight, I'm happy to oblige. I have a personal score with the vicar for causing damage in my territory, and I admit, I'm curious to meet more of the Rogues."

Laura was considering other matters. "In addition to all this," she said, "I still want Jack away from Caldfort. Harry will have to visit there, more and more as he grows up, and I will not have Jack nearby."

She had all their attention.

"What do you have in mind?" Stephen asked.

She looked at him. "Once Harry is the viscount, he — or his guardian and trustees, rather — have control of that living. It can be taken away from Jack."

"That will cause talk."

"Not if we find him a richer one elsewhere."

"A promotion," Stephen said. "Very clever, though he doesn't deserve it. I'd rather he end up in the roughest parish in a city."

"I know, but it seems he will live with his punishment, and I think he truly was horrified by the results of his actions. Also, it wouldn't be fair for Emma and his children to suffer from his actions. They are innocent. In fact, if a living could be found in the north, she would be happy to be close to her family."

"You have a very kind heart," Stephen said, and his smile was like a kiss, "but yes, that should be possible."

"There we are, then," Nicholas said. "The only thread remaining is our mysterious villains. I can't leave without understanding what they were up to."

"Where are they?" Laura asked.

"They were shown to a room last night and locked in," Stephen said. "None of us was up to a confrontation then. Nicholas and I took them breakfast, washing water, and clothing a while ago — armed, in case — but they volunteered nothing but thanks."

He looked at her. "I had begun to wonder if HG was a woman in disguise."

"Oh, no," Laura said. "Or if so, a very manly one." She puzzled over it. "It would explain a great deal, but I really don't think so. He's fine boned for a man and has those soft hands, but they're a man's hands. Much bigger than mine."

"I agree," Stephen said, but there was a strange expression on his face.

Perhaps he'd noticed what she'd noticed, but she didn't see why that should make him look almost embarrassed.

"I don't think Farouk is Arab," she said. "Last night, without his turban, and in the strange firelight, he could have been an Englishman." No one seemed surprised. "But why the masquerade? Were they pretending to have been slaves to the corsairs, and if so, why? If that part is true, why did he dress as an Arab? And why try to extort money from Lord Caldfort?"

"Perhaps they met Henry Gardeyne in the Mediterranean before he died," Stephen offered, but he obviously didn't like the hypothesis.

"The only way is to ask them," Nicholas said. "We nobly decided to wait until you were ready, Laura."

"After all," Stephen said, "any decisions are still yours to make."

She frowned. "Why? It's not a matter affecting Harry or Caldfort anymore."

"It has to be something to do with Caldfort. That letter can't have been a shot in the dark, and it enclosed something that persuaded Lord Caldfort of the claim."

Stephen rose, drawing her to her feet. "Let's go and find out."

Everyone rose. "They're in the Jason room," David said. "It has mazes on all the walls, which seemed suitable. If you don't mind, however, I will leave the questioning to you. I should go to Draycombe to give assistance."

"If you can," said Stephen, "get Jack Gardeyne away from there before he says too much."

David nodded and left, and the rest of them went upstairs and along more of the strange corridors. Stephen unlocked a door and they went in.

Laura had a vague impression of walls decorated entirely with mazes, but she paid no attention to them, only to the human puzzles. "Farouk" was standing beside the bed upon which HG lay right on the edge, propped up with pillows. They were almost touching, as if HG couldn't bear to be far away. From his protector or his master?

There was absolutely no doubt about one thing. In jacket, shirt, and breeches, Farouk looked exactly what she'd thought him — an Englishman who'd been exposed to too much sun. In Algiers as a slave? Why, then, was HG so pale?

HG wore similar clothes, and to Laura's

eyes there was no doubt that he was a man. Despite pale skin and soft hands, she could sense a strong body and see quite broad shoulders. Then he gave her one of his fluttering, wicked smiles and she was confused again. "You're beautiful, Mrs. Penfold."

"It's Mrs. Gardeyne," Laura said, and saw Farouk start, then stare at her.

She stared back, and her artist's eye absorbed what she was seeing. She'd been entirely wrong in aging that portrait because she'd been focused on frail Dyer. There was nothing frail about this man.

"*You're* Henry Gardeyne!" she exclaimed, and heard the stir around her.

The dark-skinned man made no comment, but Stephen said, "Ah, the final piece of the puzzle. I'm Stephen Ball, by the way, sir. This is my friend, Mr. Delaney. Will you introduce us to your friend?"

When Henry stayed still and silent, Stephen added, "Believe me, we wish you no harm. Quite the contrary, in fact."

"I find that hard to believe." Henry Gardeyne spoke in perfect gentleman's English, as he had when Laura had been listening through the wall, but now she thought there was the slightest trace of an accent after all, or a foreign intonation, something burned into him as the sun had burned his skin.

For nine years, Laura thought, shifting all she knew and trying to make a new picture. Why had Henry Gardeyne lingered in the Barbary States for so long when he could have bought his release at any time? Having done so, why — as Nicholas had asked before — decide to come home *now?* He hadn't needed liberating by the British navy.

She was dazzled, however, by happiness. Henry Gardeyne was alive, and so Harry wasn't the Caldfort heir anymore. He was safe!

"I'm sure you've lived where truth doesn't serve, sir," Stephen said, "but it is different here. Unless you have committed a serious crime, you have my word that you and your companion will be safe."

"And you can trust him," Nicholas added lightly. "You can trust us all, but Stephen's the most impeccably honorable."

Henry Gardeyne bowed his head then. "In Draycombe, I heard people talk of Sir Stephen Ball with great respect."

Laura smiled up at Stephen, seeing, as she expected, embarrassment.

"We can't help you without the truth, though," Stephen said. "Why did you try to extort money from Lord Caldfort when everything he possesses is rightfully yours?"

Laura saw HG grasp Henry's hand, pale against dark. "You didn't tell me, Fellow."

Henry spoke without looking at him. "It didn't matter, Des. It still doesn't. I don't want the title and estates, but we need money and I don't see why I shouldn't have part." He looked coldly around the room. "I still don't. I assume Lord Caldfort will pay to keep what he has."

"Then why not approach him that way before?" Laura demanded. "Why the offer to kill the rightful viscount?"

The hint of a smile touched Henry Gardeyne's features. "Perhaps I have spent too long in a land where indirect ways are favored over the direct. It seemed neatest. Once done, no one would ever know that Henry Gardeyne still lived."

Laura glanced around, wondering if she was exceptionally dull, if the situation made sense to everyone else.

"You were depending upon your relatives' lack of honor," Stephen pointed out. "Perhaps with reason, but you underestimated it. Your cousin set fire to the inn."

"Hal?" Henry said with a frown.

"Hal's dead. Mrs. Gardeyne is his widow."

"*Jack?* He was studying for the cloth."

"And is now the vicar of St. Edwin's, but carried away despite that on a wave of wickedness." Stephen sketched the recent events.

"Like most such people," Nicholas said, "he found himself in waters far rougher than he'd intended. He will be a concern to you, but I think his fangs are drawn."

Henry had relaxed somewhat, but now he became cold again. "He is nothing to me. I repeat. I will not claim the viscountcy. All I want, all we want," he amended, with a look at "Des," whose hand he still held, "is enough money to live in peace somewhere on this earth."

Laura looked at the two hands, absorbed the tone of Henry's voice, and understood.

"Oh." It escaped before she could stop it and she felt her cheeks burn. "I am *not* embarrassed!" she protested. "Just startled."

When Stephen laughed, she turned on him. "Do you mean you knew?"

"No. Well, not exactly." He winced and looked across at the two men. "My deepest apologies, sirs, but you see, we had the means of listening through the walls. And

last night I had to move to the room beyond your bedchamber."

Henry looked outraged, but HG laughed
with a faun's guiltless merriment. It made
Laura smile, too, but how had these two
very different men come together?

"I assure you," Stephen said, "that I
stopped listening as soon as I realized, and
even then, I thought you man and woman.
I hadn't seen you then, sir," he added to
the younger man.

"I'm glad there's no doubt," Des said
with a coy flutter that was obviously put on
for effect. He was a bewildering mix of
masculinity and beauty that Laura found
hard to fit into any slot in her mind. She
abandoned the effort.

"I'm learning a great deal," she said,
"but I still understand nothing. Could we
perhaps have a name? Des, I think?"

He cast a questioning glance at his lover,
then said, "If you wish. It's short for
Desdemona, though."

Another piece clicked into place.
" 'Thello, not 'Fellow,' " Laura exclaimed.
"The moor and his fair wife."

For some reason that did embarrass her,
especially when her mind began to fill in
some of what she'd listened to. She'd
known that some men preferred male

lovers. She'd even known some men who were clearly of that type. She'd never before thought about it as another form of marriage.

The moment was interrupted by a knock on the door. Nicholas opened it.

The thin maid bobbed a curtsy. "There's a Mr. Watcombe here, sir, looking for his daughters!"

# Chapter 45

Suddenly panicked, Laura sucked in a breath and looked at Stephen. "I'd forgotten Father. Here comes our need to explain everything."

"I admit," said Henry, not without an edge, "that I am curious as to why my cousin's widow was staying at an inn in disguise, with a lover."

Laura grabbed Stephen's arm before he could react to that. "Don't cast stones, sir. You are dependent on our goodwill."

"It seems I have a weapon to hold against you, however."

"Not equal to ours," Stephen said grimly. "Our sin is not a capital crime."

Henry jerked as if hit, and Des paled.

"You see, then, why I cannot become Lord Caldfort. I will not separate from Des. I will not marry and beget an heir." He rested his hand on his lover's shoulder. "We have come too far and suffered too much to be separated now."

"But —"

Nicholas cut Stephen off. "Not now, Steve. You and Laura have to go and pacify her father and get his blessing. We will leave Mr. Gardeyne and his companion in peace to talk things over, and resume this later." But he added to Henry, "It would lend more dignity to your companion for him to have a full name."

Henry's dark skin hid it, but Laura suspected he blushed. "You're right." He looked down at the blond man. "What name do you want to use, Des?"

"Not the one I was born with. I like being Des."

"Despard," Laura offered. "It was one possibility I came up with to fit with Des. Egan Despard, perhaps? The anagrams were very clever."

"We played with them," Des said. "'Thello and I. I'm very good at it. Draycombe, for example, throws up both *my brocade* and *cream body*. Which," he added, in that lid-lowered, wicked way he had, "are very pleasing images."

Laura couldn't help thinking of him as a naughty child, and she shook her head at him before leaving with Stephen to face her father. "What's going to become of him?" she asked as they hurried down a corridor. "He seems both wicked and unworldly."

"Gardeyne will look after him, I assume. You're not too shocked?"

She stopped to look at him. "I thought I'd shown you last night that I'm no delicate bloom. I was never wicked, Stephen, and I kept my marriage vows, but Lady Skylark moved in racy circles."

He smiled and drew her close for a light kiss. "I can't complain, but it will take me a little while to adjust. Be patient."

To prove her point, she deepened it, pressing him against the wall, moving against him, feeling his response. . . .

*Father!*

She pushed back and straightened her stern gown.

"I know," he said, "your father's waiting, and we probably shouldn't appear looking too thoroughly kissed. But," he added, "I don't think I can wait until Gaudete Sunday to rejoice again."

She smiled and suspected she blushed, not with embarrassment but with desire.

"Me neither. We'll find ways."

Breathless with need, she pulled him on and down the stairs.

They found her father in the drawing

room, which was surprisingly normal, with silk wallpaper and plaster cornices and inoffensive landscapes hanging on the wall.

Her father, however, was in a stern mood. "What's this all about, Laura?"

With a gulp, Laura plunged into the truth, leaving out only the fact that she and Stephen had anticipated their wedding.

Fortunately, he latched on to Jack's behavior. "Such wickedness! Are you sure, Laury?"

"As sure as I can be."

"And there's little doubt that he set the fire in Draycombe, sir," Stephen added.

Her father shook his head. "What a terrible thing. But to be poking around in someone's desk, Laury . . ."

"If I hadn't, heaven knows what might have happened, Father."

"But why couldn't you have told us? You always were impetuous."

Laura managed not to look at Stephen. "I wasn't sure, you see. I had no evidence, and I knew you'd be too fair-minded to act without."

She prayed that would appease him, and it seemed to. "Well, that's discreet, I suppose. And you were wise enough to disguise yourself. But if you'd been detected, love!"

"We were very careful, and see, this has brought Stephen and me back together. I hope you'll give us your blessing, Father. We hope to marry from Merrymead in December."

That turned his mind to much happier channels.

"It'll be grand to have you close, Laury. You'll be refurbishing Ancross, then, Stephen?"

The two men talked a little of such practical matters.

Then her father looked at Laura. "You'll have a complicated life, Laury, what with Stephen's political work and two estates to oversee. Those men of Lord Caldfort's said that he's in a bad way. If he had wind of his son's wickedness, it's not surprising, but Harry may be Viscount Caldfort sooner than you thought."

Or perhaps not, Laura thought. Surely Henry could be persuaded to claim the viscountcy.

"Together, Stephen and I will manage."

"Even if you end up as Prime Minister, Stephen?" her father demanded. "That's what some predict for you."

Stephen shook his head. "I have no desire for it, and it will be a long time before an uncompromising reformer leads the country. If ever."

Laura couldn't help but be pleased about that. She would enjoy being Stephen's partner in politics, but that degree of responsibility would be a burden.

Her father stood. "Well, I think I'll go back down to Kerslake Manor. I don't care for this place, and Sir Nathaniel Kerslake mentioned some bean crops that sounded interesting. You'd best come with me, Laury."

Laura was feeling as if she was back in the schoolroom, but she managed to say, "I will come down in a little while, Father. I promised Harry. But there are a few things I need to take care of here first."

She saw him begin to ask what and stop himself. Perhaps he remembered that she was a grown woman, or he may have decided that she should be allowed to do a little courting. He nodded and took his leave.

Laura blew out a breath. "Now to convince Henry to assert his claim to the viscountcy."

"I'm not sure how we can if he's resolute."

She frowned at him in dismay. "But it would be wrong for Harry to become viscount now — quite apart from the danger it puts him in."

Stephen shrugged. "We might as well continue our discussion in here. I'll go and get the others. Remember, though, that the Rogues can defang Jack Gardeyne and I suspect that events in Draycombe may have shocked him to his senses."

Laura paced the room as she waited, realizing that this room was peculiar after all. It had only one small window and thus needed lamps in the morning. She didn't envy David Kerslake the possession of this place.

But surely there was a way to persuade Henry Gardeyne to claim the viscountcy. True, his . . . intimate relations made things difficult, and as Stephen had said, what they did was a capital crime. She thought she remembered a case involving some men of the upper class, and though they hadn't been hanged they'd been put in the stocks. The mob had been so outraged that they'd killed one by throwing stones before the guards had stepped in and put a stop to it.

But if he was discreet . . .

The others came in, Henry carrying Des. He put the younger man on the sofa. "Let us be clear from the start," he said, as

Laura, Stephen, and Nicholas took seats. "I will not take up the role of Lord Caldfort."

"Please be seated, Gardeyne," Stephen said. "You're not a prisoner in the dock."

Henry sat but did not relax. Des smiled slightly and took his hand, obviously attempting to soothe him.

"Perhaps you could tell us your story," Stephen said, "and help us to understand. Then we can help you."

"Why would you wish to?"

"We're a philanthropic society," Nicholas said, "particularly dedicated to the succor of rescued slaves and reluctant viscounts."

Henry studied him. "Why?"

"For right and justice, but also I'd like to learn more about Arab ways."

Stephen groaned. "Don't pander to him. He'll pick your mind dry."

For some reason, this seemed to release all the tension. Henry relaxed at last. "Our story is one of medium length."

"We have time."

Henry shrugged. "I assume you know that I traveled to the Mediterranean, despite the difficulties in sea travel at the time. I hoped to visit Greece and Egypt. A strange Gardeyne, I, being seriously interested in antiquities.

"I took passage on the *Mary Woodside*, whose master hoped to make the Ottoman lands and bring back a rich cargo. Des was the cabin boy." He touched Des's arm, his face softening with obvious love. "His real name is Isaiah Wissett, by the way."

Des winced, laughing. "Did you have to tell them?"

Henry smiled, then sobered. "I assure you I respected his youth. He was only thirteen and astonishingly innocent, even though he'd run away from home. He could read and write, but had never read anything except the Bible and knew nothing of the world. It quite terrified me, so I read other books with him and taught him geography, history, and the like. I'd never imagined that I'd like to be a teacher.

"We made it past the British and French blockades, but were felled by a storm. The ship went down, but a few of us got away in boats. Perhaps the other boats made land, but after days adrift, ours fell into the hands of the corsairs. I need not bore you with the details. It was the usual thing, which has been described in detail in the papers here."

"We wondered," Stephen said, "why you

did not announce yourself a gentleman and arrange ransom."

"We had been some time in the boats, and I'd taken to it in my nightshirt, so there was nothing gentlemanly about me by then. I could have proved my status in time, but for the moment I stayed close to Des. Being so young, he was very frightened, and I assumed that when I arranged my freedom, I would be able to arrange his, too. Unfortunately, I didn't understand the value of his type — young, fair skinned, and beautiful. He was instantly purchased for a harem."

Even though Laura wasn't naive, it took a moment for her to understand quite what that meant. A male harem.

"Des did not go calmly to his fate. He was only thirteen, and he screamed and cried for me. His owner whipped him, but when he wouldn't calm, Abdul-Alim bought me to pacify his new 'pearl.' Like a pet. Like a dog. I was kept in the yard like a dog, but provided with shelter from the sun and given adequate food. Des was allowed to spend time with me as long as we did not touch and were in full sight of the guards."

"Couldn't you have revealed your identity and been ransomed," Stephen asked, "and then bought the boy's freedom?"

"That would have been delightful, but I soon learned that Abdul-Alim let no one else have his pearls. They were never sold. When they ceased to please, whether from bad behavior or from growing coarse with age, they were killed. So," he said with a shrug, "I stayed."

Laura stared at him. "What of your father? Your apparent death broke his heart."

Henry looked down for a moment, but then met her eyes. "I would have broken it sooner or later, Cousin. I would not have been able to hide my tastes forever, and he would never have been able to accept it. He was a Gardeyne, after all."

"So are you."

"Any family can produce an oddity. It's why I went abroad, to spare him and to try to find my place in the world. Ironically, I did, after a fashion."

"Go on with your story," Stephen said.

"I was allowed to continue Des's education, and Abdul-Alim soon came to see that I wasn't a common sailor, though he assumed me a lowly scholar or clerk. It amused him to have me to turn his English Pearl, as he called Des, into a gentleman. He even purchased European clothes for him to wear on occasion, though not quite of the sober style favored these days. It didn't matter. All that mattered was that we had more time, and even English books to read together.

"But," he said grimly, "Des was being educated in other ways. Trained for the harem. He turned to me for advice. What could I do? I advised him to cooperate, to do everything that Abdul-Alim required."

"It wasn't so bad," Des interrupted, clearly to reassure. "I liked the music and dancing, and I miss swimming in the warm pool, and the massage afterward. I made friends with other boys, and," he added with a genuine smile, "there was never any work. I could lie in bed as long as I wanted, and had servants to do everything I asked."

Laura supposed that for a child of a stern Methodist family who'd preferred the hard life of a cabin boy, this could have seemed like heaven.

But then he shrugged. "Or almost everything. We were never allowed to leave the palace. There were grilled windows, though, so we could look out."

"As you see," Henry said dryly, "Abdul-Alim was never needlessly cruel, and in our first years there, Des was one of his favorites. He doted on him, and thus became kind to me."

"Did he not suspect your feelings?" Nicholas asked.

"Probably, but if so, it would have amused him. He was quite sure that nothing could happen. Which was true. We were never alone and we both knew the punishment would be extreme and not at all quick. We witnessed it a time or two."

Des's lashes were lowered, but his lips formed a grim line. For the first time Laura wondered with horror what had caused his infirmity.

"I was gradually given better quarters," Henry went on. "By a year after our arrival, I was living in a small house close to Abdul-Alim's compound with a slave of my own. Ironically, a Greek girl with no knowledge of classics at all. I was allowed to move around Algiers freely and meet Des almost as often as I wished, but only in the palace courtyard, in sight of the guards. So there we were. I decided that I might as well use my spare time to study the place to which fate had taken me. It proved satisfying."

"But for nine years?" Laura asked.

Henry shrugged. "I learned a suitable acceptance of fate. Apart from one thing, it was not an unpleasant life. The culture, at its best, is gracious."

"And then the British came to set you free," Stephen said.

Henry's face returned to Farouk's coldness. "And then the bloody British came to set us free. No, I shouldn't be bitter, but I was furious at the time. I knew that Abdul-Alim would kill his pearls rather than let them go. Thus I would have to try to get Des out of there. Which would doubtless lead to a slow and excruciating death for both of us."

His hand had become a fist, and Des gently covered it.

"Des and I talked of escape, though he was as doubtful as I was. I delayed, hoping the British would fail." He spread his hands as if they'd accused him. "We had no hope of success in escaping, and had long since decided that the life we had was better than nothing. But then the bombardment began, and I knew the British would prevail. The slaves would be freed, as they had been in other corsair states.

"Abdul-Alim began to smuggle his most precious pearls out of the city. Des was not among the first, for he was older so not quite as valued, but we knew it would be soon. He was still beautiful and skilled at pleasing. I was desperate for any plan that had the slightest chance of success, but I hadn't found one when they came for him."

He looked at Des, who was looking away now, his expression not so much grim as lifeless, as if he did not wish to remember this part.

"He was the brave, resourceful one. He hid. It was the height of the battle and he hoped that Abdul-Alim and his men would give up the search and flee. But he was caught. He was beaten. Tortured. Not with the usual refinements, for lack of time, but they would have killed him if a shell hadn't broken down a wall to the harem. All was panic, wounded, and dead, so I took my chance and ran in to find him. What they'd done . . ." He closed his eyes for a moment. "But he was alive. He was in such pain as I carried him away, but he never made a sound."

Tears escaped the young man's eyes and he suddenly turned his face into Henry's shoulder. Henry put his arm around him. Laura felt that she should be embarrassed but she wasn't. This was a remarkable love story.

"If he was so badly injured," Stephen asked, but even his voice sounded gruff, "why not take him to the navy?"

Henry's look was pitying. "The battle

still raged, but besides, I could get better medical help in Algiers if my friends would take the risk. They did. They hid us and tended to Des until he could travel, then helped us to a boat that would take us to Spain. I'd carried Des away still wearing a collar and bracelets of jewels, and they helped us find a place where we could rest for a while. We had our freedom at last, and it seemed Des would live and be whole in time, but how were we to survive? The jewels wouldn't support us forever.

"So I decided to return to England. I would find a place for Des to live and then present myself at Caldfort, the dutiful son returned from the grave. Once reestablished, I would find a way for Des and me to be together as friends. You see, at this point I wasn't sure that Des's desires were the same as mine or simply part of Abdul-Alim's training. He deserved the chance to choose."

Des moved then and looked up at Henry, shaking his head. "He took some persuading, if truth be told."

Henry gave him a look, but wrapped it in a smile. "As it was, the briefest enquiries showed that it was too late for the return of the son. I was Lord Caldfort by right, but would have to wrest my property from my uncle. If I wanted it, which I didn't. Once I knew that Des shared all my feelings, I saw how that life would be torture. We would live under constant scrutiny and the *ton* would question his origins. I would be hunted by ambitious young women and under endless pressure to marry, as well as living in the shadow of the law. We would be almost as severed as in Algiers. So I decided we would make a new life, but I needed part of my heritage."

"What did you send as evidence?" Laura asked, fascinated by the couple, who had lived a romance more dramatic than anything Byron had written.

"A detailed description of the house, including places unlikely to be seen by outsiders."

"So simple. I am truly sorry you had to go through so much, Cousin Henry, but are you *sure* you don't want the viscountcy?"

He hesitated for the slightest moment, and his eyes flickered away, but then he said, "Completely sure."

Did part of him long for England and his home? She hoped for a moment, but then he became strong again.

"I have lived a long time in a foreign land. England seems strange to me now, and the climate is far too cold."

"This is autumn," Stephen pointed out. "You may like summer better."

"But there is autumn, and winter, too." He gave a theatrical shudder, but a smile lightened his lips and Laura saw a hint of the Henry Gardeyne of the portrait, but only a hint. He was right. He was a different person now.

She wanted him to take up the viscountcy to make Harry safe, but she could not try to impose it when he and Des had been through so much and would risk so much here.

"Where will you go?" she asked.

His smiled his thanks of her acceptance. "Somewhere warm. Perhaps we will wander the equatorial regions until we find a home. But," he added, "we do need money."

Her decisions to make. Laura looked around, then said, "My father says that Lord Caldfort has taken a turn for the worse, so there seems no purpose in distressing him. He must soon learn of Jack's injury, but it can be presented that Jack went to find out the truth, that the fire was complete accident and he a hero. If you are determined not to claim the viscountcy, Cousin Henry, then I would like you to write a letter admitting that your purpose was fraud and giving up your plan out of fear. That will lift a burden from him, allowing him to die in peace, for I fear it will come to that."

"Certainly, but we still need money. Des and I are now destitute. What small amount of money we had left went with the fire. We don't even own our clothes."

"I agree that you are entitled to support from the estate, but I can't see how to arrange it now. I have very little." She looked to Stephen for help.

"A lump sum now," Stephen said, "and quarterly payments thereafter? My friends and I will arrange it until such time as it can be drawn on the estate."

Henry looked between him and Nicholas. "A philanthropic society dedicated to the succor of rescued slaves and reluctant viscounts?"

"Something like that. You will have to take my word for it."

After a silent communication with Des, Henry inclined his head in thanks. "We are free to go?"

"Of course."

"But," said Nicholas, "you would much oblige me, sir, by paying me a visit at my estate of Redoaks. It is not far away, and as you said, you are temporarily embarrassed for funds. I would only ask to learn more of Algeria and Arab ways."

Henry looked a little nonplussed but then said, "We would be most grateful for your hospitality, sir."

"The gratitude will be entirely on my side. I will make arrangements."

He went out, leaving Laura and Stephen with Henry and Des.

It would seem that they were thoroughly Rogue-entangled, but Laura was glad of it. "I am happy to know you, Cousin Henry," she said, "and sad that we will see little of you in the future." She hesitated, then said, "Would you like to visit Caldfort House before you leave England? I could discreetly arrange that."

His face softened. "You're very kind. Yes, I would. I was happy there as a boy, and I would like to show Des my old home. There are a few things I would treasure, too, if they are still there. Nothing of any particular value."

"Of course."

"And I would like to visit my father's and mother's graves."

"You have a stone there, too, you know."

He laughed, and she realized it was for the first time since she'd met him. "How strange. I should definitely see that."

Laura turned to Des, who was looking brightly, if hesitantly, happy. "Is there hope that you will walk again, sir?"

He smiled. "Oh, yes. If I rest," he added, reminding her with a mischievous look of their discussion in Draycombe. "I can walk a little now, but it pains me and I hate to hobble in public. So ungraceful. But it gets better day by day." He cocked his head. "Do you think anyone at this Redoaks knows how to play casino?"

"*I* know how to play casino, Des," Henry said. "Is that what you were doing with Mrs. Penfold? I can teach you more complicated games. Piquet, for example."

"I will enjoy that. I will enjoy exploring everything in the wider world." He smiled up at Laura in a frank, delightful way. "Thank you, Laura Gardeyne. You were kind to me even when you thought me a villain. You have a legendary aura."

"What?" she asked, wrinkling her brow at him.

"She has," said Stephen, equally puzzled. "She is known as Labellelle."

But Laura had realized. "It's an anagram!"

In a little while, Nicholas took Henry

and Des down to Kerslake Manor to arrange transport to Redoaks. Sharing a secret smile, Laura and Stephen had made an excuse to linger, and no one had argued.

They went back up to the George and the Dragon Room.

"This is very wicked," she said as he locked the door.

"And everyone will guess," he agreed. "Do you care?"

"Not at all. But, sir, this dress fastens down the back, so I will need your assistance . . ."

He came to her and turned her, and then she felt his fingers working at the buttons for the first time. Another matrimonial moment, and sweet.

"A corset, too," he said, as if his throat was tight.

"Yes." Her heart was speeding and breath seemed precious. "An inconvenience. Perhaps I should take to wearing the soft garment Eleanor favors."

"If you wish." He spread her gown so cool air touched her back. "But there are times when a corset is part of the pleasure. I confess, however," he said, his fingernail scratching down plain linen, "that when I allowed myself wicked dreams, I imagined your intimate garments to be somewhat more adorned."

Laura chuckled but then felt herself sway, felt his hands catch her, support her. "Silk," she breathed. "And lace. Ribbons." She swallowed so she could attempt coherence. "I have a corset of red silk, very low in the back."

He began untying her laces and loosening them, taking his time, each touch sweet torture. "To wear under that red dress? I hope you still have that."

"Yes, but it's very grand. Not suited for a quiet life."

"You plan to live a quiet life?"

She remembered their earlier discussion and smiled. "Now and then."

He tugged on her corset laces, more urgently now. "And now and then, I will expect my wife to host brilliant parties in fine plumage, flying high."

"Whether I want to or not?" she asked, knowing he would hear the teasing pout.

"I will be the proud possessor of Labellelle, and will expect you to play your part."

"Tyrant."

"Master. Consider yourself my slave, required to please me in every way."

Her corset loosened and her clothing

began to slide. She wriggled to help it as she turned so she stood before him in only shift and stockings.

"Indeed?" Laura began to tear the clothes off him, buttons flying, cloth ripping. "Or I could make you my slave in all things."

"Do you think so?" But his breathing was deep, his erection strong, so she laughed as she tossed away her shift, backing toward the bed.

"Come to me," she commanded, and he obeyed.

When the bed hit her thighs, she lay back on it. "Now pleasure me, sir, and pleasure me well."

He lowered himself over her. "Tyrant."

"Mistress." She ran her nails lightly down his flanks.

He shuddered and smiled. "Beloved."

She smiled back, swept suddenly through by pleasure so intense that she could weep. "Come to me, Stephen. Love me and let me love you. Let us be one."

His eyes closed for a moment, but then he looked at her again. "Always, and forever. I promise it. Ah, Laura . . ." he sighed, watching her in daylight as they did indeed become one.

# Author's Note

The seed for this story came while I was writing *Winter Fire*, my most recent Malloren book, set in 1763. The heroine of *Winter Fire* is a naval captain's daughter and has spent time traveling with him. Now and then people will mention that Miss Smith "fought Barbary pirates."

Of course I did some research about this but I wasn't planning on using it again — until I set to write Stephen's book and realized I was in the autumn of 1816.

The newspaper item at the start of *Skylark* is my invention, but there was excitement and furor in the fall of 1816 over the liberation of the Christian slaves of Barbary. Since my tentative storyline already required the return of a lost heir — bingo!

Barbary was the old name for the states of the north coast of Africa — Morocco, Algeria, Tunisia, and Tripoli — that had been notorious for centuries for piracy.

The corsairs, as their maritime pirates were called, hunted down ships for cargo, but especially for slaves.

The harsh lands of North Africa required a lot of cheap labor, but the corsairs' religion, Islam, forbade the use of Muslim slaves. As they were close to Christian Europe, the solution was obvious, and as well as raiding shipping, the corsairs raided the shores, scooping up young, healthy workers.

In the sixteenth and seventeenth centuries they raided more widely, even pouncing on the shores of Britain, but improved navies put an end to that. By the early nineteenth century the Barbary states limited themselves to attacking crippled ships and the coasts of the weakest Mediterranean countries. In fact, by then most of their wealth came from ransoms and from protection money.

Most countries paid the Barbary pirates to leave their shipping alone, including Britain and the United States. For example, in 1812, Portugal paid over a million Spanish dollars for release of Portuguese slaves held by the corsairs and for immunity. The latter was guaranteed by an annual payment of twenty-four thousand dollars.

However, in 1815, the United States was the first to realize the weakness of the Barbary states and turned the tables. They refused to pay protection money and sent a fleet with a demand for the return of all American slaves and property. They were victorious.

There were not many American slaves, however, and the countries who had lost the most people to the corsairs had no naval power to use. It was Britain, Europe's naval champion, who was called upon to continue the fight.

The Annual Register for 1816 says: "It has long been a topic of reproach, which foreigners have brought against the boasted maritime supremacy of England, that the piratical states of Barbary have been suffered to exercise their ferocious ravages upon the inferior powers navigating the Mediterranean Sea, without any attempt on the part of the mistress of the ocean to control them, and to reduce them within the limits prescribed by the laws of civilized nations."

You have to admire such a long but coherent sentence, don't you? The writer goes on to point out that competition with the upstart America was one of the motives for action. There were others, however. The end of the war meant that Britain had time, a war-trained navy without much to do, and a leadership position to cement.

In late 1815 Britain sent Lord Exmouth to begin negotiations, backed by the threat of force, on behalf of some of the smaller and more vulnerable powers such as Sicily and Sardinia.

Tunis and Tripoli were "persuaded" to abolish Christian slavery and release all their captives, but diplomacy went out the window in April 1816 when a Tunisian corsair raided Sardinia. Not only did this violate the agreement, but Caroline, Princess of Wales — yes, the estranged wife of the Regent — happened to be there and only just escaped.

With British guns trained on Tunis, the dey of that country signed a treaty totally abolishing Christian slavery. Tripoli followed suit. Exmouth and the navy moved on to the toughest nut — Algeria.

The dey of Algiers resisted, and as mentioned in *Skylark*, treated the British consul and his family, and some naval officers sent to aid them, badly. This was an affront that could not be tolerated, and battle commenced on August 27, 1816.

The city of Algiers could not hold out

for long, and soon the dey had to surrender and sign a treaty that ended Christian slavery in Algeria and released all those then held as well as repaid recent security monies. There were 1,642 slaves, most of them Italian.

The number of British is uncertain. Some sources say none, some up to eighteen. I failed to find any account of a returning British slave, which makes me think that none is the correct number, but for the purposes of this story I chose to go with a few, even though it doesn't affect the situation Henry Gardeyne found himself in.

As Stephen says, the Battle of Algiers was not particularly popular in Britain because the slaves were nearly all peasants from southern Europe, and Catholic to boot, and the cost, especially in casualties, was quite high. However, a victory is a victory, and when it was presented as Britain liberating the downtrodden that everyone else had abandoned, it went down well enough.

Is Henry and Des's story likely?

It is certainly possible.

Young male captives did become sex slaves, so a male harem is likely, and conditions there would be luxurious to an English farm lad.

As for Henry, slaves were used for everything from the hardest labor in the salt mines to housework. Generally constrained by an iron ring on their right ankle and a heavy dangling chain, some slaves were allowed to move about the area and even to run small businesses on the side. Some ran taverns for other slaves, even though devout Muslims do not consume alcohol.

In a strange way it was a tolerant society, and some slaves who earned enough from their enterprises to buy their freedom chose to stay. Don't forget that conditions at home were harsh for many, as Stephen points out when telling Laura that some soldiers in the army in India tried to get transported to Australia in hope of a better life.

The Christian slaves in Barbary had their own hospital and even chapel. They were not persecuted for their Christian religion, but if they chose to convert they were automatically set free. It was, however, slavery. Some slaves were kept in harsh conditions and worked to death, and the punishments for disobedience and especially for attempting escape were cruel.

So that is the background which I found waiting for me as I began to discover this story, and it created a fascinating story for Henry and Des as well as Stephen and Laura.

# About the Author

Jo Beverley is widely regarded as one of the most talented romance writers today. She is a five-time winner of Romance Writers of America's cherished RITA Award and one of only a handful of members of the RWA Hall of Fame. She has also twice received the *Romantic Times* Career Achievement Award. Born in England, she has two grown sons and lives with her husband in Victoria, British Columbia, just a ferry ride away from Seattle.

The employees of Thorndike Press hope you have enjoyed this Large Print book. All our Thorndike and Wheeler Large Print titles are designed for easy reading, and all our books are made to last. Other Thorndike Press Large Print books are available at your library, through selected bookstores, or directly from us.

For information about titles, please call:

(800) 223-1244

or visit our Web site at:

www.gale.com/thorndike
www.gale.com/wheeler

To share your comments, please write:

Publisher
Thorndike Press
295 Kennedy Memorial Drive
Waterville, ME  04901